CHILDREN OF DUST

Paul Ferris writes novels and biographies. He was born in Wales and still lives there sometimes.

By the same author

Fiction

A CHANGED MAN
THEN WE FALL
A FAMILY AFFAIR
THE DESTROYER
THE DAM
VERY PERSONAL PROBLEMS
THE CURE
THE DETECTIVE
TALK TO ME ABOUT ENGLAND
A DISTANT COUNTRY
THE DIVINING HEART

Reporting

THE CITY
THE CHURCH OF ENGLAND
THE DOCTORS
THE NAMELESS: ABORTION IN BRITAIN TODAY
MEN AND MONEY: FINANCIAL EUROPE TODAY
THE NEW MILITANTS: CRISIS IN THE TRADE UNIONS
GENTLEMEN OF FORTUNE: THE WORLD'S INVESTMENT BANKERS
SEX AND THE BRITISH: A TWENTIETH-CENTURY HISTORY

Biography

THE HOUSE OF NORTHCLIFFE: THE HARMSWORTHS OF FLEET STREET
DYLAN THOMAS
RICHARD BURTON
DYLAN THOMAS. THE COLLECTED LETTERS (ED.)
SIR HUGE: THE LIFE OF HUW WHELDON
CAITLIN: THE LIFE OF CAITLIN THOMAS

PAUL FERRIS

Children of Dust

'Frail children of dust . . .'
Hymns Ancient & Modern, No. 167

HarperCollins*Publishers*

HarperCollins*Publishers*
77–85 Fulham Palace Road,
Hammersmith, London W6 8JB

This paperback edition 1995
1 3 5 7 9 8 6 4 2

First published in Great Britain by
Grafton Books 1988

ISBN 0 586 07023 0

Set in Plantin

Printed in Great Britain by
HarperCollinsManufacturing Glasgow

Children of Dust

PART ONE
Family Affairs

I

Marriage was not a state to be entered into lightly, as any idiot knew, but the world didn't stop for it. David Inkerman Buckley was glad for everyone's sake that his daughter was about to be given in marriage, or perhaps taken in it; he liked 'taken' better. The act, though, was no more than a means to an end, which itself would change, with time, into other means to other ends. Standing at the bay window of his dressing-room, he thought how agreeable it was to have fathered a sensible girl, one who knew that twenty-six was twenty-six, and chances didn't grow on trees.

Workmen were on the lawn, setting the poles for the tent. Tomorrow she would arise Miss Buckley and lie down Mrs Penbury-Holt. But when she had gone in a cloud of steam and confetti, Port Howard would be the same, and so would the Buckleys. It would still be 1904. The works would still be there, along with other people's works, and the harbour, and the coal-pits, and the future.

Driving a stud through his shirt like a rivet, Buckley squinted between the trees and made out the angularity of the moist brown stonework in the mist, a quarter of a mile away. It could have been a ruin – a few walls and black silent windows and two stacks with rooks in them. Then smoke came out of the stacks, orange light glowed along the ground, and he heard the comforting thump of bars going through the rollers.

'Dadda,' said a boy's voice from the other side of the door, 'Mamma says do the men know about joining the tent to the house, because it could rain.'

'Come in and close the door. We don't want to frighten the ladies.'

The boy stood uneasily in front of his father, aware of the bare, dark-haired legs and the yellowish underpants that hung in a thick loop at the front. The shirt above it gleamed in the gaslight. Above that were square, rough features and a smile.

'I look to you for support, mind, with all these women fussing,' said Buckley. 'You're sixteen, you're almost the man, eh?'

'Yes, Dadda. Will Margaret live in London always?'

'People do. Now this is how you can help me. Go outside and find the gaffer, who'll be Trubshaw from the works. Tell him to mind he has the extra mats and tarpaulins ready if there are showers. And make sure he measures where the band are going to go. They need six hundred square feet clear. You can't squash a band. So what do you tell him?'

'Mr Trubshaw, my father says to be sure – '

'No, Will. You call him "Trubshaw", and you don't invoke me as the authority. You are my son, so you assume it as a matter of course. I shall be listening at the window, mind.'

He wanted to please his father; it wasn't so bad, once he got going. Trubshaw nodded his head in time to the words. It was obviously the way the universe was constructed. Trubshaw didn't object to it so why should Will?

His duty done, he would have been happy to stay on the lawn, helping the men, except that this would have counted as 'familiarity'. Instead he wandered down to the summer-house, and stood thinking of his sister, trying to envisage the life she was going to.

A hammer struck an anvil; he felt a shock wave through the earth, in his knees. Upstairs, Buckley already had the window open, screwing up his eyes. The mist had lifted, and the estuary flickered with light beyond works and marshes, silhouetting the engine-house stacks. The horn of smoke above No 2 had drifted off on its own. Nothing came after it.

'Engine's stopped!' he shouted from the gallery. A maid stood frozen at the breakfast gong, the telephone started to ring, and Pomona Buckley appeared in the hall with an armful of flowers, flattening them against her chest.

'Davy, your workmen are using language,' she observed. But she was prudent enough to signal the maid to open the door. He was through it in a second, calling for Will. They all lived with the works, like a shopkeeper over his shop.

A bottom roll had shattered, one of the pairs of mangles like elongated garden rollers that took heated steel bars and flattened them, stage by stage, into the wafer-thin plates for tinning. The place had a fearful stillness. The shock had stalled the engine, despite the impetus of the flywheel as big as a house that was supposed to take the load and keep the drive-shaft turning. So one set of rolls in the hot-mill department was idle, the crews grouped like players enjoying the interval of some obscure game, aprons streaked with soot, flannel shirts stuck to their chests with sweat, the steel tips of their clogs still hot, faces turned to watch as the gantryman began to manoeuvre his pulleys over the broken machinery.

The reduction in real noise, hot-mill noise – steel slammed through rollers, steel flung across floor, tongs on steel, steel under boot – was itself like noise of a different species, debased and melancholy. It infuriated Buckley whenever it happened, but behind the fury was fear, to think he was at the mercy of the forces he was supposed to control. He wanted everything to roar and breathe flames and spout perfect sheets for the cold-rolls and the tinhouse and the world far away that depended on Port Howard for its endless boxes of tinplate, polished like mirrors.

These noises were intolerable – the furnaces, their

draught-plates shut, snapping as they cooled; warm grease dribbling and splashing from the dead flywheel into the pit that housed its lower quadrant; a doubler with watery eyes, kicking ashes off the toe of his boot and reaching into a water tank for his ginger beer.

'The rollerman will sign a paper stating the chill was wrong when we had it from the foundry,' intoned the manager, the bull-like Phillips.

'Very kind of him,' said Buckley. 'They all blame the foundry. But it was his roller. Who is it?'

'Thomas Jenkins – Tommy Spit, they call him. Piece came off and went through his hand. He's in the ambulance room, waiting for Dr Snell.'

'Right through?'

'Took two fingers.'

'Two and a half,' said the doubler, the one with the ginger beer. 'I chucked them in the coal bunker. Waste not, want not.'

A woman on the same crew, an opener with a sack around her middle, guffawed like a man.

'John Morris,' said the manager, 'Tommy Spit's doubler.'

'You're Morris Short-change, am I right?'

'First time, sir,' said the man, grinning to hear his nickname from the boss.

'I see you've opened the screws.'

'Check the extent of damage, sir.'

'And stop Mr Phillips finding out if the roll was too tight.'

'Beg pardon, sir, not with Tommy Spit. Very experienced man.'

They were all rogues, sometimes chapel-going rogues. This one had his wits about him. Buckley leaned close to smell his breath in case it was ale in the bottle and not ginger beer. The hair was chopped to nothing in a skinner-cut, except for a tuft in the front. He wasn't more than thirty, but his forearms had a dozen blue streaks of scar tissue, survivable wounds from edges of plates. Morris knew what was coming. Lost fingers weren't survivable. If the rollerman went, the doubler had his chance.

Buckley gave the nod to the manager, and Morris said, 'Thank you, sir.'

Two and a half fingers seemed a small piece of Tommy Jenkins to make such a difference.

The victim didn't look too bad when they got to the ambulance room. The place had a comforting smell of iodine and soap. Tommy Spit, seated on a stool, seemed to be waving a bloodstained fist at them. It was mainly bandage. His arm was up in the air, held there by a piece of rope around his wrist that went to a hook on the wall. A tight handkerchief cut into the upper arm.

'Let me see,' ordered Buckley, and Will stood close to him, both loyal and curious. Tommy Spit had eyes that were very blue and pale. He kept them on Dadda while the first-aid man unwound the rags, as if the hand belonged to somebody else.

It was the right hand. It didn't much resemble a hand – more like the claw of a crab, the red thumb and red little finger curled inwards around not very much. It seemed conclusive. You couldn't argue about a thing like that.

But Tommy Spit did. When Dadda said, 'Very regrettable, but Mr Phillips will see if he can find room for a sweeper,' Tommy shouted, 'Christ, give us a chance, mun! It'll mend!' Then he began to shake; the suspended claw jerked towards father and son as if it meant to nip them, and Will went outside to be sick.

Wiping his mouth with a handkerchief, he was sorry to have let Dadda down in front of the mill girls on the grass, eating breakfast out of newspapers and staring at him. But his father understood. He said blood was like everything else, it took getting used to.

'Let's have some air,' he said. 'There's plenty of time.' He bore in mind that Will was the younger son, not groomed from childhood to succeed his father. One had to make allowances. It should have been Will's brother, Morgan.

Paths criss-crossed the marsh grass and scrub that lay between the works and a sea-dyke. It was the last piece of exploitable land before a series of low hills and rock outcrops to the west, outside the town boundary, where the remains of a small mine could still be seen; there had been galleries under the estuary, and sea water got in one night.

'Feeling better now?'

'Yes, Dadda.'

Will was ashamed to be upset. It was only the dragon, sending a puff of its iron breath in his direction. When he was small, Will believed that a dragon lived there. At night its fiery mouth turned the sky red. Dadda used to joke that it was a tiny one, about the size of Mamma's terrier, and all it needed was a stroke with a whip to keep it in order. Fairy-tales were soon knocked out of Will's head. Yet over the years the works itself came to suggest a monstrous presence, a creature made of brick and smoke. Such thoughts didn't go with being the proprietor's son; he kept them to himself.

To the east – on their left as they walked towards the invisible sea – was the plateau of Tir Gwyn farm, dust rising from a field, and the flash of sun on sickles; and beyond that again the first of the cheek-by-jowl works, the Morfa, and the blur of town steam and town smoke.

Approaching the dyke, the sense of being in a shallow pit was pronounced. It overshadowed the wedge of land. At the foot of it their feet squelched in moisture. 'Hello,' said

Buckley, and dug with his heel. But the wetness was nothing new.

They climbed up the slope. The sea was at their feet, drowning the estuary sand and mudflats. The Gower coast on the other side was hazy. Ships crawled through the empty blueness like insects on a pond.

Small, abrupt waves, a few inches high, slapped the grass of the dyke. The water was rarely as high as this.

Something was different. Buckley tried to think when he had last been there. The retaining sea-wall, a few hundred yards offshore, looked uneven, with stones missing from the parapet here and there. It was just a wall to deflect the currents and deepen the channel up to the harbour.

'It's nearly covered, Dadda.'

'Equinoctial tides. Nothing unusual about that.' But the slap, slap, slap of waves was insistent. 'Do you ever come down here?'

'Not since I used to with Morgan. He said if there was a tidal wave, it would come right over the top and wash the works away.'

'Your brother has a vivid imagination. Pity he hasn't found a better use for it.'

Buckley decided he must come down again one day and bring a surveyor. 'Right,' he said, 'quick march.'

They followed a path that took them near the boundary of Tir Gwyn, a scarp of higher ground. It showed Buckley's land for what it was, a reclaimed sea-marsh.

'Will Japhet Jones ever sell it to you?' asked Will.

'Sooner or later.'

'Did you want to build the works here?'

'No option. They say the sea came up this far until a hundred years ago. Then the course of the river shifted. They built the retaining wall to help keep it there and make a deep channel. This little bay turned into a marsh. So some bright spark put up the dyke – supposed to have used

French prisoners from the Napoleonic wars – and thought he'd farm the place. Didn't work – they could never get the salt out. It was sheep grazing in the eighteen-eighties. It was the only bit of land I could afford that I could run a railway to.'

Buckley's works had a mysterious air of permanence. But that came from Buckley himself.

A voice screamed at them from the hedge that ran along the scarp. A face under a cap could be seen; it had a black hole for a mouth.

'Pretend you haven't seen him,' said Buckley. 'Japhet Jones should keep him locked up. It isn't right.'

The path led them round the back of the works. In the rail siding, tarpaulins were being tied over boxes of tinplate in wagons.

'Will you be giving Tommy Spit a chance, like he said?' asked Will. He hoped it was a man's question.

'Sweeping sheds is a chance. So is overlooking his cheek. He won't starve, if that's what you mean.'

'I meant nothing, Dadda.'

'When the works belong to you' said Buckley, 'whether it's here or at Tir Gwyn, you'll have to understand about putting first things first. This is a hard world and getting harder.'

They waited by the line for an engine called 'Jumbo' to go past in a shudder of pistons. Buckley's fingers were like hooks in his son's shoulder. 'Twenty years ago the tinworks in this town had no competition, nowhere in the world. In your lifetime you'll know nothing else. There's a wolf snaps at my back and he'll snap at yours. Slow down and he'll get you. There are thousands of Tommy Spits. They'll lift their caps, and try it on, and ruin you if you let them. Do you understand?'

The boy nodded. But what he understood was his shame at loving his father without managing to be more like him.

* * *

At Blaen Cwm Theological College in north Carmarthenshire, in a land of dairy farms and inbred families about thirty miles from Port Howard, they kept watch for a spiritual reawakening as if 1904 had already been set aside by God as a year when the Welsh underwent one of their periodic spasms.

Signs were said to have been seen in other parts of the country – a mediocre preacher who could suddenly fill his chapel, a grocer who spilt semolina on the counter and saw the face of Jesus in the grains; he confessed in public that he had been giving short-weight for years. Even in the unredeemed city of Cardiff, a preacher at a meeting with reporters present was heard to say, 'There is a sound in the tops of the mulberry trees.'

There were no mulberry trees at Blaen Cwm. If the wind of heaven ever did blow, it would come straight over the bare fields to rattle the windows, like the prevailing winds from the coast. The students slept eight to a room. Morgan Buckley was the monitor of Room Five, the coldest bedroom in the college, facing south-west. Instead of using his privilege to have the warmest bed, he slept under the window. 'What a small thing to do for Jesus,' he told the younger boys.

One of these, a farmer's son with a squint called Gwilym, decided, when the first chilly nights came in September, to move his bed away from its corner by a flue, and give Morgan his space. He trundled the beds around during cocoa-time, but was soon ordered to trundle them back again. They all had to pray that Gwilym be forgiven for his presumption.

A week later Morgan woke at dawn and, scrutinizing his charges, saw a drowsy smile on Gwilym's face. He sprang out of bed and tore away the boy's blankets. Unclean thoughts couldn't be hidden; these particular ones were visible below Gwilym's nightgown. But as the boy emerged from his dream, red-faced, Morgan practised forgiving him.

He intended to be a stern minister but not one of the absolute fanatics. 'I forgive you,' he said, under his breath. It was the power of self-denial. Instead of shaming the boy, he put the bedclothes back. 'Dreaming,' he said out loud, adding, 'Don't eat so much cheese,' as the others stirred and opened gummy eyes.

He wasn't sure about sin, least of all on the day he was going home to see his sister married. She and Y Plas and the works were the world he had left behind, beginning with the day he quarrelled with his father over supper, waking up next morning to the passionate conviction that Jesus was a better bet than industry. 'I was visited in my dreams,' he announced; it was Morgan's word against theirs.

At the wash-house tap he worked the cake of brown soap into his groin and armpits before his fellow-students got there. Beyond the wooden partition at the end, the chain clanked in the one and only flush lavatory, and young Mr Wimmer appeared with his Bible.

'Good morning, Morgan. I notice the weather is holding. I spoke to the Principal last night, and you may be excused at five o'clock.'

'Thank you, sir. I was thinking, sir. My mother said I was to bring anyone I liked from Blaen Cwm.' Morgan did up his braces, trembling with excitement at his own words. 'I wonder, sir, since it's a Saturday tomorrow, if you would very kindly come as a guest?'

'I?' said Mr Wimmer. He was stout but pale and his hands were always cold; when Antichrist came, he expected him to be a Continental theologian. 'I am not of your parents' persuasion.'

'My mother is the Anglican, sir. My father's side are all

Calvinistic Methodists. You would not be the only dissenting Minister, sir, not by any means. It would mean a great deal to me for you to meet my family. My mother has sent me two return tickets, second class.'

Mr Wimmer blew his nose sharply into the trough. 'I am sure your sister's wedding will be an occasion for Christian thanksgiving, but someone in my position might find it a trifle *rich*.'

'It will be very simple, sir, with a plain wedding breakfast to follow and one or two speeches. My mother would especially like to meet you.'

That seemed to work. The tutor rubbed his nose with a corner of the Bible, and said that if his duties permitted he would accompany Morgan to catch the 5.35 from Blaen Cwm Junction.

Boarding the train, Morgan gave way to doubts for a moment. What was he thinking of? Mr Wimmer's cardboard suitcase and a newly trimmed look about his beard suggested a man setting out on a sober journey, not going to a wedding that would have forty guests from London and a band. But Morgan had frightened himself with his boldness before, and no harm had come of it.

It was the moment of the act that mattered, when the desire for some shocking end was no longer to be resisted, any more than pain or hunger was. He had no doubt that it was one of the ways God worked. How else would he ever have got to Blaen Cwm? His father had nearly choked at the time, shouting and banging the furniture.

What protected him then protected him now, a secret awareness of the inevitability of himself, the unique Morgan Buckley. It consumed his nerves and ran through his lanky frame, reaching into the cavities of chest and loins, the bony rods of limbs, the loneliness of feet. It was all him. The doubts were upstairs in the mind, an ignoble fear of consequences. The skin-nerves and gut-nerves advised him that theirs were the consequences that counted.

Precisely why God chose to work through people in this way he wasn't sure. At twenty, he had a lifetime to find out.

'The Vale of the Towy is very lush, isn't it, sir?' he said cautiously, when they were some distance to the south, at dusk, passing meadows that fringed the gutter of yellow tidal water below Carmarthen.

'Lush is the word, as the word for many things created by the Hand unseen is lush. Mind you, Morgan, there are salmon poachers along stretches of that river. Never judge by the outward appearance.'

'I try not to, sir. Do you believe that a religious revival is to be expected?'

'Wiser men than I are saying it. We shall have to wait and see. And if it comes! . . .' Mr Wimmer hammered a soft fist into a soft palm, before opening his Bible to signal the end of conversation.

They didn't speak again until the train was approaching Port Howard, and Morgan, pointing at a mixture of murkiness and red light, said, 'Over there is my father's tinplate works, sir.'

Mr Wimmer cleared his throat and fiddled with the lock of his suitcase. He was less sure of himself than at Blaen Cwm. He was still in command in Station Road, wrinkling his nose at the stench of beer and horse manure, less sure ten minutes later when they reached the house, lights flaring at every window, and Morgan saw him surreptitiously combing his beard. Still, it was a bit early for wrath.

Mamma was too busy to notice who he had with him. 'Most kind of you to come,' she said, looking past them to the seamstress, who was hurrying downstairs with pursed lips, carrying orange silk and a tape measure. 'Dadda is at the works. There is cold supper in the dining room. *Nobody* is doing as they're told.'

Watkins, the housekeeper, found Mr Wimmer the last empty bedroom. A maid was scrabbling with coal and sticks in the grate as Morgan showed his guest into the narrow room. It smelt of damp. The curtains were undrawn; paraffin lamps could be seen moving about the lawn. A man said under the window, 'See to the ropes. There's a wind,' and when he listened, Morgan could hear it stirring under the roof.

'Would that be a tent outside?' asked Mr Wimmer.

'I believe my father did insist on a small one, sir. My sister Margaret is his only daughter. The Archdeacon will perform the service.'

'Not in the tent, I hope.' Mr Wimmer opened his suitcase and took out a flannel nightshirt, which he laid on the bed next to his Bible. 'I see I have been inveigled into a grand occasion.'

'Not inveigled, sir! No hint of inveiglement. May I tell you the truth? I wanted your moral support. I wanted to feel I had a friend.'

The window rattled in a gust and Mr Wimmer said, 'There is a sound in the tops of the mulberries.'

Someone was outside the half-open door. Morgan smelt perfume on skin. He heard lips part and a voice say,

'God in the whizzing of a pleasant wind
Shall march upon the tops of mulberry trees.'

'It's only my sister,' he said. 'Come in, Margaret, and meet my tutor, the Reverend Daniel Wimmer, BA.'

Margaret was bare-footed and bare-armed. She must have bathed not long before. Her hair was damp and a brown dress clung to her hips.

'I like a quotation,' she said.

Mr Wimmer bowed but there were sparks in his eyes. He couldn't not have noticed the bareness of the limbs.

'You are a student of religious verse, Miss Buckley?'

'Unfortunately not. I don't believe George Peele was especially religious. We did him in school for some reason.' She crossed to the window, and when her back was turned, Mr Wimmer made a snake-like movement, and the nightshirt disappeared under the pillow. 'I think Mamma will fall down in a fit and die if it rains tomorrow. Do you think one would be entitled to pray for a nice day, Mr Wimmer?'

'Not for oneself. One could perhaps do it for the sake of others.'

'Then I can request it on behalf of Mamma, Morgan can request it on behalf of me, and so on, *ad infinitum*.'

'That would be a conspiracy,' said Morgan.

'Is he right, Mr Wimmer?'

'Motive is the deciding factor, the intention behind the prayer. *Calon lân*, we say in Welsh, a pure heart.'

Drops of rain struck the glass, and Margaret drew the curtains and turned her attention to the room. Would their guest like to help himself to a light novel from the library? Thank you, he had his Bible; the manner was distant. Would he care for some cold meat and a glass of champagne in the company of whatever uncles or aunts were downstairs? Thank you, a cup of tea and an arrowroot biscuit in his room would be more than adequate; the manner was hardening into contempt.

As Morgan shook hands and said good night, he thought there was now a real chance that God would soon be employing Mr Wimmer to deliver home truths to the ungodly, or the not quite godly enough.

'You might have warned us,' said Margaret, taking her brother's arm and steering him into the library, which was on the same floor, in a wing of its own. 'This is the only place we can have five minutes' peace. Are they all like that at Blaen Cwm?'

'He's the finest man I have ever met, so let's be clear about that. Don't try and turn me against him like Dadda tried to put me off the college.'

'No need to snap. I only meant that nobody wants surprises at a wedding.' She put her hand over his. 'I had an awful feeling you weren't going to come. I thought there'd be a telegram at the last minute. You've been a bit funny about the engagement all along.' She squeezed his fingers. 'Except you're a bit funny about everything.'

'That's an expensive diamond he gave you. Where are you going for the honeymoon?'

'Germany, but it's supposed to be a secret. We shall be away for three weeks. Will you come and stay with us?'

'Your London wouldn't agree with me. He wants a pretty wife to run his dinner parties for other shipbrokers, he doesn't want her brother in a black suit, castigating the ungodly.'

'Don't be tiresome,' said Margaret. 'You know perfectly well that when it suits you to come to London, come you will. Anybody would think you were the minister of Capel Als, not a student at a Bible college.'

'You had better take me seriously. We shall never be friends if you don't.'

Below them voices murmured, doors banged, all the comings and goings of an excited house. Morgan knew that none of it signified, any more than the rows of dark bindings and gold titles that surrounded them signified. 'I spend a minute praying for your happiness every day, but half an hour praying for your soul. Shall we kneel and say a prayer now?'

'Not this minute.'

'Every minute gone is gone for ever, mind. Look, I am kneeling by myself. Won't you come down beside me.'

'You are play-acting,' said his sister. Her dress flicked him as she walked rapidly to and fro. 'Like when you were small and you didn't want gristly meat or something, you used to faint right off. You were play-acting then. It's your nature.'

Morgan's eyes were screwed shut, so tight that red and silver bars appeared under his lids.

'O God our Father, bless thy daughter Margaret and bring her within the encircling arms of thy redemption. Bless her on this eve of her wedding day, when married life with a man she hardly knows stretches before her like the waters of an uncharted ocean.'

'I have been engaged to Henry for the best part of a year,' said Margaret in a fury. 'Will you please stop playing the goat?'

'Forgive Margaret, O Lord.'

'I know you too well.'

Through his fingers Morgan could see the hem of her dress, hesitating by the door. Then it vanished. He stood up, dusting his knees.

'I think we have sown a seed,' he said to the empty room. 'Thanks very much, God.'

Abraham Lloyd, number one pilot on the roster for the night, as drawn up by the Port Howard Harbour Trust, would hardly have expected more fuss in the house if it was his own daughter that was getting married, not his niece.

'The tide will be finished by three o'clock,' he said, dumping buckets of coal in the scullery because his wife wanted the fires going all night. Villette was attending to feathers on a hat that was making her despair. 'Joe and I will be back here in bed by half past. We can both have four hours' sleep with ample time to get ready.'

'Oh, ample,' said Villette. 'We only have to be in the

parish church by quarter to eleven for the most important wedding this town has seen in years.'

'Stop moithering.' Abraham went through to the passage and called upstairs, 'Joe!'

'His name is Joseph,' said Villette, 'and I would be grateful if you wouldn't wake Theodore. I want one of you not looking like a shift worker tomorrow.'

'What's a shift worker look like, Ma?'

Joe sprang down the stairs like a thin, dark little monkey.

'Black rings under his eyes. It's a disgrace your father didn't change his turn tonight so you could both be home.'

'Superintendent Helmes said no. Simple as that. The Trust pays my wages. Quick march, Joe. The *Falcon* will be off in fifteen minutes.'

She lay at a sharp angle of wall inside the lock gate of the North Dock. The wind oozed rain, and the rungs of the ladder were slippery as they climbed down. Daddy, the skipper, was in the wheelhouse.

'What's doing?' said Abraham.

'Collier coming down from Newport. Mitch'll see to her. You'll take the *Arvik* out?'

Abraham had his hand on the ladder to step ashore when Joe rushed up the companionway and said the Mate had told him he could board the *Arvik* with his father if he liked.

'You're learning seamanship, not going for joy-rides,' grunted Abraham.

'Yes, Pa. But you want me to learn pilotage as well.'

'Come on, then.'

Sooner or later the boy would be out in rough water, off some other estuary if not this one, needing to step in darkness from one boat to another, two slippery decks heaving, a black chasm between. Better to do it the first time with Abraham beside him. The *Arvik* would drop her pilot within sheltered water. Nothing to worry about.

Abraham found the master badly disposed towards the facilities at Port Howard. He was a Norwegian, like his ship, with a triangle of beard and red glimmers in his eye. 'First they jam a wagon on the coal hoist,' he grumbled, when they were snug in his cabin with the pilotage agreement to sign. 'Then they tip a load on my deck. Dust everywhere.'

He went over the charts with Abraham, who told him there would be water in the Inner Pool soon after ten, and a safe margin over the harbour bar when they reached it twenty minutes later.

'Not satisfied, Pilot. Where's the tug I ordered?'

'Taking pilots out to the river. She'll be back in a minute.'

'Your tug is your pilot boat? Incredible!'

Abraham stuffed the papers inside his topcoat. Foreign captains came and went, indifferent to the life behind the quays. All they saw was a dock with a dog-leg channel that shipped cheap coal, cheap because the pits were so close.

At twenty, Abraham himself had had no time for the place. His father had owned a barque that worked the western coasts and crossed to Ireland. Father and son had talked of more barques or even steamers. But the fleet was never more than the *Jerusalem*, and her white ribs had rested in the cemetery of the Hooper Sands for decades now.

Presently they were in the lock channel, looking down on the stern and towing hook of the *Falcon*. Daddy emerged from his wheelhouse and bawled, 'Drop the tow at Number Seven buoy, right?'

'Aye aye,' called Abraham, but the captain said, 'No, Pilot, no. You take me to sea. Beyond the bar if need be. I make that decision when I get there.'

Abraham shouted the correction. There was just time to bundle Joe off the vessel and get him aboard the tug. But what sort of father would do that? The sea was a rough trade; danger was an education; a boy of sixteen longed to be a man.

They slid into the fairway and came up against a wall of wind. It pushed open the wheelhouse door, and flung a roll of charts on the floor. The *Arvik* dipped at the bows, and the tug hastily lengthened her tow. Too late, Abraham knew he had made the wrong decision about Joe. Nothing could save you if you slipped coming off a ship in the dark.

With the wind in their face, and the tide still running in, the convoy made slow progress. By the time they reached No 7 buoy, the swell was running against them with a heavy oiliness, broken at its peaks by white water. A distant light or two showed from houses near the tip of Gower on their left.

They passed the bar, and the tug lengthened the wire again as it felt the force of the Atlantic, rolling up the Bristol Channel. Abraham wanted to shout at the master, 'That's the open sea – nothing to you, everything to me.'

Death waited for them in the dark water as it had waited for all the crews who had picked their way through these shoaly passages, as it had waited for his father and the *Jerusalem*, always half expected, the first article of service. Except that Joe was only a boy, enjoying an adventure.

Watching him watch the steepening waves, eyes slewed with excitement, Abraham clutched at a way out – leave him on board, let him go with eighteen hundred tons of anthracite to Rouen, get the agents to send him back.

At last the master sounded the whistle to tell the *Falcon* he was letting go. The answering siren sounded like a scream. Two seamen in the bows of the *Arvik* were wrestling with chains and bolts. A sheet of water rose in the air and fell on them. When it cleared, the tow had gone.

'Half ahead,' said the master. 'Give me a course, Pilot.'

'Steer one-nine-four. Where do you plan to drop me?'

'Well clear of the estuary. I don't like this coast.'

'You've got plenty of water. This course for three point seven miles sees you clear of Worms Head. Can't go wrong.'

'To sea, Pilot. Your tug will remain on station?'

'Aye,' said Abraham bitterly.

Villette would see Joe's absence in foreign parts as wicked, a slur on her role, which had been stamped on her brow for months, sister of the mother of the bride.

The Whitford Light blinked astern. The *Falcon* came abreast, then fell back to approach on the lee side, ready to launch a boat.

The master lit a cigar. 'Ladder on the port side, Pilot?'

'If you please.'

When the *Falcon*'s longboat was in the water, Abraham took his son to a corner of the wheelhouse.

'The pilot has to be on the rope ladder,' he said, 'with the boat underneath.'

'I know that, Pa.'

'He waits till the ship plunges and the boat comes up on the edge of the same trough. Then he says his prayers and jumps.'

'It's all right, Pa. I'm not frightened.'

'It's too dangerous,' said Abraham, but the boy gripped his arm and said, 'Honest, Pa, I'm real good on ladders,' as if the only issue was his bravery.

'You can't. I can't let you.'

'Where's the ship going, then?'

'Next stop France.'

'Ma will skin us if we go to France.'

'It's not us are going, Joe. Only you.'

The boy nodded. He looked puzzled. Suddenly the door was open and he had gone. From the arm of the bridge, Abraham saw him put his leg over the side, helped by a seaman. A watery electric bulb shone down on him. Spray seemed to knock his head to one side, and then he vanished.

Everything hung in space – ships, waves, people, a nightmare painted in oils. The fear came up in Abraham's throat like cold salt water. He flung himself at the rail. Joe was crouched on the ladder, out of reach. The boat was yards away, see-sawing in the waves.

From the *Falcon* Daddy was shouting through a megaphone. Abraham couldn't catch the words. The oarsmen below pulled hard, the prow of the boat came as far as Joe, a wave swept it up, Joe swung out with one arm holding on, Abraham shouted 'No!' and at the last minute the boy pulled himself back to the ladder, as the boat was sucked astern, leaving nothing but sea where he would have jumped.

There was no more difficulty. 'Joe,' he yelled, leaning as far down as he could, 'even if you can do it, I can't. Up you come. We'll go and see France.'

Joe didn't speak till he was back on the deck. He said, 'Honest, Pa?' and fainted. Abraham waved goodbye to the longboat. He felt the tremble of the *Arvik*'s engines.

Later, wearing blankets, in a rusty cabin with black beetles and a couple of mattresses, eating stew sent up from the galley in an iron pot, Abraham started laughing.

'Well,' he said, 'this beats everything. I'd like to see your mother's face. But there it is, you can't fight providence.'

'I was scared. Were you scared, Pa?'

'Aye, but don't tell them in the *Falcon*.'

'Honest?'

'Eat up, because they live on frogs in France. You wait.' He put his arm around the boy. Death had been ready, greedy hands outstretched below the ladder.

'I wouldn't mind,' said Abraham, shaking with relief and the laughter that came with it, 'I wouldn't at all mind seeing your mother's face.'

* * *

Margaret Victorine Buckley, spinster, of Y Plas, Port Howard, in the county of Carmarthenshire, was married to Henry Arthur Livingstone Penbury-Holt, gentleman, of London W., according to the rites of the Anglican Church, dead on time, according to the Archdeacon's calculations, at nine minutes past eleven in the morning.

The usual crowd turned up. A contingent from the works, on standby-with-pay for the morning shift, stood in the fitful sun, under a banner of roses stitched on white cloth to read, *May God Bless Them.* Margaret saw it as she stepped from the carriage. She wanted to ask Dadda if it was his idea or theirs, but cheering broke out, there were problems with the bridal train, Dadda said, 'Now!' and she felt herself gliding, on wheels that seemed to have been put under her, out of the showery morning, where puddles underfoot and faces along the street both rippled uncontrollably, into the blessedly fixed world where Henry waited.

Signing the register produced the day's first serious social encounters. Too many relatives crowded into the vestry, trying to make themselves heard above the bells. Penbury-Holt and his family, including the women, were inclined to a fleshiness that made them all shoulders and behinds. Though fewer in number, they were more noticeable than the Welsh.

Mrs Lloyd, clutching Theodore, was anxious not to be thought inferior, and told several strangers that her husband was in France on business. She decided the Penbury-Holts were charming, largely because one of the bridegroom's brothers trod on her foot (it was painful for days) and said, 'Ah, you must be Margaret's favourite aunt' in the course of his apology.

Buckley and the bridegroom's father each urged the other to sign.

'I'm not bothered. I'll get you to safety and a whisky and soda presently,' said Buckley.

'Worse than the Baltic Exchange at four in the afternoon,' said Penbury-Holt.

But when he saw his chance, Buckley grabbed the pen and made sure his name was on the register for ever. He might have some relatives who weren't up to the London crowd for social graces, but it was his daughter and his wedding; he deferred to no one.

Morgan, watching the day unfold, kept to himself. Outside the church, while the photographer set up his apparatus, he made sure of seeing his grandmother, Hannah Buckley, and introduced her to Mr Wimmer, 'the famous Biblical scholar and moral theologian'.

'You sound a paragon,' said the old woman, who didn't much care what she said. 'We all know my grandson is a paragon as well, so that makes two.'

While she was telling him about her late husband Tomos, who would have turned in his grave to see his granddaughter married in church instead of chapel, a coal-owner of sorts called Albert Rees, universally known as Rees Coal, came up with two ladies, one middle-aged and one young, and said, 'The last time I saw you, Morgan, you was making mudpies in the yard.'

'And learning I had no vocation for making anything.'

'I heard you was in training for the ministry. I preach from the pulpit, y'know? The Lord's been good to me in my business.'

He introduced the women – 'Mrs Dilys Rees, my sister-in-law' (Morgan bowed and guessed she was a widow). 'Miss Aeronwy Rees, her daughter.'

A silky-haired young woman with fine eyelashes, a thread of gold around her neck and a hint of fullness lower down, smiled brightly.

Morgan exchanged pleasantries with the mother, but he

was uncomfortably aware of Miss Rees, standing there and breathing, her chest going up and down. The Miss Reeses of the world called for eternal vigilance.

'They want to take our likenesses,' said Hannah. 'Come and stand next to me, Morgan.'

Groups dissolved and re-formed as instructed. Vanity, vanity, Morgan said through teeth clenched in a false smile for Margaret's sake. A second photographer was there, a bearded man, cranking a handle on his box. 'That's William Haggar,' he whispered to his grandmother. 'He makes moving pictures.'

'What for?'

'Cinematograph lectures. People pay to go in.'

'More fool them.'

Sir Lionel Mappowder, industrialist, Colonel of the South Carmarthenshire Yeomanry, was taking an interest in Haggar's box. Haggar stood aside. The Colonel seized the handle and waved to acquaintances, telling them to step up smartly and walk from left to right.

Rhodri Lewis, proprietor of the Morfa Works, was on his way to make sure his motor car and chauffeur were ready by the gate to take the bridal couple home to Y Plas.

'Halt!' barked the Colonel, and stopped cranking. 'May we have you with your lady, please, Mr Lewis.'

Lewis looked over his shoulder but failed to see his wife.

'Won't I do?'

'Two by two makes a better picture. I'm sure Mr Haggar would agree.'

'In that case, please excuse me,' said Lewis, and his long figure walked away down the path, followed by Mappowder's disapproving eye.

Most of the guests were only too pleased to do as they were told for the new toy. Henry W. Sprewett, Town Clerk, accompanied by Mrs Sprewett and two Miss Sprewetts, performed a slow march for the Colonel and

Haggar. A few drops of rain didn't deter him. He paused and bowed to the lens, digging his wife with his elbow to make her leave her umbrella alone.

'Donkey,' said Morgan, loud enough for others to hear. He was on edge, hardly able to take his eyes from Margaret and the raiding party of the English that was soon to carry her off. As for the keen edge of nonconformist disapproval that he had hoped for from Mr Wimmer, it looked suspiciously as though his tutor was enjoying himself. Any action of a disapproving kind would have to come from Morgan.

Bride and groom sailed down the path at last. Haggar, back at his handle, turned and turned, while a boy kneeling on the ground moved the legs of the tripod so the camera could follow them to Rhodri Lewis's vehicle. Confetti exploded, and Morgan went home on foot, by himself, hearing the strains of the Yeomanry Band (kind permission of the Colonel commanding) blown by the wind when he was still half a mile away.

Passing one of the back lanes, he saw a peepot woman from the copperworks, emptying chambers into a wooden bucket – night urine was a cheap way to descale copper bars – and stopped to speak to her. He liked the surprise on her face. The stench didn't disturb him. He imagined himself as a minister, not too proud to pause and offer kind words to an unchaste woman or two, and perhaps change their lives in an instant. The peepot woman was a step in the right direction.

'What do Mappowders pay you?' he asked.

'Twopence a bucket. Why, d'you want to add a drop of yours?'

She wasn't old, probably about his own age. 'Here's sixpence,' he said.

'What's that for?' But she took the coin and dropped it

down the side of her boot. 'Who are you, then, all dressed up and nowhere to go?'

'A man with pity in his heart.' He had real tears in his eyes. 'Go in peace, my good woman. Sin no more.'

'Why don't you bugger off,' she called after him, but he strode on towards the music, uplifted by the experience.

Desolation lay about him, desolation and dirt, the wickedness of hearts.

In the gusty September sunlight, crowds swarmed over the lawns. For a second time he encountered Miss Rees. She was alone, fingering the gold chain.

'My uncle has taken Mother to see the fish in your ponds. I prefer flowers.'

'Do you have a garden?'

'A tiny one. We live in Glenalla Road.'

'Just you and she?'

'Father died several years ago. Uncle Albert's very kind to us.'

The way she said it, with a trace of huskiness – perhaps damp days brought on catarrh – made her seem unusual. He was reminded of the coarse voice of the woman he had given sixpence to. As if that wasn't bad enough, he experienced a twinge of physical excitement. He excused himself and strolled away with an angry hand in his pocket.

Almost at once he encountered the bridegroom, minus his bride, walking with Dadda.

'Morgan! You've met Henry, of course.'

'Margaret has talked a great deal about you. She hopes you'll come and stay with us one day.'

Head bowed, Morgan appeared to be agreeing. He knew the time had nearly come. Mr Wimmer was certainly going to be no use at smiting the wicked. He was chatting amiably to the London brigade. The responsibility was Morgan's. Regardless of Margaret, he had to speak out against bad thoughts and strong drink; he had to get on with the evangelical life. He glimpsed his mother, fussing in Dadda's wake as usual, and felt a pang. But whatever it was that God wanted, it couldn't be done without tears.

As the first waitresses appeared, carrying trays and wheeling hotplates from the back of the house, Morgan made for the facilities erected in a corner behind the stables. He stood between two of the London party. Cupping his hand modestly, he saw to his astonishment that his neighbours made no attempt to conceal themselves, but stood with the lower parts of their bodies thrust forward, casually spraying the gutter.

He said nothing. His stomach churned at this fresh indictment of the strangers. All through the heavy layers of luncheon in the tent, the soups and sauces, the steaming things with fins and claws and ribs and wings, the skins of ice and pastry, the debris of pulp and sugar, he brooded on his task.

Two Penbury-Holts and a Buckley sat between him and his sister at the top table, but she might as well have been in the next county. He knew he was alone. Laughter and the clatter of dishes being cleared and trails of cigar smoke rose and filled the greenish bowl of the marquee, symbol of Dadda's pride.

The champagne, undrunk, had long since gone flat in his glass. When they cut the cake, he drank a mouthful of water. When they toasted the bride, he folded his arms. When the head Penbury-Holt sat down to applause, he jumped to his feet and said, 'Friends, both Welsh and English, I am the brother of the bride, and I've come to say things no one was expecting to hear.'

The long tables gave off sounds of distress. A knuckle of wind rapped the canvas walls. His father leaned back, trying to catch his eye. The broad scarlet shape of Sir Lionel Mappowder, wearing his colonel's uniform, crouched over a cigar-cutter. Rees Coal jerked his head, and Miss Rees's bosom rose and fell. Morgan avoided Dadda's glare and stared into Margaret's puzzled face.

'I wish my sister every happiness,' and his voice carried nicely, 'but the happiness of our earthly shell isn't everything, definitely not. I know my sister'll remember what she said to me last night. "Morgan," she said, "God is going to come whizzing through the tops of the mulberry trees." She's laughing and shaking her head because she doesn't want to embarrass her husband. But we understand one another, my sister and I.'

Dadda said, 'Thank you, Morgan. Next, please!'

Laughter rippled up and down the tables. Will Probert (editor of the *Port Howard Star*, Conservative) made a quick decision to see that nothing distasteful to the Buckleys got into print. Dai Weekes (editor of the *Port Howard News*, Liberal) took out his wedding invitation and a stump of pencil.

Morgan brooded on his audience. Slowly it stopped laughing. Instead it cleared its throat. It shifted its feet.

'There's a great awakening to come in this country,' he muttered. They had to strain to hear him now. 'The guests from London must forgive me. I mean Wales. I don't know about England. For all I know the English live on champagne and keep harems. I've got my suspicions. But the Welsh,' and he raised his voice again, 'the Welsh I know. Wallow in filth, they do. Wales has her hypocrites. And her adulterers. And as for drunkards, we are the mainstay of the breweries. Even women.'

There was a commotion on the other side of the bridal pair. Mamma had fainted. 'This wedding has been polluted by strong drink and evil thoughts!' shouted Morgan. Through the corner of his eye he saw Dadda make a movement, and expected to be flung to the ground. Instead, his father hurried in the opposite direction.

It was Margaret who came to him, her face as white as

her dress, and said, 'Please. For my sake. Because Henry doesn't understand.'

'I must speak out,' gasped Morgan. Then the band struck up, full blast, and he knew he had been out-manoeuvred.

He was dripping with sweat, his limbs trembling so much that he could have fallen any second as he walked out of the tent. But the victory was like steel pins down his legs, keeping him going. He had turned his back on the guests, on Dadda, on Margaret, on compromise, on the Devil.

A rain-shower cooled his face, and he spread his arms to give the backs of his hands a share. A flame had passed over his skin; he would never recover.

'Listen, you!' said a voice, and his brother ran up, shoes squeaking on the grass. 'You get out and don't come back!'

'God spoke. I listened. Go back and comfort Margaret.'

'Mamma only has port wine as a tonic.'

'What about the bottles of stout she keeps in the bedroom?'

'She's had a fit,' said the boy.

'Pretending.'

'They've sent for Dr Snell.'

'Burn a feather from her hat and let her smell it. That'll do the trick.'

Will lunged and hit his cheekbone, and he fell over, too easily. Will was afraid. Would Morgan kill him? He was capable of anything, so why not that? Will's head swam with champagne. He didn't mind dying.

'I forgive you,' said Morgan, on his hands and knees. Blood trickled down his cheek. 'You'll be punished, mind. God will crack down on you for raising your hand against your brother. I can't do anything about that. You'll suffer.'

'Why don't you stand up and fight?'

Morgan got to his feet. He made no attempt to defend himself. This time Will only prodded his chest, but he fell over again.

'Stop it, stop it!' cried Mr Wimmer, teetering up beneath an umbrella.

'I keep forgiving him,' said Morgan, 'but he keeps knocking me down. He's only my brother. He's not used to champagne. Will you forgive him, too, sir?'

'Fighting is wrong,' said Mr Wimmer weakly.

There was no way of defeating Morgan; there never had been. Will heard his brother say, 'There is a train in fifteen minutes, sir.' He watched them go with an odd feeling of being left behind, before turning back to the chaos of the wedding.

The night boat from Harwich drew away from her berth, the diminishing lights along the quays making Margaret sad for a moment, until Henry clasped her fingers and she told herself that he was thinking the same thoughts, the mysteriousness of being husband and wife, of crossing from one life to another.

They had eaten on the train. Henry told her she ought to have been tired, but she insisted on coming up to the boat deck so they could wave goodbye to England. Wrapped in coats, they leaned on the rail, aware of other passengers nearby, yet remote from them, absorbed in the new conception of themselves. Henry smoked one of his scented cigarettes; when she asked him for a puff, he said nothing, just touched her ear with his lips, and then, to her amazement, darted his tongue inside the opening.

'How strange!' she said, glancing along the rail in case someone might have seen; but they were all shapes in the starlight and phosphorescence.

'Time to turn in, sweetheart,' said Henry.

'I'm still not tired. I could stay here all night. Nothing matters any more except you and me. That awful, awful reception doesn't matter. My unspeakable brother doesn't matter. Were we really there, just a few hours ago?'

'We shall be on the Rhine by tomorrow afternoon. My sweetheart needs her beauty sleep.'

She knew what he was getting at, and had no intention of being found wanting in that department of even deeper mysteries. About the general outline of what was to happen she was reasonably well informed. There was a this and a that and a such-and-such; the human race found it of significance, and Margaret had no doubt that she would, too. How one began she was not clear, but that was a problem she was happy to leave to Henry.

In the cabin their overnight things had been laid out like kit for a military inspection. Her silver-backed brushes were drawn up in parallel lines at one end of the dressing-table, his implements at the other, like flattened bodies.

'Germans, y'see,' said Henry. 'The ship will run like clockwork.'

'The steward missed this,' said Margaret, and stooped to pick up a single piece of red confetti from the floor.

'Or left it on purpose, so we'd know that he knows.'

It was an odd remark, but she had no time to consider it because Henry had pushed her on to the lower bunk. He sprawled on top, guzzling her face and neck. One hand was behind her head; the other touched her calf before pushing up under her clothes.

All she could think of was the need to do things properly – she ought to take off her dress and hang it up, then her stockings and underwear, and cover herself in the lace and ribbons of the nightgown that once belonged to her mother's mother. Then she would be ready to love Henry.

This was incomprehensible. She let her thighs part at his insistence. It all seemed to be putting them both to unnecessary trouble. Then his braces pinged, and just for a second, in the middle of her bewilderment, she wanted to laugh.

2

When David Buckley was a young man, in the 1870s, the art of tinplate-making still belonged to Great Britain in general and South Wales in particular. Other countries had tried it without much success. There was a knack in rolling iron as thin as paper, then barely brushing it with tin – which cost a fortune – that got into the blood. The method had changed little since the start of the industrial revolution, but now the machinery was better and the world was richer. There was easy money to be made.

Port Howard excelled at making the stuff, for no particular reason that anyone could think of. Shiploads of wooden boxes packed with tinplate went off to Europe and the Americas and the East, to be stamped and shaped into the artefacts of progress. Port Howard tinplate was in milk churns and food cans, kettles and cash boxes, gas meters and tea urns. Settlers moved across the Mid-West with Port Howard plates and bowls rattling in their wagons. They roofed their homes with the same shiny stuff, created by fiery skills, at a few shillings a box, inside smoky sheds built along a sea-coast they'd never heard of.

Once established, this new pattern of manufacturing, with its eye on a bigger world, seemed immutable within a generation. Buckley, a clerk in an iron works, wheedled money from his father Tomos, borrowed from a bank, married a girl whose father had a few pounds to spare, and built himself a works on the dried-up saltmarsh that became a bigger works, all in the expectation that tomorrow would be like yesterday only better. So much going on in so many mills and tinhouses side by side, so many flames and sparks at night, so much thumping and hammering, so many railway tracks binding them together, made the scene seem both cosy and final, a happy ending for Port Howard.

This reality, these expectations, lasted until the day the Yankees put their unspeakable tariff on imported tinplate. After that, '1891' lay like a curse on Port Howard. Although its worst effects wore off, and the industry recovered, the old certainty had gone. Whatever the knack of making tinplate was, the world had acquired it by the turn of the century.

Certainly Buckley was never the same. He had nearly gone under; he couldn't forget the bitterness he tasted then. Now, when he read that a tinplate mill in Ohio turned out two or three times as many boxes per shift as the Welsh could manage, he writhed at his lack of capital, and gave his manager a hard time. When he heard some fool insist that Yankee tinplate was fundamentally, almost mystically inferior to Port Howard's, he would go and watch the girls opening the heavy packs as they came fresh from the first rolling, and let the blemishes, the stains, the unpeelable plates that they couldn't open, remind him of the imperfections the industry had to live with.

Money was only one problem. He could always borrow it, if he had to, or even take seriously Rhodri Lewis's idea, discussed on and off for years over whiskies and sodas, that they form a combine and make tinplate under joint ownership. What he could do nothing about was the cramped condition of the works. If the rolling shed was to be longer, the sidings would have to be moved. That would interfere with the tinhouse, which was too small anyway. He needed a road for motor lorries. He needed more storage space.

And next door was Japhet Jones, with a run-down farm that had room enough for two tinplate works. Buckley called at Tir Gwyn one drab February morning with a bottle of something under his coat. Patches of snow were on the ground. The tin roof of an outhouse rattled in the wind. Guto, the son who wasn't right in the head, shadowed him from behind hedges and bushes as he approached the farmhouse, then ran forward and kicked on the door, grinning in his face.

'Thank you,' said Buckley, trying to sound kindly. He had a feeling that Guto, although a halfwit, knew who liked him and who didn't.

Japhet patted his son on the shoulder, and took Buckley into the icy parlour, where a stiff collar and shirt, which no doubt had been there since it was taken off on Sunday after chapel, lay on a shelf in front of a stuffed fox. Guto crept after them and sat in a corner. He made faces at them as they talked about the cold spell, about a suicide on the sands, about the farm.

'You know I want it, when you're ready to sell,' said Buckley. 'Top price, Japhet.'

The old farmer had eyes that might have been screwed into his head, they were so flat and deep.

'What will this one do after me? He's past forty – doesn't know anywhere else. His brothers have hopped it.'

'All the more reason to get out now and take him with you. It must be, what, five years since I asked you first.'

Buckley brought out the bottle and put it on the table. The farmer went to get glasses. While he was gone, the halfwit darted to the table and grabbed the bottle.

'Easy now,' said Buckley.

Guto pretended to drink, holding the bottle by the neck. Saliva dribbled from his mouth.

'Give it here, there's a good lad.'

The man retreated to the empty grate, rolling the bottle between his palms.

'Come along, Guto,' said Buckley, and held out his hand.

Guto grinned. The bottle popped between his fingers and burst on the stone surround.

'Oh, dammo!' roared Buckley, and drew back his hand to cuff him. He stopped himself just in time.

The man ran out howling, and Japhet came back with a long face, demanding to know what had happened.

'I spoke to him sharp.'

'He means no harm,' said Japhet. 'I won't have him touched.'

'No, but if he was my son, I'd stop him breaking things.'

'We know all about your son, Mr Preacher Morgan. Can't put a curb on him, can you?'

'Let's not quarrel,' said Buckley, and made his peace as best he could. But it had not been much of a visit.

As he left, Lewis came into the yard with a shotgun under his arm and a stained bag over his shoulder. He looked like a tall, cold bird with a blue beak for a nose.

'I didn't know you came here shooting, Roddi.'

'There's a lot of things you don't know. Japhet lets me come over and pot rabbits when I can't settle in the office.' He flung the bag towards an outhouse. 'There you are, Guto. All for you and your Dad.'

The halfwit came out of the dark building. He shook the bag, and four rabbits fell out. He went up to Rhodri, stuttering in his throat and nodding his head.

'That's all right, Guto. You get the girl to put 'em in a pie.'

'He likes you,' said Japhet. 'He likes people that's kind to him.'

Buckley kept his mouth shut. It was not an abstinence he liked to have forced on him. He smarted, too, at the gibe about Morgan. The wedding still rankled. But he would have to go on cultivating Japhet for a bit longer.

A few days later, when the tides were high, he accompanied Billy Rod – Billy Williams, Borough Surveyor – for the long-awaited inspection of the dyke.

'Solid as a rock,' said Billy Rod.

The waves still splashed at the foot of the grass, and more pieces seemed to be missing from the retaining wall offshore. Billy Rod said he'd heard that the river had shifted course again. Perhaps it was that, not the state of the wall, that made the currents stronger. In any case, the Harbour Trust would argue for years rather than pay to mend it.

'I'll come and look again in six months,' he said, adding, as they turned from the spray, that if anyone wanted a *real* problem, they were welcome to come and study the bronze statue of Soldier with Rifle, at present under oilskins in the Streets and Highways yard, which had turned out to be eighteen inches wider at the base than the plinth prepared for it outside the Town Hall.

'He's come, has he?' said Buckley. 'That means a committee meeting soon.'

Committees weren't his line, but he had let Colonel Mappowder put him on the Fallen Heroes Committee in 1902, when the South African War ended, and the town began arguing how, and even whether, the four dead soldiers of south Carmarthenshire should be honoured. It didn't surprise him that three years later there was still no statue on display. There hadn't been a proper war for so long that people were out of practice.

Collecting the money by subscription had been simple, although the usual streaks of pacifism and republicanism were visible, and some local figures – a doctor here, a shopkeeper there – gave long-winded reasons for refusing to contribute. Young David Lloyd George, MP, had come to Port Howard during the war, and packed Calfaria chapel for a fiery speech in favour of the Boers ('DISGRACEFUL PERFORMANCE' – the *Star*. 'WELSH WIZARD TRIUMPHS' – the *News*); when the Boers were beaten, the town's Liberals and Welsh Nationalists went on muttering about concentration camps and cruelties.

Buckley wasn't interested in the higher politics, or even the lower kind. Men had died and they deserved decent recognition. He supported Mappowder's proposal of a soldier with his rifle at the ready. What was there to argue about? No other war was likely in any of their lifetimes, despite the scares that blazed up twice a year in the London *Daily Mail*. They had the money for a statue, and that was the end of it. Ah, but should it not be a memorial garden, or a fund to send poor children on holiday, or avenues of trees? The Fallen Heroes Committee was bombarded with advice, and deeply divided.

Even the statue, assuming it was going to be a statue, had been far from straightforward. In the opinion of Henry W. Sprewett, Town Clerk, who was secretary of the Fallen Heroes, the soldier should be sitting on the ground, firing a Maxim gun – 'Six hundred rounds a minute, gentlemen, that's the bark of the British bulldog.' Rhodri Lewis, the most prominent Liberal on the committee, was opposed to any statue at all, but suggested mischievously that if they had to have one, couldn't it be a member of the Cycle Corps, ringing his bell and pedalling into action?

Even the rifle caused arguments – was a fixed bayonet part of a hero's equipment, or an unnecessarily warlike touch?

'Humbug,' Buckley had said, in one of his rare contributions to the debate. 'Whoever he is, he's a fighting man. He went to war with the intention of killing people. Quite right, too.'

It had taken three years to have the statue commissioned and made, more or less as proposed by the Colonel in the first place. Buckley's carriage took him up the hill to Cilfrew Castle, the Mappowder residence, hoping this would be the committee's last meeting.

A footman was ready in the Indian Room with light refreshments and apologies from Sir Lionel, who was at the copperworks on urgent business but would be with them presently. Half a dozen were there already, warming their behinds at the fire or standing near the stuffed elephant.

'I do b'lieve the Lord's against the statue,' said Rees Coal, slouching up to Buckley. 'You won't believe what's happened.'

'The plinth is too small.'

'No, no, Davy, the statue is too big.'

'The best brains in Streets and Highways are wrestling with that problem,' said Rhodri, no smile to be seen. 'What Mr Buckley and I are really here for is a quiet word about your prices. We hear they're coming down. Isn't that so, Davy?'

'Not a hope, gents. I expect to get an Admiralty contract. They don't quibble over pennies.'

'Signed it yet?' said Buckley.

'Ain't no hurry.'

'Eight and tuppence, at the pithead.'

'Are you a combine, then, you two?'

'We discuss it from time to time,' said Rhodri. 'Then again, we compare notes on the quality of the coal we're being supplied with.'

'Watch what you say about my coal. 'Tis better than some of the stuff you buy. When a roller breaks in yer works, the engine stops, like as not, 'cause the steam pressure's down. Buy decent coal, it wouldn't happen.'

He left them for the latest arrival, Tom Egge, who owned a tin-stamping works.

The room filled up. Men who lived well off a few seams of coal, or a tin mill in two sheds, or a blast furnace built before the Crimean War, or a rusty steamer, or a pottery making plates, or even a grocer's shop with mice in the flour, rubbed their prosperity off on one another. They were Buckley's friends, by and large, though he wouldn't have trusted some of them with a packet of sherbet.

He made an exception for Rhodri.

'Buckley & Lewis, right?'

'You've nearly got it. Lewis & Buckley.'

They were each proud of the family name. But it was enough for Buckley to have it on the letter-head and the sides of tinplate boxes. Rhodri wanted his in the newspapers every week as well – elected member of this body, co-opted member of that; under the crust he was vain.

He told Buckley in an offhand way that a seat on the Harbour Trust would be vacant by the summer, and he was hoping to have it.

'Excellent,' said Buckley, 'then you can do something about the retaining wall off the sands. It needs repairing.'

All around them, kites were being flown, opinions canvassed, winks tipped. T. T. Rees, wholesale provisions, slid up for a word about the Poor Law Guardians (chairman, Rhodri Lewis Esq). Tenders were due in by the end of the month. T. T.'s squeaky voice could be heard discussing currant cake, arrowroot, butter, cocoa, sardines, lentils, Welsh oatmeal, haricot beans, strawberry jam and scouring soap.

Llewelyn the Death was hanging about by the elephant's back legs, pretending to listen to Sprewett discuss the borough council's plans for electric traction, but really waiting for a chance to get Rhodri's ear and discuss coffins. February was the coffin month, and the Board of Guardians were good customers.

Mappowder arrived with a light step for a big man. His red face and white hair were tempered by a voice that was softer than strangers expected. 'Friends,' he began, and, after making his apologies, leaned against the mantelpiece, cutting and lighting a cigar, while Sprewett read the minutes of the previous meeting, almost a year ago.

Chairs of cane and leather, deep sofas and chesterfields, accommodated most of the committee. Rhodri Lewis sat upright on a plain dining chair, as if to demonstrate his independence. Buckley was in a window seat where he could see what was going on. In the grey light of a winter afternoon, the cotton carpets and native paintings on cloth that draped the walls seemed to reflect their colours among one another. A marble throne at the far end of the room burned along one side with the firelight, and a case of swords, damascened with silver, made a row of crescent moons.

It was customary to make jokes behind the Colonel's back about his curios and his elephant, but the room was part of his power. He had fought a skirmish or two in his Indian Army days before he inherited the copperworks and twelve thousand acres of Carmarthenshire. India was another world, one he had touched and they hadn't. Buckley felt the chill of the tall window-panes down his spine. When he grew old, what would he have achieved?

The Colonel was speaking. The statue, they might have heard, had arrived. The plinth – ah, my friends, the poor plinth (laughter) – but Mr Sprewett had assured him that an overhanging base would be supplied, if anyone knew what that was (renewed laughter).

The real news was that he had made an informal approach to a certain person about unveiling the statue. With the committee's indulgence, he would disclose that name.

They all sat up and looked at one another. Egge was heard to whisper, 'Does he mean the King?' That was taking things too far. Mappowder had been in touch, via suitable intermediaries, with the hero of the South African War, General Roberts, now Earl Roberts.

There were cries of 'Hear hear!' and some foot-stamping. 'Good old Bobs!' shouted Hughes of Old Castle works.

Yes, said Mappowder, Earl Roberts would be available on a date in August to come down and do the honours. Mr Sprewett had confided to him informally that the Town

Council would play its part, with decorations along the route and a triumphal arch. All that was needed was a formal invitation from the committee.

Rhodri Lewis opposed it, but the meeting was against him. Earl Roberts in the town would be good for business. A formal invitation would be sent. If anyone had ideas about the great day, Mappowder would be glad to hear them.

'I'll get the works to make him in tinplate,' said Buckley. Heads turned approvingly. 'On a horse.'

'That's a splendid offer. Life-size?'

'Why not?' In fifty years, they might remember him for it. 'I'll talk to the men.'

Rhodri clapped ironically, but Buckley didn't mind. They disagreed on most things and yet there was an understanding of temperament between them, a breath of dissent they shared, even if one was a Tory, the other a Liberal.

As Buckley was leaving, the Colonel asked him to stay a moment. A servant turned on electric lights by the fire and drew the curtains.

'I never know what you're for or against,' the Colonel grumbled.

'I'm not always sure myself. That's one reason I don't go in for committees.'

'Perhaps you should. Since democratic ideas are becoming the fashion, it behoves us to make sure we have the right kind of democrats, not the dangerous Lloyd George variety. Why not play a part in public life? There's a vacancy coming up on the Harbour Trust.'

'Rhodri Lewis wants it. I don't.'

Mappowder waved at a chair. 'Men never speak their minds. Think of this. I control the railway access to a dozen works. Every wagon has to use my lines – in some cases it's not more than ten yards of track, but that makes no difference. I see that they pay. That was my father's method and now it's mine. Do you suppose the owners of those works would ever speak out on any issue involving me? There were three or four of them here today.'

'Rhodri Lewis pays you wayleave. He spoke out. He always does.'

'Our Rhodri's an exception. The licensed jester.'

'Is that how you think of him?'

'He parades his opinions – very moral and decent they are, too, but I prefer something subtler. One of these days he'll be after the Metal Trades presidency. But he wouldn't be right for the job. You, on the other hand, would.'

It was unexpected. Buckley always thought of himself as rough-and-ready – as good as the next man, but not interested in most of the next men.

'Can I think about it?'

'Plenty of time yet. Let me know how Earl Roberts in tinplate is getting on.'

Not many men were remembered for fifty years, for anything. Turning away from the fire, he felt the chill.

The religious revival that Morgan Buckley had felt in his bones began late in 1904 and continued into the following year. Its leader was a fanatical young coal-miner turned theological student, Evan Roberts, who travelled about with an entourage of lady singers, preaching to hysterical congregations, and stirring up tales of supernatural events that amazed the newspaper reporters who followed the campaign.

While standing at her washtub, a Llynfi Valley woman had seen her four dead babies and heard a choir of angels singing 'O Paradise'. A Christ-like figure in white robes was seen walking on an aqueduct at Neath. Roberts himself saw Satan grinning in a hedge at four o'clock one afternoon.

Morgan loved the excitement. At Blaen Cwm it was like

living through a revolution. He went out preaching with bands of students, half believed in the miracles, and longed to be like Roberts; he slept badly, with disordered dreams.

One morning he lost control of himself in Mr Wimmer's classroom when Gwilym, the farmer's son, drew attention to a report in the *Western Mail* – a hard-headed newspaper read by industrialists in Cardiff – that a man who claimed to have seen mysterious red triangles in the sky, while attending a Salvation Army meeting, had really been looking at a hoarding, and the red triangle was part of an advertisement for Bass Beer. Morgan called him a squinting toad and got his hands around his neck.

Dr Jenkins, the Principal of Blaen Cwm, decided he was suffering from nervous exhaustion. He prescribed a week's rest at home, sending a telegram to say that Morgan would be there on the mid-morning train. But Morgan sent a second telegram from the post office to say 'Matter resolved. Morgan not coming. Jenkins,' and went in search of Evan Roberts.

As far as Ammanford he travelled on the prescribed route. Then he changed trains and disappeared into the maze of branch lines north of Swansea. Roberts was there somewhere, zig-zagging among the mining villages. At each wooden platform serving the sulphurous neighbourhood of a pithead or a copperworks, Morgan would lean out of the window and shout at a porter, 'Where'll I find him?'

There were rumours and false reports. He had been at one place, he was half promised at another. Tonight he might be at Godre'rgraig, or if not him, his brother Dan, or one of his lady singers. Roberts knew he could pack half a dozen chapels with a hint of his coming. So he left it to the Spirit to tell him, at the last minute, which one he ought to choose.

Late in the afternoon Morgan broke his journey at a village of two streets and a public house. Shut away in the snug he fed himself on bread-and-cheese and barley water. He felt feverish yet capable of anything. It gave him a singing noise in the head to think that until a few months ago, Roberts, too, had been a nobody, a young man in patched boots and a shabby suit, studying at a college barely twenty miles from Blaen Cwm. The Spirit, whizzing to earth like a meteor, might easily have landed somewhere else; twenty miles wasn't far in the endless geometry of the Universe.

He sat still, listening to the murmur of colliers' voices in the next bar, trying to guess Roberts's plans. According to one report, the evangelist had exhausted himself the day before and was going home to meditate. But his presence was strong in the smoke-smeared countryside.

Morgan prayed to the Spirit, hand over face. Suddenly he heard the name, 'Birchgrove'. He opened his eyes, not sure if it had come from inside his head or the next bar.

'Do they say he might be in Birchgrove tonight?' he asked the landlord.

'Hope not. Too close for comfort, Birchgrove.'

'There's a meeting over there, at Soar,' said a collier. 'More broken windows and sore knees. Newspaper reporter, are you?'

'Minister of religion, as a matter of fact,' said Morgan, and set off to walk six miles in the raw gloom of dusk. He believed that a voice had spoken to him.

He heard Soar before he saw it. They were singing 'Throw out the Lifeline'. Dim walls with lighted windows stood between a cemetery and a slag-heap. By the time he reached the chapel, a woman had broken in with a Welsh hymn, 'Ymgrymed pawb i lawr', 'Let all people bend'. A few of the Lifeline singers clung to their melody.

It was chaos; Morgan's mouth was dry. A deep voice was shouting, 'I have passed first-class examinations in the service of the damned, and even I have found mercy. Even I have. Even I. Even I.'

'Any news?' he asked a man in the porch who looked like a deacon.

The man shook his head. 'He have sent Sal Jones in his place – hear her? It's a grand meeting. We've had a rugby player already has thrown away his kit.'

'Roberts will be here tonight,' said Morgan, and pushed his way inside. The heavy air closed behind him like curtains, warm and sour. The deacon had followed; he was looking towards him and talking to another elder. Then Morgan lost sight of them and was absorbed into the congregation.

They were like people tipped off a cart – some upright, some fallen into heaps of bowed flesh, some swaying on pews, some kneeling with hands locked together, some half crucified against walls, some sitting up straight with hymn-books as if it was a normal Sunday service, some stretched out in the aisles, some hopping and gyrating, some with their heads back at alarming angles, some covering their faces.

Colliers' wives in aprons rubbed against shopkeepers' ladies with bits of fur round their necks. Men in stiff collars and men in pit-clothes bellowed confessions of spiritual weakness into one another's faces, which all wore dazed expressions. There were groups of young women, younger than Morgan, who seemed glued to one another, hands and faces brushing, breasts thrust out together when a hymn swept their portion of the floor, then, bodies suddenly concave, drawn together into a cluster of necks and dresses, emitting small, sticky sounds that might have been giggles, until the faces re-emerged and were seen to be wet with tears.

The elderly minister in the pulpit made little attempt to influence proceedings. Sal Jones, a broad-faced contralto, led the singing, but her voice was challenged by others. When a man shouted, 'Let us have more prayers and fewer hymns!' she knelt obediently.

They were aware of needing Roberts. There was an anguish about the hymns as they sang of lost sheep.

'He's coming, you know!' shouted Morgan, only to be shushed by a deacon.

They ignored him. He edged from place to place, boiling with certainty. Finding himself by a knot of girls, he whispered to one of them, 'Believe me, Evan Roberts will be here tonight.' She rolled her eyes and shuddered, and he caught a whiff of her skin. It came to him like a vision, sharp with detail, that she and her friends dreamt about Roberts every night.

It was half past nine, then it was ten o'clock. Would he come? To lose faith was to be lost for ever. Morgan remained standing, praying to himself. Upstairs in the gallery they shouted that a woman who had lived an unclean life was kneeling – was confessing – was saved. Waves of singing bounced off the woodwork and made the lights shake. A voice called out that someone had fainted. A pane of glass broke.

'I will not have damage!' shrilled the old minister.

'Let the Spirit do its work!' came from upstairs.

Columns of sound were ascending like smoke, chantings and prayings, bits of hymns that had broken loose, screamings in Welsh and English, sobbings from the younger women who sat rigid, thighs pressed together.

Morgan knew it couldn't last. For a moment he thought to force his way to the front, leap on the pulpit stairs, make himself a focus so the night could be prolonged until Roberts came. Instead he knelt, suddenly broken by the knowledge that it was too late for Roberts now.

Near him a man was crying out, 'You know me as a

schoolmaster. Some of you I have taught. I have taught you *nothing*! This is reality, *here*, tonight.'

In blackness, in chaos, Morgan prayed to be released from his visions and longings. 'I have had enough,' he said. 'I would like to be a simple minister of religion. If that is thy will, naturally.'

The schoolmaster was bringing the meeting to its climax. He had a stern delivery; you could imagine him rounding on a boy and clipping his ear. There was no philosophy in the universe to explain these things, he declared. His life had been hypocrisy and fraud. This is reality, he kept saying, reality is within these four walls, inside this split-second of time.

There was a rushing like wind, the doors of the chapel swung open, footsteps were heard, and a great moan of 'Sh-h-h!' went up from those nearest the entrance. Morgan was unable to open his eyes. Enormous weights pressed down on him, enough to shatter his spine and make the blood spurt out of his fingers. He tried to scream but couldn't. He concluded he was dying, probably of a stroke brought on by disappointment; it was the very moment of death.

In his coma a powerful voice somewhere in space said, 'I was told to come here.'

Morgan pulled himself together and looked up to see Roberts in the pulpit. He had been afraid to believe it was true, that was all. Now everything was confirmed; the Spirit that spoke to Roberts spoke to him. People were noticing him at last, nudging one another. He felt dizzy with gratitude, all peace and compassion. He wanted to send a telegram to Gwilym saying, 'You were wrong but I forgive you.'

Roberts leaned on the rail, a tall, unbearded figure, with a vague air of distinction about his arched nose and long straight mouth. A man with a yellow moustache who hadn't been there before was looking up at him, sucking the end of his pencil.

Roberts asked how many had been saved that night. A voice shouted, 'Five.' Another said, 'Six, at least.'

'You cannot tell. The truth is hard to be sure of.' A smile wavered and went out. The voice, though, remained gentle. 'Only Jesus Christ knows the truth. He knows the names and addresses of those who are saved . . . and those who are not.'

Two young women in cloaks and hats had joined Sal Jones below the pulpit. They sang of harvests and rewards. The congregation joined in. Morgan found himself singing, too. One of the lady evangelists had protruding pink lips, and he watched fascinated as they opened and closed on the syllables.

He was thinking how agreeable it must be to go from place to place with a band of pure women, who were ready to bring one a glass of water, say, or a handkerchief on demand, when Roberts cried 'Stop!' in a commanding voice, and the singing died away.

His gaze, raking the congregation, was that of an auctioneer or a politician.

'Someone laughed,' he said, so softly that at first people weren't sure if they had heard correctly. 'Or smiled. It could have been smiled. Now then, there are smiles of joy and smiles of mockery.' The voice became a shout. 'This – was – mockery!'

'No, no,' sobbed a woman, amid a ripple of unhappiness.

'I noticed a coldness as soon as I entered. There are some who are here out of curiosity. They will be bent, never fear. Their souls are in terrible danger. Pray for them. Now! Everyone pray, out loud.'

People dropped on their knees. Some stood gazing up at the roof. Shouts and groans rose above a murmur of dismay.

The evening had taken an odd turn. When a man begged

for mercy, Roberts leapt down from the pulpit, waving large hands in the air, and knelt beside him. 'The Holy Spirit says it's all right for you to be forgiven,' he announced. It wasn't clear if this was the man who had laughed.

The night grew more mysterious. Roberts was friendly now, talking rather than preaching, telling them that what they must do was stand still, and they would find salvation growing everywhere like grass. 'Never mind what jobs you do,' he said. 'I see there are miners here tonight. As you know I used to be one myself. I never cared for the colliery much. I have even forgotten the name of the seam I worked in.'

'Amen! Amen!' they shouted, and Morgan watched the long bony fingers, knotting and unknotting.

'I knew for years that I was to be the means of bringing about a revival in Wales. I kept it a secret from everyone, even my Mam and Dad. It will spread throughout the world. England first. Then America. China after that.'

'Pray for America,' someone called from the gallery. 'There's some of us have relatives in America.'

'No!' said Roberts. His mood changed again. 'Pray for England. It's nearer home. When there's an east wind you can smell the stench.'

He frightened them. They surrendered to him but they feared him. He told them they had hypocrites among them, and drunkards, and youths who preferred billiards to the Bible. A man rolled in the aisle, gasping for breath. 'Leave him!' warned Roberts. 'He has been struck.'

Morgan could have stood there all night. There had never been anything like this. He felt that he alone in the congregation understood Roberts and his method, how he had no option but to make people soft, like clay, so he could mould them. With so much at stake, kindness and unkindness didn't come into it; he was pure energy, straight from God.

Roberts was gripping the rail in front of him. 'There is someone here,' he said, 'who does not believe. I do not mean a sinner. I mean a person who should not be here.'

'I am praying for his soul,' called the lady evangelist with puffy lips.

'The Spirit has told me no one is to pray for him. His soul is lost. It is owing to disobedience.'

His eyes, searching the gallery, stopped at a pillar, travelled down it, and reached Morgan. Had the moment come? Morgan was ready to give his witness, even to help identify the lost soul, perhaps the root of the evening's disquiet.

'That one,' said Roberts.

Morgan looked over his shoulder. He couldn't see who Roberts was pointing at. A woman shook her fist at him. He turned back, his legs becoming jelly. 'That one,' said Roberts again.

'I was told you would be here,' said Morgan. He had to force out the words; they hurt his throat. 'I was told to come.'

'But by whom?'

The man was mad, of course. Morgan had his own sanity to think about. He shrugged his shoulders and walked out in dead silence. The door banged behind him. He heard a hymn start up. Poor mad Roberts.

Morgan stood in the roadway, the horizon lit by blast furnaces towards Swansea. The revival seemed to be over.

A period of recovery was called for. The formula prescribed by Dr Jenkins came in handy. 'Nervous exhaustion' meant nothing but covered everything. It left the dark puzzles unexplored; it suited Morgan, who knew that whatever he was and would become must bide its time.

The night had been one long dream in which he died over and over again, to be revived, each time, by a prod from a woman whose face he never saw, but who might have been Margaret. He watched the dawn through the window of a milk train clouded by his breath. An hour later he was at Rhydness farm, outside Port Howard, eating boiled bacon in his grandmother's kitchen, explaining that he had been working too hard at college.

'I was supposed to go home,' he said, 'but I came here instead. Can I stay a few days? I could help round the farm.'

'You been in trouble, then?' She whisked the bacon off the table so he wouldn't expect another slice. 'I hope you haven't come asking for money.'

'Have I ever, Nain?' He squeezed her skin-and-bone hand. 'What with paying Pritchard a salary, and him cheating you over the accounts – I bet he does – and the bad harvest – I daresay it was a bad harvest? – and Margaret's wedding present, you must find it hard.'

'Some people think I'm made of money.'

'What would I want money for anyway? Isn't God my reward?'

'You were always glib with God. Like your grandfather.'

'He and I would have got on. Shall I read you a passage?'

He took the Bible and read at random, about Gideon and the three hundred warriors he hid in jars. Hannah rocked in her chair, eyes closed. The tale soothed Morgan as well. It had no moral message, not even much poetry; it was just a dream and a battle full of names, Oreb and Zeeb, Manasseh and Abel-meholah. After what happened at Soar chapel, he could do without fire and drama for a bit.

'I think I'll have a lie-down upstairs, if that's all right,' he said, when he had finished the chapter.

'You look as if you spent the night in a hedge.'

'On a railway station. It's a long story.'

'Spare me,' she said. But she reached up and ruffled his hair.

He slept till the afternoon in one of the big damp beds, then went for a walk on the Twmp, the hill behind the farm. New lambs bleated at him; a ewe trailed bloody strings. The savage clamour of the night before was fading. Faith, after all, might be simple; Morgan saw himself wandering far from the paths of men, patient, whole, indifferent to everything but God, without ambition.

Roberts, mad with pride, contained the seed of his own destruction. If a voice led Morgan there, was it to show him the dangers? The thought made his heart pound. Life seemed to consist of illusions which flaked away only to reveal other equally convincing illusions beneath, progressions towards a core of ultimate reality that, if reached, might annihilate the discoverer; then the reality would be death itself.

A locomotive heading a coal train appeared below, steaming along the embankment that carried the main line across the waterlogged bottom meadows; source, it was said, of hundreds if not thousands of pounds in the bank for Grandfather Tomos when the railway company was desperate to cut the quickest route down to Port Howard during the eighteen-seventies. Did Hannah still have that money? Was there an illusion of wealth behind her illusion of poverty?

At the top of the hill he sat on a stone until his bottom got cold, unable to stop being bored by the countryside. The paths of men were the ones that mattered. God, after all, was as likely to be found in a city as in a parish of fields. Margaret had sent him a postcard on his twenty-first birthday a month earlier, showing the Welsh chapel in London's Charing Cross Road. The minister posed on the steps, teeth bared. 'What of the future?' Margaret had scribbled, after the birthday greeting.

When he got back, he recognised his father's second-best carriage in the yard. The coachman raised his hat. Morgan tried slipping upstairs, but the maid saw him and said he was expected in the parlour.

His mother was there as well, wedged into a low armchair from which she was trying to be helpful; the cups rattled as Morgan arrived.

'And where may you have been?' said Buckley.

'Doing the Lord's work, Dadda.'

'One telegram said you were coming home. Another one said you weren't. Now you turn up here, pestering your grandmother.'

'Leave him be, Davy,' said Hannah. She wore white cotton gloves and sat in state on the sofa, letting her daughter-in-law get on with dispensing the weak tea and hard yellow cake. 'You wouldn't have known if you hadn't come over with that old thing.'

'Oh, it'll be nice to have sharp knives,' said Pomona. 'And cleaned as well.'

'If the girl wants to sharpen a knife, she does it on the back step. I'm glad Davy's got money to throw about.'

It stood on the floor, next to the sofa, a drum with slots and a handle, like an engine of torture.

'Very smart, you know, Nain,' said Morgan, stooping to examine it. 'Almost brand new, I'd say.'

Dadda gave him a venomous look. 'The less you say about anything the better. The minute we get back, I am sending a telegram to Blaen Cwm to ask what's going on.'

'Leave him stay with me over Saturday and Sunday. He's a good boy, aren't you, Morgan? Read to me beautiful earlier.' Under her breath she added, 'Doesn't come wheedling with presents like some.'

Mamma was difficult in her own way. Before they left she asked Morgan to carry the knife-grinder into the pantry, and came after him. 'Charity begins at home,' she said. 'I won't have Dadda upset, so that's that. Faults he may have. But a better father never walked the earth. You're to come back with us now, and we can settle everything up.'

'Settle what, Mamma?'

'All he asks is respect. I know he's not perfect. But he's never liked telegrams. You and he are more akin than you realise. He used to pin great hopes on you. He's like all thick-skinned men, he needs flattering more than one thinks.'

Cornered between a mousetrap and the bread bin, Morgan couldn't drift towards a door. He tried putting his arms around his mother's waist and lifting her off the floor.

'Morgan!'

'Mamma!'

'You are a silly boy. This isn't some joke.'

She kicked her legs and went red in the face.

'My duty is here just now. A voice told me.'

Unable to stop himself, he kissed her on the cheek and popped her on one of the shelves.

She jumped down, twisting round to see if her dress was spoiled. 'If your father's up with his indigestion tonight, we'll know who to thank.'

When they had gone, Hannah put her gloves back in the drawer and asked slyly if Morgan would take something into Port Howard for her.

'Am I allowed the trap?'

'It isn't heavy. God gave you legs.'

'I could get back quicker with the trap and read to you before supper.'

She considered. 'Hywel shall do the driving in case you make the pony wild, like the times you were small.'

'Couldn't Hywel take whatever it is?'

'Anyone *could*. Pritchard *could*. Wait here.'

He heard her moving about upstairs. She returned carrying a linen bag with a draw-string, and Morgan sensed coins; milled edges seemed to grate in his head.

'Ninety pounds,' she said. 'You'd better count them.'

The sovereigns fell out of the bag like a lump of gold and shattered on the table. Morgan counted ninety-one but said nothing. The thick coins stuck to his fingers.

'More than a poor minister's paid in a year, Nain.'

'It's hard-earned, I'll tell you that. There's butter and eggs and poultry and mutton gone into it. A year's profits.'

He didn't believe her. It was of no consequence. He refilled the bag and weighed it in his palm.

'I'm glad you trust me.'

'I'm glad you're glad.'

Handing over the bank book, waiting while Hywel brought the trap to the door, Hannah kept her eyes on the money.

'I've a mind to come with you and see the bank manager.'

'Hop in, then.'

'But there's a cold wind.'

'So let's wait till tomorrow.'

'Mind you have the book stamped,' she said, and went inside.

He was his own master. He lounged back, savouring his wealth as they rattled down to the town. Crossing the canal bridge into Market Street, he had an urge to pelt people with gold, just to see their faces.

He told Hywel to wait for him in the yard of the Stepney.

'Mrs Buckley said – '

'Don't be frightened of Mrs Buckley. Here's twopence. Buy a meat pie.'

Morgan counted out ninety pounds to a cashier with a runny nose, and left the bank feeling full of grace. The Free Library was on the next corner. He went into the reading room, drawn to the file of *Cambrian Posts*. His hands shook as he turned the pages of the afternoon edition, and the black sludge that was inked over the racing tips,

Erased by order of the Libraries Committee, came off on his fingers.

An inner page had what he was after:

REVIVAL BOILS AT BIRCHGROVE.
CONVERSIONS GALORE.
UNUSUAL SCENE AS ROBERTS DENOUNCES STRANGER.
INTENSE BEWILDERMENT.

Morgan heard the words as though someone had spoken them; he almost expected his neighbours to look up. Reading the account, he found mistakes, as he might have expected. The time Roberts arrived was wrong. So was the description of himself ('An educated man aged about 30, wearing an overcoat'). The reporter had even failed to hear the final exchange of words correctly, attributing to Morgan an imbecile 'People told me to come,' and to Roberts, 'What people?'

An adjacent paragraph caught his eye, announcing a revival service to be held in Port Howard that evening, at New Dock chapel. Hadn't he finished with all that? Restless now, he wandered through the market, and down gritty lanes towards New Dock, which had not been new for forty years.

The pubs were busy, the corner shops open. Children ran errands or played in the dirt, women with babies in shawls stood inside doorways to avoid the wind, talking to neighbours they couldn't see; their voices blew down the long terraces, Tunnel Row and Copperworks Road, Tinworks Row and New Street. No men were to be seen. They would be sinning non-stop inside the Red Cow, the Mariners, the Halfway. Even the urchin with firewood dagger and helmet cut from tinplate, prancing under a lamp and fighting his shadow on a house, would soon be old enough for beer and swearing.

The chapel was beyond, figures converging on it. Morgan

turned down another terrace of stone houses and lost his way on the edge of marshland. He skirted a tinplate works, where flames spurted from cracks in the walls, saw a man vomiting outside the Morfa Arms (foretaste of wrath to come), and once more came in sight of the chapel. Ahead of him was a group of young women, their heavy skirts brushing the road. Their sins, actual or potential, made him feel weak.

Had he been led to this place, too? Keeping behind the women, he entered the chapel and found a seat. Kneeling, he prayed with his head buried in his arms as the building began to fill and spasmodic singing broke out.

He felt calm, ready for anything, as though he had a plan without knowing what it was. Choosing his moment as the praying fluctuated, he spoke briefly about the Revival ('I was fortunate enough to have a conversation with Mr Evan Roberts') and went on, 'I am a young man, and I think the young people have a duty to be out and about. We ought to be taking the message to the public houses. If a few will follow me, we can make a start tonight.'

A deacon spoke against it, but a tinplate-worker, still in his apron, opposed him; the minister said nothing, and Morgan led an exodus of half a dozen youths. As they assembled in the porch, two young women came out, then two more.

'Are you ready, sisters?' cried Morgan.

'Wait you,' said a girl, tying her hat under her chin. 'There's more will come when they start the next hymn.'

They stamped their feet for warmth, grinning and jostling. Soon more girls than youths were coming out. He saw the tinplate cuts on their hands and smelt the pickling on their legs. 'Who are you, then?' one of them asked, looking at him from under a shabby beret. It could have been the pee-pot woman, but the weak gas lamp on the wall left gaps in her features.

When the party was twenty strong, Morgan said, 'Quick march!' A woman in a cloak came out at the last minute, a scarf pulled around her face. 'Any more for salvation?' shouted Morgan, and led them off to the Red Cow, where they prayed and sang outside the window, and a drunk gave them a shilling.

Up and down the streets they marched, picking up more followers, getting bolder, crowding into the passageway of the Fox, arguing with the landlord of the Mariners.

Morgan hardly knew where they were. It could have been one street, one public house, one hymn. His senses were overwhelmed by the skirts and bonnets clustering around him. The pee-pot woman, if that's who she was, wore a thin, brass-buttoned coat around her shoulders. With her hair pinned back and excitement in her cheeks, she was almost pretty. She glanced at him from time to time, ignoring the stern looks he gave her.

At the Morfa Arms a woman with uncombed hair rushed out as Morgan was praying and danced an Irish jig, screeching and waving a bare arm above her head. Men laughed from the doorway. Morgan waited until the woman stopped, exhausted, and said, 'Mary, you're dancing to your death.'

The woman looked alarmed. She ran sobbing into the doorway. A man called, 'Hey, you, how d'you know her name?' He stumbled towards them, but the girls closed around Morgan, and he went back, muttering.

Beyond the lamps and corner shops, at the limits of the town, darkness pressed in on them from marshes and the bay. The joys of Jesus couldn't exist in a vacuum; they were only joys because the sins were never far away. Take the pee-pot woman. Half an hour alone with her, and he could change her life.

He had lost sight of her – the group was breaking up. Men had begun to drift back from the pubs. The keener revivalists went to pick them off, hoping for the repentance that went with empty pockets.

The woman in the cloak fell into step beside him. 'Excuse me, Mr Buckley,' she said, 'how could you tell her name was Mary?'

He went cold. 'Know *my* name, do you?' When she turned her face under a lamp, he saw at once who it was. 'Well I never. Miss Rees, of course.'

'So how could you tell?'

'She looked like a Mary. I'm not sure. It came into my head.'

They chatted like old friends. It wasn't a night for saving the pee-pot woman after all. He thought he saw her in a doorway, staring. Miss Rees claimed his attention. Her mother should have gone with her to the meeting, she said, but felt unwell. Their own chapel had seen little fervour so far.

'Was it how you expected?'

'It seems a grand thing to walk about the streets, doing good.'

'Don't hope for too much, is my rule.'

A warmth came from her. She was flushed and her eyes were brilliant. 'So was it the Holy Spirit at work?' she asked – like a child, using words it was uncertain of.

Yet she was also the self-assured young woman who had been at the wedding.

'These things are all mysteries,' he said. 'It may be human compassion. Compassion itself may *be* the Holy Spirit in one of its forms. The more I study, the less I know. I think I was just as wise when I worked in my father's office – training to be a manufacturer.'

'Ah,' she said, 'that wouldn't have suited you.'

'You can tell? Yes, a woman like you can tell everything. I want to clasp your hand. If the Holy Spirit is abroad tonight, it must have played some part in bringing us together.'

They had left the New Dock district. To their right, inland, was a wedge of works and sidings. Straight ahead would lead them to the railway station and the lower part of the town. To the left, seawards, was the marshland and Buckley's.

Fires glowed, the wind blew acrid dust into their mouths. Her hand – plump, hot, sharp-nailed – was inside his.

Crabwise, they skirted the marshes and found a path he recognised. Crossing a stream on a plank bridge, she leaned against him, the cloak flattening itself to her body.

'Where are we going?' she whispered.

'Where the Spirit takes us. It leads – we follow.'

Figures moved in the rusty glare of the rolling department, open to the fields. To the left, a row of squat chimneys showed against the sky.

'Tinhouse – not working – doesn't always,' he explained; the words thickened in his throat like cream. His arm was round her waist, his fingers touched her rib-cage. 'Miss Rees, or shall I say Aeronwy?'

'. . . what you like.'

'. . . sent to me,' he was whispering, '. . . sent to you.'

Memory went on working. The shed where they stored materials for the polishing rolls was still there. The key lived on a ledge. Cotton waste and sheepskin lay in piles. He knew by touch.

'Kneel here,' he whispered.

'Like this?'

He unfastened her cloak.

'The Spirit is here. It commands. We are all children, lost in the fields of eternity. There was nothing Roberts could tell me I didn't know already. Do you feel the Spirit?'

'Oh yes!' she breathed.

'In your soul,' and he opened the buttons of her blouse,

'in your heart,' and almost keeled over at her breasts. They were heavier than the breasts of imagination. The way they pulled away from the skin, separate entities, amazed him.

'. . . in us both,' and when they were stretched out together, he raised her skirts and slowly, ritually, pulled off her underclothes, continuing to whisper – 'This was meant' and 'power of grace' and 'lost in eternity'; the words were aimed at himself as well as at her.

When her drawers caught on a boot as she drew them clear of her legs, she said 'Damn!' under her breath, and the syllable, cutting across his 'spirits' and 'mysteries', hurled them forward to the conclusion. They slammed against one another like enemies. After he had finished, which wasn't long, she went on writhing under him like a fish.

He said 'Amen' and rolled clear. There were bits of wool in his mouth. Aeronwy was in tears. She said she was hurting. His monologue tried to pick up the thread with something about 'destiny' and 'gratitude', but petered out in the face of her frantic tidying-up. Thereafter he confined himself to providing a clean handkerchief and picking bits of wool from her clothes.

Late-goers were still on the streets when they returned across the stream. They hurried past an argument under a lamp-post in case it was New Dock evangelists with a drunkard. In Station Road they stopped for Morgan to inspect her cloak and skirt in the light.

'Have we done an awful thing?' she asked.

He whispered consolations through his teeth – her goodness, his piety, Man's ignorance of divine intention. But he had a feeling the question had been rhetorical, after all. She was Miss Rees again. She patted his hand and said, 'I trust you.'

Her desire to be seen home and delivered safe and sound to Mother was only natural. They struggled up a hilly avenue, against a wind that poured over the top, and found the front door of the square-box villa in Glenalla Road open.

'Well, my girl,' said Mrs Rees grimly. 'I do think, Mr Buckley – ' But in a minute or two she had relented, and was smiling at his account of the young people's impromptu mission.

'It wouldn't have happened when I was your age,' she said. 'But, I suppose . . .'

'I do hope I shall see you both again soon,' said Morgan, in a hurry, as he explained, because he was staying with an aged grandmother who might be worried. His fingers locked with Miss Rees's for a second as they shook hands. 'But I have my final examinations in a few months, so I don't expect to be back until well into the summer.'

He had to walk every inch of the way there. The countryside was black, windswept, vengeful. A tree might have fallen and maimed him, but it didn't. He might have slipped in a ditch and drowned, but his feet were guided safely. Whatever had happened, he knew that in some mysterious way God endorsed it. Miss Rees with her legs raised was fixed in a tableau. Nothing would ever be quite like it again.

'Thank you, thank you,' he said cheerfully, and arrived at the farm whistling.

The latch clicked and he bolted the door behind him. An oil lamp burned on the kitchen table. Hannah slept in her chair. Then he saw her eyes were open.

'Sorry I'm late, Nain. Big meeting. Had to go.'

'I thought – ' she said.

'Thought what?'

'That you'd be back soon. Hywel came home without you.'

He gave her the bank book. 'See?' he said. 'Proper stamp and everything.'

'Ninety pounds. Exactly right.'

'Only there were ninety-one. We counted them again. I brought it back.'

He put the coin on the table.

'Good boy,' she said, and he stood touching her shoulder, sleepy, watching the red coals in the grate. 'Fair do's. *Very* good boy.'

3

'Dear Mamma' (wrote Margaret), 'I hope and believe we have now reached the end, for the time being, of the round of dinner and luncheon parties at which we have been alternately guests of, and hosts to, different members of Henry's family. We seem to have acquitted ourselves satisfactorily, and as Henry said when we were eating a quiet supper last night, just the two of us, "Well, you have had your baptism of fire, or should I say cheese soufflés, and now we can think about entertaining our own friends" – not that there are any of mine so far in Highgate!

'I wrote to you at the time about how kind Mr and Mrs Penbury-Holt have been, and the magnificent weekend we spent with them at Old Saracens, their "place" in Gaddesden (in Hertfordshire), which I liked so much because it was less grand than I had been led to suppose. They dined with us a fortnight later, and the evening went without a hitch, apart from a little uncertainty over the claret. Henry insisted on buying it, from a friend of his in the wine business, and it would have done very well for the pickling department, tell Dadda.

'Tristram (eldest brother – best man – probably very clever) and his wife Charlotte (she made a face when we told her about laverbread, remember?) had us round (Kensington) to a very nice Saturday luncheon, at which we met their two female pixies, since joined by a male pixie, who will have to make sure he can scream and shout as loud as the other two (joke). Stuart (youngest brother – the one who apologised so charmingly for stepping on Aunt Villette's foot and breaking her shoe, according to Aunt

Villette) and his wife Virginia laid on a rather gay occasion at their house in Ealing. I like them best of all, I don't know why.

'I fear they found the return engagement dull, although they were as amusing as ever. Henry was showing off his orchids (he has them in a special conservatory) and Stuart ribbed him about them, christening a spiky one "Kaiser Bill" and a fat purple thing "A Royal Personage", and pretending they were having an argument about the temperature. Quite hilarious, and even Henry looked as if he was going to laugh.

'I think that completes the calendar of family engagements. The only ones we haven't seen are the daughter Daisy (ringlets) and her husband, Dr Munro Parton, LRCP, MRCS, as you may remember he signed himself when RSVP-ing. He has a busy practice in the North and they rarely come to London.

'I forgot to mention Esther, the unmarried daughter. She shares a flat in Victoria with a friend, and they carry on a furious campaign on behalf of soldiers' wives (letters, leaflets, seeing MPs). The friend is an ex-Captain's daughter. It has to do with morals (absence of their menfolk, in plain English!). Morgan, our self-appointed conscience, must meet them if ever he comes to London. (Sorry! Hope he's not sore point still.) When we went there to supper, they gave us unfermented grape juice, which Henry drank as meek as a lamb, and we had an hour's punishment drill addressing envelopes.'

The letter continued about domestic matters arising in a marriage of six months' standing, and was duly posted to South Wales.

From the start Margaret had accepted the need to be an enthusiastic Penbury-Holt, for Henry's sake. In London, with her new family, she would grow to be a different person. Not that she thought anything was radically wrong with the old person, but before she met Henry – two summers earlier, at a resort on the English Channel, where a Penbury-Holt contingent and the Buckleys found themselves staying at the same Imperial Hotel – a grim sense of repetition had begun to trouble her.

Now, when Henry said, 'I fear that Tristram and Charlotte are christening their babe down at Gaddesden the very day I had someone coming here to see me about an orchid,' she automatically took on a family role and said how upset people would be if they failed to appear.

'I daresay you're right. Though it seems only yesterday they were christening the one before.' He fiddled with his *Times* and the orchid in his buttonhole – he was about to leave for the City – and said, 'No doubt our day will come.'

Early in May she believed that it had. She said nothing to Henry, which was fortunate, since it turned out to be a false alarm. That occurred on a Saturday, the day of the christening, an unkind irony that depressed her briefly, until a post arrived with a letter from her Aunt Villette, and gave her something else to think about.

Theodore, Villette's younger boy, was convalescing from scarlet fever. His convalescence was a *great opportunity* (her aunt liked underlining things) for Theodore to broaden his education, and she hoped her niece agreed that it was the duty of someone who had the *inestimable privilege* of living at *the fountain-head of culture* to share her blessings. In other words, could mother and son come and stay for a week?

'We shall be having two visitors from next Tuesday,' she told Lake, the parlourmaid, in the guest bedroom, where she had sent for her. 'Mrs Lloyd will be in here. Her son, who's nine years old, will be in the next room, with the connecting door left unlocked. You'll see everything is got ready?'

In future times it would be the nursery, unless they moved to somewhere bigger before she had a child. Flecks of sunlight, filtered by the leaves of an elm, vibrated on the floor at the very spot where the cradle would stand.

'It certainly needs airing,' she added brusquely, and opened a window with a bang to disperse the last traces of her mood.

When she told Henry about the coming visit, in the cab on the way to Liverpool Street station, he puffed up his cheeks and said, 'You should have consulted me first.'

'Should I? Oh dear. I thought aunts were all right – you know, unobtrusive female relatives.'

'Even if your Aunt Villette is unobtrusive, a boy aged nine is hardly likely to be. I expect to have one or two business associates coming to the house.'

'I'll tell her it's not convenient next week, and you can tell me when would be convenient.'

'I believe that when it comes to purely social entertaining, of which we've done our whack so far, we should start cutting our coat according to our cloth.'

'You mean the real reason is we can't afford it?' She was distressed, ready to blame herself for extravagance if necessary. 'I shall look at the household accounts the minute we get home.'

'It is nothing immediate. I mean only that I have to think about the future. It behoves us to accumulate capital in this life. Tristram is senior to me in the business. I have plans to paddle my own canoe. I give a great deal of thought to accumulating capital.'

Anyone who confided in Margaret won her sympathy at once. She thought how fine he looked, like a songbird with a feathered chest (he went in for embroidered waistcoats), pouring out his call of 'Accumulating Capital!' There was no malice in her perception.

'My father makes me a tiny allowance – did I ever mention it?'

'I think not.'

'I shall happily make it over to you. May I use a little of it first to entertain my aunt?'

'You know how to get round me,' he said, rather stiffly, it seemed to Margaret, and before long they reached the station, and by lunchtime, Old Saracens.

'Dear Mamma,' she might have written afterwards – but didn't, this time – 'the christening was perfectly organised at what Arthur (Mr Penbury-Holt Snr) calls "the family nest" at Gaddesden, thanks to Elizabeth (Mrs ditto) who is always so cool and collected; I suppose it is the English virtue. Tristram and Charlotte were spending the weekend. Their son was given the names Horatio(!) Arthur Thomas, and apart from some vigorous bawling in church by little Horatio – and scratchings-cum-scufflings by their two small daughters (Mrs P-B gave the nanny a look, and the three of them vanished into limbo) – all went well until Stuart (youngest bro.) went red in the face and seemed to be choking. Practically ran from church. Virginia (wife) found him outside, collapsed over gravestone, hysterical with laughter. Initials of babe's given names are H-A-T. "Will be known to all as Old Hat," Bro. Stuart managed to say, when articulate. Joke not appreciated by Tristram.'

Or indeed by anyone except Virginia and, rather nervously, by Margaret. She was determined to be herself but unwilling to offend; the two showed signs of conflicting.

Back at Old Saracens, with tea on the lawn, she was drawn into the circle around Horatio, and presently introduced to the youngish rector of the parish who had done the baby-sprinkling. He was called Rees, but when she made a conversational opening, to the effect that Rees was a Welsh name, he pointed out quickly that his was spelt in the English way, making him a Reece, and added that his family had no connections farther west than Gloucester.

'A good way round the problem is to think of them as West Britons,' she said, 'and then they don't seem so bad.

But they *will* go on speaking that odd language of theirs. Is it perversity, do you suppose?'

'My dear Mrs Penbury-Holt – you yourself are . . .'

'Yes, I am.'

'I most sincerely apologise. I should have caught the lilt in your voice sooner – ' (Quite right, thought Margaret, you're being punished for not listening properly) ' – but I hope you won't think . . .'

'That you dislike the Welsh? No, I think you are merely paying them the unintentional compliment of seeing them as different, a thing the English don't much care for.'

Her father-in-law, coming to sit on a vacant iron chair, heard the last remark, and looked at her speculatively.

'Fortunately modern society has the answer,' he said. 'Travel, education, and the intercourse of nations. Intermarriage, eh, Margaret?'

She was glad when the conversation moved on to roses.

The nicest part of the afternoon was wandering off with Stuart and Virginia to find a tennis court, minus net, where they used mildewed racquets and balls from a hut nearby to play makeshift games. It was only when Henry appeared after half an hour, asking with a puzzled expression what on earth they were doing, that she was conscious of having taken another step in the wrong direction.

It seemed that Esther, the spinster sister, was looking for her. She went hurrying back. Baby, awnings, family, greenness and ivied walls were still suspended in sunlight. Esther, short and sunburnt, was standing by a pond where red fish moved below the surface. Her friend Enid, the Captain's daughter, square-shouldered, with a touch of wetness in the armpits, was with her.

'We thought you might like to see Parliament in session on Monday,' said Esther. 'That time you and Henry came to supper, you said London was a closed book. Well, if you wait for Henry to show you the sights, you'll wait for ever.

There's likely to be an interesting debate on public health. Eat with us at one o'clock and we'll walk over to the House.'

What appealed to Margaret about the sprawling city, which she had barely begun to take in, was rather different – its theatres and art galleries, perhaps, but more deeply than those, the places she had read about that seemed romantic in themselves, Soho and Hyde Park, the Pool of London and the Observatory at Greenwich, the Jews of Whitechapel and the booksellers of Paternoster Row. The Mother of Parliaments didn't qualify.

She said, of course, 'What a splendid idea. I should enjoy that very much.'

'Enid has an appointment with the Member for Aldershot, so we shall be going there anyway.'

They weren't a very gracious family. Yet Henry, on the way back to Highgate, surprised her with his tenderness.

'I heard about you and Mr Reece,' he said.

'I'm afraid I embarrassed him. I should have been more tactful.'

'Nonsense. You have every right to be proud of your little country.'

His finger was on her lips, his other hand was squashing hers against the tight cloth of his waistcoat, and he told her with a kind of level-headed passion, as the train clattered through the suburbs, that he had never been so happy as that afternoon.

This admirable Henry might have lasted overnight, or even until Monday, if the boiler in the orchid house hadn't gone out, which ruined his calculations involving sunlight, blinds, ventilation and the hotwater pipes. 'I knew it was a mistake not to have engaged a full-time gardener,' he said. He was in there for hours, stoking and checking and fussing over, in particular, a single large plant with yellow petals, purple-veined. Margaret found it menacing, like most orchids. '*Cypripedium fairieanum*,' he said through his teeth, when she tried to show an interest. 'The mountains of Assam, since you ask. And yes, it was expensive. It cost me nine guineas.'

'*Nine guineas*? For a flower?'

'Has it occurred to you that orchids might be an investment? That they might even represent our future?'

It had not. She would have to try harder, and did so, for the remainder of the weekend. But the moment on the train was not recaptured. In no time it was Monday, Henry had taken his orchid and gone, and the House of Commons loomed ahead.

Lake brought in a business card and reported a gentleman in the hall. His business, according to the card, was 'Financial Services, &c.'

'Tell him that Mr Penbury-Holt has left for the office.'

'He said it was you he wanted to speak to, Madam.'

The man was stout and jolly, with auburn side-whiskers. He had not been relieved of his hat, which he perched on his knee when invited to sit.

'This is a most pleasant house,' he said, so agreeably that it hardly counted as impertinence.

'If you wish to leave some literature for my husband – '

'I wish to ask your advice, Mrs Penbury-Holt. About your husband and his character.'

There was danger in his face. She got up to ring for Lake. A wheelbarrow squeaked outside and the part-time man went past the window.

'I'd advise you not to have me thrown out before you know why I'm here. Your husband has certain creditors, sad to say. Now, you might speak to him about it. Wives have been known to. There is a school of thought, says we are in for a new breed of wives altogether. Be that as it may, will your talking to him make things better or worse? You know his character. I only know what he owes.'

The room slipped out of focus, except for the whiskers, which remained horribly distinct and curly.

'You're a debt collector, are you not?'

'If we have to call a spade a spade.'

'I have no intention of discussing my husband's affairs behind his back. If you wish to see him – '

'Oh,' said the man, standing up and fitting his hat on, 'I know where to find your husband, and he knows where to find me. We are old acquaintances. You may be right. Straightforward summonses and old-fashioned committal proceedings have stood the test of time. But if you did think your intercession would help, remind him of Sander & Co – patience exhausted – six hundred and thirty pounds, seven shillings and fourpence. Good morning.'

The name had a familiar echo, but Margaret couldn't place it. As for the sum of money, it made her go cold. She went straight to the City. It seemed to her that Henry was in danger, and that to delay until the evening was cowardly.

The milling streets were daunting in themselves, the crush of traffic at the top of Cornhill so great that she walked the rest of the way. Clerks and runners dodged in and out of alleys. Lustrous brass plates bearing famous names shone like gold bricks in the walls. It was romantic enough to return to, one day.

Heneage Lane, where the Penbury-Holts had their offices, swirled with dust and voices, a cramped topography that took her by surprise. Admitted by a startled doorman, she was sent up narrow stairs and shown into a waiting room with a globe of the world and photographs of steam-ships. Shortly an old man in a frock coat appeared. 'Let me see, you are Mr Henry's sister . . .?'

'I am *Mrs* Penbury-Holt. His wife.'

'They are all on the floor at this time of day. They will be back presently.'

'Perhaps I could go there – wherever "there" is?'

'It has an absolute prohibition against ladies,' he said eagerly.

'There is a messenger?'

'Certainly, for an urgent matter.'

She shook her head, trying to be unruffled, like her mother-in-law; already the visit seemed unwise. 'I shall wait,' she said, and was left to the spiritless room and the grey light from a building-well. A tick revealed a clock with faded numerals. It was a few minutes past noon.

At half-past, figures walked by the frosted glass of the door. Indistinct voices and the slow clack of a typewriter came out of the walls. At twenty to one she decided to leave, then decided against it, and sat down again. Esther didn't matter. Nothing mattered but her husband.

One o'clock came. Her head was throbbing; the room had become unbearably hot. She was trying to loosen the window-catch when the door opened and Tristram appeared.

'Good lord,' he said. 'Is everything all right?'

'Perfectly.' She hadn't allowed for anyone but Henry. 'I was just passing. I looked in.'

'Forgive me, what an odd place to be passing.'

'I mean to see something of London. The Tower is quite close. You Londoners take everything for granted. I am still at the open-mouthed stage.'

'Sightseeing by yourself is hardly wise. I shall give Henry a ticking-off for not looking after you better. He'll be here directly. Is there anything you require?'

'A glass of water?'

While he was away, Henry came up the stairs, and saw her through the open door. She felt like weeping, Henry looked at her shrewdly, the water came, Tristram bowed, the door closed; they were alone.

'So what *are* you doing here? Wives in offices is rather bad form. But you shall be forgiven.'

'I wouldn't have come unless I had to.'

They sat at the table, knees touching. 'Let me make a guess. You saw someone this morning.' (She was amazed.) 'You were in Harley Street.' (What was he getting at?) 'Is that your news, dearest?' (Oh, she thought, *that*.)

'A man called. He said you owed six hundred pounds and made threats. He left this.'

Henry peered at the script. 'You?' he said. 'Him?' He ripped the card in tiny pieces, failed to find a receptacle, and put them in his waistcoat pocket. 'And you came here for that?'

'I thought you would want to know at once.'

'Then you made a serious error. Approaching the wife is a form of blackmail. You should never have admitted him.'

'But the debt is a fact?'

'The debt? The debt?' He looked over his shoulder at the frosted glass. 'Some piffling creditor employs a person from the sewer, and you come running to the office where everyone knows everyone else's business. I am disappointed in you.'

The stifling air was unbearable. 'May we talk in your private room,' she said. 'I have sat here for over an hour.'

'What private room? You are full of misconceptions, Margaret. I sit in Tristram's room. I have no more entitlement to privacy than a clerk. Why do you suppose I am anxious to accumulate capital?'

'Tristram thinks I was sightseeing at the Tower.'

She meant to comfort him, but he said his brother wasn't a fool. And Esther, what was Esther going to think? Margaret had a picture of the entire Penbury-Holt clan following her movements.

'There may still be time for me to get there before they leave.'

'Good. You are being practical.'

She was glad she was being something. Henry went into

the street to find a cab, while she waited on the doorman's stool. It took some minutes, Victoria was miles away, and two o'clock had struck from Big Ben before she knocked at Esther's apartment. The caretaker who had come upstairs with her rapped harder. But they had gone; there was nothing to do except slip a pencilled apology under the door and return home.

The orchid person whose visit should have been on Saturday was coming for supper. For the rest of the day, Margaret concentrated on her preparations. His name was Johansson; he was a Swede. His business was collecting the things, and over the meal he spoke of his adventures. His English was poor; his handsome, hollow features twitched with the effort of finding the words. Only the year before – she was half listening, half worrying about Henry – he had been on an expedition to New Guinea. Some rarity with crimson flowers was found close to a human sacrifice.

Henry's face was flushed. 'What treasures!' he kept saying. 'What treasures!'

Henry being enthusiastic was lovable but difficult. She knew men weren't boys, or if they were, they weren't the innocent sort; he and Johansson, at ease and happy together, more or less turned their backs on her. It was irritating to be reminded at your own table of the gulfs there could be between husband and wife.

She left them with their port, but they soon retired to the orchid house, and she supervised the clearing-away. They had left papers on the dining table. One was an orchid catalogue. The name of the firm was Sander & Co. So one question was answered.

Aunt Villette arrived at Paddington station with Theodore, a trunk, several cases, a haybox containing freshly boiled cockles for her hosts, and Theodore's violin. On the way to Highgate – Margaret had met the train – her aunt instructed the child to sit up straight, to keep a sharp look out for churches and monuments, and to make a mental note of all he saw so as to provide material for the first of his letters home. A post office had to be stopped at for a telegram to be sent. 'Arrived safely' would be waiting for Abraham on the mat when he came off duty.

There was to be no relaxing on their first day. Villette was inquiring about the National Gallery within an hour of arriving in Highgate, and only Margaret's intercession saved Theodore from an afternoon with the Tuscan Schools. Illness had left the child pale, and his boots were like weights on his sticklike legs.

'So where would you suggest?' said Villette. She let herself be persuaded to visit the Zoological Gardens on the grounds that they were instructive, but showed little interest in the inhabitants, and refused to let Theodore remain in the Lion House to see the inmates being fed at 4; 'there are enough nasty things in the world without our coming to London to see them,' she explained.

For her, London consisted of places, mostly buildings, that contained approved items of significance. Her interests were exactly opposed to those of Margaret, who would have swapped the daily round of gallery, cathedral and museum for bracing trips up the river in steamboats ('Steamboats? I hear enough about boats of all kinds in Port Howard, dear') or window shopping in Oxford Street. Still, Villette was the honoured guest, and it was hard to quarrel with an anxiety to improve one's son. People laughed at her behind her back, but wasn't there something noble about a refusal to accept the common clay that life handed down, generation by generation? Margaret tried to think there was, and that snobbery didn't come into it.

Henry approved of the art-gallerying, or he said he did, and Villette, after a severe attack of nerves when she was reintroduced to him, confided that he was 'a very fine type of man, you made the right decision, dear.' If his eyes glazed over when she spoke of the Wallace Collection or the ceiling of Henry the Seventh's chapel in Westminster Abbey, Aunt Villette failed to notice.

The Penbury-Holts in general found it hard to go wrong where she was concerned. Stuart and Virginia were invited round to supper, and in the course of a lively evening, Stuart pulled her leg about Welsh food (they ate the last of the cockles as a savoury), Welsh accents, Welsh weather and Welsh unreliability, all with deferential smiles and flourishes that so charmed her, she was indifferent to what he was saying.

Virginia was less attentive. Nor was she as animated as usual. When she and Margaret were alone together upstairs, she said the brothers were having 'one of their set-tos'.

'Do they often have them?' asked Margaret, refastening the suspender on a stocking.

'It's always to do with the business. Between us, I don't think they're as successful as they make out. That's why Stuart went off and joined a stockbroker. I think they want him to go back, but he won't talk to me about it – makes one of his jokes about Old Hat being groomed at the age of six weeks for the senior partnership in the nineteen-fifties, and goes off laughing. Does Henry talk to you about things?'

'Not those things.'

Virginia touched her sister-in-law's shoulder. 'Is he – devoted? In a loving sense, I mean?'

'What a funny question. I wouldn't dream of answering it. Come and see if Master Lloyd is still awake.'

The child was propped against the pillows, looking at one of Henry's volumes, an illustrated Encyclopaedia of the Empire, by what remained of daylight.

'Where's the famous violin we've been hearing about?'

asked Virginia. She sat on the bed, and Margaret saw Theodore's nostrils dilate at her perfume.

'Uncle Henry might be disturbed by it, so Aunt Margaret has had a stool taken up to the attic, and I go there to practise. I'm better at the piano, but Uncle Henry and Aunt Margaret don't have a piano.'

His thin, ugly features and embedded eyes were like Morgan's as a child. The year they tried to teach Morgan the piano he took to composing what he called 'my symphonies', banging the keys non-stop in manic outbursts that no punishment could deter him from; it got him out of piano lessons, which he swore was not his intention, insisting that the symphonies were what he could hear in his head.

Theodore was supposed to be a model child, not a little liar. Margaret kissed him goodnight, wanting to make him happy, without knowing much about model children. She wondered if Henry would have time to take them all on an outing at the weekend, but the signs weren't good.

Over breakfast next morning he said he would be dining at his club that night, which was Friday. The scrape of Theodore's violin came from the top of the house.

'I'm afraid my aunt can be rather tiresome.'

'It's nothing to do with your aunt. Tristram is dining with me. We rarely have a chance to talk alone.'

'I hope there's nothing wrong.'

'We meet from time to time and discuss a wide range of topics.'

'About accumulating capital, things like that?'

'Of that nature. I shan't be late.'

He was, though, and in a bad temper, and on Saturday before he departed for the City he shouted at Theodore for leaving the door of the orchid house open.

'I didn't!' said the child, through tears, which annoyed him further.

'English boys don't blub when they are reprimanded. They stand up straight and say "I'm sorry, sir."'

'But I didn't do it, Uncle Henry.'

Margaret, who had heard the drama, emerged to call the child and comfort him in privacy. Villette, who had also heard it, was so upset that she had to go and lie down. Ankles of clay had appeared in the Penbury-Holts.

'Theodore is a truthful boy. I have brought him up properly.'

'I'm sure Henry will accept that. He was in a hurry. You know what men are like in the mornings.'

'The damage has been done. Perhaps we should never have come to stay, if this is the effect we have on your husband.'

Irritations rose to the surface. Villette's ability, first to find Henry perfect, then to withdraw her approval instantly because of a momentary lapse on his part, seemed ridiculous to Margaret. Ostensibly as a treat for Theodore, but in part because she was tired of doing exactly what her aunt wanted, she announced that today they would visit the waxworks at Madame Tussaud's.

'Is there not a Chamber of Horrors? That sounds unsuitable for Theodore.'

'We are not obliged to enter it. I just want him to enjoy himself.'

'I assure you that he has, all week.' Villette took a fistful of underclothes from a drawer – they were in the bedroom-that-waited-to-be-a-nursery – as if she meant to pack and leave at once. 'Famous paintings will stay in his memory longer than wax statues with false hair.'

'Yes, Aunt, of course,' murmured Margaret, and went to find Theodore. He had retreated to the attic, where he was most at home, and was drawing animals with coloured crayons. A tolerable lion, seen through bars, was being fed chunks of meat.

'Is that one of the lions we saw?'

'He's eaten his keeper,' said the child, and when she looked closer, she saw with a shudder that one of the chunks had a nose. His voice lacked emotion, as it did a moment later when she told him they were going to the waxworks, and he replied, 'What jacket shall I wear?'

Resentment stirred, the thought that on their account she had been neglecting Henry. Her marriage came into focus. There were sure to be 'bad patches'; that was common sense. Yet here she was, in the first such patch, doing nothing about it. He was to be at his club again that evening, a Saturday, when clubs were almost deserted. Virginia was right: there was a crisis.

This time Margaret was more circumspect. She sent a telegram to Esther, reply paid, to ask if she might call there at 6. When they returned from the waxworks – it had not been a success – the reply was waiting, 'Yes of course.'

Mother and son were left with Lake to serve them a cold supper, and for the second time that week, Margaret climbed the stone steps. To her relief, the Captain's daughter wasn't there.

The rooms were more cheerful than she remembered, with bowls of flowers by open windows, through which electric trains could be heard.

'The note I left was hardly an apology,' she said. 'It's been on my conscience. I came to explain.'

'Kind but not necessary. Something to do with a sightseeing visit to the Tower that went wrong, I gather. Henry looked in for a gossip.'

The lie became a fact; Margaret became an accessory. Marriage was an endless conspiracy of loyalty.

'I'm still not used to finding my way around London.'

'They make exceptions for an emergency. Otherwise you would have had a chilly reception.'

‘I did,’ began Margaret, but turned it into, ‘I did think of that before I went. But you must have been there?’

‘They regard me as privileged. It would be different if I were a wife.’ Esther moistened a handkerchief and rubbed ink from her index finger. ‘As it is I have short hair and go for holidays in Greece with Enid. If they ever take the plunge and appoint a typewriting lady, they’ll look for someone who reminds them of me.’

‘I was hoping for something different.’

‘You mean grander.’

‘I mean noisier and busier.’

‘We must arrange a visit to the Baltic Exchange if what you want is noise,’ said Esther drily. ‘But you know, Henry won’t thank you for taking an interest in what he does from nine till five. They shut themselves away and make money. When they finish for the day they like to have an entirely separate life to step into.’

Margaret smiled. ‘I must have had the wrong sort of upbringing. The works were always on the doorstep. I see no reason why a woman shouldn’t be interested in how a husband earns a living – not that my mother ever has been, I admit. I thought you might have agreed with me.’

‘Oh, I do, in theory. I think equality of interests as important as equality of property. Were I to marry, which I won’t, some of my ideas would turn my husband’s hair white. But if you felt like that, I imagine you wouldn’t have married Henry. He certainly wouldn’t have married you. If he thought you differed from his basic ideas about what a woman ought to be, he must have decided the differences were slight and didn’t matter. You agreed to join the Penbury-Holts. You signed a contract. Business is business.’

She stated it without rancour, a fact of life. It was the Penbury-Holt knack again, staying calm and keeping ‘feelings’ out of it. Margaret was entangled in feelings.

'So I shall keep well away from the office – that won't be much of a hardship – and act as if money grows on trees. But what if it didn't, one day?' Her facts were as valid as Esther's; only a tone of voice betrayed her. 'One hears of business failures, even in the City. I've heard Dadda say that Barings nearly went down, not many years ago. Mightn't there be circumstances where the nine-to-five life spilled over into the other?'

'What a gloomy picture you paint,' said Esther, leaning back, her hair fiercely gold, too fierce for her skin, in reflected sunset from windows opposite. She looked what she was, approaching forty. She was listening to footsteps on the stairs, the key in the lock; her face was stiller than ever. 'Enid,' she said, almost to herself.

A tweed jacket came off and landed in a bundle on a chair before the Captain's daughter was properly in. Easing her blouse where it stuck to the shoulders, she said, 'He was too busy to see me!'

'Margaret's here,' said Esther.

'I'm not blind,' said Enid. 'Good evening, Margaret. There is a man with chambers in Jermyn Street who owns property near the barracks in Chatham . . .'

When Esther said she was going to heat some coffee, her friend followed her to the kitchen. Their voices rose and fell. The windows opposite were turning dark; it had been a wasted visit.

'You should have put it in an air-tight bottle,' she heard Esther say, to which her friend replied, 'Oh, stop fussing about your damn bottles.' The swear-word gave a flavour to the conversation, as if it was the Captain there, not his daughter.

When she returned with a tray, Esther was alone, and there were only two cups. 'I've told Enid we are talking about family matters,' she said. 'You had better finish what you were leading up to.'

A door banged somewhere in the apartment. The coffee was thick with particles, which filled Margaret's throat.

'I'm afraid Henry is worried about the firm. There has been some trouble.'

'You have been told so?'

'I have reason to believe so.'

'That's Virginia, no doubt. She chatters about everything. I blame her husband.'

'The point is, is it true?'

'If you mean the firm, it's as sound as the Bank of England. It may not have been quite as profitable of late. But you are concerning yourself with things that don't need your concern.'

'I might as well come to the point – '

'Do.'

' – the real point being Henry. I meant to be more tactful. But you like things to be black and white. Very well. A debt collector has been at the door for more than six hundred pounds. Is that a nine-to-five matter?'

'I wonder you bother to ask me. You'll have discussed it already with Virginia.'

'That's an unfair remark and not worthy of you,' said Margaret. She wished she was more fond of her sister-in-law; it was easier to disagree with friends. 'I speak to you and you alone because you're his sister. I can hardly approach his brothers. I have no intention of being disloyal to Henry. On the contrary.'

'I apologise, of course.'

'It was wrong of me to come.'

Shaking, she declined the coffee pot that Esther held out with daunting steadiness.

'There is very little I can tell you. Henry is thinking of leaving the firm – on amicable terms, naturally. He has ambitions that the Father regards as eccentric. His private debts may be connected with his plans. You see how nebulous it all is? I'm sure he'll take you into his confidence when appropriate. In a different world . . .'

'Yes?' said Margaret eagerly, always alert for the power locked up in things that might be; her marriage itself had begun as a hypothesis about a man in a straw hat, paddling on a shingly beach. But Esther didn't elaborate. They had nothing in common, after all.

Margaret went home to Aunt Villette, who was set on aggravation. She found fault with Lake's boiled potatoes ('But it doesn't matter in the slightest'), debated at length the most edifying venue for divine service the next day ('Dare I propose the Metropolitan Tabernacle in the morning and St Paul's in the evening?') and hoped that Henry would show Theodore some mark of affection to make up for his injustice ('A threepenny piece would be sufficient, dear').

Going to bed – at last – Villette remembered a clipping from the local newspaper that her sister had asked her to bring to London. It was about Morgan, 'Mr Morgan Buckley, elder son of the well-known tinplate manufacturer, Mr David Buckley,' who hoped to be ordained as a minister of the Calvinistic Methodist persuasion in September.

Margaret took it to her bedroom, where, brushing her hair and waiting for Henry, she stared at the scrap of paper as if she might catch a glimpse of the real Morgan behind 'an outstanding student at Blaen Cwm Theological College' and 'played a quiet but effective part in the recent Revival'.

Henry found her asleep with it in her hand. Lifting her on to the bed, he made love to her so gently that she hardly woke up. She told herself that he had responded, perhaps unknowingly, to the emotions that disturbed her. After that it seemed logical enough that within twenty-four hours he had told her his plans.

That Sunday Aunt Villette was left to go to divine service

on her own; when, soon after, she went back to Wales, she was full of dark hints about selfishness in marriage. But love made Margaret callous. She would have done anything for Henry, now that he had put his trust in her. He told her he meant to give up shipbroking and become a grower and seller of orchids. He would be in partnership with Johansson, who would be in charge of bringing back exotic plants from around the world. There was something called the Orchid Boom. It couldn't fail.

4

'If Rees Coal wants us back,' said Buckley, 'he'll have to take something off his price. We'll try him with fourpence.'

'Fourpence is a lot, Dadda.'

'He should have thought of that before he went round boasting about the Admiralty. The agent took one look at his pits and said No. Daft old Rees.'

Will and his father were walking from Y Plas in a summer drizzle.

'What shall I do today, Dadda?'

'Help with the wages till dinnertime. Then you'd better go in the tinhouse. We're using a new flux. I want you to keep notes.' Men coming from the despatch bay took their caps off, and Buckley gave them a friendly wave. 'Learn, learn, learn, that's what you have to do.'

They looked in to make sure Earl Roberts was well covered up in the store, where he had been moved the week before when General and horse were brought together for the first time. A team under one of the fitters, John Johns, had worked on them since the winter, cutting and bending the tinplate, even fashioning a tail for the horse and angular features for the man. All was now draped in newspapers and blankets.

'It feels nice and dry, Dadda.'

'Good. You're in charge of him from now on. Colonel Mappowder's coming over to inspect him. I'll send for you when he's here.'

Buckley had things on his mind. A mill crew had walked out the day before, complaining it was too hot to work. There had been a spillage in the tinhouse. The two things were unconnected, except that he had run a works for long enough to know that incidents were often threaded together, symptoms of unrest or bloody-mindedness. The nonsense about wanting to be paid on a Friday instead of a Saturday had surfaced again, in the form of a half-hearted petition. There was a whiff – just a whiff – of agitation.

Phillips was waiting for him, rubbing his hands; he thrived on trouble. Two of the openers had been fighting, Lizzie Wills and Fat Sara. Sara had scratches on her face. 'You know who she is?' said Phillips. 'Tommy Spit's sister.' Someone had put a dead mouse in her food tin. 'Down on the floor they were,' said Phillips. 'Men had to come off a mill to get between them.'

'Dock them a shift and give them a warning. I'll see them in here at two o'clock.'

He gave them a lecture and made them shake hands. A happy works produced more tinplate. 'Friends, remember,' he called down the stairs as they left. Perhaps it was just the weather, after all.

Colonel Mappowder cheered up the place when he paid his promised visit. Will was sent for and came running from the tinhouse, cleaning his fingers on a rag.

'Never mind the hand-shaking,' said the Colonel. 'Let's get down to business. Your father tells me you're going to show us Lord Roberts.'

'Will you follow me, sir?'

Nervous but determined not to let Dadda down, he led a procession of the Colonel, Buckley, Phillips and John Johns.

Phillips darted ahead to open the door. He climbed a step-ladder alongside the pyramid of blankets.

'Right, Mr Buckley?'

'Mr Will is in charge.'

Will gave the signal. At the same time he asked Johns to step forward and tell their visitor about the work.

'Used sixteen boxes of tinplate, we did, sir,' said the

man. He frowned, looking up at Phillips on the ladder, as the first blankets came loose, and helmet, head and shoulders appeared. 'Mr Buckley found us a coloured picture of Lord Roberts . . .'

'The face is excellent,' said Mappowder.

The General was in the wrong place, too far back on the horse. He must have moved when they put the blankets on. The hero of the Transvaal was sitting on the animal's rump.

'Give me a hand here, Johns,' said Phillips. He shinned down the ladder and the two men tore at the covering.

'Good Lord!' came from Mappowder, and Buckley went crimson.

Earl Roberts's breeches overhung the end of his steed. The horse's tail, a fine braiding of tin, had been severed. It dangled from the breeches instead.

Will prayed for a diversion – a broken roller, a man scalded in the tinhouse, anything.

Something glimmered at their feet. It was a chamber pot brimming with horse manure, neatly placed underneath Earl Roberts.

Dadda kicked newspaper over it and said that when he found who was responsible, he would see they were charged with criminal damage. He turned on Will, saying he should have made an inspection before their guest came.

'Be fair, Davy,' said the Colonel, 'why should the boy have suspected? Why should anyone? It was a joke that got out of hand.'

'I'll give them jokes. Phillips, I want him repaired within twenty-four hours, put on a cart and taken up to the house, where he'll be safe. In the meantime, put a watchman on the door, day and night.'

Someone would be sorry; he had an idea who the someone would be. As soon as Mappowder had gone, he sent for the foremen and rollermen, told them what had happened, and said it was in everyone's interests that the culprit be found. Then he went home, and sent for the union gaffer, Ben Ellis, who as usual was skulking in his poky office in town, with his clerk and his book of rules.

Ellis was retiring next year, and was even less inclined than usual to do anything to upset a proprietor.

Buckley said they were mostly decent chaps at his works. 'We don't want to be like the Rhondda Fawr,' he said, 'madmen preaching syndicalism on street corners and vandalism rampant. What they did to it was criminal.'

'Dear, dear. Poor Earl Roberts.'

'If you hear anything, come and tell me. Will you do that?'

He was back early next morning, a Saturday, fanning himself with his hat and saying he knew nothing positive.

But if he had no information, he wouldn't have come.

'Is there an agitator?' said Buckley. 'Yes. Do you know who he is? Yes. Are you going to tell me? No. You represent the men. I understand.'

'Oh, thank you, Mr Buckley. You see, they aren't sure who did it. Some of them would hand him over to the police if they had proof. Others think it was a lark.'

'We've a duty,' said Buckley. 'I propose to give a name. If I'm wrong, tell me, and I'll take your word. If I'm right, say nothing. That way, if you tell me anything, you are only doing it by way of clearing an innocent man. Do you agree?'

Ellis blinked and nodded.

'Thomas Jenkins – Tommy Spit, he's called. The one I was charitable to when he lost half his hand.'

'Well,' said the gaffer, 'I must be off. Business to see to at Mappowders.'

'It's going to be a warm day. Slip round the kitchen and have a glass of beer before you go.'

He had guessed all along it was Tommy Spit. As a punishment for Will's carelessness, one that would do him good in the long run, he made his son do the dismissing, while he and Phillips listened from the next room.

No reason had to be given. He was to be told, and that was the end of it.

Will sat at his father's desk and said, 'Come in.'

Tommy Spit stood frowning, five foot-nothing, his right hand sealed up in a black leather glove.

Will had seen him about the works often enough, but it was the first time he had looked closely since the day of the accident. There was nothing to be anxious about. Blue eyes swam above the seamed face of a workman.

'Jenkins,' he said, 'you are to get your cards from the wages clerk. You are paid up to the end of the fortnight. That's all.'

'Oh,' said the man, 'something serious, I thought it was. Just go on the parish, Jenkins. That's all.'

'I don't want lip.' Will spoke with an effort. Authority had to be learned, Dadda said. 'You're a trouble-maker, Jenkins.'

'There's nice you've learnt the words. I heard a little chap off a ship talking Spanish. The captain's family, I 'spect. Seemed funny, him so small. Same with you, Master Will Buckley. You know the vocabulary. You have had lessons from the cradle.'

'If you don't go, I shall have you thrown out.'

Still the man didn't move. 'It wasn't me, you know,' he said. 'Tell your father to take out a summons. Let him prove it in a court of law. But he wouldn't, would he? He'd be a laughing stock. General Roberts and the chamber-pot. It was somebody with a sense of humour, right enough. But it wasn't me.'

'Would you swear it on a Bible?'

'Ay, if you've got one handy.'

The connecting door flew open, and Dadda was there, giving Jenkins ten seconds to get himself down the stairs.

Some of his anger was left over for Will. He had fallen into the trap that waited for weak managers. He had let himself be drawn into a debate. If he carried on like this, he was no son of Buckley's.

'I didn't think.'

'Go and have a word with John Johns and see what he has to say about Jenkins. He was here half the night.'

Not thinking was wicked. Why was it so difficult to do what Dadda wanted?

In the afternoon Will mooched off to the North Dock to see a sailing barque aground on the sands outside. Crowds were at the pierhead for the fun. Annoyed with himself for having made such a mess of sacking a workman, he resented, too, having to sack him in the first place. How must it feel to be a Tommy Spit, with a glove for a hand and someone half your age deciding your future?

After the works, the seaside was a tonic. He didn't have to think about right and wrong.

The water was slack, the estuary a desert of mud and pools. Gulls shrieked over sandbanks, waiting for the tide to turn. The ship, the *Laverno*, lay in a belt of haze, its foremast making a Cross of Lorraine. A rowing boat scuttled under the bows like a two-legged water insect. On the horizon, smoke poured angrily from the tug *Falcon*, which was steaming up and down in deep water, unable to get close.

Friends greeted friends. A collier had his arm round a girl.

Most of Will's friends had been at boarding school. It was nearly two years since he left there to enter the works – after Morgan decided his career lay in salvation, not tin-plate, and nearly gave Dadda a seizure. That should have been long enough to make friends, but somehow he hadn't; the works ruled his life because it ruled Dadda's. There was Sam Lewis, whose father owned the Morfa works. But

Sam had gone to America, to a tinplate mill run by a Lewis who emigrated at the time of the tariff.

How cool it would be, bathing naked off the pier! That was the sort of thing Sam would egg him on to do. As a second-best, he climbed down to the sands and set off, bare-footed, with his shoes around his neck, to see how close he could get to the *Laverno*. He remembered Morgan saying, 'If you like being on your own, be on your own. Make up your own rules.' It was crude and simple, like most of Morgan's advice.

Sand gave way to mud, which squirted between his toes. The estuary was a plain, burning his eyes with its heat. In the jellied light, shapes of emptiness lay around, blocks within blocks. The works and Tommy Spit and even Dadda dissolved in them.

Details of the ship became discernible, flannel shirts hanging on a rail, and a man in a peaked cap leaning over the stern, smoking a pipe.

The rowing boat he had seen was in a creek between mudbanks. A man rested on the oars; a boy leaned over the bows, as though fishing. 'Three feet six inches,' came his voice. It was his cousin Joe, and the man was Joe's father, Abraham.

The Lloyds were their poor relations. He hardly knew them, though Aunt Villette was sometimes at the house with Mamma. 'The Duchess,' Dadda called her behind her back.

They saw him and shouted. Uncle Abraham rowed up the creek. 'Step in,' he said.

They were surveying the banks to see what had shifted since the previous month's springs. Will sat on a wet plank. His suit felt like lead. He asked politely about the *Laverno*.

'Pilot wanted to anchor, but the Master was in a hurry,' said Uncle Abraham. 'She'll be fast for a month.'

Joe teased his cousin about the suit. Both the Lloyds

wore thin cotton trousers and collarless shirts. Tentatively, Will unfastened his collar and removed his tie. He folded his jacket and waistcoat and stowed them where Joe pointed.

Joe showed him how to swing the lead. Loneliness itself dissolved into the landscape.

The haze grew bluer and thicker. Water came trickling into channels, joining up pools, brushing at the mud. On the skyline, as the boat bobbed higher, Will made out the twin stacks of Buckley's. Voices could be heard from the pier, but the rowing boat continued to occupy its own dimension, blue-white, plastic, boundless.

'Time to be off,' said Uncle Abraham. A sheet of water was filling the estuary as far as Gower, in the haze to the south. The first intimation of waves appeared, like wrinkles in skin. The *Falcon* came nearer, all foam and smoke. 'They'll wonder where you've been.'

'Can Will have supper with us?' said Joe.

'I don't see why not.'

Joe was sent to take word to Y Plas, and Abraham led his nephew into the house, one of a row of nondescript cottages at the foot of a mound of slag and dirt, accumulated over a century and now overgrown with grass, called the Bank.

The kitchen was in shadow already. Villette was making jam, which boiled darkly on the fire in a copper pan and filled the air with its sickliness.

'Uncle Abraham should have told me you were coming,' she said, glaring at her husband. 'It's fish, I hope you like fish. Theodore has it boiled with a white sauce.'

She apologised angrily for the boiling strawberries, for the heat, for the absence of garden to sit in. Theodore, she said, was in the parlour with one of his favourite books. She was sure that Will was a great reader, too.

Cousin and uncle in a boat were not the same as the

Lloyds at home. Will sat on a threadbare sofa next to Theodore, *Lives of the Poets* on their knees.

'Why were you invited?' said the child.

'Your brother asked me.'

'I learn the piano and violin with Mr Damon Stoker. Mother and I went to London and stayed with Aunt Margaret. Uncle Henry doesn't like music. He said he'd smash my violin.'

'I think that's a fib.'

'I don't care what *you* think. Mother says Uncle Henry is a vulgarian. Are you a vulgarian?'

Over supper Joe and Abraham had an argument. Will kept his head bent over the bony fish, waiting for Joe to be sent upstairs. The dispute was about refloating the *Laverno*. Joe said the *Falcon* would have her off the mud by nine o'clock. His father shook his head.

'You know everything,' grumbled Joe.

'I been here a long time.'

'Well I think you're wrong. Got a new boiler, the *Falcon* has. Skip says we could shift the *Mauretania* now.'

'Delusions of grandeur, my boy.'

No explosion came. It was Joe who had lost his temper, not Abraham. Where was the authority, then? Aunt Villette gave most of her attention to Theodore, cutting out the cod-bones and pouring him cups of milky tea. Authority as Will understood it wasn't there at all.

After the meal, Joe rushed up the Bank, taking Will with him, to see what was happening. The sun had set behind the *Falcon*'s smoke, and the tug moved in close to the barque. People were crowded along the pier and on the foreshore, lights flaring up among them. Cheering could be heard.

'She's coming off!' shouted Joe, and ran down, telling Will to follow.

Abraham sat on the doorstep, smoking a pipe. 'No hurry this month,' he called.

'I must be going home, anyway,' said Will, and thanked Aunt Villette for having him.

Surely it was wrong of Uncle Abraham not to send Joe upstairs?

In sight of Y Plas, a thudding and clanking came from the works that never slept. It was a fire-breathing animal with dark nostrils and claws of tin. Once he had learned authority, its red eyes would respect him.

He left the last lamp behind. The wall of the grounds threw shadow over the drive. Squares of window-light showed through the trees.

A figure stepped in front of him and a voice said, 'No harm, Mr Will. Don't go, Mr Will.'

'Who's there?' He wanted to shout but his heart was choking him.

'Thomas Jenkins, sir. Tommy Spit.' The insolence had gone. 'I'm sorry I spoke out of turn.'

'I've said all I have to say to you.'

'There's sickness in my house. I have little children.'

'I'm sorry, but . . .'

Should he have been sorry? 'Sorry' wasn't relevant.

'I'm asking for my job back. That's not easy for a man with pride.'

Words formed themselves in Will's head, *You should have thought of that before*. Why couldn't he say them? He managed, 'You must speak to my father.'

'Save my breath, couldn't I? You could speak to him, sir. You believed me when I said I didn't touch Earl Roberts.'

Dadda saved him, calling from the house to ask what the voices were, and Tommy Spit was gone in a second. 'Man lost his way,' said Will.

The lie haunted him for days. What gave him the right to have twinges of conscience for a workman? What stopped him learning the lessons that Dadda taught so patiently? Rogues were cunning, men were deep, life was hard.

The fiery animal across the marshes was the answer to all arguments. Only by serving it without question could he hope to be a worthy son. Nothing mattered but the clank of the rolls, the flashing circle of the flywheel, the doubler leaping with his tongs, the furnaceman at the bellows – scarecrow-like shapes in the glare of smoke, more savages than men. All servants of the iron dragon.

Morgan passed his final examinations, received a telegram from his mother, spent hours on his knees, and went student-preaching whenever he could at villages around Blaen Cwm. The term had another month to run. In the autumn they would all return to be ordained in the chapel. By that time the best men among them would be hoping to hear calls to chapels that wanted new blood.

Not that he had any intention of burying himself alive in Llan-Llyn-Llwyn-somewhere-or-other. But for the moment he played safe – took tea with ministers, inquired after wives, bowed obsequiously to deacons, and made sure his sermons were vigorous and good-tempered, just scorched with hellfire.

Even in the heat – maggots in the bacon, the drains playing up – Blaen Cwm was sweet. Hard beds felt soft, the clanging bell was music. Disasters, perhaps, had been lurking below the horizon. Low marks in his exam papers would have been a storm signal. Miss Rees had never quite left his thoughts. Only now, with a good diploma in his pocket, was she finally eradicated.

Unselfish actions became easier. 'I'd like to coach Gwilym in my spare time, sir,' he said to Mr Wimmer, the torpid Gwilym having failed to appear in the pass lists for anything. 'He might have better luck next year.'

'Pigs might fly,' said Mr Wimmer, made morose by the

petering-out of the Revival. 'The only call Gwilym is likely to receive is from his Dadda's farm. Still, blessed is he who maketh a kind offer.'

Morgan persisted, and was to be seen on warm evenings under a tree in the woods nearby with Gwilym, explaining what Jesus meant by the words 'Son of Man', or why St John's Gospel was the least reliable of the four. Morgan even tried the experiment of loving him – blackheads on nose, rank yellow hair, grubby shirt and all. He tried it on a Saturday afternoon, taking with him a present of some melting Pegler's chocolate and a Penny Monster to wash it down.

There had never been anyone less lovable than Gwilym. He had no sooner devoured the chocolate and taken a swig of the pop than his sweaty frame began to emit little farts and belches. But the flesh was corrupt by definition. Somewhere inside Gwilym was a soul that didn't break wind.

As though by divine command, letting him know that nothing more was expected of him for the moment, he heard his name being called. Dr Jenkins was shouting from a window. Morgan told the hopeless Gwilym to work hard on what the disciples would have understood by the word 'Christ', and went back hoping it was a telegram from a chapel, asking him to preach at short notice.

It was something else. 'Your friends have come to take you out for the afternoon,' said the Principal. 'Hurry up and put your best suit on.'

It was Rees Coal, colliery proprietor, Mrs Rees, widow, and Miss Rees, spinster. They had 'driven over' in Rees's de Dion-Bouton, lately acquired. The college buzzed, and everyone came out to see it.

Morgan's first instinct was to lock himself in the bogs or say that God had told him to spend the afternoon coaching Gwilym. But all seemed happy, even hilarious. The ladies wore gauze face-masks, and there was an extra pair of goggles for Morgan, who sat up in front next to Rees Coal. Cheers went up as they drove away, taking him off to tea, and Rees Coal missed a chicken by inches.

Conversation was limited on the journey, but Morgan gathered that Mrs Rees and daughter had read about his success in a local paper. They were staying a few days with her brother-in-law, and suggested, 'on the spur of the moment', that they visit Blaen Cwm.

That was reasonable enough. But he was not at ease. Through the goggles the landscape was burnt yellow, as if fires of punishment had visited these well-slaked hills.

It would be unfortunate if Miss Rees had ideas, merely because he and she had been involved in a mysterious outpouring of the Holy Spirit. After all, he was on the brink of a future. He had said goodbye to her months ago.

Rees Coal's house, called The Mount, was sunk against a hillside. A bird that Rees Coal said was a kite circled high overhead, watching this new thing on wheels. White table-cloths dazzled in the sun. Servants hurried out with food, and Mrs Rees, going indoors to freshen up, called, 'Show Mr Buckley the swallows before tea.'

Behind the house, the cobbles glittered like glass. The swallows nested in what had been a coach-house. She walked ahead of him. Forked shapes swept in and out, whistling faintly. It had been a serious mistake to leave Blaen Cwm.

'Mother is very fond of you,' the girl said.

Only eighteen inches of stifling semi-darkness lay between him and her bosom.

'I think we'd better go back now.'

'Is that all you've got to say to me? After all your promises?'

'All what promises?'

'We mustn't argue. I had to see you. I haven't told a

soul.' She seized his hand and held it against her stomach. 'Oh, Morgan, my darling Morgan.'

He felt he was choking.

'I may be in Port Howard next month. I'll call on you then.'

'Don't you understand?' she said. She pushed his hand away. 'I thought you were supposed to be clever. I'm going to have a baby.'

'Not possible' – not possible, he meant to say, that an obstacle like that could be put in his path.

'How do you think babies are made, then? Not by what you did to me in your father's tinworks?'

'I meant you have to be sure about a thing like that.'

Had they all died on the way? The motor car had swerved off a bridge. It had taken them to a spectacular death. Eternal punishment was beginning.

'Women make mistakes, I know,' he said.

'Morgan, listen, I have got to tell my mother soon.'

'But not yet, eh?' Any breathing space was acceptable. He knew that every large town and probably small ones as well had ladies who specialised in these matters. The dirtier-minded students at Blaen Cwm (Gwilym, for example) smirked over advertisements in the *Carmarthen Journal* for 'Pennyroyal Tablets, woman's unfailing friend', and such like. 'There may be something we can do.'

'I have had hot baths till I couldn't sit and spoonfuls of brandy from the medicine chest. It didn't work. It's too late now. I'm four months gone. It's you and me now, Morgan.'

'You and me,' he repeated. 'Well, the first thing I will have to do is tell Dadda.'

He had been snared like a rabbit. 'Give me a few days,' he said.

'Mm-m-m.' It was a hollow humming, like a bee inside a flower. 'I've missed you' (face upturned), 'have you missed me?' (arms around his neck), 'we were meant to meet, like you said' (lips parted, sweetish breath).

Unable to stand much more of this, he tried the Gwilym Experiment, to see if he could feel some love for her of the love-thy-neighbour variety. Anything, really, to save himself from being swept away. She tidied her hair, he wiped his lips, and they walked to the top lawn, where Rees Coal was saying that the swallows were a b. nuisance.

But it was harder than it had been with Gwilym. In the end, with the Gwilyms, there was always some drop of charity to be squeezed out with the pity. To consider the bare-headed Miss Rees, her throat gold-lit, her little hands at work on sandwiches, was inexorably to dwell on what was happening under her skirt. The rounded belly, the puff of hair, the juices in the crevice, had no connection with loving thy neighbour. They were carnal truths, a woman's machinery; they made her self-sufficient. She was an antagonist.

When he put it like that he felt better. But it was only a beginning. The world was coming to an end. Dadda would order him to marry and be damned. And when they heard at Blaen Cwm, what would happen to the sacrament of ordination in September?

'Don't eat much, do 'ee?' said Rees Coal. ''ave a Welshcake, my boy.'

At last it was time to go. The car was to take him to the nearest railway station – the road journey to Blaen Cwm and back couldn't be completed before nightfall. They gave him a food parcel for his friends.

'Shall we see you in Port Howard?' said Mrs Rees.

'Soon, I hope. Goodbye, Miss Rees.'

The station yard was empty but the train was signalled. A bleached poster on a wall, torn down the middle, announced the coming of Evan Ro, months ago.

'Well,' said Mr Rees, 'I wish 'ee the best of luck. Fond of my niece, ain't you?'

'Yes, indeed, sir. Of course, I have to think of other things at the moment.'

'The Lord first. Young ladies second. That's the ticket.'

Morgan prayed on the train, and again in the dormitory while the other students were gobbling the food. He knew he was wasting his time. Whatever God was up to, he had ceased, at least temporarily, to intervene on behalf of thy humble servant. To put it bluntly, he had given this humble servant a boot up the bum.

He wondered if he had a vocation, after all. He could hear Margaret laughing if she heard that. 'Morgan,' she would say, 'you're *hopeless*.'

He wished he could see Margaret now.

'Are you enjoying that, Gwilym?' he called.

'Bit thin this bread is.'

'We shall all eat thin bread and butter in the house of the Lord for ever and ever, Amen,' he said, and fell into tangled dreams about his sister and about London.

To relax with in the evening, David Buckley liked an empty room, a glass of brandy and a London newspaper. Failing that, he could make do with the homegrown *Star* or *News*. Not long after the Tommy Spit episode he glanced at a column in the *News* headed 'PEOPLE SAY . . .' and saw they were saying:

. . . That overcrowding at the Intermediate School is disgraceful, with one class being taught in the fireplace and another in the coalhouse,

. . . That two men were heard arguing how many funnels the *Falcon* has. On being told, only one, his friend inquired about the other long thin object, and was told it was Poyntz, the dock policeman,

. . . That a certain well-known manufacturer in the town found that his tinpot* effigy of a famous General on horseback, who is shortly to visit us in the flesh, received additions of an indelicate nature during the night.

*Our printer is sorry, he means *tinplate* of course.

'Stupid rubbish!' he said out loud, but he failed to put it out of his mind, and even consulted Oscar Harris, his solicitor, as to whether the paragraph was libellous.

There must have been gossip around the town or it wouldn't have reached the flapping ears of Dai Weekes at the *News*. He hadn't forgiven the editor for reporting the daft things Morgan said in his speech at Margaret's wedding. Oscar sent off a stiff letter, which did no good. Weekes replied airily to say the Harbour Trust had to put up with jokes about the stranded *Laverno*, and he hoped Davy Buckley wasn't losing his sense of humour.

Buckley had no time for such games. They trivialised the hard-won achievements of the town, which had risen from nothing on a marshy plain, and could sink back to nothing tomorrow if men let it. He liked things plain and straight, as they had always been; works, pits and docks were no laughing matter. Without its smoke and railway lines, the place was nothing.

Now that some of the bigger shops had gone in for plate-glass windows, Stepney Street was becoming quite metropolitan. He and Will walked through it on their way to see Soldier with Rifle arrive on his plinth at the Town Hall. Goods were dangled in front of passers-by – hats, dresses, stockings, shirts, sofas, cookers, bird cages, butter coolers, machines that were unheard of when he was a young man, vacuum cleaners, even a typewriter at Ben Rees, Stationer and Printer.

But Stepney Street was only the varnish on the surface of Port Howard. The red smoke from Mappowder's stacks continued to drift overhead, and the murmur of mills and furnaces, punctuated by shrieking whistles, clanging bells and the restful plink-plonk, like a distant xylophone, of wagons being shunted, rose continuously from the lower end of the town. There, everything was cut and dried. It was the engine that drove the rest, and, like all engines, it worked to natural laws, whether they concerned steam pressure or human necessity. Down that end of the town, you knew where you were.

Sprewett and some of the committee were in the park adjoining the Town Hall, watching Soldier with Rifle being lifted by derrick from the back of the council's motor lorry. His top half was draped in tarpaulin. Buckley poked with his stick and had a look. The bayonet had a nice sharp point.

As the Soldier was lowered on the rebuilt plinth, an elderly workman, holding him steady as he swayed in the ropes, collapsed in the heat and cut his head.

Roddi Lewis, who had come to disapprove of the statue, made sure he was taken care of, and walked over to Buckley, saying, 'Poor fellow. By the way, does the name Tommy Jenkins mean anything to you?'

'I dismissed him, as you well know. I dismissed his sister last week, too, for giving cheek. Why, have you taken him on?'

Even in a heat wave, Roddi looked cold. His blue chin was shaved down to the bone. 'There are still men I can't employ who were with me before the slump. No, his case is before the Guardians for parish relief.'

'Would you like to be a parish guardian one day?' Buckley asked his son, sarcastically.

'Somebody has to do it,' said Rhodri. 'I take my share of civic responsibility. Now, about Jenkins. The Secretary needs a character. It's on the agenda for this afternoon's meeting.'

'He'd better look elsewhere. Tommy Spit is a dangerous man. Will knows all about him, don't you?'

'Yes, Dadda.'

'Come to the Union now. Leave the works for once. Phillips knows how to crack the whip. You owe it to Will to let him see all sides of a question.'

'Roddi Lewis is a Liberal, you see,' smiled Dadda. 'We all know he rules his men with a rod of iron, but he butters it up with nice words like "responsibility".'

'No need to be offensive, Davy.'

The Soldier was on his stand. Workmen were putting a wooden fence around him. A stretcher had come and gone.

'None meant. Lead on, my friend.'

The two tin-masters discussed trade and the American competition as they walked through town. Will listened and hoped he was learning. He was more interested in hearing about Sam, Rhodri's son, who would be home next year from Indiana. 'He'll come home full of ideas,' promised Lewis senior.

The only idea he had passed on to Will so far was a postcard of a young lady in bicycling costume standing beside her machine. Her knee-length frock was embroidered with cycling motifs, among them wheels that fitted neatly on each breast, pointed hub-caps in the middle. Prudently, Sam enclosed it in an envelope.

The Poor Law Union was ten minutes away, on a strip of land with room for vegetables and cows. The barred windows might have been painted black on the inside.

The Secretary, a clergyman, tried to show Buckley the wards, but he said they all knew what the destitute looked like.

'I thought I might raise the case of Thomas Jenkins,' said Rhodri. 'The committee is against relief. But the man is in difficulties. If he goes under, we may have his family here before long.'

'We are full to the doors.'

'Exactly. But twenty shillings a week would keep Jenkins afloat. So what character would you give him, Davy?'

Tommy Spit was neither here nor there. He was part of a long argument.

'Am I supposed to have my common sense perverted by the sight of poverty? He gets a bad character from me,' said Buckley (the clergyman ran his fingernail along his hair-parting).

'A reformed man, according to him. Prepared to toe the line. Hopes to find work as a clerk one day' (the clergyman grunted).

'Then you put him in your office, Roddi. I wouldn't have him if he paid me instead' (the clergyman went to the window and shouted at an old woman).

You knew where you stood with David Buckley; he liked to think that would be his epitaph.

On his way back to the works with Will, he asked his son what he thought. Had he done the right thing?

'Yes, Dadda.'

'You see what Roddi Lewis does? He dares me. Look, he's saying, I am a humanitarian. We are old friends – but like all old friends, we're old enemies, too. I, Rhodri Lewis, vote Liberal, because I've got one of those new-fangled consciences you read about, and I dare you to ignore what you see around you. The truth is . . .'

Larks were rising over Japhet Jones's fields. Tiny marks on blue paper, they struggled in the down-draughts of cooler air between the rising heat from the works on either side.

It seemed to Will that Dadda and Rhodri Lewis were birds of a feather. Is that what Dadda meant?

A rabbit scuttled from behind a shed, two women in pursuit. Why did the stupid creatures choose to live alongside death and cruelty?

The women saw Buckley and hesitated. He waved his consent, and a moment later they cornered it and knocked its brains out with a stick.

'The truth is,' said Dadda, 'those papers about Billy Protheroe's lungs are on my desk again. The union says it's acid fumes from the tinhouse. Send 'em off to Snell and see what he says.'

Phillips handed him a telegram, rubbing his hands. It read, 'URGENT WE MEET AT MY SISTER'S HOUSE, 33 GLENALLA ROAD. I AM THERE ALL DAY,' and was signed 'Albert Rees'.

'He's come round,' Buckley told his son. 'Fourpence a ton off – remember?'

He took his time going there. No doubt Rees had come down for a chapel outing or a mission, and was staying with his sister-in-law.

In the passageway the yellowish wing-collar was the most visible bit of him. The house was silent, muffled, as if a death had taken place. 'In b'here,' whispered Rees Coal, and they entered what might once have been a dining room – it contained a sideboard carved with flowers and archangels – before it acquired armchairs and a piano. A black marble clock like a gravestone with a dial ticked heavily. Drapes of green velvet kept out most of the light.

Silk rustled and Mrs Rees rose from a chair. Buckley hadn't seen her until then. He bowed and assumed she would leave them. Instead, she sat down again.

'Here,' said Rees, and turned two high-backed chairs away from the table so that they were facing his sister.

Was Rees dying? Was it something to do with the future of his coalpits?

'This ain't easy,' said Rees.

Buckley nodded encouragingly. One way or another, fourpence off a ton wasn't beyond the bounds of possibility.

'Your son, Davy – '

'Yes?'

Now it dawned on him. He had been slow. There was a Miss Rees, was there not? Will must have met her in the past, and certainly at Margaret's wedding. They had an understanding. What a sly young man! *He was being offered a marriage between the two families*. Think of the potential – tinplate and coal.

Having lost Morgan, the son and heir he missed more than he ever admitted, it was just what he needed.

A combine cemented by love. And he had failed to think of it himself!

'Of course. Will.'

The collar was fading into the gloom of Albert's neck.

'Morgan. Your boy, Morgan.'

How could that be? 'Does this concern Miss Rees?'

'You know 'bout it, then?'

'I know nothing. I thought – '

The silk stirred itself.

'My daughter and your son, Mr Buckley. There it is.' The silk made a noise like sandpaper. 'These things are best put plainly.'

'What things, madam, what things?'

'He have ravaged my niece and left 'er expecting a child. Is that plain enough, David Buckley?'

The news, stunning in one sense, was so much in keeping with Morgan that as soon as he heard it, Buckley had no doubt it was true. It wasn't merely the lechery. From late childhood there was a hint of a wider dissipation in Morgan's eye. He must have his own way. Thus, no knuckling under to the discipline of the works. Thus, the mad fancy for Jesus. Thus, a girl on her back in some field.

The shame of having a son who behaved *like that* gave him a pain under the ribs. It took him a moment to recover. Rees was muttering a date and a place. The date was months earlier. The place was a shed by the tinhouse at Buckley's own works.

More shame. But anger was close behind. It made him feel better to know the Jesus episode was over, that Morgan had come up against reality at last.

'Does he know?'

'He knows all right. The girl's been waitin' for him to speak. My sister had her 'spicions a week since. Taken till now to drag it from her.'

'Is the girl here?'

'We got a doctor's paper,' said Rees. 'Gone to The Mount, she has, where she can be looked after and learn repentance. My sister'll join 'er there as convenient. The fewer tongues wag in Port Howard, the better.'

There was just time for a train that got Buckley to north Carmarthenshire by nightfall, and to send a telegram before he caught it.

At Blaen Cwm Junction he was surprised to see the Principal waiting on the platform.

'. . . unfortunate development . . .' he heard through the steam and slamming doors.

'Gone? Are you saying gone?'

'Disappeared when I said you were coming. The ticket office says he booked to London, second class, one way. He was on the ten past five. It connects at Swansea. Are there things I should know?'

'One or two.'

'If he's had another breakdown, the Lord can forgive him.'

'The Lord can do what he likes,' said Buckley. 'I shan't.'

What did it matter where you lived as long as you were happy? Margaret, who was moving, had said it to Virginia, who wasn't, and Virginia had said it back again. The furniture men in their green aprons were like the assistants in a stage illusion. Under Margaret's eyes, her home in Highgate was being reduced to a shell, and under Henry's eyes, at the other end of the trick, home was being re-created in a far-off land three miles away called West Hampstead.

'Don't brood,' commanded Virginia, and began to talk about babies – she was pregnant again, another Penbury-Holt keen to get on with making Englishmen.

Babies, as it happened, was a subject guaranteed to make Margaret brood that morning – had she conceived on the honeymoon, the room she stubbornly called the 'nursery', already reduced to bare boards by the green-apron squad, would just have been coming into use. The move itself was a relief. Henry being realistic about orchids – deciding to rent a jerry-built place because it was cheap and included a wired-off field for his nurseries where the streets stopped – was sweeter than any well-appointed residences in Highgate.

'Here's this awful photograph of them all,' said Virginia, poking among odds and ends on Henry's desk – the women had taken refuge in the study – that had survived the packing process.

The brothers, clad in striped bathing costumes, stood in a row outside a deserted bandstand. Tristram's hand was on Henry's shoulder, Henry's hand on Stuart's.

'How ugly men are, don't you think?' said Virginia. 'In a pleasant kind of way, of course.' She studied the figures. 'Henry's legs are thinner than one would expect. Come on, cheer up.'

'I am cheerful, you silly. I'm excited about making a fresh start.'

'Does Henry ever,' and Margaret sensed one of those departures from decency that she wished Virginia didn't make, yet couldn't help being fascinated by, 'ever love you downstairs? In here, for example?'

'How *can* you say such things?'

'I wish we could be free to say anything we wanted. I

talked about freedom of that sort to Esther once – it was she took this photograph, by the way – but she was shocked. You only pretend to be.'

'Nonsense,' said Margaret, 'and put that photograph down before you break it.'

'Free!' murmured Virginia, pressing her bosom against the window, giggling and flapping her arms at the garden. 'Free like a bird. Stuart wants to take up ballooning. Men are free. You and I – ' She drew back. 'Oh dear,' she said, 'there's a man in the garden.'

Margaret looked over her shoulder. It was Morgan. He wore a black suit and carried a bag with a clasp. He stood like an apparition, staring up at the house.

'Hello, Maggs, fancy seeing me,' he called, but she knew something was wrong.

'You remember my brother at the wedding?' she said, when he was inside.

'Don't I half,' said Virginia. 'You're going to be a minister – or have they made you one already?'

'Not quite. I felt like a holiday first. Where are you moving to, Maggs?'

'Not far. Henry needed a piece of land . . . I don't know how well up in the family news you are.'

'I had a sister who got married. She sent me a picture-postcard of a chapel on my birthday. The rest was silence.'

'Now, Morgan.' She wanted him to laugh and make it easier for them both. 'I ask you. I'm still waiting for an apology after the way you played the goat at the wedding.'

'Bother the wedding.'

The door closed behind Virginia. Morgan was still holding the bag. It was hard to tell if he was acting. Distress was in the hard line of his mouth and the pallor of his skin. If he laughed, she could say, 'I know you, Morgan. You've had another row with Dadda.' She could tease him and he could tease her back. Love, if there was love, could stay in the background where it was safe.

'Be nice to Henry, that's all I ask.'

'You're happy?'

'I shall be happier when we're there. You won't mind chaos tonight? Do stay a while. I take it term's finished at Blaen Cwm?'

'I'm not going back to Wales. The Revival failed. I failed. God failed.'

It had to be play-acting. 'Tell the truth,' she said, 'you mean to look around the chapels because you've always had your eye on London. *Good opening for assistant preacher* – that's what you're after.'

'You'd like that, would you?'

'I'd like to know you were here, within ten miles. People in London think ten miles is nothing. We could meet in the afternoons. You could take me to Hampton Court. I could explain the Underground railway.'

He flung the bag on the table. It broke the glass of the bathing-costume photograph.

'All over,' he said. 'No joke.'

Margaret was frightened – for Morgan, not for herself. She put the bag on the floor and collected the splinters of glass. Her hands weren't steady and she cut herself. When he saw the blood, he held the finger to his mouth and licked it clean with his tongue, keeping his eyes on her.

'O God,' he said, 'forgive thy servant Margaret for doubting the word of her brother, who isn't a bad chap really.'

'That sounds more like Morgan.'

He bent over her, his mouth on the side of her neck. She could feel a pulse against her skin. 'There was a woman,' he said. 'They'll tell you if I don't. She set a trap for me. Thy servant left in rather a hurry. Now you know.'

Someone tapped the door. It was Lake, who had been

asked to bring tea and toast. Virginia's voice came from the hall, telling the foreman to be careful with a mirror.

'Ravenous,' said Morgan, and disposed of the toast in seconds. 'I spent the night at a fearful place for Welshmen by Paddington station that said "Gwalia" on a glass globe. Do you forgive me?'

'I don't know what to forgive you for yet. We can't talk in here.'

'Don't be so big-sisterly, Maggs. If you give me a hand, I can look on the bright side.'

'We'd better go in the garden.'

She took him into the orchid-house, now stripped bare. Crushed flowers lay on the floor.

'Who is the woman? As you say, I'll hear soon enough.'

'You wouldn't know her. A Miss Rees, Glenalla Road.'

'Of course I know her. She was at the wedding. And you've asked Miss Rees to marry you?'

'Not exactly.'

'Either you have or you haven't. Was there an engagement ring?'

'Nothing like that.'

It could only be some muddle involving God and a silly romance and overwork.

'So you never said anything to make her think you had serious intentions?'

'For heaven's sake, Maggs' – he screwed his eyes shut – 'the girl's pregnant. Give us a kiss and say you forgive me.'

'Oh, Morgan!' She felt sick, and in an odd way, hurt. If it wasn't Virginia and babies then it was Miss Rees, Glenalla Road, and babies. 'Don't try your soft soap on me. Does Dadda know?'

'Yes, and so does everyone else by now.'

'What have you said to Miss Rees?'

'As little as possible. Now don't start lecturing me, Maggs. For all I know, Satan was mixed up in it.'

'Never mind him. You're going straight back to Wales and you're going to get decently married to that girl.'

She snapped at him; she couldn't help it. Think, she said, of Miss Rees's future, in ruins unless he married her. Life consisted of swallowing what had to be swallowed. There were worse things than a coal-owner's niece.

'Are you listening, Morgan?' she said.

Even the ministry might still be possible in a year or two if he got married and behaved himself.

'I didn't come for advice. I came so I could be the one to tell you.'

'Well, you've told me. I suppose that's better than nothing. But don't expect me to make excuses for you. You're behaving disgracefully. Have you thought what you're going to do next?'

Henry, who should have been in West Hampstead, appeared. He was looking for a thermometer that had been left behind. 'I came back with the motor lorry,' he explained. He remembered Morgan. He shook hands and nodded, his mind elsewhere.

'Would you be so kind?' said Morgan. 'Margaret and I have some urgent family business to discuss. This is the only place with any privacy.'

Henry flushed, picked up a handful of instruments and went away.

'How could you!' said Margaret, but Morgan only smiled.

'You mustn't worry about me. I have twelve pounds in the post office. I shall think of something.'

'Worry about you? The less I see of you the better from now on.'

'No outings to Hampton Court? Come on, Maggs, nothing's changed.'

'Oh yes it has.'

She wanted him out of her sight. She told him to go, to

let her get on with her own life. Henry was worth ten of him. His parting line, 'Don't forget, it was my sister I came to, because I trusted her,' rang as false as the rest of him.

A week later, seen from West Hampstead, it might have been a genuine cry from the heart; with Morgan, you could never tell. But by then it was too late.

The *Port Howard Star*, 31 August, 1905:

It would be impossible to conceive of a more hearty reception than that accorded Lord Roberts on the occasion of his visit to Port Howard on Saturday. The memorial he unveiled to the local men who laid down their lives for King and country in the South African war represents a soldier with rifle in hand, ready for action. The Fallen Heroes Committee is to be congratulated on the arrangements, which included magnificent decorations, and a life-size figure of Lord Roberts on horseback, made by the men at Buckley's, thanks to the public-spiritedness of Mr David Buckley. It attracted much attention, and Lord Roberts himself commented favourably.

The *Port Howard News*, same date:

PEOPLE SAY:

. . . that General Roberts was asked if he would care to take Mr Buckley's masterpiece in tin, or tinny masterpiece, with him when he left the town by train on Saturday night, but that he declined with thanks, on the grounds that it might frighten the horses.

When the celebrations were over, the statue, already tarnished by its day in the open, was removed to the works. Will made himself responsible for having it wrapped in rags and brown paper. He locked it away in a shed and put the key in a drawer of his father's desk, with a tag attached to say what it was, and before long it was buried among the bits and pieces that accumulate around busy men.

PART TWO
The Quick and the Dead

5

Pomona Buckley dreaded gossip, respected her husband and loved her sons, especially Morgan. Didn't men all have a drop of wickedness in them somewhere? She grieved for Morgan.

As proof that he was a good boy really, a postcard arrived from him once a month, depicting places like The Albert Memorial and The Botanical Gardens, Kew, with a pencilled message on the back – 'All well. Assisting at local church' or 'Bought a waterproof hat. Stormy weather'. Of his whereabouts and career, if any, nothing was known. Christmas 1905 brought a postcard of Highgate Cemetery.

At The Mount, the fruits of misdeed had arrived on time. Pomona tried to shut her mind to it, but even a glass or two of invalid's champagne wasn't proof against her fear that everyone in Port Howard was oo-ing and ah-ing about it behind her back.

It was called Isabel. It was her flesh and blood, and Davy's. But that was beside the point. It had not come about in the proper way. She had to forget all about it and pray that nobody found out.

Given half a chance, she would have stayed inside the house. Davy could reassure her till he was blue in the face ('I even went back to Blaen Cwm, my love, and left a donation for the roof'). She felt the gossip in her bones.

Nor was it much consolation that the scheming girl, the scheming girl's mother and Isabel (Was she a healthy baby? Did she have the straight Buckley hair?) were far away in the countryside.

The countryside wasn't far enough. It was only another

word for the place that began where Port Howard ended. Twice a week trainloads of farm-wives and farm-daughters arrived for market, baskets crammed with dairy produce. They were strong, noisy women, chattering among themselves in Welsh, acting as if they owned the place – as if their chickens and cheeses were the real business of the town, not those upstart tinplates. Pomona, like her husband, had been brought up in rural Carmarthenshire. She knew how gossip could travel between isolated farms as if they were houses in a terrace.

Her closest friend, Ada Lewis, wife of Rhodri the tinplate maker, made her do things. They worked together on Lady Mappowder's committee to provide winter breakfasts for children of destitute families. They went shopping for linen and gloves at Bradford House, as they had always done. They went to the market on Saturdays instead of sending their servants, because they were both only one step away from the farm women and farm lives of their ancestry, and it satisfied some nostalgic craving to stroll past the trestle tables piled high with produce, the Swansea fruit sellers, the Carmarthen butchers trading from their carts, and the herring sellers from Cardigan whose trays of fish were sewn with red eyes.

A stallholder with a leather apron who had been selling cockles from the estuary for years, and knew many of her customers by sight, greeted Pomona one Saturday with a shrill 'How is you-ar boy, Miss-is Buck-ley?'

This upset Pomona so much that she hurried off, dragging Ada with her, without being sure whether the question was an innocent one about Will or a cruel one about Morgan.

Ada, who had shared all the secrets about Morgan, was furious. 'Oo,' she said, when they were back at Y Plas, and could have a nice quarrel in private, 'you are so *silly* sometimes. I wanted to buy cockles, for goodness sake.'

Ada was small, even smaller than Pomona. Their quarrels were fierce and frequent, like children's. 'Fine friend *you* are,' cried Pomona, and ran upstairs, banging doors, to watch from behind the curtains as Ada stalked down the drive.

That evening she locked the bathroom door and consoled herself with half-bottles of the invalid's companion.

Buckley had to ask Dr Snell to look in. The doctor had wet eyes like a rabbit and hair that trailed back over his head and interfered with his collar. Under Buckley's gaze, he fingered the varicose veins buried in Pomona's plump calves, prodded her liver, and prescribed sedatives and three glasses of milk a day, warm from the cow.

Alone with Buckley, he murmured about women undergoing the change of life, and how, besides, they often missed their daughters when they married. 'You're like all of them,' said Buckley. 'You describe what we know anyway. The question is this: should I stop her drinking or not?'

'If you think you can, Mr Buckley.'

And that was going to cost him half a guinea.

His wife was propped against the pillows when he returned to the bedroom, patting the sheet for him to sit down. She would stop being silly, she promised, but would Davy mind very very much if she didn't go with him to the engagement ball for Colonel Mappowder's son Aubrey next month?

'But that,' said Buckley, 'my dear little potato Pomona, is what being silly is.'

As a consolation he slept in her bed that night – stayed there half an hour, amid her fluffy pillows and feather mattress, pulling his pyjama trousers down with a snap, and sinking into the rosy folds of his dear little potato, who once had pleased him beyond all his adolescent dreams of lust, and still sighed and rolled as if she was torn between throwing him off at once, and keeping him at it until morning.

He was adamant about the Mappowder ball – even when it turned out that Pomona did have something to worry her, after all.

He found her sobbing over a copy of the *News*. The vile innuendo was in the usual place for innuendoes:

PEOPLE SAY:

. . . that the rumours about a young evangelist who used to be in tinplate, and a young woman who used to be a young lady, are not without foundation.

Mappowder had warned him, more than once, that Federation politics were even dirtier than the Westminster variety, and he mustn't expect bouquets from the Liberal interest. But Morgan's scandal was in the past. Dai Weekes and his rag had gone too far this time.

He went to the newspaper office and burst in on the editor, who happened to have a steel ruler in his hand, measuring galley proofs.

Weekes backed away, holding the ruler like a sword.

'Don't you come in here. There's a free press in this country.'

'Free to print filth. What do you think this will do to Mrs Buckley?'

'I got a duty.'

'Whatever happened is dead and buried. I'll have you shut down. I'll have you put away.'

'The people in this town don't like goings-on.' Sweat dripped off the editor's chin, on to his waistcoat. 'Only last year there was that married man from Hendy, at the carnival with a young woman. Remember that? The crowd chased them to the York and started breaking windows. Be fair, Mr Buckley. It was all in the paper.'

'Which is only fit to wipe bottoms with. You are conducting a vendetta against me because you know I might be up for the presidency of the Fed one day.'

'But it's true!' wailed the editor.

'I'll give you truth.'

A police constable arrived, saying, 'Now then, gentlemen,' and Buckley became aware of faces in an outer office, peering over frosted glass.

He strolled down Market Street, nodding at acquaintances, taking off his hat to Mrs Sprewett outside Bradford House, popping into the reading room of the Conservative Club so that members could see him glance unmoved at the offending page of the *News*; taking his time, reasserting his dignity.

It was much the same at the Cilfrew ball, where Pomona wore a yellow gown and danced once with the Colonel. Buckley kept his chin at the attack, and stared back at anyone who stared at him. Besides a sprinkling of notables from London, there were Dillwyns from Swansea, Butes from Cardiff and coal-owning Davieses from the Rhondda. The lesser fry were well represented, too, the likes of Egge and Hughes. Buckley didn't put himself among them, although it was undeniably true that Hughes' Old Castle works made more tinplate than he did. Buckley felt he had a destiny. That was the difference.

The company swirled among the banks of flowers like coloured liquids in a glass, and Buckley swirled with them, his mind on tinplate. In the gentlemen's lavatory he met Henry Sprewett, looking at himself in the mirror as he buttoned his trousers, and congratulated him on the appearance of the Sprewett daughter, Lucinda, whose engagement they were celebrating. Sprewett boomed at him about the virtues of daughters, but as they strolled back towards the music they paused in the Indian Room for a smoke, two plain men again with no time for fairy-tales.

'We shall presently have a vacancy on the Harbour Trust,' announced the Town Clerk. 'You might care for your name to go forward. No gold cups are awarded, I fear.' Gobs of smoke fell from his mouth. 'One would think the action of the tides was a personal shortcoming on the part of the Trust. We have had the captain of the dredger in tears in front of us because the public, which never understands anything, has been misled into believing that a little effort on his part would enable the White Star line to send its vessels into the Burry Estuary.'

'It must be somebody's fault,' said Tom Egge, who flitted from behind the elephant's back legs, a thin shadow. 'Mud is universal. Why are we so bad at getting rid of it?'

'Buckley and I are having a private conversation,' rumbled Sprewett.

'Then you'd better go somewhere private to have it in. I was admiring the great beast.' He struck a match on its rump and lighted a cigarette of his own. 'Hello, Davy. You won't have time to make tinplate, what with the Fed nomination when you get it.'

'If it's any business of yours,' said Buckley, 'I wouldn't dream of joining the Harbour Trust. I'm flattered to be invited, Henry, but I understand Rhodri Lewis is hoping to be elected. He and I are old friends. Let it go at that.'

'Public spirit, no less!' crowed Egge.

'Selfless men have made this town what it is,' said Sprewett. 'What have you ever done for it?'

'Paid my rates and given employment to men. What have you done? Got yourself appointed solicitor to the urban council as well as clerk, and pocketed the fees. Not to mention what the Harbour Trust pays you.'

'That,' said Sprewett, 'is common slander, and if I hear it repeated, steps will be taken.'

Other men drifting in, tired of music and women, put an end to the unpleasantness. Such ripples were always on the surface. Buckley would have enjoyed the evening, if Mappowder had not found time for five minutes in one of the conservatories closed to guests, and told him he would have to wait a while to be nominated for the presidency. Not this year, certainly, and not next.

'First you put the idea in my head, then you take it away again.'

The Colonel stooped to sniff an orange flower. 'Your marching into Weekes's office and threatening physical violence – that's what tells against you. Your temper, Davy. Never fear, the presidency'll come.'

But why covet things that were in other men's gift? The experience changed his mind. To hell with being president. At the next meeting of the Federation he saw the following year's candidate making himself agreeable to everyone, and vowed to keep clear of such things: unless of course he was pushed.

Speak your mind, make a profit, and be no man's servant. Had he made that up, or had he heard it from his father, old Tomos? The past was harder to pin down these days; slices of time became interchangeable, confusing who did what and when.

The meeting debated 'Friday Pay', the old chestnut that the union was trying to reopen. Buckley sat through one of Roddi's famous 'reasonable' speeches, examining both sides of the issue but not reaching any conclusion. Then he let them have it.

'We are told it will be fairer to the wives,' he said. 'Is that the purpose of tinplate manufacture, to be fair to wives? I've never been fair to mine,' and there were chuckles up and down the table. 'Pay the hands Friday and they go out and get drunk. I have no objection. That's their affair. But the result is they have no Sunday morning to lie in. So they miss the shift, we lose boxes, and the proprietors are on a slippery slope. Reject this motion. It's common sense.'

Afterwards, in the street outside the Metal Exchange in Cardiff where the meeting was held, Rhodri said gloomily, 'The forces of reaction have won again. I hope you're pleased.'

'No more than you are. You like to be seen as forward-looking, but you don't want to pay the buggers a day early, any more than I do. Let's form that combine, you and I. Now, this year. Before the spring.'

'You sound in a hurry.'

'What if I am?' Winter rain came down like arrows, smelling of coal dust. They both hated Cardiff, an upstart, full of foreign money. 'I'm an old reactionary and proud of it. I'm nearly sixty. So are you.'

Next day the Lewises came to supper. Afterwards, while the women shut themselves away in Pomona's sitting room, the owners talked business in the library.

Rhodri was dubious; he was always dubious. 'We are crossing a Rubicon,' he said. 'Hundreds of men will depend on us. Neither of our sons will forgive us if we make a wrong decision. It will have to be give and take.'

'I've just given you a seat on the Harbour Trust that you were keen on.'

'My dear Davy, the seat was mine for the asking.'

'I won't argue.'

'If you think I'm going to agree to "Buckley and Lewis", you are wrong. I am senior to you in the industry.'

'By about six months. But I won't argue about that, either. We can leave our names out of it. I got Oscar Harris to register a title this morning. "Burry River Combine" – how d'you like it?'

The beak nodded over the whisky and soda. 'It might do.'

'It will do. Now come and sit my side of the table.'

On a sheet of cartridge paper they drew up a scheme for a works to be built on Tir Gwyn farm, between the old Buckley's on one side and the old Lewis's on the other. With a blue crayon, Rhodri delineated the new mills and tinhouse. With a red crayon, Buckley turned the Morfa works into rail sidings, sawmills, boxing plant and despatch house. His own works would keep the rolling mills, and send the tinplate next door for finishing.

'It'll work!' he said. 'The next thing we shall want is a coal mine.'

'One step at a time' – but there were spots of colour in the pale Lewis cheeks, and soon he was marching up and down the library, talking about Rubicons again. 'Is it business acumen you are showing, Davy?' he asked, out of breath. 'Or is it pride?'

'Both. Come on, take the plunge.'

Rhodri found a Bible, stood it on the lectern and opened it with a dramatic flourish.

'For shame,' said Buckley. 'I thought you despised superstition.'

Rhodri stabbed his finger at a page. He narrowed his eyes and read aloud, 'I will give them an everlasting name, that shall not be cut off. Isaiah chapter fifty-six, verse five.'

'There you are. Couldn't have a better omen. You don't believe in such things, I know.'

'Weakness,' said Rhodri, and his mouth looked as if it had sucked a lemon. 'We live in a scientific age, but we are still sheep inside.'

'Yes or no, then?'

'Yes.'

The library was cold but they were both sweating. They sat slumped, gazing at one another.

In the morning they visited Japhet Jones.

The farm shivered in the frost, and the straw underfoot

in the yard snapped like twigs. Guto cackled with excitement when he saw Rhodri. He stuck out a skinny arm to stop Buckley entering the house, and Rhodri had to come back for him. Japhet was in bed, coughing his lungs up. He wore an overcoat under the blankets, and a cap with his hair sprouting at the edges. Their breath formed clouds in the bedroom.

'If I see the winter out,' Japhet said mischievously, 'I'll sell it for a thousand pounds.'

'And if you don't?' said Buckley.

'You can ask Guto then. Second thoughts, best let Mr Lewis ask him.'

Rays with no warmth in them shone through a hole in the clouds as they left, shadowed by Guto. In the fields the mills and furnaces shimmered with heat, visible only to the two men. Only they could smell the tinhouse fumes behind the icy tang of the air. They paced out the crayon lines, gazing through the invisible brick and iron of the sheds to Gower on the grey horizon and the *Falcon* making smoke. They stumbled along ruts left by carts where the ice already gleamed like rail tracks.

They waved to Guto, and he threw them a dead rabbit over a hedge. It was frozen stiff and its throat was cut. But Rhodri said they must take it, so as not to give offence.

Rees Coal looked after his niece's interests, so he and Buckley had to reach an understanding. Money changed hands about the time the child was born. It was a token. Rees took it and made it clear that no more was expected. 'Scrub floors and do the laundry, she must,' he said with satisfaction, and went on trying to sell coal to Buckley.

He arrived unexpectedly one afternoon. Buckley was with Will and Dr Snell, discussing workmen's compensation. The union's new district secretary was due in half an hour. Medical reports were piled on Buckley's desk, each one marked 'No' in Snell's red ink on the cover.

Will was making an inventory of the plant to help Oscar Harris draw up the legal agreements for the combine. The lists were endless. Chains, paint, girders, rollers, pots, brushes, shears, tongs – he yawned and spilled ink and thought anything would be preferable, even the back-breaking labour of the men on the hot rolls.

Then Rees Coal put his death's-head round the door and said, 'Buckley, we have opened the Fiery seam at Glynvale Number 2, and I might take a penny a ton off.'

Anything to do with the Reeses excited Will. He remembered Miss Rees from Margaret's wedding. From the moment he knew his brother had seduced her, she took on a peculiar quality, as if he, too, had been involved in the affair. He couldn't shake it off. He had even been to the shed where it happened. The thought of her lying down there with Morgan made his heart pound.

He got to his feet when he saw who it was. Dadda's only response was a casual, 'Dear me, have you come all the way here to say that?'

'Penny a ton is serious.'

Dadda took his hat and the three of them went for a stroll to the dyke.

'Staying in Glenalla Road I am,' said Rees Coal. 'My sister-in-law have come back to look after me. The Calfaria Baptists have big meetings every spring. They ask me down to preach.'

'Is your niece with you?' asked Dadda, and Will sprang up the damp-sided dyke ahead of them.

He heard Rees Coal say, 'On no account. She'm too fond of living in a town for her own good. She stays at The Mount and works for her keep.'

'And the child?'

'Sickly. I 'ad the doctor and he wasn't encouraging. But I done my share. God is my witness.'

'Now, about your threepence off,' said Buckley. 'Worth discussing, that.'

'I said a penny.'

'But we hope you meant threepence, don't we, Will.'

'Ain't you fortunate to have this fresh young chap in the business.'

'My right-hand man. I want you to go back and hold the fort, Will. Rees Coal and I will be a while discussing pennies. It'll be an opportunity for you to deal with that new trade union fellow when he arrives. Haycock's the name.'

'What shall I say?'

'What's right and proper.'

It was better than the inventory. Going upstairs to the office, Will pretended the works was his. Phillips, with the purple cheeks, would get the sack on Friday. He pleaded for his job, but Will told him there would be no more bullies at Buckley's. Trubshaw, whose moustache drooped like wet string, would be promoted. Every mill girl would get a box of chocolates as a present.

He had no business thinking such things.

Phillips regarded him with eyes like pips and said, 'Due any minute, sir. If Mr Buckley isn't back, I'll handle him.'

'I am to do it myself, thank you.'

'Slippery customer, this Haycock. Not like old Ben Ellis, who knew which side his bread was buttered. I'll sit in, anyway.'

'There's no need to. Dr Snell and I will see him alone.'

'If you're entirely sure.'

Will talked to Dr Snell about the pickler who said his teeth had rotted, and the doubler whose boot caught fire, burning a toe off. Dadda would say – had said – that they were cheeky stratagems by the union. But were they not real teeth and toes?

You could make an inventory of scars and stumps.

'And this one,' he said. 'Willy Protheroe, tinhouse. That's the one they call Willy Lungs. What have you written here?'

'May I see? Oh, yes. "Union will press this case." If they know what's what, they will. He's badly affected and likely to die. Any pension would be of short duration. They might think they have a chance. But of course, they can't prove anything. They never could and they never will.'

A locomotive hooted and the flywheel drummed in the floor, in the walls, in the bones. Steam drifted past the windows. The dragon devoured them all.

Will said, 'So there is a case, if they could prove it?'

'There's a case for everything, is there not? The Liberals believe that folk should be insured from the cradle to the grave. I fail to comprehend their case, but I believe there is one, of a sort.'

'And Willy Lungs? What does the case consist of there?'

'Sulphuric acid is nasty stuff, Mr Will. Get the fumes up your nose and you'd see.' The doctor's wet eyes looked sideways to make sure he wasn't giving offence. 'In your position you naturally have to take a wider view. Many spend their lives in the tinhouse and suffer no ill-effects. This fellow happens to be unlucky. Again, no one *made* him work there. He was offered a job and he took it. *Caveat actor*.' He bowed. 'But I hardly need to give lessons to David Buckley's son.'

'Haycock will argue it's unfair?'

'When was life ever fair, excuse me. If I may be personal, is it fair I can't boast a brass plate in Harley Street? He sendeth rain on the just and the unjust,' and the head clerk came in with Haycock.

He was too recent for Will to have met him; he was a

surprise. The brisk step, the trim beard, the schoolmaster's spectacles clipped on the bridge of the nose, were a long way from Ben Ellis. His age was somewhere round the forty mark. He carried papers held by rusty pins inside a cardboard folder.

Will introduced himself and they all sat down. Haycock's voice was deep and quiet. He said he came from the Merthyr area and was a newcomer to West Wales. They must bear with his ignorance. He hoped they would get on well together.

It was a formal speech; perhaps impudent as well. Phillips was clearing his throat next door.

But Haycock lapsed into silence. He sat with arms folded, chin on chest, while Snell dismissed the cases one by one. 'Half of them were argued in your predecessor's time,' he said. 'Vernon Harris, Dai Spring, Tommy Spit . . .'

'Who was sacked for gross misbehaviour,' added Will.

'The famous Earl Roberts case,' said Haycock, raising his head. 'Even I have heard of that. Jenkins continues to deny it, naturally. In any case, he's now a clerk with the Great Western. Encouraging, that.'

'I don't think the proprietor's son wants to hear your views!' spluttered Snell.

'Then no doubt he'll tell me himself, doctor.'

'Please get on,' said Will hastily, anxious not to be thought interested in what this strange fellow was saying.

'I hold no brief for Tommy Spit. Or for trouble-makers in general. If I am to convince proprietors of the moral and practical arguments for industrial compensation, I want cut-and-dried cases.'

How would Dadda reply? He said, 'Willy Protheroe, for example.'

'You know the case.' Haycock searched his bundle. He got the man's age wrong, said 'enteritis' instead of 'emphysema', and scratched his thumb on a pin. 'Forgive my ignorance,' he said, when Snell corrected him. 'I shall learn quickly. Willy Lungs has been thirty-six years in the tinhouse – '

'Thirty-five,' corrected Snell.

' – and now he can't breathe. He's dying by inches.'

'Which is unfair?' asked Will.

'Unlucky, certainly. No one asked him to work there – if I don't say it, you will. But unjust. Unjust that he gave Buckley's good service. Unjust that now he's finished, he ends up destitute.'

'Look here, this is disgraceful,' cried Snell.

'Hold on,' said Will, and took the easy way out – he sympathised with Haycock, he couldn't dismiss him off-hand, so he left it for his father to decide. 'We'll consider the case of Willy Protheroe,' he said, 'and let you know in a week.'

At once, Phillips banged and came in. 'Are you off, then, Mr Awkward?' he roared. His ear was red where it had been pressed against the wall. 'Wasting the proprietor's time, indeed. Willy Protheroe was a bad workman, so you can write that down on a paper, too.'

'I'm glad to have had a hearing,' said Haycock, and shook hands with Will.

Phillips followed him out, and was heard to say, 'I'd like to kick your bottom.'

Authority was what mattered; Dadda would support him, whatever he did.

'Mr Phillips,' he called, 'will you kindly ask Haycock to step back for a moment?'

In his anger at Phillips, he lost his fear. The room went quiet. Only the engine continued, thundering in all their heads. 'About Protheroe, Haycock,' he said. 'Five shillings a week.'

'Five – shillings,' repeated Haycock, writing it on the back of his cardboard file.

'Granted from today.'

Dadda laughed when he heard what had happened. He talked to Will about it at home. 'You nearly gave poor Phillips heart failure,' he said.

'And you'll let the pension stand?'

'Just this once. You spoke with my authority. I was negotiating twopence a ton off with Albert. There's nothing I can do now. I shall take it from your wages, naturally. Five shillings a week out of your own pocket will remind you next time you feel like being generous. I like your spirit. But things have a price. Including principles.'

Sam Lewis came back from Indiana. He blew into the office at Buckley's one summery morning with a Yankee accent, his red hair cut short, wearing a soft shirt and spotted bow-tie.

Will had been finishing off the inventory. His father was with Rhodri Lewis in Cardiff, meeting the directors of the South Wales Bank. For company there was Phillips on the other side of the wall, swearing under his breath.

Sam shook him out of himself. 'It's a great little town when you've been away,' he said, 'but it needs a bomb putting under it. Know what the Yanks say? Great Britain needs a bomb putting under it, too.'

The accent soon faded; the whiff of adventure didn't. Sam told wild stories that couldn't have been true. With his own eyes at his father's cousin's works at Elwood he had seen a single mill produce a hundred boxes of tinplate in an eight-hour shift.

In Port Howard they were lucky to make forty. Sam might as well have talked about unicorns.

In hot weather, he told Will, they used fans to cool the air, so that production never stopped. He went near the edge of credibility by saying that when millwrights were changing a broken roll, the replacement was running within twenty minutes, and the men wore gloves while they worked. It was the gloves more than the twenty minutes that emphasised the distance between Port Howard, Carmarthenshire, and Elwood, Indiana. Gloves in a tinplate mill!

Sam and Will had been friends since they were small. They went to the same boarding school at Llandovery. Morgan had gone there, too. 'And how is the saintly Morgan?' Sam wanted to know.

The scandal had to come out. Sam thought it a lark. Within days, he knew more about it than Will. He claimed to know it was still being gossiped over by the mill girls.

'Don't be such a stick,' he told Will. 'I know fellows who do it all the time. Morgan was unlucky, that was all.'

'It was a rotten thing to run away like that. I don't have any time for Morgan.'

'You never did. Your Pa was fond of him, though. I'd like to see old Morgan again. He and I could swap stories. Here, I haven't told you about the lady who took my virginity.'

Will went red.

'Well, it was like this,' said Sam, and Will was transported to the Lewises' fine wooden house at Elwood, with roaring stoves and hot-water pipes to keep the place like an oven in the depths of winter. A friend calls, a married lady – the visit is unexpected – everyone is at church except Sam – he has a cold, sitting huddled over the fire – they talk – she touches his leg with her leg – next minute she is stripping off her clothes – he does the same – the hot pipes gurgle – they are on the carpet – he is in paradise – he is terrified – there are servants – they are nearly caught.

He never sees her again.

'You're pulling my leg,' said Will, without conviction. So now he had two stories to inflame his imagination: Sam in America, Morgan and Miss Rees.

In a way that he could never have admitted to anyone, certainly not to Sam, he was in love with Miss Rees.

The two young men went about together. Soon, when the lawyers had finished their work, they would be partners. The future looked brighter.

Sam's father even let them take the car sometimes. It was a Simms-Welbeck in green and yellow trim that made Will's mouth water. One Saturday Sam drove them the eleven miles to Swansea – one puncture, due to furious driving – and left the car parked outside the Palace Theatre, in the charge of a youth who received sixpence to guard it with his life. They enjoyed a show of Magnificent Bioscope Pictures, including *The Man Who Swallowed a Clock*, *The Burglar and the Cat*, *The Female Desperado* and, best of all, *Sweet Suffragettes*, where a band of animated young ladies tried to wallop a policeman, and ended up rolling on the ground and showing glimpses of leg as high as the knee. It beat anything Will had ever seen.

On the way back they saw a car at the roadside near the Loughor Bridge, steam pouring from it. There was no driver, only a figure in the passenger seat, huddled under a cloak and blankets, crowned with a hat like a chimney.

Sam stopped – 'Automobile drivers have to stick together,' he explained – and Will saw it was Rees Coal. The engine had boiled over and the chauffeur had gone for help.

'Blessed machine!' Rees kept saying, while Sam looked under the bonnet and burnt himself on a pipe. They took him on to Port Howard, and Sam dropped his passengers at Y Plas.

No one was about. Dadda had gone to a cricket match, Mamma was resting. Will sent the coachman to see about the car. Rees Coal wanted a mustard bath to warm his legs, and messages sent to his housekeeper.

When Will telephoned, he imagined the bell ringing in

the house under the Black Mountains, within earshot of Miss Rees.

A runner came up from the works with a report on a damaged gantry. Will scribbled an instruction for the maintenance shift and sent him back.

'Yer Pa works you hard, does he?' said Albert, dipping his toast in the blackcurrant cordial he had ordered.

'No harder than he works himself, sir.'

'That's a good answer. I've worked hard all me life. There was only a dozen men in Carmarthenshire had a motor car before I did. If you work hard you're entitled to rewards. Nobody else is.'

Will rang for more hot water, and Albert gave a groan of pleasure as the steam rose between his knees.

'There's some believe otherwise, but the Lord catches 'em in the finish. D'you ever hear from that brother of yours? I know yer Pa doesn't, but brothers stick to brothers. Has the Lord swiped him yet?'

'He writes Mamma a postcard every month. We think he's with an evangelical mission.'

'There's rewards for hard work and there's rewards of a different colour for sinning. My niece – but I won't refer to her. Has yer Pa ever spoke to you about keeping yerself clean?'

Will stared at the old man's skinny legs.

'I can see you're on the right track. Yer body is a temple – I read that somewhere, and I've always remembered it.' He lifted his feet out of the bowl and buried them in the towel that was waiting. 'You couldn't give 'em a rub, young Will? Ah, that's the style. Don't forget between me toes.'

His nails were lemon-tinged, like his face. Will felt sorry for him.

Rees Coal presented him with a ticket to an Evangelical Mission Supper in Swansea, which he threw away. He knew instinctively that religion was a fraud.

Will hardly thought the visit worth mentioning. But a week later Dadda said he had made an impression on Rees Coal – 'He wants you to go and visit one of his pits – see how they do things up there. Even dropped a hint about joining forces one day. I daresay he's got wind of the Rhodri scheme.'

'Would it make sense?'

'To have collieries and tinworks under one management? It might. Anyway, Roddi doesn't like the man.'

'Do you like him?'

'I could tolerate him for profit. Ask your friend Sam what the Americans will do for profit.'

Sam and Will often talked about the combine. The obstacle of Japhet Jones remained. Rhodri took Guto shooting rabbits and let him use the twelve-bore, but Japhet wouldn't budge. It was fine weather; he had a harvest, of sorts, and he could sleep without coughing. When the gales and frosts returned, he might decide that at his age a dry house was better than a wet farm. Nothing would happen till the winter.

'See this?' said Sam.

The *Cambrian* newspaper, 17 August 1906:

> We understand that Mr Jim Larkin, the well-known Socialist and trouble-maker from Liverpool, will be in Swansea next Sunday to address a meeting of dockers, railwaymen, etc of a 'militant' tendency. We welcome free speech in Wales, but we would remind Larkin that the Welshman is also a true Briton, whose loyalty precludes his swallowing the half-baked theories of Syndicalism and Anarchy that, if realised, would undoubtedly bathe his land in the blood and tears of a revolution utterly alien to his nature.

'Sounds a lark,' said Sam. 'You should have heard what went on in Chicago when they set up the Workers of the World. People said they had dynamite.'

'Will we get in?'

'Sure, if we wear cloth caps and mufflers.'

They took the train, and managed to push their way into the hired rooms without anyone asking for union cards. Sam was soon bored. He said in Will's ear that the sooner they could get outside, the better. He had a plan, elaborated on the train, to pick up a couple of nursemaids or shopgirls.

Sun and cloud alternated at the windows. Will was absorbed by the strangeness of the meeting – the intensity of the voices, the title of 'Brothers' bestowed on them all, the boos when one of the preliminary speakers declared the need for 'co-partnership between capital and labour', the stamping and clapping when Larkin took the floor, to roar at them with his fist raised, telling them that the weapon of Man's deliverance was a simple undertaking called the General Strike.

Did they believe it? What, anyway, was the 'it' they believed in? Would the world come tumbling down and a better one arise by magic? And if the Jim Larkins had their way, would there be anything left for the owners to own?

Yet Will was stirred by the speech.

As the speaker reached his peroration, a scuffling was heard from the back, and someone shouted that a man was making notes – 'Plain-clothes bobby, like as not.' Stewards moved to eject him – he said he was from the *Cambrian*, but that didn't help – and he was flung into the corridor.

'That's the stuff to give 'em,' said Sam, but he forgot to keep his twangy voice down. In a moment they were being stared at, surrounded, asked who they were –

'Interested parties,' said Sam. 'If you don't want us, we'll be glad to go out for a breath of air.'

'Cheeky devil!' shouted a steward.

Their coats were grabbed at. Sam went white and his knees seemed to give way. Will put up his fists to defend himself but he was seized from behind.

A voice said, 'I know them.'

'Who are you, then?'

'Saul Haycock, Metal Workers, Port Howard district secretary. Here's my card.'

The hands let them go. Haycock's sharp-cut beard was comforting. 'They're two young sparks from my town. No harm at all, but I'll take them off your hands. Safe conduct, please. Make way, now.'

In the porch a man was holding a bloodied handkerchief to his nose. Sam recovered himself and said it was a good job nobody had aimed a punch at *him*, or there might have been a case of manslaughter to answer.

'We're grateful to you, Haycock,' said Will. Jim Larkin's voice could be heard – 'affairs of men . . . ranks of labour . . .' An electric tram went past, bucking on the rails like a ship. 'Don't leave the meeting on our behalf.'

'The motions of solidarity come next. I can give them a miss.'

'We must be away,' said Sam. 'Young sparks, you know. Come on, Will, and don't forget, I get first choice.'

'You go.' He was curious about Haycock – no more curious than he was about the girls who might be promenading on the West Pier, but at least Haycock was there in the flesh; the nursemaids were unproven.

Sam gave him a pitying look. 'Suit yourself,' he said, and went off whistling, his cap pulled down over one eye.

Applause was heard; Larkin had spoken. The two strolled towards the station, helped by a sea-breeze from the docks. Commerce imposed itself on the landscape more harshly than in the winding lanes of Port Howard, where the fields could still be sensed underfoot. The earth was dead here. Coal exchange and shipping headquarters had flattened it with their marble.

An asset to the trade union movement, the dockers were, said Haycock, as they reached the sooty station and entered a sooty carriage; he spoke with an easy impartiality, not exerting himself, sprinkling his speech with 'Mr Buckleys'. They needed brute force in their jobs; it followed that they were useful men in a test of strength.

'I thought the unions believed in argument and peaceful persuasion,' said Will.

'They do, if anyone will listen. But what if nobody does?' Haycock polished his spectacles. 'I like to hypothesise. Take no notice. Violence is alien to our culture. I am merely a cog in the nice, quiet tinplate industry. I have a lot to learn.'

Yet he liked to keep an eye on movements, he said. He was a man for movements.

Will listened carefully. It was wise to know your enemy. At the same time, he found it hard to see Haycock as anything but a schoolmasterly man with sound ideas. If Haycock thought that oppressive labour crushed men's spirits, that was no more than Will believed.

Haycock said they had movements in the eastern valleys, right enough. Why, the Chartists hid in caves north of Newport sixty years earlier, the men whose revolution could have overturned the State, and very nearly did – though that was in a more primitive society, before *democracy* took root.

He spat out the word as if he disliked the taste of it, but at the same time he was smiling. 'I have much to learn,' he sighed.

Where was he? Ah, in the valleys, like the Rhondda – those tortured accidents of geography where the coal mines with their twisted seams and flooding and deadly gases bred antagonism. Why, he had friends who regarded him as a traitor for moving to a backwater like Port Howard. But was there not an obligation for all men to be given an equal chance to fight for their deliverance?

So that was Haycock – bold as brass. The train dashed

them along Swansea Bay and up a wooded valley, trailing the shadow of its steam.

'Do you believe in revolution?' Will asked politely.

'I like the sound of it in theory. But not the blood-spilling sort. Dear me, no. Would I be in Port Howard if I were that way inclined? I ask you, Mr Buckley.'

'I don't think your predecessor Ben Ellis even liked it in theory.'

'Oh, him,' said Haycock. He slapped his hands on his knees and leaned towards Will. 'He was corrupt, Mr Buckley. We all know that.'

The train pulled up at a small station, Killay. Two men with terriers got in, putting an end to conversation. Haycock closed his eyes and dozed. An air of danger clung to him.

The morning fixed to sign preliminary contracts for the Burry River Combine was unfortunately the same morning Buckley had promised to be at the Royal Institution in Swansea to hear his nephew Theodore compete for the Daniel Jones Gold Medal.

'You did promise, Davy love,' said Pomona.

'In a weak moment. The boy has got his own father and mother. Why should I have to go and hear a lot of piano-playing? Anyway, I thought it was the violin.'

'Mr Stoker says he has found his vocation.'

'If he wins, I've promised him two guineas. Tell the Duchess he can have the money even if he loses. Will that satisfy her?'

'The judge will know who's there. They'll think, oh, Mr David Buckley has come with him, the boy must have talent.'

'You are very naive,' said Buckley, impatient at her and it, but touched, all the same. 'I'll try and arrange the signing earlier.'

So it was to be at nine o'clock in Oscar's office, all parties to be present. The purchase of Tir Gwyn was still not settled, but the partners had decided it was time to show their faith in one another and form the combine.

Buckley felt the solemnity of the occasion, and hoped that Will did, too. Clerks hovered in the background with blotting paper and sealing wax. Oscar stood by the window with Harker, solicitor to the other side, looking out for Rhodri.

The Town Hall clock struck nine. '*This agreement is made between David Inkerman Buckley of the one part and Rhodri John Lewis of the other . . .*' Will was frowning at the carpet, far away, as usual. '*Inasmuch as the Burry River Combine aforesaid is to be capitalised in the sum of thirty-two thousand pounds . . .*'

'Here he is,' said Harker, and they heard a motor-horn.

Oscar said, 'You need glasses. That's the Colonel's chauffeur taking Lady M to buy a hat.'

After ten minutes there was still no Rhodri. 'If you had installed a telephone,' complained Harker, 'we could find out what's happening.'

'I prefer to spend my money on a typewriting machine and a lady to operate it, which is more than you've done.'

'Let me tell you something, Harris. The telephone – '

'For heaven's sake send a messenger,' said Buckley. 'I am supposed to be in Swansea in an hour. I have Mrs Buckley waiting in a carriage. See if there's been an accident.'

The messenger returned to say Mr Lewis had been at the Morfa works at eight, and gone by half past. Nobody knew where he was.

'Will, I suppose I must go to this piano-playing,' said Buckley. 'I leave it to you to find out what's happening. I shall be back by the afternoon.'

On the way to Swansea, he wondered if Roddi had been

struck down by a seizure and carried unconscious or even dead into someone's house. Without intending any harm, he sized up the situation – Roddi's estate would pass to Ada, who would hand over the works to young Sam, who wouldn't have the faintest idea how to run a business. Buckley's would swallow up the Morfa. He would be sorry if Rhodri had been taken from them. He was not being a hypocrite. It was simply that Rhodri dropping dead might be part of Buckley's destiny.

They were late, or at least too late to meet the judges beforehand, as Villette had intended. Piano music resounded through the entrance hall, which was crowded with children, mothers and music teachers, talking in whispers.

Villette presented Mr Damon Stoker to her brother-in-law.

Buckley's private opinion was that a fit middle-aged man with a red nose and a frock coat should have better things to do than teach music.

'You must be proud of your nephew,' said Stoker.

'What shall we hear him play?'

'What they are all playing, the Chopin Barcarolle. You will be astonished when you hear the trill with the right hand!'

The child himself, mercilessly washed and combed, wore kid gloves and stood very still, listening to the music. To Buckley it was less music than bunches of notes, some agreeable, some not, disconnected in the air.

Applause was followed by a call for 'Miss Daisy Tremlett', and a nymph in a brown frock was whisked away with her supporters. Theodore was next. Buckley went outside for a smoke by the Crimea cannon on the grass, and Stoker came after him, his coat steering him like a rudder.

'Is there music on your side of the family?' he asked.

'I had an uncle who sang in a choir. I have come to show

willing, as they say. If I can do anything for the boy, I shall, if it turns out that he has real talent. Do you know it infallibly when you hear it?'

'He perceives the structure of the music. I don't tell him. He knows it. What does Pushkin say? Inspiration is a disposition of the soul toward an acute perception of impressions and their reasoned understanding.'

Life was too short for all that. 'Is he unique?' said Buckley. 'Is he going to be famous?'

'Those are impossible questions to answer, Mr Buckley. He is going to win a gold medal today, I can tell you that.'

Buckley smelt whisky. It pleased him to know that lurking behind fine words about dispositions of the soul was a bottle of liquor. Men were all the better for being reduced to common denominators.

Mr Damon Stoker swept back to the hall, frock coat wobbling, and nearly fell over the top step. Miss Tremlett was being applauded. Presently Buckley and his party were at the back, watching Theodore adjust the piano-stool and remove his gloves.

The same bunches of notes came sailing through the air. Buckley leaned on his cane. Behind him, the door opened, there was some fierce 'Sh-sh-sh-ing', and he turned his head to see Will waving at him.

He caught the Duchess's look of dismay as he went out. What did such people know of the real world?

Will had come on the next train. 'Bad news, Dadda,' he said.

'Dropped dead, has he?'

'No, he's bought Tir Gwyn himself and means to lease the land to the combine. He was with Japhet this morning, signing the papers.'

'He can't do it. Either we have a combine or we don't.'

'He says he owes it to Sam to keep something back. Says

Japhet would only sell it to him if he promised you wouldn't own it. He'll lease it to the combine at a peppercorn.'

'He's up to tricks,' said Buckley. Before Theodore got to the end of his Barcarolle, he had decided to explore the possibility of a combine with Rees Coal instead. He wouldn't make an open break with Rhodri yet. He would pretend to talk about it. He would try to change his mind.

But he would never compromise. If Rhodri wanted to be his enemy, why, then he could arrange that easily. Friend and enemy were two sides of a coin.

A necessary part of the process was to make Will an emissary, but a discreet one. To be eager with Rees Coal wouldn't be wise. Let Will visit him as a hint.

An early-morning workmen's train took Will to the uplands on the fringe of the Black Mountains, where the pits squatted under their slag-heaps. Rees had suggested he visit Glynvale to see what a well-run colliery was like.

Will was excited, but not in a way that Dadda would have approved of. His dreams the night before were full of Miss Rees.

A trap was sent to meet him at the station, and Rees Coal was waiting on the steps of the manager's office at Glynvale No 2. 'Nice place, ain't it?' he said, revealing a different Rees, the proud proprietor.

A colliery was a colliery to Will. He showed polite interest in the washery and the screens, where graded coal for Buckley's was being loaded into wagons in his honour, before being given a suit of old clothes to change into, fitted out with helmet and lamp, and taken underground.

For hours, with an overseer ahead and Rees Coal behind, he scrambled through galleries, stood back in alcoves to let trams go past, was soaked to the knees in icy water, breathed air that was suffocatingly warm, and eventually, when he thought they must be under the middle of the mountain, came across men at a face, hacking the stuff out of the Fiery vein. On the way back, the heat and claustrophobia made him vomit. 'Don't worry,' said the overseer, 'there's worse things underground.'

'More than you bargained for,' said Rees, when they were back on the surface in a cold wind. The afternoon shift was taking over. They had come up in a cage packed with black-faced men, eyeing the bosses and not speaking. They were grimy themselves.

'I wouldn't have missed it for anything.'

'That's yer good upbringing makes you say it. If you was my son, you'd ha' cursed the mine every day of yer life, but never turned yer back on it.' His motor car was waiting outside the office. Brown-paper parcels with their clothes in were on the back seats. 'Jump up an' we'll have you back for a hot bath.'

The road climbed towards a distance that crumbled into blues and greens, a disturbing emptiness.

'You'll meet my sister-in-law at The Mount,' said Rees. 'Nice woman. Poor 'ealth. Her daughter nearly killed 'er.' He looked sideways. 'Don't say much, do you? Pit too dirty for you, was it?'

'Depends what you're used to, Mr Rees.'

'Butter wouldn't melt in yer mouth. Try 'ard to keep yerself clean. That's been my religion. You can't avoid dirt, mind, don't think you can. But I like you, Master Will. If me and your Dad ever join forces, you'll see a lot of me. You can come an' hear me preach. Why weren't you at the Mission Supper I gave you a ticket for?'

'Dadda says one religious son is enough for any man.'

'You mind what you say about the Lord. He never sleeps,' said Rees, and blew the horn for the gates to be opened. Smoke blew level from the chimneys. Every room had its fire, stoked up with limitless coal.

Will was handed over to the housekeeper, a Mrs Evans,

quick-eyed, bunch of keys at her plump middle. Two maids ran up and down a passageway with buckets of boiling water, and Will was left in a downstairs room where the bath stood alone in mid-floor, its granulated surface rough to the skin. His clothes had gone to be pressed. But as he was drying himself, someone entered the ante-room, and he saw a shape through the frosted glass in the door, laying out the suit.

The clothes were still warm from the iron. Lacing his shoes, he heard a woman scream. Then footsteps, a man shouting, a door slamming. It could have been an argument or an accident.

At once he thought of Miss Rees. For all he knew, it was she who had ironed the clothes; it could even have been Miss Rees who brought them. He imagined her creeping from room to room, lonely, in rags, seething against her fate and the unspeakable Morgan.

Would she come if he called? What would he say to her if she did?

Reality was there to be tested. The corridor was dark and smelt of coal fires. The living quarters were on the right. Will hesitated, then turned to the left. Walking softly, listening, he heard a woman's voice and a clink of dishes. He put his hand on a door. His curiosity was about himself as much as about the girl.

The shadowy kitchen could have concealed a football team. A cook was scraping a glutinous substance on to plates. A woman with grey hair and pinched features stood with one hand on a cold tap, gulping water from a glass.

'I'm Will Buckley,' he said. 'It's Mrs Rees, isn't it?'

'Does my brother-in-law know you're here, Mr Buckley?'

'He brought me up from Glynvale.'

'I mean in this part of the house.'

'I must have taken a wrong turning. I haven't been here before.'

A door opened on the far side of the kitchen. Rees Coal appeared. He was holding a handkerchief to his cheek.

'Couldn't wait for yer vittles? I don't blame you. Men who've been down pits need something in their bellies.'

His face was scratched. He pushed Will ahead of him to the dining room, where three places were laid. The handkerchief had blood on it. 'Kitchen maid saw a rat an' started screaming. I gave her a splash of water to cool down with an' she got her claws out. But I shan't sack her, shall I, Dilys?'

Mrs Rees had come in and was taking lids off bowls of vegetables. 'No doubt you'll do as you think best,' she said.

Rees tucked into his food, talking about coal and money. 'My sister-in-law don't concern herself with pits, do 'ee?' he said. The woman took no notice, picking at her plate, brushing wearily at strands of hair over her eyes. 'Like you, Master Will, when you come up in the cage. Oh, nasty filthy place, you was saying under yer breath. But it don't seem so terrible now you're all pink and white again. 'Tis a vital matter that women don't understand. All them tinworks and ironworks might as well be scrap without coal. Must respect it, Dilys. It's bread and butter, d'you see. It's a roof overhead. Master Will Buckley here respects it.'

Her unwellness was like a shadow on the table. Will leaned across and said, 'Mamma asked me to send her kind regards,' though what Mamma had said was that she hoped Will might catch a glimpse of little Isabel.

'My sister-in-law don't see much of Port Howard. She stays here and looks after me. Tongues wag in towns, don't they, Dilys?'

'I'm sure Mamma would be glad if ever you were to call on her.'

'The boy's got a kind heart,' cackled the old man.

'If there's anything I can do . . .'

'Tell me about your sister,' said the woman timidly. 'She had such a lovely wedding.'

'They live in London.'

'And is she happy there?'

'Is she happy there?' mimicked Rees. 'Married persons is mostly happy to begin with, I'm told. Leastways, they all *pretend* it. He has to say she's happy. I don't s'pose he knows more than this pear in a dish if it's true.'

'What does anybody know about anybody?' said Will. 'What do you know about me? I about you? I about this house?' The mission he had come on didn't matter. He stood up abruptly and his chair fell over. 'It's time I went back.'

'So it is, if you can't be civil.'

'I hope I shall see you again, Mrs Rees.'

She was dumb; nodding at her plate.

'You an' me must be friends,' said Rees when they were outside, waiting for the chauffeur to bring the car round. 'Yer Pa and me have got ideas.'

'Should I ever see my brother, what shall I tell him about Miss Rees?'

'Tell him the babby's cared for, which is no thanks to him.'

'The girl . . .'

'What about the blasted girl? She's well fed and well treated. Do you want to see 'er, is that what it is?'

'I don't want her thinking we're all like my brother.'

'Back inside and wait in the gun room, then.'

The room was cluttered with fishing rods and saddles. It was a long time before Rees Coal returned, his niece by his side. She was a thin face above a shapeless blue dress; no rags, no flashing eyes. Her long silky lashes seemed out of place.

'This is the young woman ye're bothered about,' said Rees. 'Go on, child, he won't bite.'

She held out her hand but wouldn't look at him. He saw black nails and raw knuckles with wet-looking cracks. Where were the tears? The imploring bosom heaving with emotion? He had no plan for dealing with a waif. 'I – I'm very glad to see you, Miss Rees,' he said, unhappily aware that she wasn't glad to see him. 'My family was very upset.'

'Ay,' chuckled Rees, 'especially yer Pa. Cost him poun's and poun's, it has.'

'If there's anything I can do – '

'Tell him if ye're treated fair.'

'Perfectly,' she whispered.

'There you are. Run along, Miss,' and he let his paw rest on the back of her dress, ''cause you got yer little one to look after.' She walked away, head bent. 'Satisfied now, Master Will Buckley? She's got a roof over her head and fresh milk for the babby, not having none of her own. She's a girl that did a bad thing, and don't let's forget it.'

Will left it at that. He had enough sense to know that maltreatment was hard to prove. It didn't occur to him to do anything but go straight to Dadda and tell him what he had seen, then trust in his judgement.

It was well into the evening when the train reached Port Howard. 'Connects at Swansea for London Paddington,' he heard them shouting, and thought of Morgan at the other end of the rails; a void from which surely there was no return.

The long day blew out like a candle. He was ready for Dadda. What he hadn't expected was that Dadda was ready for him.

Watkins said he was to go straight to the library. It was the room for formalities. The blue-black bindings of history and literature were rarely disturbed. Only the cases of technical writings received regular attention, the *Mineral Statistics*, the *Returns of Wages*, essays about tin-making, polemics on the Tariff.

Dadda was at the far end, by the shelves of modern novels. That in itself was an event. Less tightly packed, they leaned dissolutely at angles. Dadda had one in his hand. He heard Will and spoke without turning.

'Some of these books are improper,' he said. 'Your sister should have taken them with her when she left home.'

He replaced a Thomas Hardy and turned to face his son. He had removed collar and tie, adding belligerence to his square, scowling figure.

'A man must accept it when his children grow up and decide to lead their own lives,' he said. 'I expect nothing of Margaret. When a daughter finds a husband, you wave her goodbye. As for your brother, I must have been mad ever to have expected anything of him. That leaves you. What should I expect of you, Will?'

'Loyalty, Dadda.'

Loyalty, yes. So was it loyalty to accuse Rees Coal, as good as, of ill-treating his own flesh and blood?

The telephone had been busy. Instead of confiding a secret in Dadda, he was having to defend himself against having behaved improperly.

'Rees Coal and I are half way to an agreement,' said Buckley. 'You will write him a letter before you go to bed tonight, apologising for your behaviour.'

'May I speak?' said Will.

'There is nothing to say. Go and find pen and paper.'

'He has made Miss Rees into a skivvy.'

'No doubt he believes in hard work as a way to salvation. There are worse creeds.'

'I'm sure he strikes her, Dadda. I saw her. She's terrified of him.'

'Her own mother is with her.'

'Mrs Rees is unwell. There's nothing she can do.'

'I am warning you,' cried Dadda. 'Whatever happens at The Mount is neither your business nor mine.'

'We should make it our business.'

'Don't speak to your Dadda like that,' came a shocked voice from the doorway. His mother was there, in a striped nightgown. 'He has worked himself to the bone for you boys. Next thing, he'll be having heartburn in the night. Now kiss your Dadda and say you're sorry.'

'You should be in your room, my dear,' said Buckley.

'How can I sleep when you're upset?'

Childhood had been like this. Will felt himself a child again, told what Duty was, led where Virtue flourished. Alternatives didn't exist. What was decided within the four walls of Y Plas was absolute. How could one hurt the feelings of the sanctified, St Dadda and St Mamma?

'Kiss your Dadda, there's a good boy.'

Reluctantly, he touched his father's bristly cheek with his lips. The quarrel was over. Mamma went back to her room, and Will wrote the letter. How could he be sure what was right? He made excuses for himself: a son's duty to his parents, and all that.

But he couldn't stop thinking about Miss Rees. He searched his pockets in case she had slipped a scrap of paper with a message into his clothes. If he had found a 'Help me' or an 'SOS' he might have acted. Days became weeks. He told himself he was biding his time.

One afternoon, shortly after, Buckley strode through the New Dock area, picking his way across the nexus of railway lines at the Mappowder bottleneck. Locomotives whistled hoarsely down side-streets, slow-trundling wagons on parallel tracks made alleyways for the brave to walk through, drivers leaned out of cabs, bells clanged, steam rose.

On the far side of the tracks he recognised Fat Sara, the sister of Tommy Spit, who had found work at the Morfa. A man had stopped to speak to her. It was Sam, Rhodri's boy. Sam must be ticking her off about something. He saw Buckley and waved, before wagons blotted him out.

How many years before Sam and Will's generation took over? Ten? Fifteen? It seemed only yesterday that he went for walks with his small sons, showing them rival works, getting them to read the names painted in white down the chimneys.

As they skirted the marshes, the little ruffians would disappear. They would hide from him on the banks of creeks, creep into tinhouses and bring out crickets in their handkerchiefs, steal a rollerman's bottle of ale from its hiding place in a water tank. Once, at their own Dadda's works, they pinned a length of sheepskin to the back of a foreman's jacket, and everyone went 'Ba-a-a!' as he walked past.

Buckley reached the Morfa. Where the rail sidings ended, Tir Gwyn farm began in a tangle of hedges. It was unchanged. A horse shivered between the rails of a cart with Guto at the reins, bumping over frozen earth. Buckley remembered the little ruffians doing something to a horse . . .

But that wouldn't do. Only a fool would remember his sons as they might have been, not as they were. He growled at the Morfa gateman that he was on his way to see Mr Lewis. It was Morgan who put pepper under the nag's tail unaided, Morgan who stole the rollerman's beer. It was always Morgan. Will was an ordinary child, no better and no worse than most. Morgan was the little devil that people remembered. He was the son who was 'shocking', who'd 'be rich if he wasn't hanged first'.

'This way, sir,' said the manager.

Until God and the angels came along with their specious promises, it didn't occur to him that his elder son, for all his waywardness, would ever be anything but the next owner of Buckley's and Y Plas. In his own youth he had been wild enough. Morgan would calm down.

'You're a stranger,' said Rhodri. 'You have been very stubborn. I had no option. Japhet sold me the farm or he sold to nobody. He's there now on a six-month lease, renewable. We can start building next spring.'

'It must be within the combine,' said Buckley. 'You Liberals are all the same – say one thing, do another.'

'We've never brought politics into our friendship before.'

'Time we started.'

Their voices had risen against the clamour of the works. All around them, on the other side of thin brick walls, the storm of a tinplate mill was raging, thunder of rolls, clatter of plates, roar of furnaces, indefinable screams and shrieks of metal. The bump of steel bars was like a heart stopping for a second.

'I've come to tell you that Rees Coal and I are forming a combine. You can do what you like.'

It was a gamble. He hoped it would bring Roddi to his senses. Instead, the beaky nose quivered. Roddi was laughing.

'Are you serious?' he said. 'Rees Coal? That old duffer?'

'He has some good seams. We have plans. There's a steel works we have our eye on.'

'Which one?'

'Mind your own business.'

Rhodri had stopped laughing. 'There's nothing more to be said.'

It happened all the time. In a small town, in a cut-throat industry, enemies were as natural as friends. Buckley had a moment of regret. Then he said, 'I agree, nothing,' and within a minute he had left Morfa and the friendship behind. A gust of smoke from the mill licked at his throat. The gateman touched his cap.

Guto and the cart were far off, silhouetted against the metal sea. A faint 'Hoi!' and 'Hup!' came over the fields.

Morgan was the root of it all. If the son had stayed, the father would have been content with things as they were. Even when he fled to London, Buckley waited for a word from him. He could have come back to the works. He would have been forgiven.

But all he ever sent were those bloody postcards to his Mamma.

6

Morgan had come down in the world. The only consolation was that he had barely started to go up in it. One minute he was at Blaen Cwm, getting ready to save the souls of the ungodly, with special reference to the materialists of England. The next, he was dragged down to their level. God had let it happen, so that was that. Though it would have been a lot easier for everyone if the message had been sent earlier.

London teemed with the Welsh, all of them busy bettering themselves. Half the dairymen with their carts of milk were Jones or Williams. Drapers, too, spoke through their noses with Cardiganshire accents. Small hotels, like the one he stayed in near Paddington station on the night he arrived, attracted severe Welsh landladies who ran model establishments, free from sin, no alcohol permitted. Welsh teachers and Welsh clergymen abounded.

Morgan shunned them all.

Life was opportunity; is that what it boiled down to? London SW, the wedge of suburbs beyond the Thames where he had settled, was no better or worse than any of the other wedges. It teemed with potential men of affairs. They travelled to and fro in electric trains and horse-buses, dined out once a month, and took summer holidays in English watering-places with piers. Somewhere in these south London hills and vales, a villa with a parlourmaid and a flower-bed was waiting for Morgan, and had been for eighteen months. As – in Port Howard, before he left the works – Y Plas and the roar of furnaces had waited, a future lying in ambush.

A vocation had saved him the first time. What would save him now?

He would have tried anything. Perhaps he was lucky it was only the Church of Christ the Atomist. The church – prosperous enough to advertise in south-western newspapers, where Morgan read of it – was to be found in a road off Wimbledon Common. A patch of grass and cinders had escaped the villa-builders, who had already covered most of the slope, leaving just enough room for the Very Rev 'Practical' Hastings to erect his corrugated-iron temple.

A board above the railings declared in red letters,

THERE IS NO VOID!

Christ Risen proves that the
Atoms of the Body and the Soul
are interchangeable!

Let the Very Reverend 'Practical' Hastings,
Pastor and President, be your
Spiritual Scientist

Morgan knew he might have found nothing. At first, one of his daily duties was to use a damp cloth on the board. There was also attending to a hungry coke stove, cleaning the floors and selling copies of *Spiritual Science News* door-to-door.

He didn't mind; he hardly noticed. He was still getting his breath back. Surveying the unbroken roofs of suburban London from the poky window of his room, which he rented from a diligent young couple called Clegg, he saw nothing he knew, nothing that knew him.

To begin with, he contemplated suicide. If God treated his servants shabbily, he could hardly be surprised if they responded accordingly. Promotion saved him from the razor on the shelf or the swirling surfaces under Putney Bridge; it would have been such a waste, anyway. One day he was putting out hymn-books for the evening service when a man in gold-rimmed glasses appeared with a police sergeant in tow, complaining of fraud. In his hand was a medicine bottle wrapped in the red and black label that Practical Hastings got from a printer in Balham –

THE GREAT ATOM.

Will open your spiritual pores.
Price five shillings and sixpence.

Morgan rose to the occasion. 'Mr Hastings is in meditation,' he said – the Pastor was never at his best after lunch. 'I'm his assistant. Is there something I can do?'

'This gentlemen is making a complaint about a substance he purchased here,' said the sergeant.

'I have had it analysed,' said the man, no doubt a trouble-maker of the Established Church, 'and it contains no active ingredient except a weak solution of laudanum.'

'Permit me to turn the bottle,' said Morgan. 'What does it say on the other side? *Praise to the Transcendental Chemist.* You see, Officer, the contents of the bottle are inseparable from the theology that comes with it. The entire universe – according to Mr Hastings – is made up of atoms which may combine in molecular or non-molecular form. Under certain conditions, the atoms we can see become the atoms we can't see. This process is known as transcendental chemistry.'

'Utter nonsense!' cried the trouble-maker.

'Could I have your name, sir?' asked the sergeant.

'I am the Reverend Morgan Buckley, graduate of the University of Wales.' It hurt him to say so; it would have hurt him even more to tell the truth.

'These are only informal inquiries' – the sergeant looked more reluctant every minute – 'but do I understand that this bottle is sold as part of a course of treatment, as it were?'

'Exactly. Spiritual treatment.'

The law had had enough; there were wickeder crimes to be found in the streets of Wimbledon. The visitor was persuaded to leave, muttering about solicitors.

Stirrings came from the vestry, and Practical Hastings emerged in his silver robes. He congratulated his assistant for putting things in a nutshell; the voice was only slightly slurred.

'Clever,' he said.

'Too clever to sweep floors, anyway.'

So Morgan was promoted to giving short addresses about Cosmic Gas, wearing a frock coat and morning trousers that Hastings lent him, and taught how to sell bottles of laudanum-flavoured water. The Church had no more than a hundred and fifty true adherents, but there was a floating fringe; and the long suburban streets continually threw up the curious, the triers-out, the almost-willing-to-believe.

No Mrs Hastings was ever seen, only Miss Poppy Foster, an agreeable young woman of twenty-eight or nine, described as 'a relative'. Poppy sang and waved the tambourine. She was fond of Hastings, as were many women, who formed the backbone of the congregation.

They were respectable folk, undone by the urge to try things. They had tried Christian Science, or Theosophy, or Spiritualism, or Mesmerism, or even the Salvation Army. Now, catching echoes of the half-baked news about science that they read in popular papers, they were ready to be told that the Supreme Being lurked on the other side of a curtain in a cloud of invisible atoms, accessible through scientific jiggery-pokery.

Morgan knew that whatever his need – even arriving more or less penniless in London – he wouldn't have carried betrayal as far as Cosmic Gas if God hadn't taken it into his head to abandon him. 'So why *did* you do it, God?' he would ask, looking from his rented room over the rooftops towards Crystal Palace.

Presently, in the silences of London that newcomers hear, the question sank to a whisper, just one among all the whispers in his head. 'Find your true level, is my advice to you, Mr Buckley,' his landlady's husband used to say, dancing around the kitchen with a small daughter clinging to his neck. Mr Clegg was a clerk at the gasworks, and offered more than once to find an opening for their lodger.

But establishing one's level was the question of questions. Was it Practical Hastings? Had a tin chapel always been his destination? Was this permanence? He found he could write pages of stuff for the *Spiritual Scientist* that read so well when the printer in Balham set it up in type, Morgan almost believed what it said. One Sunday he conducted a service (Hastings was indisposed) that had half the congregation in tears, and Poppy broke her tambourine. When they went out on a Practical Mission (selling elixir and pamphlets in other districts south of the Thames), he could dispose of almost as much as the Pastor. There was undoubtedly money to be made. Quite often he had the jingle of sovereigns in his pocket.

Now and then Hastings went up to the West End 'on business' and stayed away all night. Poppy was restless and inclined to sulk on these occasions. She was a likeable woman who described herself, when asked, as housekeeper to the Pastor. The house was a two-up, two-down near Wimbledon railway station; 'he sleeps up and I sleep down,' she told people firmly when the subject arose, and for all Morgan knew, that was the truth.

One of the trips upset her more than usual. Poppy said it was his birthday. She had spent hours making him a cake. But he pleaded 'urgent business' and did his vanishing trick. In a temper, she threw the cake in the dustbin and went round to the church, where Morgan was in the vestry sticking labels on bottles of The Great Atom.

When she had finished grumbling, Poppy announced that for once she meant to enjoy herself. There was just time to see if Mrs Squale – he must have heard of Mrs Squale – had a vacancy at her Tuesday night table. She would send a telegram. She supposed that Morgan wouldn't care to accompany her?

Mrs Squale was a medium who practised at Putney, a twopenny train ride away, holding private seances at which marvellous things were said and done. Once a week she held a popular evening for as many as eight or ten sitters. It was three shillings and sixpence a head. It was really nice.

'You believe in all that stuff, Poppy?'

'Promise you won't tell Mr Hastings. He goes barmy if anyone mentions the spirits.'

The reply said 'Two vacancies, eight sharp,' and they arrived early at a modern house with bay windows, and a flight of steps up to the front door. An afterglow of sunset showed through trees alongside, and the air smelt of bonfires.

The river was near. A steam whistle shrieked. Banjo music from a pleasure boat filtered through the streets. In Wales, a year earlier, there would have been witnesses to swear it was angels singing. That was a world of innocence now. Had Morgan ever believed in stratospheric choirs and Christ walking on the aqueduct at Neath? The question belonged with Evan Roberts in the past.

After a maid took their coats, a man with thick eyebrows wearing dark formal clothes, who was Squale, produced a visitors' book for them to sign. Money changed hands at this point, collected in a plate lined with blue cloth. They were in a church, it implied, and the three-and-sixpences were an offering.

A drawing room, with people already present, continued

the illusion; no one spoke above a whisper. A stern old couple (experienced sitters?) looked at them sharply. A woman with swollen eyes (a bereaved mother?) was comforted by her husband. A cool young fellow in a cravat wrote on a piece of paper (calculating Mrs Squale's annual turnover?). Finally a woman in a dirty blouse arrived as eight was chiming on a clock in the hall, and Mr Squale asked them to follow him.

Seances were held at the back of the house. The medium was seated on the far side of a table, which was draped in black cloth. She was younger than Morgan expected, somewhere in the mid forties, her pretty, puffy features framed in coils of dark hair. Her dress was black, and immediately behind her – they moved when she moved – hung black curtains on a rail along the front of a cabinet, four or five feet high, that stood against the wall. Even in the bright gaslight, the effect was that of a face suspended in darkness.

'Mrs Squale has asked me to say that physical phenomena may or may not occur tonight,' said her husband, and the financier frowned. 'We shall begin with a hymn. This may help conditions, as you know.'

A harmonium stood near the heavily curtained window. Mr Squale gave a loud rendering of 'Abide with me', and the company sang intermittently, standing in the places he had indicated; Morgan and Poppy were opposite the medium, who had the elderly couple on either side of her.

Morgan knew it was fraud. When everyone was seated, Squale opened the curtains to the cabinet, revealing a small table on which stood a handbell. Before Morgan could get a proper look, he closed them again.

Everyone held hands, except that Mrs Squale kept hers on the table, one above the other, and her two neighbours laid their free hands on top. Her eyes were closed.

'If there are no questions,' said Squale, 'we are ready to begin.'

'I have a question,' said Morgan. 'What is the purpose of the cabinet?'

There was a murmur of disapproval, and Poppy tugged at his hand. He saw Mrs Squale's eyes open for a second, and take him in. She looked unconcerned.

'You may be unaware that many spirits need a cabinet to concentrate and hold the magnetic fluid,' said Squale. 'This is the fluid used to produce phenomena.'

'I see. Thank you,' said Morgan. The explanation seemed on a par with Cosmic Gas, but everyone else seemed to believe it. He felt his interest stirring, in their beliefs as much as in the phenomena.

A candle was lit on the mantelpiece and a red shade placed over it. Squale closed the lid of the harmonium, turned off the gas, and padded to the door on soft soles. Light from the hall shone in briefly. Morgan saw him go out.

Hoarse breathing came from the other side of the table. Otherwise there was silence for several minutes. Poppy's hand sweated into his.

Suddenly a bell tinkled above their heads. Morgan thought he could see something move, but it was impossible to be sure in the dim redness. Then it sounded beside his ear. Poppy gasped and dug her nails into his hand. A faint swishing through the air was followed by silence, which lasted as long as before. It was broken by a soft thud on the table, and almost immediately, Mrs Squale began to speak.

'Dr Oliver has brought us roses.' The voice was shrewd, with a trace of a northern accent. 'He says the influences are waxing and waning tonight. He says . . . he says it is not that man shall conquer matter, and build the idols of material worship. He shall go on beyond the stars and planets with new companions of knowledge and wisdom. We are citizens of space and time.'

Dr Oliver was succeeded by personal messages from assorted spirits. An 'Arthur' came through and was promptly identified. An 'elderly gentleman, a schoolmaster type', brought a murmur of recognition. The less convincing it all was, the more it interested Morgan. 'A classical man,' Mrs Squale was saying, 'good at Latin. Fond of children. I hear a child laughing.'

A woman began to sob. In the darkness, the noise was terrifying. The man's hand on Morgan's right was withdrawn, and his voice could be heard comforting her.

'The circle is broken,' said Mrs Squale.

In a whisper, the man said, 'The schoolmaster was our Ruth's grandfather.'

'She is happy now.'

It was the ultimate fraud. The room had grown colder. Mrs Squale groaned, and 'Abide with me' burst from the harmonium. Poppy was shaking. The mother of Ruth wept noisily. The music stopped, and Morgan smelt bonfires – from the window, of course, where Squale must have climbed in for the grand finale, and now had climbed out again.

A minute later Squale reappeared and lit the gas. It was all over. A bunch of shrivelled roses lay on the table. Mrs Squale, looking exhausted, had to be helped out by her husband and the maid, but recovered in time to say parting words to each sitter.

'I'm glad you could come, Mr Roberts,' she said to Morgan.

'It's Mr Buckley, Cordelia,' said Squale.

'How strange. You know someone by the name of Roberts?' He shook his head. 'And Birchgrove, is that a place?'

'I couldn't say. Good night.'

On the train Poppy wanted to know what it meant. 'Nothing at all,' said Morgan, but he wondered, too. Even if Poppy were in collusion with Mrs Squale, which was unlikely, she knew nothing of his life. He had never mentioned Roberts, or Blaen Cwm, or anything else about his past. So where had Mrs Squale got it from? What was the illusion behind the illusion?

Morgan could have slept with Poppy that night. He saw her to the door of the house behind the railway station, but she was afraid to go in by herself until the gas was lit. Seances made her nervous, she said.

In the darkened hallway, kisses came at him like teeth. He resisted her calmly. He told her he had taken a vow of chastity until he was twenty-five, which wasn't just yet.

It was so absurd, they both burst out laughing.

'Get on,' she murmured, and put his hand on her breast.

'No, I'm serious,' he said, 'I can't do it, Poppy.'

Ever since Miss Rees, one half of him had wanted badly to go on doing it, and had done it more than once, in extremis, with women who hung around the courts off Leicester Square and the Charing Cross Road. But the other half was wary, blaming Miss Rees as the mysterious agent of his fall. It was hard to accept that he was the victim of an everyday mishap. He felt better if he thought dark forces were at work.

'It's not that I don't like you, Poppy,' he said.

She let him go. Her face was scarlet and her dress was sticking to her shoulders.

How could she understand that in the beginning the earth was without form, and void; and darkness was upon the face of the deep? God, having created one new Morgan Buckley in six days, or whatever it took to turn him for ever against Dadda's tinplate works, was faced with the task of creating a new version – or, more likely, had given up and left the task to Morgan himself.

Morgan Buckley was without form, and void. The blatant worminess and crawliness of his lust was too terrifying to be given a free hand until he knew what would become of him.

He liked Poppy and the things that Poppy had to offer, but she wasn't important. The performance at Mrs Squale's was what caught his imagination. That winter Morgan decided he couldn't spend his life standing in a tin shed, shouting about God the Scientist to a scattering of pinched faces and February coughs – Practical Hastings was laid up with bronchitis, writing the *Spiritual Scientist* from his sickbed, and mixing new supplies of The Great Atom ready for the spring campaign.

He even thought to visit Margaret. Like Mamma, she was on his list for postcards – once he had sent her a picture like the one she had sent him, of the Welsh chapel in the Charing Cross Road; he signed it with an exclamation mark; he wanted her to think he hadn't lost his nerve. He missed Margaret.

One Sunday he got as far as West Hampstead station before turning back from the wilderness of cheap houses that mirrored his own south London streets. How could he visit her with nothing to show?

He went to Mrs Squale's again, without telling Poppy. He had a soft spot for the darkness and fraudulence. Or was it more than that? Another group of believers sat in a circle, holding hands. So much faith in miracles was worth conserving.

He was ready for the bell and the roses, but neither of them happened; the table gave some preliminary rattles, lights were seen above the cabinet, and a spirit called Rameses declared that if Cleopatra's Needle was not returned from the Thames Embankment to Egypt and the sacred city of On, London would be devastated by fire.

'Believe, believe, for it is written,' said the spirit, and Morgan wondered how mediums dealt with sceptics.

Dr Oliver was there, as before. Mrs Squale invited questions, and the doctor was asked about a dead father, a paralysed brother, a friend who had emigrated to Canada. The answers were shrewd, but were they anything more?

'I am worried about my grandmother,' said Morgan.

'Is she in the body or the spirit?' inquired Mrs Squale.

'I thought Dr Oliver knew everything.'

A neighbouring hand tightened on his wrist.

'Spirits are only the dreams of the dead,' said Mrs Squale. 'We must help them if we want them to help us.'

'She's in the body.'

'An old lady,' said Mrs Squale. 'Bent over a table, with a shawl about her shoulders. She misses you. Her time hasn't come.'

'I could do better myself,' said Morgan.

The harmonium gave a cough and a wheeze, 'Abide with me' got under way, and Morgan pulled his hands free of his neighbours, and kicked his chair backwards.

'Stop him!' shouted a man.

Rapping noises came from the cabinet. Morgan ran for the harmonium, which had stopped playing. Halfway there, his ankle caught in something. He fell with a crash, full-length, and seemed to go clean through the floor. Still in darkness, he could hear himself trying to breathe. Then there was only the sensation of falling towards a square of light, far away.

Mrs Squale held a handkerchief soaked in brandy to his lips, and said it was a miracle he hadn't hurt himself. He was in the drawing room, on a sofa. Mr Squale hovered by the door.

'There was a tripwire,' said Morgan.

'Don't be foolish, dear.'

'Where are the others?'

'They've gone.' The eyes were like beads of glass. 'What were you trying to do?'

'You know perfectly well. Find evidence of fraud.'

'Silly boy,' she said, and the door closed behind Squale. 'Do you suppose I'm performing scientific experiments?' She took a sponge from a basin, squeezed out the cold water, and wiped his forehead. 'You, of all people. You see, Mr Buckley, you have a psychic's head. No, that's untrue. The signs are never physical, but one is tempted towards the concrete – towards the trick, the demonstration. Let's say I knew when you first came here. I told Mr Squale, and he said, "Cordelia, you are never wrong."'

'Why did you call me "Roberts"?'

'I thought it was your name. It enveloped you. Mr Roberts of Birchgrove. There is such a place?'

'As it happens.'

Morgan's knee was stiff and his shoulder ached. He had solved nothing. He said goodbye in the hall.

'You'll be back soon,' said Mrs Squale. 'You can't fight it for ever.'

Morgan's bruises kept him in bed next day. He was there when a detective called to see him in the evening. Mrs Clegg showed the visitor upstairs and tip-toed away; in living memory there had never been a policeman in the house.

The detective was young, with bitten fingernails. He opened his notebook, asking to be enlightened about the Great Atom mixture.

'Again?' said Morgan. He explained that Hastings kept it secret, although everyone knew the important part was the opium. 'But the elixir is inseparable from the theology,' he said, getting into his stride. 'He's had complaints before. People expect miracles.'

'They don't expect to drop dead.'

In the kitchen below, Mr Clegg had arrived home, and his small daughters were squealing and laughing.

'Never hurt a fly,' said Morgan.

'Until now.'

A member of the congregation had collapsed and died of asphyxia. They thought it was laudanum poisoning. Practical Hastings was in a cell at Balham. Hundreds of bottles had been impounded.

'Unfortunate accident.'

'Some accidents are manslaughter. You may be required to give evidence, and you will be interviewed further.'

When the detective had gone, the Cleggs hurried upstairs. Mrs Clegg had a dread of anyone being in what she called Queer Street. Her husband had a daughter on each shoulder. They were pulling his hair and giggling. 'Do you know what Queer Street is, Miss Muffet?' he said, and they both jumped on the bed, screaming 'Queer Street, Queer Street!'

Next morning Morgan found Poppy at the church. She had been arrested with Hastings, but released overnight.

'He must have forgot to put water in or something,' she said. 'Did you ever?'

'He may get off.'

'He's not had a lucky life. It's you and me'll have to keep things going for a bit.'

She urged him to wear the silver robes for their midweek service. They smelt of dust, and an inner pocket under the armpit contained a quarter-bottle of whisky and a small rubber object in a plain packet.

God was laughing at him. This was permanence, after all. A crowd turned up, made curious by the death. They were disappointed not to see the Pastor, and a woman jeered at Morgan.

'Those who mock condemn themselves!' he thundered. 'They disturb the molecular balance of the universe. Christ is implicit in every atom of hydrogen, oxygen and carbon that Man is made of. Yea, verily.'

It was when he saw the detective in the congregation that he decided to make a run for it. Running would become a habit if he wasn't careful. After the service he packed his belongings and left the Cleggs' without saying goodbye. Poppy had invited him back to the two-up, two-down for supper. Most probably the detective would be outside, standing under a street lamp, nibbling a fingernail.

Only when there was no escape did the future become bearable.

The evening's seance was over. Mrs Squale, wearing a loose flowered garment like a dressing-gown, was sitting alone, playing patience.

'I want to start a new life,' he said.

'Is that all, dear?'

'You seem to think I have talents. Very well. I would like to find a use for them.'

'It will be a long apprenticeship. One progresses slowly from plane to plane.' But she patted the sofa encouragingly.

Postcards with noncommittal messages were all that Margaret heard from Morgan. When his first card arrived, she looked at the SW postmark and made a wild guess at Battersea. She walked there for hours, until her feet hurt and she lost her temper. Anger was the best way to cope with Morgan. Apparently he wasn't starving or in prison. Margaret had her own life to lead. She let London SW get on with itself.

She had her home (in West Hampstead), her husband (when he was there) and the Penbury-Holts (for ever, she supposed). They were her family; she was in them and of them, and if she still looked at them from time to time with the same uninhibited eye, she kept her observations to herself.

There was the business of Esther and the Suffragists. A year or two earlier Margaret might have written, 'Dear Mamma, The blessed Esther, having tired of her campaign for soldiers' wives, has now joined the jolly Suffragists, and on entering her flat one instantly falls over a banner saying *Votes for Women*.'

Now, that would have been disloyal. She laughed about it with Virginia instead, and commiserated with Henry, who said gloomily that a fellow found it difficult enough to build up a high-class business like orchids, without having it known (as if it was!) that his sister associated with women who had been in prison.

In an odd way, Henry-as-one-of-the-family was less of a problem than Henry-as-my-husband. Not that the family did much, or anything, to help. The firm of H. Penbury-Holt, Growers and Importers of Fine Orchids, with three steaming hothouses beyond the residence, not to mention the romantic figure of Johansson the Swede who appeared from time to time, was left to make its way in the world. But Margaret sensed that Henry had always been a potential source of anxiety to his father and elder brother, the son with faulty judgement who might, just might, turn into a black sheep one day. She, as his wife, now took the day-to-day responsibility.

No one expected her to interfere. Yet she was there – perhaps – as a moderating influence, in their eyes. Was that what Esther had meant by 'signing a contract when you agreed to join the Penbury-Holts'? And if the family could look to her in extremis, she could look to the family.

Extremis, however, was not what Margaret normally had in mind. It seemed not impossible that Henry was going to make a success of his orchids. He had contracts to supply what he called 'leading hotels in principal cities', and if these were chiefly in smoky parts of the Midlands and North, at least they were regular business. The hothouses had a staff of two (or one and a quarter, said Virginia, when she saw the size of the boy who assisted the man).

And there was Johansson, who six months earlier had almost acquired an exclusive consignment of a new species of giant Cattleya from the Colombian forest. Margaret had lived with the suppressed excitement for weeks. The cattle's ear (it was how she thought of it) would make them rich, except that she suspected all along that it wouldn't. Its flowers were 'like purple velvet', according to the Swede's letter – which had to be translated from the Swedish – and 'I propose to name it *Cattleya penburiana*, in honour of our founder.'

Sadly, a rival traveller from the firm of Frederick Sander outwitted him (or a filthy dago cheated him, if one listened to Henry). Johansson brought back hundreds of other plants, and the expedition made a small profit. But the real prize, a new variety that could have been offered to Nathaniel Rothschild or the Pope – Johansson could name all the leading buyers – eluded them.

Henry told her often that it wasn't Johansson's fault, that he was the kind of man one needed to have faith in. All they had to do was be patient, and the firm would be as famous as Sander's. Margaret did her best to believe it; she would have found it easier if the aspects of Johansson she could see with her own eyes were as impressive as Henry seemed to think.

Staying in London after one of his trips to the Continent, Johansson insisted that Henry bring her to dine at the hotel. A female cousin from Stockholm was also in England, and they would be 'a jolly party', in Henry's words; the phrase, though, sounded more like his partner's. Margaret's main impression of the evening was how lavishly the Swede spent the firm's money on fine wines and dishes, and how Henry appeared to be so under his spell that he forgot to worry about money. What upset her wasn't the spending, though, but the fact that she preferred Henry as he was, even his morose aspects, rather than see him dancing ponderously to the foreigner's tune.

She had her doubts about the 'cousin', too, who was pretty and full-bosomed, and poured little bursts of Swedish whispers into Johansson's ear. Again, it was Henry who might have been expected to spot any latent impropriety. But his partner could do no wrong.

When the evening ended, and the two cousins waved them off from the steps of the hotel, Henry sat back in the hansom cab and said, 'I'm a lucky man to have a partner like that.'

'Mr Johansson seems to be the luckier,' said Margaret, before she could stop herself.

Henry puffed his cheeks at her. 'You will have to watch your tongue, my dear. You were less than attentive to him all night. He will make our fortune. Kindly remember that.'

Squashed, she turned to the passing streets as they went up past Regent's Park, and felt the chill of strangeness that London still offered when she was not on her guard. The melancholy bulk of the city swept under the wheels, unknown, unexplored, unsettling. Margaret's solitary expeditions in search of some imagined London were a thing of the past; they had never come to much, no doubt because you needed a companion for that sort of thing, and when she went about these days, it was either sedately with Henry or frivolously with Virginia.

London was merely a pile of stone and humanity, accruing over centuries; what she noticed now were the sharp edges and loose ends. With Morgan it might have been a different city. But Morgan had cut himself adrift. Morgan didn't bear thinking about.

Virginia was coming to lunch tomorrow; that was something to look forward to. Henry had to leave early on one of his expeditions to the north of England. He was still yawning as he set off for King's Cross. Margaret wished it was the done thing for wives to go with their husbands on business trips.

Cobwebs on his shoulder showed he had been in the orchid houses. Margaret brushed them off, listening while he repeated the instructions about temperatures and boilers. The daily man was reliable only as long as he was supervised. Henry explained, as he had done twenty times before, what a gauge was, and Margaret said, 'Yes, dear,' as she always did. 'Autumn is in the air,' he said, sniffing at the blue mist over lawns and hedges. 'Frost is a devil.' His trouser-legs were stained with dew.

Margaret whispered, 'Come back quickly. I shall miss you,' but he ducked his head nervously and jumped into the cab, as though afraid that the driver, sitting aloft with the reins in his hand, might have heard.

At half-past eleven Virginia came. She found Margaret in her sitting-room, with a pile of ripped-up paper on the floor.

'Let me guess,' said the visitor. 'Henry is away, so you thought you'd have a nice read of your various lovers' letters, only you took fright when you saw how passionate they were.'

'What strange ideas you have. Neither of us has lovers. We're not the kind. These are from my mother. She writes every week. Why fill the house with litter?'

'I can see a man's sort of writing.'

'Postcards from my brother, that's all,' said Margaret, and pushed two halves with her foot to indicate that Virginia could look.

The letter-burning mood had descended without warning, connected, though certainly not for Virginia's dotty reasons, with Henry's departure, and his worried expression, and the wet trouser-legs, and the orchids, and their life together that demanded her care and attention, overriding the marginal needs of a family she no longer belonged to. Getting rid of letters was a gesture.

'*Making headway*,' Virginia read, holding the two halves together. '*One day we shall meet again, though not on Gwalia's shore, God help. What a second-rate summer, eh? Bought a silk umbrella. Your loving bro., M*. He's a card, your Morgan. Tell me, what happened to the woman and the child?'

'I have no idea,' said Margaret, reaching over to rip the two into four and then eight. 'The fruits of sin were a girl. The rest is silence.'

Lunch, signalled by a whiff of burning fat from the kitchen where a Mrs Haynes (who came in to help with the cooking) was at work, was almost due when they had a surprise visitor – Johansson, who bowed, grinned, then rapped his knuckles on his forehead for having forgotten that his partner was out of town.

'Please,' he said, 'take pity on lone gentleman. I travel you to luncheon, both.'

'And where's your cousin?' asked Margaret firmly.

'En route to Stockholm. Permit you to choose me a luncheon house, dear ladies.'

'The Hotel Cecil is extremely nice,' said Virginia, and it dawned on Margaret that the only way she could now avoid this absurd expedition was by snubbing Henry's partner. That being out of the question, she went quietly. They lunched on oysters and veal at the Cecil, and Johansson paid five shillings a head without a murmur. Five shillingses out of Penbury-Holt profits when they could have been eating bread and omelettes in West Hampstead seemed scandalous. Margaret smiled brightly and said it had been a pleasant meal.

No sooner had they finished than their host was proposing an afternoon trip to the Crystal Palace, again eliciting sympathy for plight of lone gentleman in large city. There is something fishy about you, my boy, thought Margaret; but Virginia seemed fascinated by all that broken English and the use he put it to, mainly flattery and tall stories about orchid-hunting, and in no time they were down at Sydenham, strolling about under the glass and greenery, and the thought was crossing Margaret's mind that Virginia was not behaving quite as properly as a married woman should. She basked in Johansson; her face looked hot.

Most of Margaret's attention, though, went on wondering if she might see Morgan around the next shrub or at the far end of the Roman statues or in the crowd listening to the hydraulic organ. That would be Fate; they were in south London, after all; sightseeing with the odious Swede (it was no use, she couldn't like him) made her thirsty for the real thing.

Returning on the train, she was still looking for Morgan at stations. Victoria brought her back to earth. The platforms heaved with homeward-bound clerks and managers, Virginia caught a smut in her eye and made for the ladies room, and Johansson said, 'Mrs Penbury-Holt, excuse me to talk, may we do in private when she leaves to go? Very importance.'

His manner had changed, the blue-grey eyes had a sinister greasiness, it was her duty to listen. Virginia smiled faintly as she left in the cab that Johansson summoned from the rank, and Margaret waited with her heart hammering for the confidence that could only be to do with Henry. But first came the finding somewhere private.

'My hotel' sounded proper enough. It was not until she realised that he didn't mean the West End establishment where they had dined the night before (and certainly didn't mean the Hotel Cecil) that Margaret faltered. Around a corner from the station, he hurried her up three stone steps, into a gaslit lobby where a porter was setting a mousetrap behind a tub; the man didn't look as they crossed the carpet, which stuck to the soles of her shoes.

Alarmed, now, she tried to halt their progress upstairs, but his 'Trust me!' got them to a landing and a door with dirt around the handle, and into a room with a wardrobe, a wash-stand and a bed that sagged.

'I would have thought a tea-room more appropriate,' she said, as coolly as she could, and Johansson put his hand against the door before she could open it again.

'Please,' he said. 'You are sportive woman, no doubt of it. I learn of the Suffragistics, of whom you like.'

'Kindly tell me what the matter of importance was.'

'You and me,' said the Swede, with a smile.

She told him he was mad, he made some ridiculous statement about husbands of lovely women who them failed to deserve, he tried to kiss her, she pushed him in the chest, he persisted, she overturned the wash-stand which broke the pitcher and sent water pouring under the door, and Johansson suddenly collapsed, moaning and apologising and saying there had been dreadful mistake.

Margaret said, 'You are never to come near my house, do you understand?' and squelched into the corridor.

Going to the police was out of the question. Telling Henry was possible, in theory; to keep silent was surely too high a price. Pondering the question that night, she forgot to watch the temperature, and a frost shrivelled the weaker blooms. Henry was furious. To tell him then would have been like making excuses for her lack of vigilance.

His reproofs for her carelessness, when he returned the following afternoon, weren't severe. Technical matters like temperatures and gauges were a man's concern. He was even more tender in making love to her. Enjoyable though that was, Margaret found it a ridiculous by-product of events.

Henry had to hear all about the Hotel Cecil and the jaunt

to Crystal Palace, of course. He thought it 'quite a lark for two staid married women'. Margaret couldn't help thinking how much foolishness there was in men. She was learning her own weaknesses, and her strengths.

In his bedroom under the eaves, Morgan copied out notes from *Burke's Peerage*, and waited to see what opportunity would bring in the shape of his old friend Poppy Foster, whose ring at the front door was expected any minute.

Presently he heard Squale call, 'Please to come down!' and descended one floor to the study where the safe, ledgers, letters, books, and unmentionable artefacts were kept. Squale was fussing again – seemed to think information grew on trees. He hummed and hawed about ninepence for a sexton who helped locate gravestones and an entry in a parish register.

He was only being officious. Cordelia Squale had an insatiable need for information about the dead. She was Morgan's real employer.

Grumbling, Squale ticked the item in red ink, and turned back to the papers that never left his desk.

Morgan returned to the attic. On the ground floor, Poppy had arrived and was being shown in. 'Oh, there you are, dear,' Mrs Squale would be saying. 'Mr Buckley is so sorry, but he has had to go on a business trip at short notice. Do sit down and have a cup of tea, and we can have a nice chat.'

Morgan was still fond of Poppy. It was a pity to have to deceive her, but she would come to no harm, and those of us who had to fight for a living (through no fault of our own) were compelled to use the best means at our disposal, were we not?

An hour later he heard Poppy leave. Silence closed in. Mrs Squale had retired for her quiet hour, as she did every afternoon, recharging her energies.

After more than a year in the Squales' employment, Morgan had learned more about spirits than he ever dreamt of at Blaen Cwm. He was discreet; he was trusted. Even before he was taken on, he realised that Mrs Squale knew enough about him to make her feel safe.

'It was Poppy Foster brought you here, wasn't it?' she said. 'A woman with a nice figure. Aged about thirty, frightened of the future. Is connected with an old rogue called Hastings – like you are, dear. Oh, you aren't any more? Very wise. I hear he'll go to gaol.'

His duties were to write letters, keep card-indexes, occasionally pop up to the West End for phosphorised oil and Balmain's Luminous Paint – but most of all, to acquire information. He visited libraries to consult reference books. Sometimes he was at provincial newspaper offices, reading the files going back for generations, paying special attention to the deaths. At cemeteries and graveyards he glided among the headstones, notebook in hand, looking for names and dates that Mrs Squale needed to embroider her messages.

Morgan was at home with the spirit world. He liked whisperings in dark rooms, breezes that stirred flowers when the windows were shut, shaking of tables, spirit fingers cast in paraffin wax. They demonstrated how easy it was to deceive, yet they had a mysterious life of their own as well.

'I sincerely believe that the phenomena produced by Cordelia Squale are genuine, actual and beyond human explanation,' said a statement that Squale handed him on the first day of his employment. He had to sign two copies, one of them undated.

Squale, who described himself as his wife's manager, handled the money and kept up the social contacts. He certainly arranged some of the phenomena as well, but at any hint of complicity he would threaten legal proceedings.

When Morgan said he knew a servant in a Mayfair house who might be used to ensnare an important sitter, Squale said, 'Stop. There is a law of slander. You know that Mrs Squale would not be party to such an affair.'

Mrs Squale had to speak to Morgan in private later on, and tell him that the tactful way was always to have a word with her first. Who was this servant and what was the house?

'Poppy,' said Morgan. It wouldn't have surprised him if Mrs Squale had known all along. 'Poppy Foster. She and I have kept in touch' ('How nice, dear!' said Mrs Squale). 'When Hastings went to prison, she got on an agency's books, and found work with a family called Leuchars in Charles Street, in Mayfair' ('I do know where Charles Street is, dear,' said Mrs Squale). 'I'm talking about Lord Leuchars, ninth baron. She's a cook's assistant there. You can get her talking. You mesmerise her.'

The ninth baron dabbled in archaeology and photography – and spiritualism. Two Irish housemaids had given notice, saying that 'something' had entered the house as a result of a seance, and the same something had got as far as their bedroom, where it was hurling underclothes and opening wardrobe doors.

'And you thought of me at once!' said Mrs Squale.

'I thought of us both. Now that I've told you about Leuchars, will you do something for me? Let me have a sitting of my own here? One afternoon, perhaps.'

'You must ascend more planes before you're ready.'

'At the worst I can make something up. I know how to do the lights and bells.'

She wagged a finger at him. He was a naughty boy, she said. There were lights and lights. There were bells and bells. Any fool could learn tricks. But as he knew full well, there was more to it than that. He must have patience. It didn't do to rush things.

Morgan was tired of being patient. Now that Poppy had called – poor Poppy, frightened of the future – he itched to know what Squale had got out of her.

Sufficient, it seemed, to write one of her Important Letters.

'My Lord,' it began. 'Your Lordship must forgive this gross intrusion, but certain events concerning my mediumship compel me to solicit your attention . . .'

Morgan read on admiringly. A Discarnate Spirit had manifested itself in her seance-room, seeking release to a Higher State. Said Spirit was connected with a house in Charles Street, name sounded like 'Lucas'. 'On consulting the London Street Directory, I observed your Lordship's title and concluded . . .' etc. (a brilliant touch). There had been a medium at Charles Street, had there not, but the Psychic Power was clearly insufficient.

Spirit confessed to playing mischief with the telephone connection a week ago (out of order on a Saturday morning, information from Poppy), and had moved objects in the maids' quarters (information ditto). Spirit deeply sorry, in despair, needed Eternal Rest, but had to return to Charles Street now; Mrs Squale willing to help, if your Lordship, etc.

Morgan read it in the presence of both Squales, in the sitting room with flowered wallpaper upstairs that Mrs Squale kept for herself. Behind diamonds of glass in locked bookcases were works on spiritualism and conjuring, and wooden boxes of the candied fruit she loved. The letter was in a thin green script.

'Impressive,' said Morgan, 'but dangerous.'

'Stop,' ordered Squale. 'You are hinting at malpractice. I would remind you of certain laws on the Statute Book. It is perfectly possible that the spirit world has chosen your acquaintance with Poppy as a means of inducing Mrs Squale to visit a troubled house where her services are needed. She wrote this under their influence.'

'There you are, dear, in a nutshell.'

Anything, perhaps, was possible. Christ walking on an aqueduct in Glamorganshire had seemed possible once. Morgan would have liked a fire to burn in him again, as it burned at Blaen Cwm. He missed the satisfying distortions of a faith.

He could stay with Mrs Squale for years, a dog on a leash.

Or he could try something. He had thought of something to try.

Leuchars had accepted her offer. An evening had been arranged.

'There is nothing to assist me with,' Mrs Squale said, when Morgan asked if he could help.

'I'd like to be there, all the same. If I think hard enough I shall help concentrate the fluids – isn't that what happens?'

'I daresay it is, dear.'

Once it was agreed that Morgan should remain with the sitters, he had preparations to make. He bought twenty yards of silk veiling from Arding & Hobbs, washed it seven times (it had to be seven), then treated it with Balmain's paint, varnish, benzine and lavender oil. The formula was in one of her books that he borrowed when she wasn't looking. He left the silk to dry for three days, before washing it with naphtha soap to remove the smell.

Using the kitchen at night, and an outhouse for drying, he worked unobserved and was ready in time for the Charles Street seance. Soft and luminous, as promised, the silk folded into a modest pad, which he laid across his loins, inside his trousers, like a rheumatic's flannel band.

The sitting was at nine o'clock. They ate supper in

Putney and travelled to Mayfair by carriage, Squale clutching a Bible. Their host, an excitable man with a food stain on his lapel, received them in a morning room that met Mrs Squale's requirements, thick-curtained and with space for a circle of upright chairs.

Was Leuchars convinced of the spirit world, or did twentieth-century scepticism lurk below the surface? Being wealthy made it harder to tell; he had one thing less at stake. Born 1844, married into an East Anglian banking family (Morgan had been busy at the public library), was he looking for spiritual comfort as he got old? Or was he that tougher proposition, an inquiring mind? His interests were antiquarian and photographic. Morgan made sure there was no camera in a corner.

In the end, one had to gamble. The rest trooped in, fed and full of expectation, and were introduced. Morgan was the plain Welsh boy, well-behaved, acting calmer than he felt. He bowed low to Lady Leuchars. Moon-faced and sulky, was she bored with a lifetime of her husband's hobbies? The Marshalls, an American railway-owner and his English wife, might be there for fun – Mrs Squale had received advance notice of the sitters, but the Marshalls weren't in the reference books.

Major Thorn, married to a sister of Lady Leuchars, looked as unpromising in the flesh as he had in Morgan's notes – equestrian, hero of a minor skirmish in the Sudan, a director of the bank. 'So you are one of our Celtic cousins,' he said, and Morgan cracked his finger joints.

'We are gathered here in the sight of God and the heavenly hosts,' announced Mrs Squale, and Squale arranged eight chairs in a wide circle, each a yard apart. 'I hope we are all in psychic harmony' ('No doubt about that, Ma'am,' growled Leuchars). They would sit in total darkness, she said, since darkness gave the best results.

'What would a sceptic say to that, Mr Buckley?' murmured Thorn, standing beside him.

'Oh dear me. Are you a sceptic, sir?'

'I had experiences in Africa. I keep an open mind. But not even a candle under coloured glass?'

'Well, sir, what would a stranger to the human race think if he heard that it spent a third of its life in the dark, engaged in something called "sleep"? Demand to see it happening with the lights on, is it?' and the Major laughed. 'He'd be very suspicious, sir, when he learned that darkness was a prerequisite.'

The folded silk was like iron around his kidneys, and he ached with anxiety. Mrs Squale was in fine form; why not leave her to it? Before they began, her bold northern voice explained how the spirit that had troubled the house was not evil, only lost and unhappy. She could promise nothing, merely make herself a channel through which discarnate beings could speak and act – when she said 'act' she spread her fingers on the card table in front of her chair, and Major Thorn cleared his throat.

Not to take risks was to be like the rest. At Birchgrove the congregation of sheep baa-ed obediently for Evan Roberts, and the finger had pointed at Morgan. Whose finger, exactly, on the end of whose arm? Where was Roberts now? Gone into hiding, it was said, a broken man, the Revival a memory. However you looked at it, the supernatural was a high-risk business.

Morgan took his place in the circle, between Thorn and Mrs Marshall. He had a feeling that Squale put him next to the Major on purpose. Mrs Squale and her card table were yards away, across the circle, between her host and his wife.

Squale would go outside, to the ante-room, ready, in theory, to fetch help should the medium become ill. His real function was to watch the door. As he left, turning off the electric lights, Morgan saw the quick movement of elbows and a second's pause as he put sticking plaster over the switches.

Wind sighed in the brickwork, a distant horse clip-clopped, and Morgan, lifting his chair and holding it against his bottom, moved stealthily backwards – not far, but far enough to be out of reach if the Major used his leg to search for Morgan's. Darkness disoriented people. An occasional cough or sniff would convince him that Morgan must be there, as indeed he would be – at first.

For some minutes nothing happened. Morgan thought he heard a movement from the direction of the Major; he leaned forward and obliged by blowing his nose.

Soon after came a dozen sharp raps from the direction of Mrs Squale, as fast as a boy running with a stick along railings, and she began to groan. The air was cold, though one always thought so at a seance. In the blackness, one moved beyond the edge of reason. He heard the deep tones of Dr Oliver – a privilege, this, since only on rare occasions did he speak directly through Mrs Squale's vocal cords.

He had come, the good doctor was saying. He brought news. There was a plan far greater. There was a perspective far broader. Science was bankrupt at the edge of the grave. Even spiritualists were in the Galvani period – facts without explanation. Soon, very soon, they would enter the Faraday period – laws established by experiment.

Morgan made a final gesture of coughing and scraping his shoes together. Slipping off his chair, he crept clear of the circle on hands and knees, and made for a sofa he had fixed in his memory. He missed it the first time, and clawed about in a panic, guided only by Dr Oliver. Then he bumped into the back. Had he given himself away? The fright produced an overwhelming urge to pass water. Restraining it, his penis burned as though dipped in quicklime. Even now, the Major might have left his chair; the darkness worked both ways.

What did Mrs Squale once say? Morgan clung to her words – 'Rich or poor, dear, those who want to believe *will* believe. Don't talk about gullibility. Call it faith.'

It sounded well enough at the time, but not behind the sofa, with his legs crossed, trying to pull out the stage props without getting them caught in his braces. Was this God amusing himself? Stubbornly, fighting back, he extracted the last of the luminous gauze and stuffed it under his jacket.

He knew by now that it was going to fail. The enormity of his schemes never dawned on him until they were under way.

Crawling into the open, Morgan was defiant but without hope. Savagely, he lay on his face and tugged the first fold of silk from under his body. A patch of whiteness, too hazy to be called light, barely a lessening of the dark, appeared on the floor. As more of it tumbled out, the luminosity began to swell and rise above the ground.

He heard a woman gasp. Dr Oliver's voice faded away, and Mrs Squale said, almost conversationally, 'Well, dear, we are very glad you are here.'

This time the woman, or another woman, gave a cry, then choked into silence. An icy quietness had settled on the room. Morgan felt a surge of energy, as if his anger at these fools, this trickery, had got the better of him. He put his head under the last of the silk and stood up slowly, so that the fabric shivered and spread out. A faint whiff of benzine caught his nostrils, where he hadn't applied the soap rigorously enough.

Damn them, damn them, damn them! Even now, a hand would be stretching out to seize him. Taking a deep breath, Morgan accidentally sucked the gauze against his face – nose, chin and forehead. That seemed to settle the matter.

As he let the gauze drop to the carpet, the Major's voice said quietly, 'Don't go, Bella.'

'Bella's message is one of forgiveness,' said Mrs Squale. 'She was unable to come before. The energy was lacking. Tonight we have full power. She forgives her family. She begs her family to forgive her. Then she can rest.'

Morgan bundled up the gauze and turned away from the sitters. He wanted to laugh and jump in the air. He walked to the sofa. If he stubbed his toe and said 'Ouch!' they would only think it was the ghost being clumsy. Once behind the sofa, he stuffed the silk down his trousers, and walked back to his seat, pausing for long enough to identify the places by movements and whispers.

They were in a turmoil. Mrs Squale was still giving a farewell message from Bella. But the climax had passed.

'Of course we forgive,' said a woman's voice.

'Each one of us,' said the Major, and Morgan, who had brought his chair forward by this time, said, 'Amen.'

'She has gone,' said Mrs Squale, matter-of-factly. 'I am going to call my husband.' She shouted, 'Mr Squale!' and within seconds he had entered. A moment's hesitation at the switches, and the lights came on.

The women were in tears. Lady Leuchars was biting her lip. Her husband helped Mrs Squale to her feet. The Major said that he had just looked on the face of his sister.

'I have seen her photograph,' said Leuchars. 'I am something of an expert in matters photographic. There is no doubt it was her.'

Major Thorn added that if anyone was interested, the young Welshman hadn't moved from his chair. He had been aware of his presence throughout.

In the carriage returning to Putney, Squale said that he saw nothing remarkable about a materialisation. 'It is not Mrs Squale's first,' he snapped.

'Nor my last,' said Mrs Squale, and Morgan felt the unmistakable pressure of her leg against his.

'Who exactly was Bella?' asked Squale.

'A younger sister of the Thorn family, dear. They wouldn't let her marry some young man so she drowned herself in the River Orwell. It was a while ago, in the nineties.'

'I was lucky to find the newspaper report,' said Morgan, out of devilment.

'Stop,' ordered Squale, 'in case you say something you regret.'

No doubt Mrs Squale wanted a private word with Morgan as much as he wanted one with her. 'Come to my sitting room for a moment, dear,' she said when they got back, and Squale said stiffly, 'I shall retire at once. It has been a long evening.'

Morgan was left there alone for five minutes. When she appeared, she had changed her black dress for a peach-coloured robe, and was nibbling a crystallised fruit.

'How could they imagine it was a woman?' he began.

'Wasn't it, dear? Didn't you feel the energy all around you?'

'Mrs Squale, you know perfectly well what I felt around me. I'm sitting on it now.'

'You are a very naughty boy,' she said. 'But remember that you are a psychic. An event may have more than one explanation. Are you saying the sitters were hallucinated? Perhaps they were, but who can tell what other powers were at work?'

He could feel the heat from her plump little shape. A roll of fat under her chin glistened like melting butter.

He said, 'I must have ascended an astral plane or two this evening.'

'You did very well. But life isn't all work, you know.' Her lips were sticky with syrup. She wetted them with a purple tongue that darted in and out like a lizard's. Even after using a handkerchief, they were still shiny. 'The spirits churn me up,' she whispered, and squeezed against him on the sofa, locking his nearest leg with her thighs. 'Those breeches must be killing you with all that silk inside. Why not pop them down?'

'Is there a bed?' he asked.

'Never mind beds,' she gasped.

'I would like to do it in a bed, if it's all the same to you.'

'Funny boy,' she said, and led him into a room next door with a crimson bedspread and the gas turned down to a glimmer.

Her eyes were riveted on his bottom-half as he took off his trousers. He waved his shirt over his head. 'Am I flesh?' he cried. 'Am I a discarnate being?'

'Why tonight?' he asked sleepily, when he was about to return to his own bed. 'Why not six months ago?'

'Higher planes,' she whispered, running her fingers over him. 'You have to progress. In everything.'

7

Will had to buck up his ideas once the Burry River Combine was in being. All that stuff about dragons gobbling up men was inappropriate. Dadda pointed out that he was now a director of the company, owner of a single share (paid for with his own money), participant in a great enterprise. A board meeting was a privilege. The Burry River was the shape of things to come.

The room had been hastily converted out of clerical accommodation. A combine had to do things properly. High-backed chairs, sharpened pencils and water bottles were provided. The place smelt of leather and cigarette smoke, as befitted a forum for discussing larger issues, such as buying another works or borrowing a thousand pounds.

At first Will enjoyed being a man among men. Sprewett, who held forty £100 shares, was the combine's chairman, because it was sensible to have a fellow like that as a figurehead. He was always at board meetings and so was the Colonel, who owned another forty shares and was much happier with the combine now that Rhodri Lewis had nothing to do with it. The real boss was Dadda, who was managing director. He had a hundred and ten shares, ten more than Rees Coal.

Buckley had big, extravagant ideas. 'Who shall we have next?' he would say at board meetings, and name a steel-works twice their size or a fleet of cargo ships that sailed from Cardiff. It was bravado – greeted with smiles, or with Mappowder saying 'Let's walk before we can run,' but it also told them all that Buckley meant business. 'This time next year,' he told Will, 'we shall be making our mark.'

The winter was long and harsh. There was skating on the Furnace pond for the town at large, and on the lake at Cilfrew for Mappowder's friends. Haggar the cinematograph man was there, cranking his camera, turning it on the frosty turrets – 'We could film a grand drama in your garden, in the fine weather,' he said.

Aubrey Mappowder, when he heard of it, declared what a lark it would be to make a moving-picture about a castle and a maiden, who would naturally have to be his fiancée, Lucinda Sprewett.

All through February, charity breakfasts at New Dock school were in demand. Despite the breach between their menfolk, Ada Lewis and Pomona Buckley clung to their own friendship. Ada said the men were a pair of sillies who needed their heads knocking together. The breakfasts were a convenient meeting place.

Will took his mother there sometimes, at half-past seven, when the kitchen fires were just lit, and a dull yellow dawn was spreading behind the chimneys. Even at that hour, children waited in the yard, hands in pockets or under thin coats, a pale luminescence about their faces, turned towards the gaslit windows.

One morning, when Will helped his mother cross a patch of ice outside the kitchen entrance, Ada saw them coming and insisted he stay for a cup of tea. Once inside, he helped stoke fires and stir porridge, regarded with interest by the matrons.

Ada Lewis said she would tell Sam he must follow Will's example. Mrs T. T. Rees, whose husband supplied the margarine and porridge oats at special prices, professed to be amazed at his dexterity with a spoon. 'A veritable whirlpool,' she said, and Will, enjoying the attention, stirred faster and faster with the iron spoon, making the cauldron rattle the top of the range.

He gave one stir too many. The cauldron tilted, and two gallons of porridge cascaded on the floor.

'Whoops!' cried Ada, and the women began to scoop up the mess with tin dishes, shaking their heads and saying that that was what came of allowing men in a kitchen.

Then a girl with grey eyes he hadn't noticed before said quietly, 'If the gentleman has stopped wasting porridge, perhaps he would be kind enough to help me move some tables in the hall.'

'That young madam had better watch her tongue,' Mrs T. T. Rees was heard to say.

Will followed the girl. She hurried in front of him, a slim figure in a plain dress. Before he had a chance to speak to her, she was lifting one end of a trestle table and saying, 'Under that window, if you please. The trustees have decreed that gas is not to be wasted for the mere purpose of eating, so I want the children to have as much daylight as possible. They will thus be more likely to see any cockroaches in their food.'

'You are very young to be a teacher,' he said, when they had moved most of the tables.'

'The younger we are, the cheaper we are to employ.' She pushed a streak of fair hair behind her ear. 'You haven't extended the legs at your end. It'll collapse if you don't take care.'

'May I ask your name?'

'Miss Haycock. You had better get back to the kitchen now or you'll miss her ladyship's weekly visit. I've just heard her carriage,' and Miss Haycock vanished through another doorway.

'Is your father Saul Haycock?' he shouted after her, but there was no response.

In the kitchen, Lady Mappowder was expressing a hope that the porridge wasn't lumpy. She had a hat that knocked against things. A crumb of bread with a speck of margarine was brought to her on a china plate and she pronounced it delicious.

Will noticed how the women, his mother included, wore fixed, subservient smiles for Lady Mappowder's benefit. He could feel humility attacking his own face muscles.

She made a short speech. What a fine work they were engaged in, she said, and hoped that the ladies would feel it was some recompense if they came up to the Castle on a day to be arranged in the summer, when a most unusual event would take place. Mr William Haggar planned to make a cinematograph film of an historical drama. He hoped to show it at theatres throughout South Wales. They were getting to be quite modern in Port Howard, said Lady Mappowder.

'I'm sure we all know the story of Princess Gwenllian, who died for the honour of Wales. Lucinda Sprewett has agreed, after much persuasion, to play the part of the princess.'

'Little baggage,' Will heard Ada whisper to his mother. 'I hope they keep her in a dungeon.'

'The period is the twelfth century, so any ladies who have tall hats and flannel petticoats will be much in demand. We shall have costumes especially made for our leading players. As for the men,' and she nodded graciously towards Will, 'we expect breastplates and swords and goodness knows what.'

Hearing her talk of Gwenllian and that particular piece of romantic Welsh history made Will think about Miss Rees in the house under the Black Mountains, and Sam Lewis's America, and Morgan in London – things perceived but beyond his grasp, perhaps for ever. He had a flash of insight into his nature, condemned to follow and conform. He should rebel against such a degrading destiny – thrust aside impediments, even if they were St Mamma and St Dadda.

Then a bell tolled, there was the sound of bolts being

drawn, shrill voices of children came in from the cold, and Will realised it was past the time he should have been at the works.

Tinplate production had been down all winter. There were epidemics of flu and measles, and a weariness in the bones of the older men as March came and the icy weather was slow in retreating to Russia or wherever it came from. They were into April before the spring arrived, and daffodils sprang up around the cooling ponds.

Buckley looked for an immediate improvement in output, but none came. Will was told to keep an eye on the rollermen and see what they were up to.

He made himself unpopular, spying on them. Once, a doubled plate, red-hot, came slithering at him across the floor when his back was turned. Men shouted, and he jumped clear in time.

The dragon's tail had nearly got him.

An accident, of course.

Dadda took him for a walk in the garden one evening after supper. 'Those men,' he said, cigar end glowing between his teeth, 'are too big for their boots. We are going to give them a surprise.'

'Catch them not working?'

'Better than that. There's a mock execution at eleven. Phillips got wind of it.'

Executions were rarely seen these days. The union frowned on them. Will knew of them only by hearsay. A workman, accused by his fellows of exceeding his quota of boxes, would have his trousers stuffed with bran and be hoisted in the air for public derision.

The works was traced against a sheet of stars. The sea scratched at the mudflats beyond the dyke.

'We can get into a store room next to the tinning shed, where they'll be,' said Dadda. 'Like mice, now.'

At first, creeping through pitch-black sheds, all they

could hear was the noise of the engine and the mills. But soon there were voices, coming from the tinhouse.

A rickety door in a rickety partition had cracks they could see through. The victim was Morris Short-change, the doubler who was promoted rollerman when Tommy Spit had his accident. A makeshift harness was under his arms, and he swung a few feet in the air, suspended from a beam in the roof. Half a dozen men held the other end of the rope.

There must have been thirty watching, with Hughes Aberdare, a six-foot rollerman, in charge. He was ordering Morris to recite the penitent verse. A voice, trying to sound brave, said,

> 'The sheet that we make, as good tinplate men,
> Is twenty by fourteen or twenty by ten.
> But woe betide him who rolls it and tins it
> Disregarding the rules we have set for the limit,

Come on, boys, a joke's a joke.'

Hughes replied that he hadn't spoken with sincerity. They hoisted him higher, till he looked like an insect trying to fly, arms and legs waving feebly. One of his clogs fell off, and men ducked as it clattered on the floor.

To Will's relief, his father whispered, 'Enough is enough,' and burst in through the door, shouting 'Thank you, gentlemen, thank you.'

Everyone froze. The men holding the rope must have slackened their grip for a second. They could be seen grabbing at a snake that danced between them and out of reach. Morris hit the floor with the thud of iron going through a roller.

By the time he was laid on a frame and carried to the ambulance room, he had stopped breathing. Buckley put a handkerchief over his face and said a prayer with the men.

'The behaviour of savages,' he said to Hughes Aberdare.

'You had better come and see me when the doctor is here. It may be we can say this was an accident in the course of work and save you and one or two more from prison.'

Waiting for Dr Snell, he took Will outside. 'Now I've got them,' he said. 'Hughes is filling his pants at the thought of the inquest. With any luck he'll concede new quotas for his team. Some of the others, too. Morris Shortchange hasn't died in vain.'

'Isn't that blackmail?'

'Don't be mealy-mouthed. Don't make me ashamed of you.'

Dadda was always Dadda. It wasn't enough to manipulate the living, he had to try the dead as well.

The night seemed to crush them all. Men spoke in whispers; Morris's clog lay where it had fallen. Snell, pyjama legs showing, was closeted in the ambulance room with Buckley, the body and Hughes Aberdare, debating whether the injuries could be reconciled with falling into an inspection pit.

Will left them to it. He prowled through the sheds, half in love with the place, half terrified by its cruelty. The tinhouse drew him back. Entering, he sensed a different mood. Men looked at him over their shoulders. A stern figure stood in the middle of them, writing in a notebook. It was Saul Haycock. He said, 'Good evening, Mr Will. I should have made my presence known.'

'Quite right, Haycock, you should.'

'Forgive me. I had information about tonight. Unfortunately I arrived too late. I've been informing myself. The men will have to be legally represented at the inquest.'

'Come with me,' said Will. They walked to the rolling mill. No one was working. 'You'll have to talk to my father.'

'I hear the plan is to make it seem an ordinary accident. It won't work, you know. I can't let it.'

'It's to spare the ringleaders.'

'And give Buckley's a hold over them. Push up the quotas, I shouldn't be surprised.' The spectacles caught the red of a furnace and were like monstrous cat's eyes. 'Be honest, Will Buckley. Nothing very drastic will happen to the men. Buckley's is out to win a point or two. It's all bluff.'

They were at the big doors of the mill, which stood open to catch the cool westerly winds. The sucking of waves on the sea-dyke could be heard.

Will was tempted to agree. But owners' sons didn't agree with union gaffers.

'Those are serious allegations,' he said. 'I wouldn't make them if I were you.'

They approached the ambulance room. A window looked out on the mill floor. Will could see Snell's bedraggled hair moving across the glass. Then Dadda's proud features, the tumble of grey hair, the thrust chin.

Will rapped the door. He said the union secretary had been questioning the men.

He thought Dadda was going to have a fit. Whose works were they in? Was it Haycock's, perhaps? Had he been present at the so-called mock execution? He hadn't? Then please to shut his trap.

'I was taught that politeness cost nothing,' said the sad voice, and insisted that the men would take their chances, that whatever Mr Buckley's motives for concealment, the truth must come out.

'Concealment?' shouted Dadda. 'Concealment?'

His fury could burn up a hundred socialists. But nothing happened. Turning, he knocked against the table where the corpse was stretched under a blanket, and a shower of bran fell out of a trouser leg.

'Dr Snell was quite happy,' he said, and the rage was already ebbing, leaving behind a map of red veins, bleeding into the cheekbones. 'Dr Snell concluded that a six-foot fall could have fractured the skull and contused the body – do I do you an injustice?'

'Well, Mr Buckley, well,' and the moist eyes looked down at the fingers that should have been in Harley Street. 'Medicine is an inexact science, more's the pity.'

'Dr Snell would say he died of cholera if need be,' said Haycock.

'I'll have the law on you if you don't leave this works,' growled Buckley, but he was weary now; he had lost.

They were there all night. The police came, and so did relatives of the dead man. Will didn't move from Buckley's side. The day shift was arriving as father and son walked home. Men looked up in surprise, stepping aside into wet grass to leave the path clear.

At the gates of Y Plas, Buckley paused and said, 'That Haycock is a dangerous swine. He's a threat and the Fed will have to get rid of him. But remember, in the end, Haycock is nothing. Only the works matters.'

The iron dragon was roaring from its bed of flames.

'All Haycock can be is a nuisance. A dead man from the start. The combines and the works will outlive him. Can you imagine this place without its tinplate? Fields and marshes. Wheat growing in Stepney Street. Sand dunes in Market Square. Leave it to the Haycocks and that's what you'd see. You know what we do? We create the future. You be proud of that always.'

Dogs barked, welcoming them home.

The inquest verdict was unlawful killing. Hughes Aberdare and another rollerman were charged with manslaughter, and committed to the Carmarthen Assizes, where they were sent to prison. Saul Haycock had been too optimistic. 'I told you he was nothing,' said Dadda.

* * *

Mr Haggar's epic, to be called *The Tragedy of Princess Gwenllian* and filmed on the morning of August Bank Holiday, weather permitting, caused excitement.

Villette was commissioned by Lady Mappowder to sew costumes for women of the court. Instead of treating it as a way of making a few pounds, she spent hours studying medieval dress at the library, bought extra cloth and buckles, and ended up out of pocket.

It was understood that a deadly-looking scimitar, once the property of an Indian potentate, was being kindly loaned by the Colonel to use for beheading Miss Sprewett.

Will, with his dark complexion and smaller stature, was down as a Welshman, helping to defend the castle. Sam, whose skin was pale and freckled, mustered with the Normans. The two met infrequently now. It was inevitable, given the quarrel between their fathers.

Both were among the dozen or two young men from well-to-do families invited up to Cilfrew by Captain Aubrey, some weeks before the event. There had to be officers to lead the rabble – the tinworkers and colliers.

'Long time no see,' said Sam coolly.

'I wondered if you'd be here.'

'What are your plans for the day, after we've slaughtered one another?'

'I haven't any.'

'We might have an outing. For old times' sake.' He wouldn't say more.

Captain Aubrey, hands behind back, addressed them as 'fellow actors'. He said he hoped to see hand-to-hand fighting when the Normans stormed the castle and dragged Gwenllian to her death.

'Mr Haggar has suggested that I be the Norman baron,' he said, baring his teeth below a moustache that looked like a poor shave. 'It will be my job to ask the princess where the Lord Rhys has taken his army. When she refuses, I point to the block – the words will appear on the screen – "You must pay the penalty" – "My lips are sealed" – "Reconsider!" – "I have the blood of kings" – "Prepare to shed it" – "One last wish" – "Granted" – "The Welsh flag to kiss" – she holds it to her lips – "Executioner, do your duty" – a tear rolls down my cheek.'

Sam squinted at his thumb to show what he thought of such nonsense, but Will wasn't so sure. Even after centuries, didn't the tragedy of a beautiful woman deserve to be taken seriously?

August Bank Holiday was a day for tried and tested entertainments – Sunday School outings, a cricket match, a fishing competition from the pier, the Swansea paddle-boat to Ilfracombe. This year was better still. Word had got round that Haggar was holding court up at the Colonel's. Volunteers would be immortalised in a moving picture.

Free beer was widely hoped for. By eight in the morning, groups of men and boys were trailing up the long hill to Cilfrew Castle, in response to Mr Haggar's request for an early start to rehearse the battle scenes. Norman soldiers in tinplate armour jeered at ragged Welsh archers in their shirts. The sun bounced off breastplates and antique swords. Garden staff were on the lawns, strategically placed to stop riff-raff going where they shouldn't.

Haggar was out on the terrace, his toe prodding a ten-foot battering ram cut from a larch, pondering, with Captain Aubrey, the interesting question of how it could be used to assault the front door without hurting it. The Captain wore a leather jerkin with coat of arms, woollen hose from a theatrical costumier, and a skirt of genuine mail. When he moved, he clinked like small change.

Sam had the motor for the day. He caught up with Will, who was on foot, at the bottom of the road up to Cilfrew. He had a picnic hamper in the back.

By the time they arrived, bands of armed men were

rehearsing, milling about and shouting, egged on by Haggar through a megaphone. On the terrace a party of odd creatures wearing tunics, cloaks, blankets and what could have been items of flannel underwear were huddled together. Some had legs bare to the knee.

Sam whistled through his teeth. 'If those are the Welsh women,' he said, 'they have nothing to fear from the Normans.'

Will, a Welsh daffodil pinned to his shirt, shouted, 'Well done, Aunt Villette!'

'You're late, Lewis and Buckley!' said Aubrey Mappowder.

'Horse wouldn't start, my lord.'

'Move the blessed thing round to the garage and collect your breastplate. Buckley, your HQ is at the base of the West Tower. You'd better rub some earth on your face. Haggar doesn't want the Welsh looking too spruce.'

Behind the house, a pair of horses were saddled up outside the stables, together with an assortment of nags. Banners and pennants rested against walls. Welsh bowmen were flirting with girls in red flannel and black hats, the traditional dress that came out only at pageants. An arrow thudded into a stable door, and a coachman offered to knock the block off any other joker who started being clever.

'Departure of the Lord Rhys!' shouted Haggar through his megaphone.

Men and horses swirled around the front of the house. Lord Rhys, whose castle this was meant to be, kissed Princess Gwenllian goodbye, embracing her with gauntleted arms; embraces were in order, since he was her elder brother, Timothy Sprewett. Unlike the ladies of the court, Lucinda Sprewett wore white muslin and looked ready for a garden party. Mrs Lloyd, who was talking to her sister on the terrace, had already told several people that the girl showed no sense of history and could do with a smacking.

'Kiss her once more,' boomed the megaphone, and the assistant cranked away. 'Gwenllian, you may never see him again. Anguish is written on your face. He mounts his horse. Anguish is replaced by pride. You are brave. You want him to go in search of the enemy.'

Miss Sprewett's expression of elaborate ecstasy didn't change.

'Do leave go the horse or he can't move,' pleaded Haggar, and Timothy Sprewett, wobbling dangerously, cried 'Forward!'

As the column of men shuffled away, Miss Sprewett held out her arms and seized a Welsh banner as it passed.

'Good, good,' said the megaphone. 'Turn around so the camera can see what's happening. You kiss the flag. You bathe it in your tears.'

Aubrey Mappowder, who had come up to watch his fiancée, led the applause as the scene ended. Then he returned to his Normans, who were behind the rhododendrons, practising hand-to-hand fighting.

Before the enemy arrived, the Welsh had to be filmed doing things. Miss Sprewett sat in the doorway plucking a harp, lifelessly pretty, surrounded by her women in tunics and red flannel. Will was second-in-command of the castle guard left behind with Gwenllian. He brought her a bird he had shot; it was a stuffed ptarmigan from a Cilfrew attic, with half an arrow glued on to make it realistic.

'Just put it down over there,' she said, not bothering to look up from the harp. She plucked it with the finger that wore the diamond engagement ring.

Cousin Theodore, wearing a sailor suit, loitered behind the camera. He was carrying a football bladder, half inflated.

'What have you got there?' said Will.

The child shook the bladder, which made a gurgling noise.

'Guess.'

'Something unpleasant?'

Theodore seemed delighted with this insight. 'As a matter of fact, it's got pig's blood in it.'

'I see.'

'A beheading was awfully bloody. It splattered everyone's clothes and went in their hair. When I put it on the block it should burst.'

Haggar and his assistants moved to the yard outside the kitchens, where a cauldron of steaming water hung from chains over a fire of sticks. Will was surprised to see Haycock. He wasn't wearing his glasses, and was dressed in a butcher's apron. He was lobbing bones into the water, at which he peered short-sightedly.

Servants went through the motions of sweeping and carrying. 'Drop those sacks as hard as you can,' commanded the megaphone, and everyone disappeared in a mist of flour, light relief before the battle.

Surely it was time for the Normans? Lady Mappowder's party of breakfast ladies was having refreshments under an awning. Will went to talk to Mamma and Aunt Villette, and missed his cue for the next scene, Miss Sprewett addressing the guard. 'The Normans are advancing down the coast,' she declared in a shrill voice. 'Your Princess exhorts you to defend the castle until my Lord Rhys returns. You must . . .' – the megaphone waved encouragingly – '. . . must fight with your last drop of blood.'

Even Will found it hard to make a heroine of the Sprewett girl. In his mind, he had cast Miss Rees for the part. He wandered back to the kitchen yard, empty now except for Saul Haycock, standing sleepily in the sun.

'Beautiful morning, Mr Buckley,' he called. 'I see we are on the same side for once.'

'Is that how your Chartists kept alive? Boiling bones in their caves?'

'Not at all. The local people saw they went without nothing. It would make a better subject for a moving picture than this fairy-tale.'

'If it isn't to your taste,' smiled Will, 'why take part?'

'It never does any harm to see behind the enemy's walls.'

'Is that the revolutionist's creed? You won't find much here. Colonel Mappowder has stated more than once that he's a friend of the working man.'

'Everyone is, these days. We hear it all the time. The worker is the salt of the earth, as long as he behaves himself. Not if he's a Jim Larkin, though. Not if he's one of the sparks from the Rhondda lodges.'

Give them an inch, as Dadda said, and they'll take a mile.

The guard wandered back. Two bowmen were escorted into the house so they could shoot arrows from the battlements.

'You should have a sword,' said Will.

The fire had died down; the cauldron was off the boil.

'Who's Princess Gwenllian to me? I'll keep my apron on, thank you very much, ready to make dinner for the Normans when they arrive.'

At last it was time for the siege. The invading column came up with cries of 'Gertcha!' and 'Look out, mun!', trampling all over the grass. Gardeners with shovels followed the horses (later, when the picture was shown to cheering audiences, the shovellers appeared on the screen, if people knew where to look). Arrows fell from the battlements at a safe distance from anybody, but a bucketful of something from the same quarter splashed over the Normans who were pretending to attack with the battering ram. Infuriated, they ran the log hard against the studded door with a thump that brought Sir Lionel out, asking for Captain Aubrey.

But there was no stopping Haggar. 'The Welsh counter-attack!' echoed under the walls, and Will and his fellow officers led a ragged assault around the side of the house. Some of the younger soldiers lost their temper and began punching one another. Nobody punched the officers. Will saw Sam waving a sword, and waved a rusty sabre back at him.

'Begin to drop dead!' ordered the megaphone. Will fell to his knees. All around were bodies. The victorious Normans charged out of sight, led by the clinking figure of Captain Aubrey, and Haggar said the Welsh could get up now.

Only the beheading was left. Captain Aubrey was soon back on the terrace, waiting for his fiancée to be dragged out resisting. Will drank a glass of the mild beer that was being handed round from a barrel. The battle had stirred him. Looking for Sam, he passed the kitchen yard. Haycock was sitting propped against a wall, a trickle of blood down his forehead. The cauldron had been overturned, and wet ashes were being brushed up by a servant.

'Funny things, battles,' said Haycock. 'You don't happen to have a clean handkerchief?'

He got to his feet unsteadily and took off the apron, revealing a waistcoat with watch-chain; the buttons were done up lopsided. 'Alas, poor Gwenllian,' he said. He was pale and his beard was dusty.

Normans had charged into the yard, he said, shouting 'Put them to the sword!' The servants had run inside giggling, leaving Haycock at his cauldron. He was hit with a scabbard and knocked unconscious.

It was a long wound, oozing blood. Will found water left in the cauldron and moistened the handkerchief. 'Captain Aubrey will see the culprits are reprimanded,' he said.

Haycock frowned, mopping at his scalp. 'It was Captain Aubrey did it.'

'I can't believe that. Others would have seen.'

'And they'd keep their mouths shut. He said something like, "You've got a cheek, Haycock." I ducked, but I wasn't quick enough. Fighting wars is a young man's game.' He took out a steel comb and ran it through his beard. 'Behind the enemy's walls, Mr Buckley, remember? Perhaps I found what I came for.'

Will said, 'Do you think the blow confused you, and you had an hallucination? It could have been some young collier. There's been drinking already.'

'The very thing! An hallucination and a drunken coal-miner. I'm obliged to you for putting me right. I'll have your handkerchief washed and sent back.'

Princess Gwenllian could be heard in the distance, shrilling defiance at her captor. 'Executioner, do your duty!' sang the Norman, and somebody blew a trumpet, off-key.

Miss Rees's small, soft neck was on the block. Would no one save her? Will had a mad longing to return to The Mount and settle his curiosity once and for all.

A roll of drums ended abruptly. At the front of the house, Miss Sprewett was fainting in Captain Aubrey's arms. She had red stains down the front of her dress. The executioner said he knew nothing about a bladder of blood. His instructions were to wave the scimitar in the air and whack it on the chopping block, which the camera couldn't see, Miss Sprewett having withdrawn to a safe distance. Nobody was sure how the bladder came to be hidden in the groove in the first place. A number of people had blood on their clothes. Theodore was nowhere to be seen.

When Will reached Sam's motor, a servant was polishing the brasswork, and hens pecked at the wheels.

'Was that Haycock, the union man, I saw?' asked Sam.

It was none of Will's business. He said, 'I believe he got knocked on the head.'

'So did some of our lads. All clean fun, as they say.' He had goggles for them both. 'Are you joining me on the picnic? Or is it no longer safe for the Buckleys and the Lewises to be seen together?'

The servant cranked the engine, and it spluttered into action.

'I can be seen with who I like.'

'That's the ticket. Do what you fancy.' The motor crept down the drive, with Sam honking at tipsy soldiers. 'Work a little, play a little. Make tinplate. Enjoy life. Take a lady's drawers down when you get the chance.'

'Do you ever think of anything else?'

'Not on a fine hot afternoon with game pie and claret in a hamper and somebody waiting for us down the road.'

'Who's waiting?'

'Have patience and trust in Sam.'

In the distance, at the foot of the hill, two figures in white stood outside a row of cottages. 'Yours is the well-built one,' said Sam.

Clouds of dust accompanied their arrival, and the two young women who were waiting held their sleeves over their faces. 'Jump up!' ordered Sam. Will had an impression of pink flesh and scent and stockings, and the well-built one was saying in his ear, 'We've only come for a ride in the motor car, mind!' When he turned to look, it was Sara Jenkins – Fat Sara, Tommy Spit's sister, who used to work at Buckley's. 'How do,' he said, glad he had the goggles to hide his shock. 'I'm William.'

'You can call me Sara. I like motor cars,' and she sat back with a crunch of silk, podgy hands folded in her lap.

The other girl, who was called Kitty, rested a hand on Sam's shoulder and urged him to go faster. They roared along the Pembrey road, several miles out of the town.

That was harmless enough. Then they turned to roar back again, but this time Sam went down a road that led to an old gunpowder works and a beach.

The car bumped along slowly. Sandy grass and bushes were all around. The tumbledown walls and cracked chimney of the powder works came into view, surrounded by scrubland. Heat shimmered over the coast. Through a belt of trees was the coppery sheen of the sea.

'Can't drive much further,' said Sam.

'Won't you go on the sands?' demanded Kitty. She was a lean, stringy girl, with a curved hat and a hook nose. 'We could all drive it then.'

'My Pa would kill me.'

'Are you frightened of your Pa?'

'It's his motor. Now behave yourself, Kitty.'

The vehicle slowed and stopped. Sara complained that it hadn't been much of a spin. She took off her hat and fanned herself with the straw brim. Smells of oil and grass mingled.

'Well,' said Sam, 'who wants to do what?'

'I only come for the motor car,' grumbled Sara.

'See if you can change her mind, Kit.'

'She's stubborn.'

'I suggest we take them back,' said Will. The goggles were enclosing his eyes in fire, but he didn't want to push them up, as Sam had done.

'Back?'

'This young lady behind me made it plain from the start.'

'I'm parched,' said Kitty. 'I'd give my soul for a penny monster.'

'Home it is, then,' announced Sam, and got out to restart the engine.

Through the trees the sea vibrated. Will imagined the coldness waiting under its coppery skin. He and Sam could come back afterwards and bathe.

'Don't you have *nothing* for a thirst?' demanded Kitty.

'There was to be a picnic,' cried Sam, swinging the steering wheel, sending them bumping over the grass, 'bottles of wine, fizzy ginger beer, pie with a handsome crust, juicy peaches . . .'

'We could just stop for a swig,' gasped Sara, and Will felt her breath on his neck, like a tongue. 'An' a slice of pie.'

In no time, the men were advancing on the sand dunes with the hamper held between them, the women chattering behind. Will had left the goggles in the motor.

'What now?' he said, when Sam indicated a hollow in the dunes where they should drop the hamper.

'Have a dip, I'd say.'

Sam shouted to the girls to unpack the food. He seized Will by the arm and ran them on to the beach, loosening collar and shirt with his free hand.

Will unbuttoned his trousers on the edge of the pondlike sea. Sam's naked form splashed ahead. Behind him, Will heard one of the girls laugh. He pulled his legs clear and plunged forward.

'Clever move,' said Sam, 'saying we'd take them straight back. Called their bluff. I don't know I'd have risked it. But we're all right now.'

They swam in waist-deep water, their shadows below them on the sand, and rushed from the sea shaking off arcs of spray like dogs. Will stopped trying to reduce the day to terms he could understand. He was on a beach with a woman. It wasn't a dream. The fact that she was Fat Sara didn't matter.

On the dunes – bodies half dry, clothes sticking to them – they knelt to uncork wine. The two creatures had begun to redden in the sun. Sara removed her hat and loosened the neck of her dress. She looked at Will slyly, and he knew that she knew who he was. Her freckled jaws worked non-stop on mouthfuls of pie washed down indiscriminately with claret and ginger beer.

The heat and food made Will drowsy. A gull screaming nearby woke him with a start. He and Sara were alone.

'Where are the others?' he said.

'They went for a walk.'

'Shall we go for one, too?'

'Suits me here.'

Her hands were behind her head, scarred along the forearms by mishaps with sharp tinplate.

'And what are *you* looking at?' she asked.

'Your openers' cuts.'

'Got most of them at Buckley's.'

'Did you know it was me who was coming?'

She shrugged her heavy shoulders. Her breasts wobbled like water. 'Why should I care? Sam Lewis, he's a good sport. They say he always gives a girl a present afterwards.'

'You mean he pays women?'

'Presents isn't paying.'

It was no good, he had to lean over and kiss her, and when she parted her lips so that their teeth scratched together, he kept on trying until he got it right.

Her arm came around his neck and pressed their faces together. Her cheeks were burning hot, and when he put his hand on the front of her dress, so was that.

'Are you taking advantage of me?' she gasped, pulling her mouth away for a second.

'How long will the others be?'

'Long enough.'

His hand slid elsewhere. His heart nearly stopped when he reached the bare skin above her stockings. Presently she was helping him. She lay like a starfish, all limbs, skirt over her head. It made the performance almost anonymous. Close his eyes, and he could have been in a shed at a tinworks.

Will gasped and shivered. The thing had happened.

'Did you like it?' she said, making herself decent.

He nodded, but 'like' was hardly the word for his mixed feelings, the pleasure, the repugnance, and the melancholy when he thought of other women doing the same thing – capable Margaret, for example, and disembodied Lady Mappowder, and, piercing him with sadness, the lost and forgotten Miss Rees.

He handed over a coin.

'Oo, a sovereign!' she said. 'That's a lovely present.'

The others came back, Sam whistling, the hook-nosed woman trailing her hat. She and Fat Sara whispered together, walking to the motor car.

'Good news, I hope?' asked Sam, as the men followed.

'Will she go talking?'

'Not if you gave her a decent present. Glad you came? Let's go to Swansea tonight. There's a bodega down the bottom of Castle Street where we can have a sirloin and a bottle of wine, and a piece of skirt as good as guaranteed afterwards.'

'I have to go to see Rees Coal on business. Lend me half a sovereign, if you will, and drop me at Burry Port station.'

'You're a dark horse,' cried Sam. 'Business on a bank holiday?'

The women waved goodbye from the station yard. A porter said there was an up train soon. In a world where princesses had died for honour, all he could do was pay a sovereign to have Fat Sara on the sands.

What he meant to do was take a down train and go to The Mount again.

For months he forgot about Miss Rees. He put her to the back of his mind. She was an inconvenience. Then, when it suited him (*lying on top of a mill girl going 'Oo!' and 'Ah!'*), he dragged the poor creature into the dirt with him – pretended he was Morgan and thcy were lying on their roll of sheepskin, performing the momentous act.

Hanging was too good for him.

Once he got to The Mount, he would have it out with Rees Coal once and for all.

Like hell he would. He was Will Buckley who made tinplate and lived the kind of life that was expected of him. He went to see his grandmother instead – took the up train and hired a trap at Port Howard.

As a child he had enjoyed the farm well enough, though he always found Hannah cantankerous – unlike Morgan, who had some bond with her, or pretended he had for his own scheming purposes.

She was in the kitchen, counting spoons as if they were money. 'Let me see,' she said, 'you must be a Buckley. Ianto, is it? John? No, Will, that's it. Such a long time since you were here.'

'We're busy these days, Nain. You have heard about the combine?'

'With that Rees Coal. I told your Dadda, there's a whited sepulchre, if ever there was.'

'Why's that?' said Will, alert at once.

'I could tell you things about Rees Coal, but I won't.'

'Concerning Miss Rees?'

'Miss Rees, Miss Rees?' She folded the spoons in a cloth and told him to put them on the dresser. 'Is that what you've come here for, to talk about that hussy? I might have guessed it wasn't to see an old woman. Your father comes here to try and find out who I'm going to leave my money to. I don't tell him, though.'

'Would you like me to read from the Bible?'

'No, thank you.'

'You used to like Morgan doing it.'

'Morgan has faith. You're like your Dadda, believe in nothing.' She pulled her shawl tight around her shoulders. 'Tomos, Tomos, you did the sensible thing, dying young.'

'Don't go upsetting yourself, Nain.'

'I'll upset myself if I want to.' She put a toffee in her

mouth from a bag down the side of the chair, without offering him one. 'Morgan found the Lord at Rhydness. He used to go for great walks up the back, thinking about his vocation.'

'Pity he didn't think about it a bit harder.'

'You sound like your Dadda. Morgan was a good boy. The Devil takes more satisfaction out of leading good boys astray.'

She knew exactly how to annoy Will. That breakfast cup on the hook was the one that Morgan preferred. Up past those trees was the way he walked. That red sunset was what he called God keeping his eye on us.

On and on she talked, with the determination of the old, only a fraction of a life left to say it all in. Morgan this, Morgan that. Then, satisfied with her victory, on to the fairy-tales of their past, told so often that the memories of her telling them seemed as ancient as the events themselves.

The March a pack of dogs savaged forty lambs.

The December Tomos saw corpse lights coming up the road.

The night Dadda was born, with snow drifted up to the roof.

The day Dadda took her and Tomos to see the neck of salty grassland where he meant to build his works – 'If we could lend him the money, that is. Your grandfather told him not to be a fool, but he handed it over all the same. He'd have handed over more if it hadn't been for me. I was the one with the head for figures.'

In the firelight, the flames were almost touching her sleeve.

'Time I went,' said Will.

'Your brother ought to come. It's only right. He must tell me himself what he did. I can't sit here for ever. I shall have to join Tomos one day.'

He supposed she was the key to them all. He didn't even

like her much. She was too devious, too old, too cruel. But she contained them all within her memories.

If he could only talk to her about Miss Rees and Fat Sara, she would take the stories and absorb them into herself where they could do no harm.

It was too big an if.

He kissed her goodbye and walked home.

The night shift, the first after the holiday, was due on. Buildings came back to life. Light streamed out over the marshes.

A whiteness on the ground startled him. The works stood in a sheet of water. Then Jumbo the engine puffed around the side of a shed, the bottom half of its wheels invisible, and he saw it was sea fog, drifting in over the dyke.

'How was the battle, Mr Will?' asked Trubshaw.

'I think we lost,' said Will.

People said it was a gamble, pouring his money into a combine instead of being content with what he had. But there was no denying that Buckley got himself talked about, or that the Burry River Combine intrigued the small-scale tinplate masters and coal-owners who peppered the landscape in this south-west corner of industrial Wales.

He burnt his boats. That was what gave him the moral advantage over the other investors, none of whom was committed to his extent. Both Mappowder and Rees Coal were richer than he was. They backed him because he backed himself. He tried hard in the early days to have the copperworks itself brought inside the Burry River. 'For the moment the nature of the family trusts precludes it, I fear,' said the Colonel, but Buckley took that as a hint: one day they might get the copperworks.

His first acquisition was to be a steelworks. Loughor Steel would suit him nicely. Two brothers called Ricketts had inherited it. James was a dentist in Swansea; Luke kept a shop in Merthyr, but sold it when the works came their way, and installed himself at Loughor, a village by the river where it widened into the Burry Estuary. Their furnaces needed relining and their steam hammers were antiquated. Buckley heard them gossiped about, and made an appointment with James Ricketts, LDS, at The Dental Rooms. There he had a perfectly good tooth attended to, and began negotiating while he was still in the chair.

The board were amused at his story, though he told it without a smile. They agreed to invite the brothers to visit the combine. Buckley wanted quick results. It was no good the Colonel telling him that industrial empires weren't built overnight. After David Buckley would come Will Buckley, and Will was still a learner. The only person you could be sure of was yourself.

The visit began at a pit and moved down to the coast. It was marred; that was the only word for it. To begin with, Sprewett and the Colonel were not themselves. Their respective offspring, Lucinda and Aubrey, had broken off their engagement shortly before. The men were seen having heated words behind the washery at Glynvale No 2.

A fire-damp explosion shook the ground while they were there, and injured colliers came to the surface. Buckley was furious. He asked Rees Coal what he was playing at, and Rees said, 'If you want to abolish natural 'azard, you better start praying to the Lord pretty 'ard.'

They were late for lunch at Y Plas, and in the afternoon were no sooner at the works than an engine broke down, halting a group of hot-rolls. Mill-men, half naked in flannel vests and pants, emerged from the smoke for ginger beer and a breath of air. 'Same sort of problem we have with our steam hammers,' said Luke Ricketts. Buckley was so upset, he sacked his best foreman, who happened to be in the mill.

The brothers promised to go away and think about

joining the combine. The dentist, in particular, seemed keen. He told Buckley that he had hoped to see the famous Cilfrew Castle. 'That could be arranged,' said Buckley. But nothing happened, until one day the other side's solicitor wrote to ask if it was true that Buckley's stood on a site that was threatened by the sea.

At once, Buckley was suspicious. It was a lie, but who had been talking to them? Was there a whispering campaign?

A paragraph about coast erosion, due to changes in the course of the Burry River, was printed in the *News*. 'I hope you're convinced now,' Buckley told his colleagues. 'There are no prizes for guessing the source of these scurrilous rumours.'

'Who's he mean?' asked Rees Coal.

'You don't need me to tell you. A man who's eaten up by envy. A man who sits on Tir Gwyn farm, not developing it himself, not letting anyone else do it either.'

'Come, now,' said the Colonel. 'I don't like Rhodri Lewis. But in my experience he's straight.'

'He beats his breast, that's true. I've known him thirty years, remember. If he can spite this combine, he will. It would serve him right if you stopped his wagons using the lines at Copperworks Junction.'

Mappowder was frowning. 'He and I have a legal agreement.'

'Renewable every few years, if I remember.'

'I don't think we should be discussing it.'

''e's having us on,' declared Rees Coal.

'I've never been more serious in my life,' said Buckley.

Sprewett calmed them down. Will kept his mouth shut.

The board asked Billy Rod for a surveyor's certificate, guaranteeing the dyke. Buckley got his brother-in-law to take a look at the old retaining wall, and the obliging Abraham went there in the *Falcon* one day when there was not much doing. Abraham and Joe rowed to it in the ship's boat, and Abraham shook his head and said, 'Like a sieve. Cost a fortune to put right.'

Joe lost an oar as he was fending them off. An ebb tide swirled them away, and they had to wave a sock on the other oar as a distress signal.

A minute later the tug blew her whistle and started making smoke. They were in no danger, except there was always danger.

The current sucked them away as Carmarthen Bay emptied into the Bristol Channel, the same current that took the barque *Jerusalem* and Abraham's father to their violent end on the Hooper.

They were rescued after some complicated manoeuvres and half a mile of black smoke. When they returned to the North Dock, Helmes, the Harbour Superintendent, was waiting at the lock gate, demanding to know where they had been. A gas buoy needed mooring. What were they doing, making smoke down the coast?

Abraham owned up at once. He had told the *Falcon* to take him alongside the retaining wall; he didn't say why, but everyone knew there were conger eels to be found there. Helmes suspended him on the spot for wasting coal and ship's time.

Abraham waited to tell Villette until the boys were in bed, and they were sitting by a fire of coal dust and driftwood. She said he was a donkey.

'You can talk to your sister in the morning,' he said, 'and Davy will see it's all right.'

'I wish I was married to a capable man. You may know about boats and suchlike. But not things that matter.'

'Fair do's, love. I never pretended to be what I wasn't.'

'You should have been superintendent yourself by now. We should have a house with a bathroom and a proper piano for Theodore, not that hurdy-gurdy. I used to think you had ambition. You have let me down, Abraham. If it wasn't for Theodore I'd have nothing to live for.'

'Be glad,' he said. 'Not every woman has a Theodore. What d'you think your sister has got?'

'Leisure. You can do nothing without leisure. I hardly have time to read a book from one week's end to another.'

'She doesn't read books, Villette *fach*, she opens bottles.'

His wife threw a shoe at him, which missed, and retired to bed. She was asleep or pretending to be when he joined her, to make two thin nightgowns, side by side. He lay awake for a long time, thinking of the Hooper Sands by moonlight, and the whitened spars of the *Jerusalem*, bare bones of lost hopes.

Complicated wheels had to be set in motion to end Abraham's suspension and return him to work with his character unstained. Sprewett, as chairman of the Harbour Trust, tried to have the matter quashed without discussion. When Rhodri Lewis got to hear of it, the Liberals did their best to drum up a scandal. Weekes of the *News* wrote columns about the need to stamp out favours and shady deals. 'Now will you believe we have enemies?' Buckley asked Will, and got Probert of the *Star* to write columns about hypocrisy.

In the middle of the row, Will sent a message to Sam, and they met on a Sunday morning at Swiss Valley, the town's beauty spot.

The walks among pine trees and around the lake were deserted; the crowds didn't come till after chapel. It was no longer wise to be seen together, even to be together.

They tried being honest with one another.

'Dadda thinks your father wants to do him down.'

'I know. Spreading rumours. I ask you, Will. As if we care whether you buy a tuppeny-ha'penny steelworks or not.'

'Nice little steelworks, by all accounts.'

'Pa says the Harbour Trust affair has gone to your old man's head. He thinks he and Sprewett can get away with anything.'

'You make it sound like bribery and corruption. The Liberals are giving him stick because they think they can make political capital. The Harbour Trust's a red herring.'

'Try and see it from our point of view. We all know the dyke leaks a bit.'

'Billy Rod says it's safe.'

'He'd say anything.'

'Quite right,' said Will. Spring air poured through the valley. The path shone with pine needles. There seemed hope for them yet. 'What are we arguing about? They're both old rogues, my father and yours. I know it, you know it. Another thirty years, you and I'll be the same if we don't watch out.'

'I don't care for that kind of talk,' mumbled Sam, and in a flash he was as parochial as the rest of them; he had ceased to be the great adventurer.

They circled the lake.

'Lot of these in America, I expect,' said Will.

'Thousands. Millions, probably. There's one near the plant at Elwood. I took a lady there once.'

'Of course. By the way, here's the half sovereign I still owe you.'

They parted at the road, more strangers than before.

The affair blew over. The Trust concluded that Captain Lloyd had not been bribed by his brother-in-law, and he was reinstated. Buckley sent fifty pounds for the Widows & Orphans Fund. He wished he had never heard of the wall. The Ricketts brothers and their blasted steelworks were no nearer than before, though he kept trying.

The afternoon the Harbour Trust matter was settled, Will went round to Bank Cottages to tell the Lloyds. Abraham and Joe were out on the sands looking for a free supper of shrimps. Theodore was playing the piano in the parlour.

'So we can breathe again,' Villette whispered, and asked if he wouldn't mind whispering too, so as not to disturb Theodore. 'Please thank your father from us all.'

'There's something else,' said Will. 'Dadda says that before too long the combine hopes to have its own steamer so we can ship our coal and tinplate. We want Uncle Abraham to be captain.'

He said 'we' but he meant his father. He was beginning not to trust him.

'Oh, Will!' said his aunt. 'I can't tell you what that means.' She forgot to whisper, and Theodore's voice came from the parlour, 'I can't play with all this noise.'

She made an 'Aren't I silly!' face at Will and stood by the window, looking at the grimy slope of the Bank, smiling to herself. He couldn't remember seeing her like that. Her straight whaleboned body seemed to loosen. Hair slipped over her face. The ghost of someone youngish and prettyish hovered.

Then a bugle sounded, a loud inexpert call, followed by the opening notes of a local song, 'Sospan Fach', in deep bass tones. Theodore started banging the piano in a rage.

'Oh!' shouted Villette, 'those children!'

She went to get hat and coat, the ill-tempered aunt again. Twice a week they had to put up with this from a hut on some waste ground.

'Let me go,' said Will, wondering where children from Bank Cottages got their musical instruments.

The hut was more of a shelter, a three-sided contraption, its back to the sea, made of planks and chipped bricks, and roofed with tinplate. Some urchins were listening to a man in a long overcoat play a curly brass instrument that he held upright and blew into from the side.

He stopped playing and lowered the instrument so they could see his fingers on the valves. The wind sighed outside.

When he saw Will, he said, 'Evening, sir. Are you the landowner, by any chance?'

'Why, shouldn't you be here?'

'That's a moot point, sir. The lady'll be over in a minute.' Sheets of music, held down by a stone on top of a box, flapped in the wind. 'We're only here temporary like, until we get proper quarters.'

'Who are you, then?'

'Budding musicians, they are, they hope.' He looked over Will's shoulder. 'Here she is now.'

It was Miss Haycock, the schoolteacher. She wore a beret and a cloak and carried a basket; Will thought of Red Riding Hood, or even the wolf. The grey eyes held him.

'What a surprise,' she said. 'This land doesn't belong to you by any chance – you *are* one of the Buckleys?'

'I am, but it doesn't. I daresay it belongs to nobody.'

'Don't you believe it. If we were to put up a proper building here, somebody would come and charge us rent. I suppose there isn't an empty hut at your works we could use? We could pay a sort of rent, say threepence a week? We could afford threepence, couldn't we, Mr Mokes?'

'Ha'penny each. You're talking big money.'

'We mustn't stop the lesson. Mr Buckley and I will go outside and talk business.'

They walked a few yards over grass and cinders. Lamps shone at windows in Bank Cottages. Washing flapped on lines. Mokes played scales while his pupils followed the notes on a sheet of music. One of them shouted, 'Can we have our cake, Miss?'

'At the end of the lesson.' She looked at Will, head on one side. 'So may wc come to Buckley's? It would make such a difference.'

'It wouldn't be possible.' Outside the farthest cottage,

Will thought he could see Aunt Villette among the dancing shirts, looking his way. 'I'm here to ask them to stop playing. My aunt lives over there. Her son plays the piano – wins gold medals. He says he can't practise for the noise.'

'How ironical. You live at Y Plas, don't you? Your cousin could practise there with an orchestra and nobody would hear. But he happens to live – you must explain to me one day how that comes about – within earshot of the one place where I am trying to give children a broader outlook on life.'

'My uncle is a pilot. Not enough ships use the docks. They're poor and they're independent. It doesn't need much explaining.'

'What a strange man. I don't care a hoot about the ins and outs of your family. What I'm discussing is basically the plight of the industrial classes.'

'You'll be discussing it with my Aunt Villette in a minute, because here she comes.'

Will moved to intercept her. 'They'll stop in a few minutes,' he said. 'This lady has brought them here from her school to have lessons.'

'We have a perfect right – ' began Miss Haycock.

'I've said I'll help them find somewhere else.'

She didn't finish the sentence. A boy asked again if it was time for cake, and she pulled the cloth off the basket and distributed a puddingy slab to everyone, including Mokes. Before he ate it, he snuggled the instrument inside a case and tied up the music with string and brown paper.

It was a euphonium, said Miss Haycock. All they had so far was that and a bugle. Mr Mokes was retired from Old Castle, where, after a lifetime, he had risen to be a furnaceman. He once played his euphonium in a brass band, long since extinct.

Will walked with her towards the town. Aunt Villette

had returned to the cottage. Piano music came through the dusk.

'Did you try using the school?' he said.

'The trustees wouldn't hear of it. School is for arithmetic and geography between nine and four. What do the children want music for?'

'The ones today weren't over-keen.'

'Why should they be? They don't have many expectations – that's their trouble. I have to change them first. Until then they come for the cake.'

Will wondered what he was letting himself in for. As he had guessed, her father was the trades union Haycock, the fellow he had to be wary of.

Helping his daughter was – what, a bit of bravado? He was showing off, that was all. A week later he sent her a message to say he had rented a room at the back of Market Hall, Mondays and Thursdays. It cost him half a crown a week. Dadda would have been furious. His mind was supposed to be on the steelworks they still didn't have, not on making himself agreeable to unsuitable young women.

When he was next in Swansea, doing business at the Metal Exchange, he visited Brader's and bought two second-hand cornets. It was a Monday; he went straight from the station to Market Hall. The class had grown to five. She wasn't there. He thought to keep the instruments, but Mokes was already eyeing the cases. Will dumped them on a table, saying, 'These any use to you?'

Mokes knew what they were, before he undid the clasps. 'Cornets, boys,' he said. '*Cornets*, no less.'

He insisted on shaking hands with Will, and made the boys do the same, one by one. He was mesmerised by the gift. 'Used to practise one of them things till my lip bled,' he said. As Will left he was still repeating, '*Cornets*, boys.'

A letter came to Y Plas:

Dear Mr Buckley,
I have heard from Mr Mokes of your most generous gift. Coming on top of your earlier kindness, I hardly know what to say. Do look in at the music class whenever you can.
Most sincerely yours, Flora Haycock.

Pomona told her husband that it looked like a woman's writing on the envelope, but at that moment, Buckley wouldn't have cared if it had been one of Sam Lewis's improper postcards. He had finally persuaded the Ricketts brothers. He had had to promise them expensive new machinery, a directorship for Luke, and a place for James the dentist at Colonel Mappowder's shoots. None of this made him popular with the board. But he drove through the acquisition with the fierce pride of a creator.

And all the time Port Howard went on making tinplate and hewing coal as if nothing had happened, or ever would, to stop its traffic of railway trucks and motor lorries and steamers, tiny threads that bound it to the manufactories and routes and markets that covered the map of the world with their sooty symbols, and showed how capitalism was civilising the world with trade.

Down Mappowder Street, Will strolled to Market Hall past shop windows packed with signs of the new age of *things* that people spoke of. In the shadows under blinds huddled the bicycles and corsets, the kettles and straw boaters, the patent floor cleaners and bars of Lever's soap, that were the very heart of progress – or so it said in the *Daily Mail*.

Miss Haycock had written him another letter. Two cornets, a euphonium, a bugle and a flugelhorn mended with wire were ready with a test-piece for the patron to hear, if he could spare ten minutes.

They were waiting for him, the boys in their Sunday suits, Mokes, even, with a collar on his shirt. Miss Haycock gave the signal as he walked in, and they let him have 'Sospan Fach', 'Little Saucepan', at full blast.

'Not perfect, boys,' as Mokes said afterwards. 'But the tune was there somewhere.'

Cake was no longer handed out. They were serious performers. Miss Haycock said it just showed.

She invited him back to tea.

'You mean tea at your house?'

'We have cups and saucers,' she said gravely. 'It's a squash in the kitchen. But you must be used to families.'

It was Haycock he was nervous about, but Mr Awkward wasn't at home. The rest of the family were at the kitchen table – plump-faced Mrs Haycock, whose accent was nearly Welsh but not quite, two younger daughters, Hetty and Alice, and an afterthought called Kenneth.

Chairs were scraped, introductions made. 'Well, this *is* a surprise,' said Mrs Haycock, and it dawned on Will that he hadn't been expected.

The meal was hard going. Mrs Haycock was over-solicitous with the cold meat and pickle. Afraid of silence, she told a long story about a great-great-uncle who presented a bugle used in the Crimean War to the Liverpool city council (so Liverpool was the other bit of her accent). When she finished, Kenneth rolled up his hand to make a tootling noise, blew crumbs over Will, and was told to leave the table.

'Pa's round with Hughes Aberdare, I suppose?' said Flora.

'He didn't say when to expect him.'

The girl turned to Will. 'The rollerman, you know? The one who went to prison for manslaughter at Buckley's.'

'I know.'

'He came out of Carmarthen Gaol this morning.'

'Is that so?'

'They've lost their home. Living with a brother, aren't they, Ma? About ten of them in a house this size.'

'I'm sure Mr Buckley doesn't want to hear about all that.'

'I must be off, in any case,' he said, hiding his anger. 'Thank you for an excellent tea. It was very kind.'

A lithograph on the wall caught his eye as he was going. A group of men in ragged clothes sat around a fire of railway sleepers. Light came through an archway, where a figure leaned against a rock with a musket at his feet.

'It's those old Chartists,' said Mrs Haycock.

It was left to Flora to see him off. The front step led straight to the pavement. She pulled the door after her. Children ran past with hoops.

'Was I invited so I could be lectured about Hughes Aberdare?'

'He was at your works. Two of his children are in my class. Is it a subject not to be mentioned – the ruining of a man's life because of an accident?'

'The fault was his.'

'The fault was the system that he, and you, and I, and all of us subscribe to. But I'm sorry if you think you were invited under false pretences. I assume that we shall now be asked to stop using our rehearsal room.'

She infuriated him. Who did she think she was? But he couldn't take his eyes off her.

A hoop whizzed between them.

'Play on,' he said, and walked down the street.

When he turned back to wave, she had gone in.

8

Margaret was never troubled by Johansson again, except indirectly, when she worried that Henry relied on him too much. The mad Swede still went on expeditions that didn't turn out as expected – his latest was to Assam, and he and his crates of orchids were coming back through Germany. This was for reasons of secrecy, said Henry, who had rushed off to meet his partner in Hamburg, where the plants would be trans-shipped to London.

Margaret had a shrewd idea that the secrecy was a game he enjoyed. Both men would be back in a day or so. She would share in the excitement, and who could tell what would happen next? A transformation? Henry's schoolboy-ish dreams come true?

Margaret still hoped for things. But she felt her life falling into a rhythm, the future taking shape around her. The house, like its predecessor, had a room that she thought of as 'the nursery'. Bits and pieces accumulated there; Henry, not thinking, called it 'the glory hole'. If it was too early to be pessimistic, as Virginia was always telling her, it was too late not to be concerned.

Virginia would stop her brooding while Henry was away. She was making plans for a visit when Lake announced a Miss Enid Wilkinson, and the Captain's daughter strode in, gloveless and hatless, shook hands, and sat down with a thump.

'I take it,' she said, 'that you are not aware of what has happened to Esther? I thought not. She is in Holloway Gaol. The family know, but are not disposed to lift a finger. She has been there for forty-eight hours, having been sentenced to thirty days by a beast of a magistrate. Her only crime was to jostle a policeman outside Palace Yard.'

'I suppose one shouldn't go round jostling policemen. But I'm very sorry to hear of it. Was she not given the option of a fine?'

'My dear Margaret, we were marching on the House of Commons crying "Parliament or Prison!" We had the words of that scoundrel Winston Churchill ringing in our ears, "regretting" that "good-hearted ladies" should "pursue courses" which would "bring them suffering and humiliation". Those who were arrested were hardly in the mood to pay forty shillings and go home meekly.'

'In that case,' said Margaret, 'I take it Esther achieved what she intended. I think the Suffragists are very brave – '

'Suffragettes, if you please. The newspapers may have thought up the word to belittle us, but we are proud of it now.'

The Captain's daughter had her jowl thrust forward, ready for a quarrel.

'So what can I do?' asked Margaret.

'Visit her, because no one else will.'

'Not you?'

'I am undesirable to the prison authorities. I am not her family,' and the broad chin with a sprouting mole on it sank to her chest. 'The authorities refuse visits from political associates. I have taken the liberty of applying for a visit in your name. You must be there in less than an hour.' She blew her nose; it was like a snore. 'I am being very foolish. Please forget that I came. I will leave you some pamphlets. Esther will survive. She's made of steel – far stronger than I.'

Margaret found herself comforting the woman. Blow the family. Of course she would go. The dress she had on, a plain green velveteen, would do. Armed with papers to establish her credentials, she set out in a cab with the

Captain's daughter. Only when it stopped at the prison entrance half an hour later, and she stepped up, alone, to the small door studded with nailheads painted black, did she pause to wonder whether 'Blow the family' was the right response; and by then it was too late.

The visit had its comical side, or so Margaret kept telling herself. She was treated with polite suspicion, as though she might have a bomb concealed about her. Perhaps there was no established practice yet for receiving the families of well-bred Suffragettes.

The gatekeeper summoned a wardress who took her to a waiting room with stone-coloured walls, where another official, in a holland dress, with keys jangling at her waist, stood over her while she completed a printed form. As her pen scratched the answers (such vital information as 'Married woman' and 'I have known Miss Penbury-Holt for three years'), doors clanged far and near like multiple echoes, and the grey afternoon light got greyer outside the barred window.

The next stage was an office occupied by the assistant governor, a young man with fierce expression and squeaky voice who fitted nicely into her 'comical' category.

'May I have your word,' he said, 'that you will not speak to Miss Penbury-Holt of political matters? If so, the wardress has instructions to terminate the interview.'

'In that case my word is superfluous. As it happens, I have no intention of discussing politics, my sister-in-law's or anyone else's.'

'It's not easy,' he said crossly, 'having more than twenty women from respectable backgrounds here,' and he rang a bell to have her sent into the heart of the gaol. 'They are infinitely troublesome.'

If he weren't to be comical, he would have to be sinister. Trying to see the lighter side was only a trick to keep her spirits up. Vistas of whitewash and black ironwork led to a room with a trestle table and benches. Beyond was a cell block, visible through a barred door at the end of the corridor, its floors jutting out in shelves; whispering rustled through it.

'Madam is not permitted to touch the prisoner,' said the wardress who brought Esther in. 'Fold your arms in front of you, Twelve.'

They sat opposite one another. Esther wore ordinary clothes; her blouse was crumpled. The whiteness of her face made her nose stand out, and her hair was badly combed. She took a deep, shuddering breath and said, 'You are the kindest person in the world. I thought I should lose my senses last night. Today is better.'

'Enid called, or I wouldn't have known.'

'They will certainly have told Henry. Tristram attempted to pay my fine. I refused.'

'Henry's in Germany on business. I'm sure he'll understand my coming to see you.'

'I wouldn't rely on it. There is something about us that maddens people – men, at any rate,' and the wardress stirred. 'Most of us were thumped in the back in Parliament Square until we were black and blue. Enid certainly was.'

'Stop talking politics, Twelve.'

'Enid wants you to know the cat is well,' said Margaret. 'She hasn't tried to eat the canary once since you've been away.'

'Dear Enid. Tell her to remember the window-boxes. The primroses are out. I'm afraid she has the opposite of green fingers.'

It was the smallest of small talk. Margaret would have liked to ask, 'Tell me *why*, exactly.' The wardress would have rattled her keys, but it wouldn't have been politics, only curiosity about the strangeness of lives.

'So how is your family in Wales?'

'Still manufacturing tinplate. I see little of them.'

'Your brother must have been ordained long since.'

Margaret shook her head. 'There was a scandal. Though why I should tell you that now, I can't imagine.'

'Things sometimes hurt less when spoken of,' said Esther, smiling. She leaned across the table and kissed Margaret on the cheek.

A moment later she had been thrust back on the bench, an electric bell was ringing, the wardress was shouting, and the visit came to an abrupt end. Esther had time to mention some toilet necessities she wanted sent in, before she was hauled off in one direction, and Margaret was escorted away in the other.

Half expecting to be ticked-off by the squeaky voice, she was led in silence to the gatekeeper's lodge, and stepped back into the world, where cab and Captain's daughter waited, and a glow of light from the busy streets to the south, licking the underside of clouds, made her think of Port Howard.

'What a marvel she is!' boomed Enid, when she had heard the story. At her insistence the cab took them down the Caledonian Road, where the Great Northern and Piccadilly could be boarded. She kept a plan of the tube railways in her reticule and said that all sensible women should use them whenever possible.

Her cloak and bobbed hair went swiftly down the station steps; she was ridiculous yet there was something admirable about her as well. London had no terrors for her. Margaret huddled back in her seat. An electric tram went by in a hail of sparks, and the gusty wind brought a low, troubled bellowing of animals from the Cattle Market as the cab turned for home.

Lanes and churchyards lay in pools of shadow. A piano tinkled from one public house; blinds shone red in another as though it was burning. Shops were still lit, people were about, through grimy windows she saw men at work-benches, and once, when the driver stopped at a street junction, a woman wearing a man's cap pressed her face against the cab window and left a trace of spittle on the glass.

Nearing home, she had a faint hope of finding that Henry had returned a day early. But the hothouses – she could see them over the fence as the cab approached – were in darkness, and if he had arrived, he would be there inspecting his treasures. She would drink a glass of milk and retire early.

Tired, as she let herself into the hall, she turned up the light and looked at herself in the gilded glass. She touched her breasts; they were sore, and she knew her period was about to start. The months ticked away like minutes.

Lake appeared, saying 'Madam – ' and at the same moment the door of the morning room opened and Morgan said, 'Hello, Maggs. I thought I heard you.'

She unpinned her hat before she kissed him. Calmness of manner could be acquired, like deportment; wasn't she a Penbury-Holt by adoption?

'Still in one piece, then. I must let them know at Y Plas. Lake, will you bring me the pad of telegraph forms from Mr Penbury-Holt's study, and then I shall want you to go out to the post office.'

Her brother made no objection – grinning at her, hands in pockets, while she scribbled the message. He was oddly immaculate in grey suit and speckled tie, with snowy shirt-cuffs and a high shine on his boots. It was a long way from the crumpled Morgan who arrived in the garden that morning. All the more reason not to let him get round her.

'You could have been dead,' she observed, when they were in the drawing room, and she was sitting out of the light, so he wouldn't see her hands trembling. 'As it was, you were very nearly the death of Mamma.'

'Is she still on the bottle? Sorry, Maggs. I'm quite genteel really. I have become a confidential secretary to a husband and wife – you're not to laugh – by the name of Squale.'

'I'm sure you're doing well for yourself. It's your nature. But you can't drop out of everyone's life and then expect to overwhelm us with your prodigal's return.'

'I sent postcards.'

'You did what suited you. Never mind the worry you caused Mamma.'

He knelt beside her, as dangerous as ever.

'Here cometh the thoughtless boy. How is Mamma, seriously?'

'She has good days and bad days.'

'And Will?'

'Dadda's right-hand man. Just as well somebody is.'

'And Nain?'

'I only hear through Mamma. Counting her sovereigns, as usual.'

'And you?'

'Never mind me. You left a woman to have your child, remember?'

'That,' said Morgan, holding her wrist hard, 'is a closed book.'

'Not for her it isn't.'

'Still the same old Maggs. Because I talked to God once, I have to be reminded of the extent of my fall. I thought you cared for me. I thought you understood that I have been in the wilderness, working out my salvation. How often do you think I've wanted to come and find you – or wanted you to come and find me? I knew nobody – *nobody*. I knew less than nobody, because I'd lost the One.'

'Histrionics, my boy,' she said firmly.

'I used to hear your voice in the middle of the night – like a dream, only I was wide awake. Rain on the slates of my little room used to wake me up. Then I'd hear you,

> God in the whizzing of a pleasant wind
> Shall march upon the tops of mulberry trees,

and I'd lie there sweating in my nightshirt.'

'Too much cheese for supper, as Mamma told you many times.'

He chewed his lip.

'Can we be friends?'

'We are always *friends*. What you'd better think about is going back to Port Howard and making your peace with everyone there.'

'One thing at a time. It's you I'm in need of, Maggs. I make no secret. I only wish I thought that *you* needed *me*. But you have a house and a husband. You have all those Penbury-Holts.'

She remained calm. 'I used to be upset when you sneered at Henry's family. Now that it's my family too, I just find it tiresome. Really, Morgan, I'd have expected living in London to make you less prejudiced against the English.'

'Rock-of-ages Maggs,' he said lightly, and went to stand with his back to the fire. 'I admire you. I salute you. I thought you might have lost your edge – you know the way married women go?' He surveyed the room. 'You seem very comfortable here. I daresay you'll be starting a family.'

The question took her unawares, if it was a question. 'That's hardly a matter I want to discuss.'

'I thought it was something the New Woman took in her stride,' he said, going up and down on his toes.

'I don't know where you get your ideas from, but I'm not one of the New Women. I'd have thought that was obvious.'

'It was your not surrounding yourself with babies I meant as being New Womanly.'

'Who said anything about babies? I intend to have them. Now are you satisfied?'

She had been outmanoeuvred. She felt tireder still, and the pit of her stomach hurt.

‘I want us to see London together,’ Morgan was saying. ‘It hadn’t occurred to me that a city could be beautiful. Sinful, yes. That was about all. Now the weather’s getting warm, we can go for picnics in Richmond Park. There’s a ridge above the ponds where you can see the whole of London. This house, even, if one had a telescope. I saw the sun flash off a window, up on this slope, one day. I wonder if that’s Maggs, I thought. Dear old Maggs. I couldn’t get the thought out of my head.’

‘Morgan!’ she said warningly, but in the very act of fending off his nonsense, she succumbed to it and went to join him by the fire. ‘I missed you,’ she said, ‘I can’t say how much.’

His jacket brushed against her breast; the tenderness made her flinch. She let him rub her hand against his cheek. She felt at peace.

A sound in the hall startled her.

‘Your husband?’

‘He’s in Germany, not due back.’

But it was Henry all right, red-eyed from a third-rate hotel or a bad crossing, his heavy frame shabby, needing affection.

‘You remember my brother?’

‘She’s been worried about you, Buckley.’

‘She has been telling me what a bad fellow I am.’

Margaret rang for Lake, ordered a hot bath, asked that Mrs Haynes be sent for, poured a whisky, unlaced Henry’s shoes, produced his slippers; saw, too late to do anything about it, that the Suffragette literature left behind by the Captain’s daughter was on the sofa-table. Morgan had taken a leaflet and retired with it to the other side of the room.

‘Did Johansson not arrive?’ she began.

‘He brought back more than twelve hundred plants.’ From his pocket Henry drew out a handkerchief, folded in on itself. ‘*Cypredium fairieanum*, a new Dendrobium – so he claimed – and more Odontoglossum than I could grow in years.' As he spoke he unwrapped the handkerchief to reveal a slimy white flower with yellow spikes, like a suppurating star. 'They all bolted on the voyage – someone got at them before they were put on board. Johansson says we can prove nothing. He was broken-hearted. I sent him home for a holiday.'

His pale, heavy misery drew out her sympathy. She would do anything if he asked – shovel coal in the boiler room, sell orchids on street corners; she already packed them in cellophane and brown paper.

'We shall have our own cattle's ear yet,' she murmured, but the intimacy fell flat. Henry asked if she would excuse him while he bathed and changed.

Passing the table he saw the leaflets and picked one up. His lips moved as he read. His neck seemed to thicken inside his collar.

'This – *document*,' he said. 'Do I understand my sister has been here?'

'Not exactly. Her friend Miss Wilkinson called to tell me something. I think we had better have a word in the study, if Morgan will excuse us.'

He was angry when she told him, but beyond the anger was incomprehension. The inevitable had happened to Esther, but his wife had entered a *prison*. She had *demeaned* herself.

'I did what I thought right,' Margaret said. 'I have no more sympathy with their aims than you. But – I might as well tell you and get it over with – no one else in the family would go to see her. So I decided I should.'

He turned his back, and look what happened. 'The Father,' he warned, departing for his bath, 'will take it badly.'

Margaret felt, at the very least, like a woman caught in adultery.

Leaving Morgan to his own devices while she went to supervise Mrs Haynes, whose speciality was underdone meat and overdone vegetables, she feared what he might become, an affliction for Henry, that odd brother of yours who comes here when it suits him and makes himself at home. But Morgan behaved himself at dinner, as they ploughed through Mrs Haynes's bloody chops and liquefied peas (when spoken to, she went to pieces) in silence.

She left them with decanter and Stilton. Ten minutes should have been ample, but the coffee went cold in the drawing room and she had to ring for more. She began to hear the occasional rumble of Henry's raised voice, and Morgan's answering bark. Appalled, she looked at one of the Captain's daughter's offerings, but found herself reading the same sentence over and over, 'Women should vote for the laws they obey and the taxes they pay,' without understanding it.

The voices grew louder. 'Never!' she heard Morgan shout, and they came in laughing.

Henry was flushed and full of himself. 'Used to think the Welsh were scallywags,' he gasped, and Morgan said, 'Or *scalawags* as the Welsh language aptly puts it,' winking at Margaret behind his back.

'Now, be serious,' said Henry, and spilled coffee in his saucer. 'How many?'

'Fifty blooms a day? The circles I move in think nothing of orchids right through the house.'

'I should have to sub-contract. This is a step towards accumulating capital, Margaret.'

'Are we thinking of Mr and Mrs Squale?' she asked Morgan, still puzzled, but trying to enter into the spirit of whatever was going on.

'The Squales for one. Lord Leuchars for another. He has a place in Charles Street.'

'Are you pulling my leg, you scalawag?'

'Number thirty-seven. He and the Squales have business connections.'

Henry said he wished his partner Johansson was there to meet Morgan. He invited him to inspect the orchid houses.

'Another time, if I may. Please excuse me if I stay and talk to my sister.'

She went with Henry as far as the hall. 'Am I forgiven?' she asked, out of deference to his feelings.

'It hardly rests with me. It's a family matter.'

'Off you go, then,' she smiled, sending him out to play with his orchids, and went back to the deeper mysteries of Morgan.

'I'm delighted to see you and Henry getting on like a house on fire,' she said. 'But what *is* all this about places in Charles Street? I still know nothing of your life, remember.'

'Best not to, perhaps.' He looked at her with eyes that seemed darker, in a face that seemed longer; the sharp severity of his stare took her by surprise. 'You won't approve.'

'You know you're dying to tell me.'

'It's perfectly respectable. Cordelia Squale is a spiritualistic medium who practises in Putney. She tells me I have a gift for that sort of thing. Her clients include one or two of the nobs. The Lord Leuchars one could say is Nob Number One.'

'You mean table-rapping? Oh, Morgan! I liked Evan Roberts better.'

'I liked him myself at one time. That's not the point. And think of all the introductions I can arrange for Henry.'

'You're not to do anything to hurt Henry,' she said. 'Ever. Promise me that.'

'I promise,' he said, too casually to put her mind at rest. He told her an anecdote (it couldn't be true) about a spirit hand cast in plaster of paris that hit Squale behind the ear and knocked him unconscious.

'Is that what you and Henry were laughing at?'

'No, he'd been telling me how his plants were killed off. It appears that orchid merchants have a deadly formula. I made him see the funny side of it, that was all.'

'What do they do?'

'Pee on the enemy's plants.'

She was stunned; then she started laughing. She couldn't restrain herself.

'How disgraceful!' she gasped.

'Now you know.'

They leaned on each other, shaking helplessly. The knot in her stomach dissolved. They were still laughing when Henry returned. She had to pretend it was about something else.

The higher planes were as far off as ever. It was Mrs Squale who reaped the benefit from the Leuchars family, anxious for more private sittings. They weren't interested in Morgan. Why should they be?

Determined to try everything, he made inquiries about Marshall, the American railway proprietor who had been at the seance, and found he was still in London. He also learned that the *Chicago Daily News* had an office off Trafalgar Square and kept a file of back numbers.

Walter Marshall was staying at the Cavendish Hotel. He received Morgan with surprise and said he could give him five minutes. He remained bent over cables and letters.

'I am a protégé of Mrs Squale,' said Morgan.

'A formidable lady,' said Marshall, and wrote several noughts in a margin. 'As to whether we saw what we thought we saw . . .' His spectacles flashed and he rubbed his cheek; it sounded like sandpaper. 'I was brought up in New York State. My late mother was a keen spiritualist.' He crossed out one of the noughts. 'She met the Fox sisters more than once – went on believing in them after they were discredited. We have some clever mediums in the United States. But your Mrs Squale . . . one could feel the power.'

'Exactly,' said Morgan, and explained how hard it was for a young psychic to start on his own, in the shadow of an established medium who might be envious of his success. 'Take the phenomena you witnessed,' he said. 'I don't wish to detract from Mrs Squale's undoubted gifts. But if I hadn't been present, things would have been different.'

'You mean it was you, not her?'

'I believe I have certain gifts.'

'Then time will prove it, young man.' He crumpled telegrams and dropped them in a basket. 'Either way, you don't need me.'

'I wouldn't be here if I didn't.'

'You won't get a cent from me.'

'I don't charge fees. I'm inviting you and your lady to a sitting.'

'Why us?', and the fountain pen scrawled an angry dollar-sign.

'You're American. You're influential. I live behind bars, like most people without resources. Chance, Mr Marshall. You were at Lord Leuchars'.'

'You'll waste my time.'

'One hour.'

The American put down his pen and regarded Morgan. 'Tell me the truth. Was it genuine? That materialisation?'

'No,' said Morgan.

'Clever, all the same.' He started writing again. 'Very well. You've got your hour.'

A Saturday afternoon was the only available date; the Monday after, the Marshalls were sailing for New York. 'Thank you, God,' Morgan said, out of habit, Margaret already having told him, when they had their picnic in Richmond Park, that she and Henry were going to spend the weekend with the family at Gaddesden.

Now all he had to do was talk her into letting him stay there. 'You see, Maggs,' he said, 'everyone needs a change of scenery.'

'Why not go to Wales? I keep telling them you will.'

'Some change, that would be. Mamma weeping, Dadda growling, half the town peeping through their net-curtains to see if I've grown horns in my head. I will go, eventually. But I know hypocrisy from the inside, remember. The fallen sinner has to be careful about returning. If he isn't on crutches or starving, it may look as if he's cheated the righteous by surviving the divine wrath.'

'They're your parents.'

'And I'm your brother. Just a couple of days – read books by a roaring fire, hear the dawn chorus on Hampstead Heath' ('You'll have to stretch your legs for that,' she said), 'ponder imponderables.'

She gave in; she wasn't his keeper. 'You will behave yourself, won't you? No table-rapping?'

'Now, Maggs, would I? By the way, will you tell Henry I'm sorry the orders for orchids are slow coming through. I'll take a dozen for myself when I come to stay – you choose them for me. A nice mixed bag.'

Morgan had money, twenty pounds in banknotes, crackling against his shirt. It was a loan from Cordelia, who believed him when he said his married sister was in a distressing financial state. Or perhaps she didn't believe him, merely let him have it because she was fond of him.

At the *Chicago Daily News*, he managed to see the newspaper's London correspondent by pretending to be a journalist from Wales, and heard some useful gossip about Marshall, especially about money and marriages. Marshall's first wife had died in a street accident. In spiritualism, tragedy never came amiss.

The afternoon was an experiment. Nothing elaborate, thought Morgan. He was embarking on a career. He guessed that cosy fireside chats with the spirits would turn out to be as useful as the apparatus in Squaley's locked cupboards. In the end they all relied on their wits. He couldn't help hankering after unearthly draughts and a few spirit-lights to help with the atmosphere, but that was weakness. His instinct told him to be simple.

'I can promise nothing,' he told them when they arrived, and hoped he had sufficient wits to rely on.

The second Mrs Marshall kept her furs and said she was charmed with the house, which must have been several sizes smaller than she was expecting. Morgan had filled the hall and drawing room with orchids. 'And these young ladies,' he said, 'are lifelong spiritualists' – it was Poppy and a respectable friend, brought in to make up the numbers.

Lake had been given the afternoon off, to get her out of the way. A butler, hired by the hour from Murchison's Domestic Agency, brought tea and drew the curtains. Morgan moved a card table to the middle of the room and arranged five upright chairs. That was all. He asked the Marshalls to sit either side of him, where they could hold his hands. Poppy turned out the gas, and they sat in a glow of light from the fire, burning low and red.

He had no idea what to expect. He had to have faith in himself. He sat quietly, eyes closed, trying not to think. Words came to him. 'There is a spirit here . . .' he said. 'Her name is Catherine. Handsome features. A determined manner.'

'Your first wife was named Catherine,' said Mrs Marshall.

'She says you are still impetuous in your business affairs. Be less impetuous, she advises . . .'

It wasn't difficult to embroider his facts. If he was hesitant, it was because he had to strain to catch what the voices were saying. Wasn't there a beloved parent no longer in the body? (likely enough). Here was a name beginning with 'J' (as so many did). There was a relative with weak lungs or possibly stomach (fairly comprehensive). Marshall gave him no help, but a grunt or a movement told him when he was on the right track. Morgan began to relax. He said the power of Marshall's business rivals was on the wane.

'This is poor stuff, Mr Buckley,' the American said suddenly.

'The voices beg your pardon, I'm sure.'

The interruption threw Morgan off his stride. He felt for a strut of the table with his toe. 'The voices are confused. I hear Catherine. All will be well, she says.'

In the failing redness from the fire, Poppy's features were like a mask. Morgan felt unusually tired; remote from everyone. 'She says there is no more pain. The little imp is happy.'

Marshall's hand tightened on his. 'What was that?'

He could have sworn he heard a woman scream. A coal fell in the grate, a flame sprang up, and instead of Poppy facing him across the table, it was Miss Rees. Words seemed to condense on his tongue. 'In prison,' he heard himself say. 'My child is very ill. In the prison.'

He must have kicked the table over. It fell with a crash. Poppy and friend were sobbing. Marshall stumbled to the window and dragged the curtains apart. His wife said, 'Is the farce at an end?'

'What happened?' said Morgan.

Marshall stood rubbing his cheek, and again there was the sandpapery noise. He put his hands on his wife's shoulders. 'Catherine was carrying our child when she was killed. We had a secret name for it, as people do.'

'I told you not to come here,' she said.

'Don't you understand? We called it Little Imp. In private, the two of us.'

'It brings nothing but unhappiness, Walt.'

Her husband wasn't listening. 'What was the prison and the child?' he asked Morgan.

'Something else. Not meant for you.'

'How could you have found out?' said Marshall. 'Damned clever. Or damned something else. I want you to keep in touch. This address will find me.'

Morgan took the card. He was trying to work out if he could be in South Wales that night. In the hall the butler stood with Marshall's hat and gloves, looking ironical.

There was a commotion on the steps outside. The door opened, and Margaret appeared. Henry was on her heels. He nearly fell over her when she stopped.

'Good afternoon, Madam,' said the butler. 'Who shall I say it is?'

'Morgan, you devil!' she cried, but he pushed her into the dining room and kicked the door shut. Henry could be heard announcing that he protested most strongly.

'Miss Rees's child,' said Morgan.

'You promised me. There has been vexation enough over Esther, and now I come back to *this*.'

'The child,' said Morgan. 'Of what sex was it? The child, Maggs, *my* child.'

He frightened her. A girl, she told him. He collected his coat and hurried from the house, passing the butler, who stood implacably in the hall, asking Madam how many there would be for dinner.

The concentrated green of early summer at Rhydness soaked into the landscape, leaving the farmhouse darker and stonier than ever. Cloud-shadows, roaring up the valley, alternated with streaks of brassy sun, making the narrow rooms dark one minute, bright the next. The past was concentrated in them, a scoured pan, the bronze clasp of the Bible, the white of Hannah's hair; memories catching the light.

'Since you're here,' she said, 'you can take me to Bethania at eleven.'

'I can't. I have urgent business. Work of the spirit, you might say.'

'Pride, that's been your trouble always. Thought you could do what you liked. But God is not mocked.'

'You're right, Nain. You're always right.' She was carved into her chair, unchanged; the same soft coal hissed in the grate, under the same chipped kettle. 'I came down on the mail, and you are the first I've come to see.'

'Now you've seen me.'

'I did a terrible thing. I expect you know. It was the night I took your money to the bank. I had the Revival in my blood. It was like a fever . . .'

'If you were telling me properly,' she broke in, 'you would be down on your knees. That's what wicked boys do.'

The stone floor was painful and not very clean.

'. . . had seen the great Roberts. My heart was breaking.' He was in the pitiful streets at New Dock. A boy with a firewood dagger was dancing under a lamp. 'I led the young people. A woman called Miss Aeronwy Rees . . .'

It had happened too long ago to matter. But it was part of Hannah's entitlement to know. At Rhydness, the wicked boy was at home. He smelt the soot in the chimney and the sour milk from the dairy gutters. '. . . and her voice was like the serpent's. I lay with her in the store room behind the annealing shed. Then I fled from God's wrath.'

'Not to mention your Dadda's. And what have you been doing since?'

'I've taken up with some religious people.'

'Not Church of England I hope?'

'Dissenters, through and through.'

'God forgives in the end. But not till he's convinced.'

'What about you?'

'Me? I'm too soft with you, that's my trouble.'

Morgan dusted his knees and sprinkled coal on the fire. The minutes were ticking away. But he had to be patient, to pretend that his life ran at the same speed as the old woman's.

Putting his hand in the niche by the hearth where Grandfather used to keep his gunpowder, he felt for the smooth, square lump of blackened oak, the first toy he remembered. Marks on one of its surfaces resembled windows and a door.

'I could play with it but never keep it.'

'I found it the day I was eleven.'

'On Pendine sands. Your mother told you it was driftwood. You said the sea had left it there for you to find. You brought it home in a handkerchief.'

'Burn it when I'm gone,' she said.

'Stay a month, shall I?' he said, pretending he was the *parch* of a chapel in a posh London suburb. 'Eat that crusty bread of yours.'

'I don't bake these days.'

'Drink some of your elderberry.'

'All gone.'

'I have to find Miss Rees. Will you tell me where she is?'

'Don't be a fool. What's done is done. You could have stayed and married the creature. You chose not to. Leave it at that. If you won't take me to chapel, the least you can do is read a passage.'

He did as she wanted, on edge now, and asked her again about Miss Rees. Her lips tightened on the gums. 'Please,' he said, and stooped to put his cheek against hers. She smelt of sweat and old age. He began to rock the chair. 'Please, *cariad*, I trust you beyond everyone.'

'Then do as I say. I never liked that family.'

'I had a dream,' he declared, and rocked the chair harder. 'Or a vision. It said my daughter was ill.'

'Visions now, is it? Stop what you're doing.'

'Is Miss Rees in prison?'

'Not that I've heard,' she gasped. 'For your own good, it is. Now stop this minute!'

He had to make her understand. 'I've only got you I can trust,' he said, arm and chair moving fast.

'Stop, stop, stop!' she cried, bouncing like a doll.

'Nobody else, Nain,' and he swung the chair with such violence that if he hadn't thrust his arm across her chest, she would have shot into the grate.

Bending over her, he stroked her hair. 'You must know. You know everything.' A trickle of saliva ran down her chin. 'I'm desperate, Nain. I was told it for a reason. God or the Devil, I don't care.'

'You are a wicked boy,' she groaned, but it was over. He wiped her chin and straightened her shawl. It was Rees Coal's house in the middle of nowhere. Miss Rees lived there with Isabel.

Morgan shaved with his grandfather's razor and rummaged in cupboards where nothing had been thrown away for decades. A mildewed silk hat, an ebony cane and a Gladstone bag were adequate for what he had in mind. Outside, Hywel had the trap ready. 'A long drive,' said Morgan, and as they followed the lane down the back of the hill, he glimpsed the dark mass of their destination, like rubble on the horizon to the north.

He had no time for Wales. The ping of chapel bells, the hurrying worshippers at the roadside, were useless attempts to win him back. He was haunted by old speculations about what was meant to happen. *My child is ill* drove him on like Hywel's stick drove the pony. How could anyone avoid the events that lay within him?

Starlings whistled from the edge of a wood and he

whistled back at them. There was nothing to fear, not even from a naked Eve with apple-juice on her thighs, ill-met in a tinworks. What he had lost was innocence, and with innocence, fear.

Hywel and the trap had to be left half a mile away, under a cluster of elms. Chimneys were visible, their smoke curling. Morgan went across fields to approach The Mount from behind. The grounds lay empty, Sunday-afternoonish, sleeked by wind.

To emerge by the outbuildings meant crossing a strip of bare hillside. A stream ran through the peaty earth, visible, much higher, as a white thread down a rock-face.

The wilderness ran up to the sky. How did people manage without London? High over the cliff a bird was circling, as it had done years before.

Through a fence, past a heap of ashes and a kitchen garden with magpies busy, and he rounded the stables and arrived in the yard.

Everything had to happen quickly, fist on door, frightened-looking skivvy, 'I'm the doctor,' hesitation, 'The sick child, *now*,' entry, bare flagstones, 'This way, sir,' a passageway, a cellar door, the skivvy faltering, 'Down here?' 'Please sir, wait sir,' 'Get out of my way' –

Then the housekeeper, or some such, a plump woman with a hand-print on one cheek where she had been dozing in a chair.

'What doctor?' she said. 'No doctor has been sent for.'

'More's the pity for your master. Fetch him here.'

In his hurry to push past, he forgot his tall hat; the lintel knocked it sideways. He clattered down whitewashed steps, the house stirring around him.

If he was lucky he had two minutes to see whether the voice had been telling the truth.

Miss Rees put her hand to her mouth when she saw him. She was real enough. So was the cradle she was sitting beside. She was a thinner, less complicated Miss Rees. The bosom and soft neck of his memory were concealed by what looked like calico and could be presumed not to exist any more. The cradle contained a fringe of dark hair and some rags.

'I'm sorry,' he said, and she stared at him and through him. 'I had a message that the child was ill.'

'You?' she whispered.

'We can resume our acquaintance later. What's wrong with her?'

'The poor lamb.'

There was no life in Miss Rees. The eyes were sunk in the face. Morgan peered into the cradle. Isabel's red cheeks looked healthy enough. He touched the head with his fingers. It was on fire.

'Her chest,' the woman murmured.

'Chest, I see.' He didn't like the sound of chest. He heard the breathing then, hard and irregular.

A door slammed and there was shouting. 'Does your uncle keep you here?'

He could hardly catch what she was saying – 'Lucky to have a roof,' it sounded like.

'Is your mother here?'

'Joint Counties' – whatever that meant.

Already Morgan felt the room's cold clamminess on his skin. Its walls were whitewashed, lit by two candles. Miss Rees had bruises on her bare forearm. He was grateful for the bruises.

'Does he abuse you?' (Someone had reached the door above.)

'Does he take advantage of you?' (The person was on the steps.)

She shuddered and bit her knuckle and nearly spoke. He knew what had been happening. It wasn't evidence for the magistrates, but the magistrates were a weapon he could use.

Rees Coal was raving at him. Morgan said, 'I want my daughter and her mother moved to a room with a fire. I want a doctor called.'

'You brazen monkey. They're sending for the p'lice.'

'I hope for your sake they're not. You've kept her a prisoner. This is the prison.'

Morgan unclasped the bag and tipped out half a bottle of brandy and a child's christening robe, more treasures from Rhydness. He wetted the woman's lips.

'I'll send for yer Pa.'

'While you're doing that, I'll find a magistrate.'

'Y'er a fine one, *Mister* Buckley. It was you ravished her.'

'Remiss of me, no doubt. But not a criminal offence.' He put the robe over Isabel because Miss Rees showed no sign of doing so. 'Think about criminal offences. There was an ironmonger in my part of London, excessively fond of his niece, came up before the beak last year. Twelve months with hard labour he got. That would kill a man of your age.'

'I been good to her,' panted Albert. 'Her and her Ma. Who'd have took 'em in? Not a penny you ever sent. Yer Pa and I did the necessary. I s'pose I get no credit for that. There's plenty of women lose their virtue and find 'emselves cast out like rubbish.'

'I know your sort,' said Morgan, 'only I'm not sure if you know mine. Get them up to the kitchen while the room's being prepared.'

'I'll 'ave the law on you,' snarled the old man. But he retreated up the steps on his thin shanks. 'I got testimonials from ministers of the Gospel from Brecon to St David's,' echoed down.

'And arrange for me to have a room near to theirs,'

Morgan shouted. 'I shall stay until they're well enough to leave.'

It was unthinkable that he should have been told about his child, if the child wasn't meant to live.

The doctor who came from Llandovery said he didn't like the chest. He meant pneumonia. The room with its fire and medicines and a brawny young nurse called Mrs Harry, a miner's widow, who slept on her own iron cot – they had all been conjured up for a purpose.

In the middle of the night he woke suddenly, tormented to think the purpose might be that he should witness his daughter's death. The fumes of camphor and wintergreen sickened him when he went in. The child's cough was harder and rougher. Miss Rees and the nurse were talking in whispers. Behind the door the christening robe hung like a shroud.

He longed for the cruel sanity of London, where even the spirits were straightforward compared with the ancient evils that lay in wait here.

Next day Rees Coal took him aside, half wheedling, half threatening, and said the child was a child of sin. If it died, wasn't that God's way?

No wonder they said madness was rife in country districts.

Mrs Harry said the crisis would come that night. She was pessimistic. Her patient was worn out, indifferent. 'She won't have the child in her bed, and the child knows it. She was asking me for her own mother last night, but I'm told the poor thing is in the madhouse.'

Morgan learned what the Joint Counties was, the lunatic asylum in Carmarthen. Mrs Rees had been there for the best part of a year.

Morgan went to Carmarthen. He was meant to save the child; to go to any lengths. It was a mart day. The town was full of farmers in stained gaiters. He bought himself a clerical collar, walked round to the asylum, and waited in the yard while they went for the medical superintendent.

A line of women shuffled out of one building and into another. They wore blue-black smocks, with peeling stockings and incongruously polished boots. The last of them lagged behind, and a female attendant flicked her on the thigh with a bunch of keys.

Morgan passed himself off as a relative, and his dog-collar got him past the regulations, as he knew it would. But it was hopeless. Mrs Rees, curled up on a dirty mattress, sucked her thumb and stared at him.

'A bad case,' said the superintendent, a thin tube of a man called Jones. 'She had an immoral daughter. But you'll have heard the story.'

On the way out, he insisted that Morgan look in on another bad case, a fellow minister. 'Mad as a hatter,' he said. 'But the sight of a clergyman invariably has a calming influence.'

A male attendant was called to open a barred door.

Inside was Mr Wimmer, late of Blaen Cwm Theological College, in a strait-jacket. He sat on a heap of straw, his back to a wall draped with blankets, naked except for vest and underpants.

He recognised Morgan at once. 'Thank heavens!' he said. 'Now I can proclaim the Lord.'

He struggled to his feet and turned away. 'There,' he said, wriggling his shoulders, 'the tapes are at the back of this contraption. Untie them and we can go. Come along, they are expecting me at your sister's wedding. In the hand of the Lord, there is a cup, and the wine is red. I shall say to them: The Revival is upon us.'

'Funny, you seem to have excited him,' said Jones. 'The Revival, of course, is what destroyed his mind. These hysterical movements have a lot to answer for, if you'll pardon my saying so.'

'I have said so myself.'

Mr Wimmer, when he realised he was not going to be released, jerked his head at Morgan and shouted, 'If nobody will denounce this man, then I will! He is an imposter. He is unclean. He has committed fornication.'

'That's enough of that,' said Jones, and the attendant picked up Mr Wimmer and dropped him on the straw.

At The Mount that night, Morgan felt the horrors crowding in. He had no allies, apart from Mrs Harry, and she was resigned to the worst. She said the doctor had been there during the day, and left shaking his head.

Morgan took off his boots and lay on the bed beside Miss Rees. He talked to her about her mother – 'I saw her today,' he said. 'She was much better. They'll let her come home soon. She said that if you were to keep hold of Isabel all night, sitting up in bed, you could save her.'

At first he made no impression. Then he tried stroking her hair while he talked. It was the first time he had touched her. He was there to save a child, not a woman.

She turned to look at him. The dark eyelashes seemed to belong to a different face. She smelt of milk – they had been pouring it into her all day, at the doctor's instruction. 'Will you stay here, too?' she said timidly.

'If you wish.'

He told Mrs Harry to let her have Isabel. The nurse brought a pan of warm water and a pile of cloths. Isabel's breath wheezed faintly.

'Well,' said Miss Rees, 'what a poor little bundle you are.' She wiped the child's face and gave her a sip of barley water.

The future was never as you expected.

Mrs Harry, sensing a change, busied herself with kettles and steam and swabs and cordials. But it was Miss Rees who held the child, soothing it and whispering, hour after hour.

Morgan slept, woke and slept again. In each state he imagined himself in the other. He dreamt he was stroking the woman's hair; Mrs Harry brought him a cup of tea, and he realised he was awake. He dreamt the breathing had stopped. It was too real for a dream. Miss Rees said, 'She was dead to begin with. Fancy you couldn't tell. I had her stuffed with Mr Wimmer's straw.'

He woke in terror. Grey dawn-light filtered in. Mrs Harry, paper curlers in her hair, was seeing to the fire. The child was still in Miss Rees's arms. Its forehead was cool.

He could think about going back to London.

In Swansea that morning he inquired about lodgings for a woman and child, found rooms in a genteel house in Brynmill Terrace – he guessed she would want the anonymity of a big town – and telegraphed to Squaley for another thirty pounds.

When he returned to The Mount, Mrs Harry was bathing Isabel. Morgan saw the forked shape of his daughter upside down, the sexual parts raw-red, before she dabbed on the powder. 'Here we are, hold her if you like,' she said, and for a moment he did.

A week later, mother and child were well enough to leave. Morgan, who had been back to London in the meantime, leaving Mrs Harry in charge of the sickroom, collected them in a carriage. Rees Coal sulked and watched from a window as they left. The nurse came with them.

By the afternoon Miss Rees was mistress of four rooms and a view of a park.

She was more as he remembered her now; that was a good reason not to stay a minute longer than necessary.

He had told her the truth about her mother, and she said she would visit her.

'Am I safe here?' she asked him.

'The rooms are paid for. Mrs Harry will stay as long as

you like. You have a Post Office savings book. I shall come to see Isabel once a quarter.'

'You've not given me your address.'

'I'll give you my sister Margaret's. I go from place to place.'

'One day, can I bring her to London?'

'One day, I expect.'

She kissed him eagerly. Isabel beamed at him from under her black fringe, and Mrs Harry, who joined in the goodbyes, said, 'She knows you already, sir.'

Before leaving Wales he paid a brief visit to Mamma, when he knew the men would be at the works.

She was in her sitting room with a glass of something. After a while he calmed her down, telling her about Isabel and how she and Miss Rees were safe in Swansea.

When he was going, he sat her on a chest of drawers to make her smile. But she looked at him sadly and said, 'Oh, Morgan! You have broken your dear father's heart.'

When he asked for her forgiveness, she gave it, without hesitation. 'So will you come back now?' she said.

'No, not ever.'

Leaving Y Plas, he didn't even glance across the salt-marsh to the works.

9

Cordelia Squale said, 'You're a wicked man, do you know that, but I forgive you,' when Morgan told her about the young Welshwoman and the child. He left out sordid details like religion and Rees Coal. As he described the affair, it was a youthful escapade for which he had decided to make amends. Nor did he say anything to her about the voice that told him to go there. He didn't want her to know how sure he was of his powers.

A telegram came from Margaret: 'IMPERATIVE WE MEET AT ONCE.' But he knew her Morgan-hating moods. He didn't reply. Behind the scenes he was busy.

Cordelia thought they might try levitation. 'Hardly anyone does it nowadays,' she said. 'You can practise it ready for the autumn, when Lord and Lady Leuchars come back from abroad. I have high hopes of our Leuchars connection.'

In summer, London seances were at a low ebb. People were in the country or at the seaside. Morgan, planning his future in secret, read books about D. D. Home. He was the medium who convinced kings and journalists. Cordelia said he was a sickly little man, attractive to women. She saw him once, when she was a child; blue lights flashed around him while he held an accordion with one hand under the table, and it played 'Home, Sweet Home'; she thought he smelt of chemicals.

Dead, now, for a quarter of a century, he was never detected in fraud. His tricks, if they were tricks, were of the highest quality. Curtains billowed, furniture danced, birds sang, shadowy figures rose up. The head of a dead infant was laid in a woman's lap. Once, a tiny hand appeared, holding a pen; it wrote, 'Dear Papa, I have done my best.' Home caressed red-hot coals and put them on people's heads.

Morgan devoured the accounts, lying in the sun on Putney Common. Another telegram came from Margaret. This one said, 'YOUR BEHAVIOUR OUTRAGEOUS. KINDLY ACKNOWLEDGE. REPLY PREPAID.' Morgan replied, 'WELL BUT TIED UP. REMEMBER ME TO HENRY,' and went out on the common to read more about the great Home.

If they were tricks, why was he never caught? He could lengthen his body by nine inches; respectable Victorians, anxious to believe, crawled about with tape measures as he grew and shrank to order. Most marvellous of all, he could levitate. One night at a fashionable address he sailed out of a window, stiff as a board, and sailed in at another, watched by two noblemen. He floated across a Hampshire lawn in a rainstorm and returned to the house bone-dry, carrying a rhododendron.

Who could tell what the truth was? It suited Morgan not to be sure. A convenient fog of uncertainty clung to them all, D. D. Home and Cordelia Squale and now Morgan Buckley. If spirits walked, well and good. If messages arrived, like the one about his daughter, one could act accordingly. In the meantime, spiritualism being a business like any other, one took steps to ensure success.

Without letting the Squales know, he went down to Kent to visit Major Thorn, the one who thought he saw his dead sister at the Charles Street seance. Thorn was suspicious; no doubt remembering a gawky Celt, not this smart young fellow who claimed to be receiving messages of his own from the dead Bella. But Morgan had been studying newspaper files of thirty years before, finding scraps of family information. He slipped them into the messages, and the Major became attentive.

The vision at Charles Street had disoriented Thorn; that was the secret of a medium's success, Morgan was sure. At the time the Major spoke only of seeing something. Now he was positive he had heard something as well. He remembered a whispered 'Goodbye, goodbye,' as she faded from sight. He told Morgan it was irritating that Mrs Thorn refused to remember that she had heard it, too.

Emily Thorn was a purposeful woman with the same clay-baked skin as her husband. Did she want to protect him from what she feared were charlatans?

In case she did, Morgan cultivated her. If he was to be a famous medium, he had to perform among friends, not enemies. Daniel Home was fussy about the guests at his seances. The Thorns' money was on Emily's side of the family, where the bankers were, and she was tight-fisted. So it was politic to let it be known that under no circumstances would he, Morgan Buckley, ever take a farthing for his mediumship. That, he hinted, was the reason he might be leaving Mrs Squale's household to begin his own career.

The Thorns had friends who took a sympathetic interest in the spirit world. A professor of mathematics and a solicitor came to Morgan's first seance at Grubb End, the Thorn house. Lights were seen and there was table-rapping. Spirits were present in force. By luck or good judgement, Morgan gave messages into which his sitters read themselves and their loved ones. In due course, the solicitor held a seance of his own.

Morgan remained cautious with his phenomena. He liked simple things. After insisting that partners on either side secure his hands on the table, he could confuse them into holding one another so that he was free to toss an orchid into a woman's lap, or do things with extending rods. The solicitor was followed by a retired stockbroker. The stockbroker begat a publisher. The publisher begat a man who had held high office at the Board of Trade. The former official begat a Member of Parliament called Booley.

Soon Mrs Thorn was saying, 'You must stay with us. You are becoming quite a celebrity in our part of the world,' and Morgan had to pretend to the Squales that he was on holiday with his sister.

In Booley's honour, Morgan unveiled his first great effect, a levitation. Cordelia had talked of importing an American contraption of springs and rods to hold the medium aloft, but that was too elaborate to be safe. Morgan did it with no apparatus at all. He rose towards the ceiling in a room with a faint, very faint, red light on a table. People touched his shoes and his trouser legs as he floated near the table. The shoes were on his hands, and his arms were encased in tubes of trouser-like material. His head was thrown well back. 'I am rising,' he moaned, as though airborne against his will, 'rising . . . rising . . .'

Since money seemed no object at the Thorns', or at any of the houses where he performed, Morgan saw an opportunity for Henry and the orchid business. He told Major Thorn that orchids had a spiritual quality. Orders began to go off to West Hampstead, and boxes arrived, express delivery.

Now that his address was known again, he was not surprised, soon after, to receive an invitation to dinner from Mrs Stuart Penbury-Holt. Morgan had a vague memory of a pretty woman called Virginia, and accepted at once. He expected Margaret would be there. He was right.

'We are all family tonight,' said Virginia, while he was still in the hall, having his hat taken, 'so we can excuse you and Margaret for ten minutes. I believe she has something she wishes to discuss with you. Stuart's study is empty. I have left a decanter of sherry there.'

Margaret's face had a fine, glossy flush. He went to kiss her, but she held him off with the decanter.

'I owe you an apology,' he said. 'I hope you can forgive me for using your house for a seance. I'm not my own master yet, you see. I have to make shift as best I can. It was your drawing room or nowhere.'

'You know perfectly well that we have a more serious matter than that to talk about. Don't wear your puzzled look. I see right through you, Morgan. You have dumped that wretched woman and her child in some lodging house and left her there – alone, in a strange town. What do you have to say?'

'Dear old Maggs,' he said, 'you always have it in for me. She has a nurse and she has money. I don't know what garbled version you've heard from Y Plas.'

He saw there was nothing he could do about it, though. He was the black sheep; it was the way Margaret thought of him. Her affection lay precisely within the limits of his black-sheepiness.

As to *why* he had decided to take Miss Rees from her uncle's house, he amused himself by telling his sister the truth.

'You heard a *voice*?' she said.

'Yes, and I obeyed it, and I found Isabel seriously ill. So I concluded it must have been a supernatural voice. Or at the very least, telepathy. Wouldn't you?'

She said she had heard enough wicked nonsense for one day, and would he kindly give her Miss Rees's address.

'If you'll give me a kiss to show I'm forgiven.'

'The address, Morgan, please.'

'The kiss, Margaret, please.'

She pecked his cheek and snatched the piece of paper. 'You might be interested to know,' said Morgan, as they left the study, 'that I gave a seance for a Member of Parliament recently.'

'No wonder people ask what the country is coming to.'

Esther had been invited as his partner, but at the last

minute Miss Wilkinson came as well. 'We call her the Captain's daughter,' whispered Virginia. 'She is Esther's friend. You will have to take them both in to supper. Do you think you can manage?'

Sitting next to Esther, he asked what it was like in Holloway.

'Extremely unpleasant. I was not forcibly fed when I went on hunger strike – people always want to know, so I tell them in advance. I was discharged after five days. The Government was having one of its periodic outbreaks of cold feet.'

'And is the moral satisfaction of going to prison for a cause as great as one hears?'

'I take it you don't approve of female emancipation.'

'I can't say I've studied the arguments.' He told her about Mr Booley, MP, who thought feminism a dagger at the heart of the Empire. 'Show me a woman who can bear arms like a Man! – and defend her Country! – and I'll give her the vote tomorrow!' he said, mimicking the MP.

'And you are prepared to follow that specious line of thought?'

'I know nothing about politics.'

'We all lead political lives, like it or not.'

His hostess, on the other side, interrupted to ask whether he knew many Members of Parliament.

'No, Booley was at one of my seances,' said Morgan, and saw Margaret glaring at him. 'He wasn't there officially, of course. Mediums are used to it. Many well-known figures conceal their interest in spiritualism.'

'Who, for instance?' asked the host, Stuart Penbury-Holt, from the other end of the table.

'Editors. Clergymen. Barristers. Heads of industry.'

'You mean you don't know their names?'

'I mean I know them in confidence.'

'You give seances?' said Virginia, hunching her naked

shoulders, large and white in the candle flames. 'You are a medium? Heavens, what fun. Why have you kept it quiet, Margaret?'

'Should I have made an announcement? *My brother has gone in for the spirits. Reasonable rates.*'

'I charge nothing, Maggs.'

'But what happens?' asked Stuart. He had a blond moustache and was better looking than Henry; and his eyes were sharper. 'Do they still have voices coming through trumpets?'

'There are phenomena, sometimes.'

'You sit there in the dark, and events take place because of you? Could we do it here? Extinguish the candles? Hear chains rattling and suchlike?'

'It would depend on your attitude of mind.'

'Do you remember the ghost of Old Saracens, Henry? Down by the lake on a misty night with a moon? The Mother was terrified.'

'It turned out to be a swan,' said Esther.

'Ah, but was it?'

'Stop teasing Mr Buckley,' she said.

'No, I'm fascinated,' said Virginia. 'I think ghost stories are the best of all. If I saw a ghost, I would try and talk to it.'

'I would take a little revolver and shoot it,' murmured Stuart.

'But Mr Buckley is a Celt,' said Esther. 'They have a different view of these things. We poor Anglo-Saxons conquer the world, not the soul.'

Morgan had to smile at the English, determined to be urbane about matters they didn't understand, waiting for him to do something odd and Welsh.

When Virginia, rosy and mischievous, asked him for his most thrilling experience, he didn't hesitate. Under the right conditions, he said, he was able to levitate.

'Levitate?'

'I float. Above the ground.'

'Like a balloon?' said Stuart. 'Most useful.'

Morgan went on staring at Virginia, willing her to believe him. In a perfect world he would produce all his phenomena for women. They were the mysteries who appreciated mystery.

She looked transfixed. Because he had deceived Booleys and Thorns and the rest, it didn't mean that levitation by spirits was impossible. Lord Adare and the Master of Lindsay were with Daniel Home in a room on the third floor, eighty-five feet above the London street. A voice said in their ears, 'He will go out of one window and in at another.' It was nine days before Christmas, 1868. They saw him floating outside in the moonlight, standing upright and revolving slowly.

'Don't look so amazed. Levitation is nothing to the spirits.'

'Oh, I see.'

Virginia bit her lip. She began to laugh.

'Sorry,' she said, 'I can't help it.'

'I think it's Morgan is pulling our legs, rather than the other way round,' said Esther.

'Not at all. Levitation is an ancient art.'

Stuart wiggled his elbows and made a clucking noise. 'Do things fall out of one's pockets?' he inquired.

'What a shame you didn't float out of Holloway, Esther,' said the Captain's daughter.

'He *is* pulling our legs.'

He was silent, brooding, frowning at Margaret. He would let them hang themselves with their silliness.

In the drawing room later, Stuart and the Captain's daughter proposed a game with wine glass and alphabet.

Margaret objected, but Virginia said that no one need play if they didn't want to. Henry took Morgan aside and asked his advice. Was it a dangerous practice? Morgan said he thought that any self-respecting spirit would need more than a wine glass to draw it out.

Apart from Margaret, who sat apart on the sofa, they all joined the circle. Six finger-tips rested on the glass. Morgan relaxed, his eyes closed.

The glass moved briskly and spelt out 'ORCHIDS FOURPENCE EACH.'

'Stuart!' said his wife. 'You are pulling poor Henry's leg.'

'Wasn't me, I swear.'

'Is there anyone there?' demanded the Captain's daughter.

Meaningless letters followed, and then, all at once, the word 'HOLLOWAY.'

'Our spirit seems to have a warped sense of humour,' said Esther dryly, and at once the glass jerked again.

'C,' chanted Virginia, 'U, N, T.' Her eyes opened wide, and she whispered, 'Oh, golly!'

'This is monstrous,' said Henry, and scattered the letters.

Both the brothers had risen. 'I enjoy a joke as much as the next man,' said Stuart icily. 'But this has gone beyond the limits of decency. You will apologise to these ladies, Mr Buckley.'

'You'd better try asking the wine glass. I had my eyes closed.'

'It's true,' said Virginia. 'His eyes were tight shut all the time.'

Morgan left the table. The company couldn't have been more upset if a phantom had come through the wall. 'If people play games with the spirits,' he said, 'they must expect the spirits to play games with them. That's only fair.'

The french windows were open. He walked into the garden. Daylight had gone, but the suburban glow on the bellies of clouds enabled him to see a path, a rockery, a tree.

Someone was following. He felt Margaret like a wind down his neck, part love, part hate.

'I can't believe you capable of such vulgarity,' she said. 'But nor can I believe it of the others.'

'So we are all agreed. Blame the spirits.'

'You won't tell me the truth, will you?'

'That *is* the truth. I don't know what happened. Perhaps we all conspired to write a forbidden word without realising we were doing it. I have been reading about the subconscious. I feel at times I'm sailing out of my depth. That's why I need you, Maggs.'

'You need me so badly that when I send you telegrams, you ignore them. What is it you want, Morgan?'

'To make a name, at any cost. Now you know my last and most awful secret.'

She put her arm around his waist. Another quarrel was over. 'Shall we go for one of our outings soon?' she said.

'Why not? In September, while it's still warm.'

But as it turned out, there was too much to do. He was no sooner back with the Squales than Lord Leuchars returned from abroad, and within a week, the news of Morgan's seances in Kent had reached Cordelia.

'You are bound to us by contract,' said Squale. 'There are courts of law, you know.'

'You wouldn't risk the publicity.'

'Don't ruin yourself, dear,' said Cordelia. 'Ambition is a fine thing, but you still have a lot to learn. You and I, working together, will travel far. You've been lucky down in Kent. Let us consolidate the good work hand in hand.'

'In addition to which you owe myself and Mrs Squale the very large sum of one hundred and ninety pounds.'

In bed, Cordelia renewed her temptations. If he weakened once or twice, it was only because she worked on him with all the tenacity of a woman caught between youth and age, her lust flaring up.

He avoided the real traps. When she whispered questions about his levitation, he maddened her by saying she must ask the spirits.

Before the autumn, he was living with the Thorns at their town house in Clapham.

The news that Aeronwy Rees and child were respectably settled on the outskirts of Swansea was a relief to Will. She was neither a Princess Gwenllian nor a slut. The feverish dreams of his adolescence were over.

Rees Coal no longer offered him mission tickets or made favourable references to his character, no doubt because he thought that Will had had something to do with Morgan's visit. Will heard him once at Y Plas, muttering to Dadda about 'your boy Morgan and 'is lies,' but Dadda shut him up. Morgan was never mentioned at Y Plas if Buckley could help it. He was the fallen angel.

Will almost envied him. The trouble with being Will Buckley was that he had to conform or get out; every month that passed bound him more closely to the place. The dragon hadn't vanished, after all. Soon he himself would be part of that alien creature with furnace-light for eyes that inhabited the sea-marsh and preyed on men, its metals in his veins, its dust on his skin. When he spoke, it would roar. There was no escaping the fate that waited for the master's son. It was, and could only be, to be the master himself.

Flora Haycock was someone he thought about, that summer, but not as a mystery to brood on, like Aeronwy Rees.

The band didn't meet in August. Then the schools went back, and he looked in at Market Hall, hoping she would be there.

The room was empty. Flies buzzed inside the windows. A smell of stale fish from the market lingered. A coloured picture of Miss Lily Langtry, cut from a magazine, had been stuck on the wall; beneath it was written in neat capitals, 'WHAT A CORKER!'

Everything was hostile, the deserted room, the grimy corridors, the market benches outside with wilting cabbages and bowls of cockles. For all the prosperity of the works, and those shop windows full of bicycles, there was something in the air and stone of the town that defeated hope.

He made for the terrace where the Haycocks lived.

The same children with the same hoops dashed up and down the pavements. The parlour curtains were drawn, looking out of place in the daylight. But the front door was open. He could see through to the kitchen, and two women's heads, set close at the table.

'Oh, Mr Buckley!' called Mrs Haycock, and the heads came down the passage. 'This is my sister, Mrs Nolan. This is Mr Buckley, whose father owns a tinworks. He's the one who helps Flora with the band.'

Mrs Nolan was from Liverpool; a darker, severer version of her sister.

'I believe I never shook hands with a tinplate owner,' she said, and he felt a claw had nipped him.

The front-room door opened, and Haycock appeared in his shirt-sleeves. 'Thought I knew the voice,' he said. In the gloom, someone was rustling papers. 'Behind the enemy's walls, eh?' he added, smiling.

'I trust I won't be knocked on the head.'

'That only happens to dangerous characters. I suppose it isn't me you've come to see?' and a man coughed in the darkened room.

'Of course it isn't,' said Mrs Haycock. 'He's looking for Flora, aren't you?'

'I wondered where the band was.'

'Good day to you, then,' said Haycock, and the door closed again.

'She went down New Dock Terrace to see Mr Mokes's bad leg,' said his wife. 'Didn't even stop for her tea. Heart of gold, that girl.'

The address wasn't far from Bank Cottages, where his cousins lived. He could hear voices inside the house. He waited on the pavement, watching the women in doorways watching him.

A ragged child hopped up and asked for a halfpenny, but he refused; the street had too many ragged children.

She was surprised to see him. Why was he hanging about like a pickpocket instead of going inside? The working class wouldn't bite him.

'Poor Mr Mokes broke his leg last week,' she said. 'We have had to suspend the band classes.'

'But you mean to start one day?'

'We certainly do.'

They walked slowly down New Dock Terrace. Behind them a boy's voice piped, 'Kiss 'er, mister.'

She said, 'We have to seize every opportunity. Nothing's too small to be of use. They don't have long, these children. They are gone at thirteen, into your tinworks. If they carry with them some conception of a world beyond the work-place, the bedroom and the public house, then they stand a chance.'

He liked to hear her talk; he thought most of it was nonsense. Passing the end of Bank Cottages, he steered her towards Aunt Villette's, and insisted they look in. 'You can meet the young genius,' he said.

'I have no interest in young geniuses. The exceptions don't matter. They find their own feet, especially if they have rich relations. Which of our schools does the young man attend?'

'He has private tuition from his piano teacher.'

'Exactly.'

But she was friendly enough when they were inside. The kitchen was smaller than the Haycocks'; an iron bowl of jam was bubbling on the fire again, and the place reeked of it. Aunt Villette was the one who looked upset, glaring at Will, apologising for the state of things.

The men were at sea in the *Falcon*. Theodore lounged in a chair, watching the jam boil over and his mother rush to save it.

'Is Miss Haycock your lady friend?' he demanded.

'I think,' said Will, 'you should mind your own business.'

'The answer is no,' said Flora. 'I'm too busy to be a lady friend.'

Tea was prepared hastily, while Theodore was told to show Miss Haycock the grand piano. Its gleaming blackness filled the parlour. Theodore said it was a gift from his rich Uncle Davy, grinning malevolently, as though he knew he could cause trouble if he tried hard enough.

'You are very lucky,' Miss Haycock said grimly.

'He thinks I'm talented, which is kind of him, considering he knows so little about music himself. He's what my tutor calls . . .' and he rippled the keys with one finger '. . . a graduate of the university of life.'

'Miss Haycock is a schoolteacher.'

Theodore returned to the subject when they were in the kitchen. 'She's a teacher, Ma. She hasn't said what school.'

'New Dock. The poorest of the poor.'

'Aunt Pomona goes there to serve the charity breakfasts, doesn't she, Ma?'

'Do your parents know the Buckleys, Miss Haycock?' asked his mother.

'Good gracious, no. My father's a trade union official.'

'That must be interesting,' said Villette, and Theodore sucked jam off his fingers, looking pleased with himself.

Will saw the girl home. He wouldn't go in. The parlour

curtains were still drawn. They were both laughing about Theodore.

It didn't occur to him that news of the visit to Bank Cottages would reach Y Plas almost before he did. But Villette thought it her duty, and here was Mamma next day, weeping to her husband with the news that Will was 'walking out' with the daughter of Saul Haycock the Socialist.

Will explained about the band. He tried to laugh it off; a donation of cornets and a half-crown rent hardly counted as intimacy. Dadda was unmoved. What could his son have in common with a family of socialists.

The two spent half the evening in the library, down by the novels that no one ever read, unable to see one another's point of view. Somehow Will never got round to saying the obvious things, that of course *he* wasn't a socialist, that of course he would inherit the hundred and ten shares and do his duty. Accused of things that weren't true, he found himself arguing as if they were. The heat of the dispute distorted his views.

Next morning, a Saturday, he overslept, and was not downstairs until half past seven. Through the landing window, he could see his father walking to work on the marsh road, a blurred figure in the rain.

Mamma was in the dining room in her dressing-gown, red-eyed. She rarely appeared for breakfast nowadays. Will kissed her and she said, 'Neither your Dadda nor I slept a wink last night.'

'I mean to tell him I'm sorry.'

'I should hope so too.'

The post was on a tray, by the coffee pot. He glanced at it and saw a letter addressed to him in Flora Haycock's hand. Mamma was watching him. He picked it up and felt the crinkles at the back of the envelope, slightly damp.

'This has been steamed open,' he said, and Mamma gave a little shriek and said, 'As if anybody would!'

Miss Haycock wrote to say that on Sunday she was going to a ceremony at the Chartists' Cave in east Wales, and wondered if he would care to go with her. Her father, she wrote innocently – or perhaps not innocently at all – had mentioned that he was interested in Chartists.

He wouldn't have gone. What did he care about those forgotten revolutionaries? Besides, the weather looked like being nasty.

But the letter had been opened. He had been challenged. He had no option.

The Chartists' cave at the valley-head was no more than a hole in a low cliff, amid the remains of quarry workings where moorland tumbled down towards roofs and pitheads. A crowd of men straggled up in the rain that had been falling since before it was light. From railway station to cave was almost two miles. Bandsmen with capes billowing over their instruments slithered on the muddy paths, cursing their lack of balance. A man with a sack over his head, only lips and whiskers showing, blew a series of 'Ta-ra-ras!' on a silver cornet, but the sound lacked substance. Some of the younger lads had beer on their breath. In the mouth of the cave, far above, Will could see red spikes of fire.

He and Flora had met in the dark at Port Howard station and caught the first train to Cardiff, changing to a valley line that climbed northward through a landscape of pit-wheels. Her father had gone the day before to meet old acquaintances at Merthyr. She had been brought up there, in the town, now respectablised, that she said they still referred to jokingly as 'China' from its early days, at the start of the industrial revolution: an alien place, unlike anything seen before, a huddle of pits and foundries that sucked in men, crime and vice. So this other-world, the heart of the old Merthyr village, where police wouldn't go, became 'China'.

They still missed the town, she said, her father in particular. So why had he ever left? Because he felt obliged, she said. Because the tinplate men advertised for an official, and at a Workmen's Institute debate, someone happened to advance the argument that socialism would never thrive as long as socialists all stayed in one spot. They needed to be missionaries.

'Are you telling me Saul Haycock has come to convert Port Howard?'

'Well,' she said, her face turned sideways to the rainy window, half stern and half beautiful, 'it's true that Ken, my young brother, suffers from a bad chest in winter, and the doctor said sea air would cure him. So it was Port Howard all round.'

'In other words, it was the sea air was the *real* reason.'

'You must believe what you want to. Your class takes a cynical view of other people's idealism.'

Flora had been trying to educate him on the train, telling him more than he wanted to know about the Chartist gun clubs and debating societies of the eighteen-thirties, and their shadowy plans to seize power with a few bold strokes; the nearest thing to a revolution since the Civil War, she said.

As they approached the cave, he felt sorry for her sake that it wasn't a better turn-out. According to Flora, it was sixty-nine years since the march on Newport, when the colliers and iron workers were to launch their Silurian Republic and signal the uprising throughout Britain. She didn't dwell on the bit he knew already, that the revolutionaries looked down the soldiers' muskets and ran away.

They reached the fire; an old man was feeding it with railway sleepers. Banners between poles rested against the rock face, where a lean-to of tarpaulins and more sleepers gave shelter. Lights flickered inside the cave.

Saul Haycock moved from group to group. It was hard to tell if he was talking or listening. A hatless man, bald from the ears up, with a whippet on a rope, dug him in the ribs with two fingers. Haycock pointed at the sky, where damp rays of sun were breaking through.

Presently he came over to his daughter, brisk and businesslike. How was Kenneth's cough? He hoped she had put cardboard in her shoes against leaks. He was catching the 1.12 train.

Their guest, he said, should have been there the year before, when they had fine weather. Rain had a lot to do with the failure of '39. It always favoured the authorities, which had the means of keeping dry.

'So umbrellas for the working class would be a useful slogan,' said Will, and Haycock fingered his beard.

He took them inside the cave, which was lit with paraffin lamps. It slanted into the cliff, low-roofed, dripping with water.

Men were playing dominoes, watched by a scraggy figure on a wooden box who was, according to Haycock, the last survivor of the '39 insurrection. 'He doesn't remember much,' Haycock said, and shouted, 'You kept your weapons at the back there, didn't you, Grandad?'

'We trounced 'em,' said the old man. 'Ay, we did.'

'He thinks they won, you see,' said Haycock.

As they were going out, Will saw a black-gloved hand stretch to pick up a domino. It was Tommy Spit. To Will's relief, he didn't look up.

Outside, the band played a hymn and then what sounded like a republican song, with a chorus of 'Penderyn, Penderyn, where was you that day?'

The speeches that followed had to compete with wind and showers. Not everyone was listening. The high spot was the bald man with the dog, who spoke about the plight of the coal-miner in 1908, and said there were pit lodges not five miles from where they stood that would vote for a revolution tomorrow.

Saul Haycock confined himself to bringing fraternal greetings from the comrades in the west – a figment of his imagination, thought Will. Tommy Spit appeared briefly on the plank-and-boxes platform to say that the railwaymen would play their part in the industrial strife that lay ahead.

More hymns and ballads followed, sung with indiscriminate fervour. This time Flora joined in, her voice high and piercing.

A tricolour flag was hoisted on a pole; the wind turned it to striped tin. A shotgun was unwrapped from a piece of sacking. The bald miner held it aloft in both hands.

Everyone was silent. Will felt Flora's nudge, and took off his cloth cap just in time, like the rest of the men.

'The martyred dead and the lost generations!' shouted the miner, and the chorus of voices shouted it back at him like a multiple echo, 'The martyred dead and the lost generations!'

Far off, from the valley floor, came a murmur of engines and wagons. The gun, raised to the miner's shoulder, gave a hollow bang. Will heard the lead shot falling in the grass.

Shouting and stamping followed. One lot of voices cheered. Another chanted, 'The republic, the republic!' Unexpectedly, Flora slipped her hand into his. When she cheered, he cheered with her.

He hadn't meant to. But he was in enemy country.

An attempt was made to roast rabbits at the fire. Pieces of charred flesh were handed round, and there was evil-tasting cider in a barrel. The wise thing was to leave now. He had an opportunity when everyone crowded to the mouth of the cave, to drink a toast to the Chartist veteran.

He walked to a clump of bushes that men had been using for calls of nature, then hurried down the slope of the hill.

Someone came after him, slithering on grass. The first row of cottages was far below. Would he be any safer when he got there? This was a land of secret societies.

Unwilling to look round, he took a short cut over a ridge, and found himself standing above thirty feet of sheer rock.

When he turned, Flora was behind him. She was angry; she had mud on the hip of her skirt where she had slipped. Couldn't he have waited? Was it tactful to run off and invite questions about who he was?

'I thought we might have Tommy Spit on the train with us,' he said, and regained the path.

'Would he have bitten you? Or my father?'

'I don't know it's safe being seen with *you*, come to that,' he grinned. 'Not after what happened up there. Do they do it every year?'

'I suppose it offended you. You don't like to think they have such strong feelings.'

'I can go and see rugby at Stradey Park any Saturday if strong feelings are what I want.'

The wind carried the tang of chimney smoke. A pit wheel was spinning.

Flora's face had a clean, polished look, as if the skin had turned to bone. 'You came to laugh at us, didn't you?' she said.

'Not at all. I was curious.'

'Did you learn anything?'

She sounded eager; the teacher, wanting prizes for her pupil.

'That they might mean business, after all.'

The station was down the road. A train was approaching on a viaduct; its plume of steam twisted like a genie.

'I must go back for my father,' said Flora. 'Won't you wait for us here? It's only one train later than this.'

'Thank you, but I feel like a bit of comfort after that mountain. First-class ticket this time, I think.'

The waiting room, with its robotic urn and chipped marble, confirmed the wisdom of his decision. She stood with him on the platform, a blonde curl waggling under the edge of her beret.

'Give my regards to your father.' The train was clanking in. 'By the way, why did he want me to come?'

'Silly,' she said. 'I was the one who wanted it.' Her hand caught his shoulder and she kissed him on the mouth.

At Port Howard, lamps were lit along the platform. Rain was falling again, with a gale behind it.

At Y Plas, he learned that his father had gone to Cardiff with Colonel Mappowder to do some gentle lobbying for the presidency of the Fed. The Colonel was determined he should have it one day. Buckley used a wry smile and a shrug whenever the matter was raised, as a sign that he supposed he would have to go along with the idea. He was dining there, not returning until the morning.

Will telephoned the works to make sure there were no maintenance problems. The craftsmen had nearly finished; the Sunday night shift would begin on time.

'No need for you to come over, sir,' said Phillips.

'That's my decision.'

His mind was on Flora, not machinery. More than ever, he felt disturbed by her. Still, if he stayed at Y Plas, Mamma would emerge and be tearful. Time enough for rows when Dadda was back.

From the marsh path he saw spray coming over the dyke, and shouldered his way to it through the wind. The ground softened underfoot. Visible in the last traces of daylight, a half-moon of water lay inside the dyke.

He splashed through the pool; it reached his knee.

Clawing his way up the embankment, it was slimier than ever.

At the top he couldn't stand against the wind. The tide was still some way out. Spray blew off it like bits of glass. Sitting on the edge, he explored the angled stone face of the dyke with his heels, and found what might have been a rift in the stonework.

Billy Rod always said not to worry. Will told Phillips to get hold of him now, and cycled over to the Lloyds. Abraham, having supper, chewed kipper and listened. High tide was ten past nine, he said. The port was already shut for the night, anticipating the worst of the storm.

'Does it sound dangerous to you, Uncle Abraham?'

'Big springs, today and tomorrow. The gale behind could add a couple of feet, and keep it piled up for an hour.' He pulled bones from his teeth. 'Joe and I will come over with you.'

'Remember, you are taking Theodore to his music!' cried Villette, who had a cold.

But Abraham said the lesson would have to wait.

In ten minutes they were all at the dyke. Billy Rod was there, dressed for chapel. 'Spray, most likely,' he shouted above the gale. 'Blown over the top, d'you see?'

When he tried to inspect the seaward side, the wind knocked him down. His hat blew into the lake. Fitters, seeing the lights, came out to find what was happening. Lively arguments about the strength of the dyke got under way.

'There's a big crack and some stones have gone,' yelled Joe, who had crawled over and back without telling anyone.

'She have stood the test of time,' Billy Rod was declaring, while Phillips said they would post a watchman if Mr Will was anxious, and then please could they get on with making tinplate.

Will tried telephoning to Cardiff, but the lines had been blown down. A telegram might take hours.

What would Dadda have done? He ran back to the dyke. Waves were thundering up the beach now. All Abraham would say was, 'The sea is a pig, don't underestimate it.'

The crisis was his alone. 'I want every available man down here,' he told Phillips. 'Night shift, day shift, round 'em up from the town. With picks and shovels.'

'You can't, Mr Will. Think of the production.'

'Never mind the production. Do as I say.'

He got through to Captain Aubrey at the Castle, and within half an hour a lorry-load of empty sandbags arrived from the Territorials' depot, and men to help fill them with earth. Aubrey, in his element, said it was how the home forces would respond if the Germans got cheeky. He even conjured up a searchlight, and directed its blue beams at the working parties.

Men came running in, excited at the thought of a catastrophe. Stan Screech was in charge of digging and filling. He gave signals. Shouting was useless. The noise was too great.

From the chaos emerged a rhythm of arms, legs, shovels, buckets. New buttresses rose, a bag at a time; it was terrifyingly slow. Joe and a party tried dumping sandbags on the seaward side, but the waves were there already, bursting like cauliflowers. A split-open bag sailed over with a sheet of spume and landed at Will's feet.

He was shovelling earth, working next to his uncle. Billy Rod had gone. His hat still bounced on the lake. Was there more water now? 'Seeping under, could be,' Abraham shouted in Will's ear.

A furnace-glare from another works lit the sky – Morfa, perhaps, safe and dry, preparing the fires for the night shift.

In desperation, he sent men to the Despatch for boxes of

tinplate. Phillips intervened and forbade it. One touch of sea water and they were ruined. He stood like a great haggard bull, defending his boxes from sacrilege.

Aubrey Mappowder, behind Will, shook water from his cape. 'Stand away, Phillips,' he said.

'I take orders from Mr Buckley senior.'

'Do as Mr Will instructs you, there's a good man. I have six Territorial soldiers who'll put you under arrest and lock you in a store room.'

Phillips backed away. Trolley loads of tinplate were sent to the dyke. It was still half an hour to high water. Suddenly Joe was seen to leap sideways. A geyser of water burst from the earth. Mud and stones spattered everyone for yards.

Sucking and roaring, the sea boiled through. But at least they could measure it now; the gangs of men had a target to aim at. Sandbags, tinplates, boulders were thrust into the wound. The sea widened its breach, the embankment above began to go, the grass sank into liquid mud.

Stan Screech organised fresh parties to dump material from above. Men scoured the yards for iron billets, old rails, lengths of chain. Behind them the sea came hissing over the marsh.

More helpers arrived from the town. Will set them to digging a trench and bank around the works, a last line of defence. He saw Dadda's face when he heard the news; he shouted at the men to work faster, and someone shouted back. 'Don't worry, Mr Will, we'll stop the bugger yet.'

Truth and fiction were inextricable afterwards. Men swore they saw Dai Kidwelly and two friends wading through water, carrying a steel roller that needed a crane to hoist it; they tossed it into the hole as if it was a plank. Ben Garibaldi was packing bags with earth. He was timed at one bag per twelve seconds.

Aubrey Mappowder and the boiler were the subject of at least two poems and a song ('Said Captain Aubrey, "Now

I'll foil her! Just help me shift this rusty boiler!"') He found it behind the engine house. Manhandled to the dyke, it was filled with earth and scrap metal where it stood, until its weight drove it down like a plug.

In retrospect, that was the turning point. The sea was at full flood. It was slow to turn, as Abraham had warned. The waters – never stopped, only slowed – came up to the last-ditch defences, and broke through in one place to lie an inch deep in a corner of the tinhouse. But that was all.

An hour late, the sea hesitated and fell back. The tons of iron that had rebuffed it were clanging and rattling until after midnight. Then the dyke went quiet, and a procession of liquefied men, mud-brown from hair to boots, trooped back to tea-urns and chunks of bread.

The mill was full of slumped figures. They reminded Will of the Boer War drawings in Harmsworth magazines, showing the aftermath of battles. In a few hours the sea would be back, gale or no. But the matter was out of his hands.

Sprewett was there, pink in the face, enjoying himself being chairman. 'Will Buckley, man of the hour,' he boomed. Billy Rod, trying to make amends, made plans for the day ahead. An army of fresh workers was on its way. So were pile drivers, concrete mixers, water pumps and train loads of colliery slag.

As the furnace-warmth soaked in, an odd delirium came over the men. For once they had not been at the mercy of events. 'Three cheers for Mr Will Buckley,' called Aubrey, and when they had finished with Will they cheered Captain Aubrey, and finally they cheered themselves.

Stan Screech and his team tied a chair on planks. 'Better let them,' said Aubrey, and Will was carried back to Y Plas. He was falling asleep as they lifted him down.

He woke to find Dadda in the bedroom. The wind had dropped; a pile driver thumped in the distance.

'Are you all right, Will?'

'Feel I've been kicked by a horse.'

'I'm too full for words. But everything will be different now.'

Their quarrel didn't matter any more – that was what he meant. His father embraced him, as he hadn't done since Will was a child, and said it was a new beginning for them all. That was fine as far as it went, but it left the matter of Flora Haycock unresolved. Did the new beginning include her?

The Burry River board voted him a testimonial and a hundred pounds. Then they debated what to do next.

Repairing the dyke was a stop-gap. The site would never be safe again. But next door was Tir Gwyn farm, thirty acres crying out to be developed. Rhodri Lewis wouldn't sell it. Buckley lit a cigar. 'Unless he's made to,' he said, and Rees Coal and Luke Ricketts nodded enthusiastically.

'Couldn't we build somewhere else?' asked Sprewett.

'There isn't a decent site for miles. This is a great opportunity. Fear sharpens the mind, doesn't it, Will?'

'I agree with Mr Sprewett,' said Will.

'Agree to what? To sit on our bottoms and face destruction? The combine could have been dealt a fatal blow. We have been made aware of our vulnerability,' and Will wondered how vulnerable his father was himself, behind the glaring eyes.

This time Colonel Mappowder listened to Buckley's argument about denying Rhodri his right of wayleave. Next day the board made a civil approach through solicitors, offering to buy Tir Gwyn, and got a prompt refusal. Parts of the letter appeared in the *News*, in what purported to be the story of an imaginary industrialist called Blockley, who longed to be president of the Federation of Rusty Nail Manufacturers, and expected everyone to do what he told them.

The board didn't find it funny; the Colonel changed his mind. Learned counsel pored over agreements whereby the locomotives, wagons and other conveyances belonging to or contracted by or otherwise serving Rhodri Lewis Esq and that manufactory known as the Morfa Tinplate Works or other works owned or controlled by the said Rhodri Lewis and his heirs and assigns may pass over that section of permanent way built on land owned by Sir Lionel Mappowder, Knight, of Cilfrew Castle, coloured red on the accompanying map, on payment of such wayleave as is demanded with due notice by the said Sir Lionel Mappowder, his heirs and assigns . . .

The Morfa's railhead crossed seventy-five yards exactly of copperworks land. The five-yearly agreement came up for renewal in February 1909. 'We've got him, Davy,' said Mappowder. 'Either he sells it to the combine, or I squeeze him for ten thousand a year. Twenty, if I like.'

As Buckley pointed out to anyone who listened, it was the realism of business. When the Yankees and Germans did their damnedest to undercut Welsh tinplate, they didn't worry if it brought misery to Port Howard. Industry was a battlefield. What was the South Wales coast before the days of hard men with vision? Nesting place of sea birds, haunt of cocklers.

Will didn't like it, but who cared what he liked?

After busy days and nights when the board seemed to be perpetually in session, he slipped away for an evening to call on Flora.

They sat in the parlour to talk, as if he was already a suitor. She knew about the dyke and how he had saved it; she wanted to hear the story from him.

'It was like a dream,' he told her. 'I did things automatically. We all did.'

'And now you're a capitalist hero.'

He didn't mind being laughed at, or at least he was

willing to put up with it. The room was cold. She wore a woollen cardigan tight across her breasts.

She knew about the combine's designs on Tir Gwyn, too – the papers had been full of it – and the threat to Rhodri Lewis if he didn't sell.

'Can we talk about something else?' groaned Will.

'Why? It's fascinating. It's the law of the jungle. Not that I'd shed any tears for Lewis of Morfa. But to see the naked machinery behind the profit motive is an eye-opener. You tear one another apart.'

No doubt it was true, but he didn't see why he should have to listen to her on the subject; again he felt he was being lectured.

'Do shut up,' he said amiably. 'I don't keep on at you about idle workmen.'

'Are you ashamed of being what you are?'

He coloured and said he was ashamed of nothing.

Their conversation burnt itself out. They lived in different worlds. There was no point in staying.

'You prefer not to talk about things that matter, then?' she said, when he was leaving.

'I came to see you, not to have a political debate.'

'Can't have one without the other.'

'I'm glad we've got that clear.'

So his affair with Flora Haycock was over before it began. His mother, who was still perceptive enough when it came to her own family, must have detected something, because he found himself partnering Amanda Sprewett, a younger sister of Lucinda, at a supper party in Y Plas. She ate an entire chicken at the buffet, and talked, when she talked at all, about dogs.

His only response was to go into Swansea the following Saturday and pick up one of Sam's famous shopgirls. Her skin smelt of face-powder and she wore a hat with a hatpin like a knitting needle. But she had a nice smile and quick fingers, and she knew how to get into the vestry of a derelict chapel. It was quick, cheap and satisfying. He was sorry about Flora.

The combine won. Buckley rubbed in the victory by getting the board to agree that he buy Tir Gwyn in his own name, for the satisfaction of putting his signature to a personal contract. A separate parcel of land came with it, a stretch of dunes and scrubland, miles outside the town, that had been in Japhet Jones's family for centuries. Buckley sold Tir Gwyn on to the combine next day, but kept the scrubland as a memento. He made Will a present of the title deeds. 'Go and pot rabbits there if you ever feel inclined,' he said.

The day the combine took possession of Tir Gwyn, Buckley visited the farm with Oscar Harris and Trubshaw. Japhet Jones must have seen them coming, and wouldn't answer the door. Oscar had to kneel down and shout through a cat-flap, 'The Burry River Combine is now the legal owner of this property, and you are given formal notice to quit in six months from today. I am giving you notice in writing,' and he thrust the long envelope through the flap.

Seconds later it shot out again, in two pieces. Oscar left them on the doorstep.

They walked to the far boundary of the land, keeping a look-out for Guto. At that point the Morfa sidings were only a hundred yards away. A locomotive jerked at a line of trucks, wheels slipping on the icy rails. Wild geese, escaping from someone else's worse winter, floated on a cooling pond amid threads of steam.

The general offices were next to the mills. In the dull light, the windows were opaque.

'We'll be building right under his nose,' said Buckley.

'Yes, indeed,' said Trubshaw.

'Don't approve of me, do you, Trubshaw?'

'I have every respect, sir.'

'He didn't want to build a new works. He hung on to this place to spite me. The combine had every right to do what it did. I feel no conscience.'

'Why should you, sir?'

'Yes, why should I? Come on, let's not waste time. We'll get surveyors here next week without asking.'

The directors were going to have to dig deep for capital to finance the new works. It would take every penny he had. But that didn't worry him. He was giving people something to remember.

Margaret and Henry went to stay at Y Plas, not long after the great storm. She had been planning a visit to Wales since the summer, in order to call on Miss Rees and her child in Swansea, but the orchid business made too many demands.

They both needed a holiday, Henry more than herself. 'Boy,' she would say, when he came back worn out from Coventry or Nottingham, 'you'll knock yourself up if you go on like this.' In the past she had often thought of him as 'Boy', but the word seemed inappropriate for the City shipbroker, and after that, for the orchid magnate.

She did her best to believe that that was what he was on the brink of becoming. As time passed, and the rare plants from the ends of the earth that would make them rich remained firmly where they were in jungles and up mountains, 'Boy' crept into use. It even seemed to cheer him up. He liked to be made a fuss of.

It was Henry who suggested they visit Y Plas. The fearful Johansson had written from Sweden to say he was planning to venture forth on an expedition that would astound the trade. On the way he meant to spend a few weeks in

London, and would be delighted to help with what he called 'administrating the business'.

Henry said, 'I expect you'd like to see your family after all their excitements. We can go when Johansson is here. He may have that nice young female cousin of his in tow.'

He was unusually jovial about the visit. His spirits rose above the downpour they arrived in. He allowed himself to be taken on an immediate tour of works and dyke, while Margaret talked with Mamma, and then, alone, sat on their bed, hoping Henry would behave fondly once they were inside it.

The arrangements were those thought suitable for a young married couple, a wide, sensible bed like a barge, brass rails at head and foot, powerful springs beneath the mattress. It gave a comfortable creak when shaken. There was no second bed for a husband to retreat to, or remain in all night without ever leaving.

It had been her parents' when they married. She had high hopes of it, which she kept to herself. To her delight, Henry, when the night came, appeared to desire her as much as she desired to be desired. It could have been the novelty of a strange house, a different routine. He seemed stirred by the thought of her girlhood there. He asked her an indecent question about what interest she took in seeing her brothers stark naked – he put the words in her ear with his tongue, and she gave him an indecent answer; it wasn't true but it was obviously what he wanted.

Her true thoughts might have put him off. She couldn't expect him to share her own concern with the baby she meant to conceive under the wet blue slates of Y Plas (surely biology could bow to the appropriate?). Babies didn't cross Henry's mind as he overspread her, fingers digging into her hips, the creakiness becoming a single vibration. He was blind to the pinhead of fire inside her, waiting to be blown into flame.

Margaret imagined her life resolving itself at Y Plas. In London it seemed she had been married for ever. Here, they still talked about the wedding as if it was yesterday. Four years and a bit was nothing. 'I said married life would agree with her,' said Dadda.

Sensible entertainments were laid on for Henry, among them a day's shooting with Colonel Mappowder that the men went to, followed by a dinner party at the Castle.

Having heard a serious account of how the works was saved, Margaret heard it made into a comical story by Aubrey Mappowder, whose long straight face was often turned towards her. The jokes were at his own expense. He became serious only when he mentioned Will, who sat flushed and uneasy, and looked as if he wanted to slide under the table when Aubrey got them to drink a toast to 'The Hero of the Combine'.

Talking to Will wasn't easy, Margaret found. He was withdrawn and had little to say. They had never been close, but she liked him, and thought she might like him more, now that he had grown up and no longer looked at Dadda in that hang-dog way.

The day after the dinner party she tapped the door of his bedroom, early in the evening, and went in. He was lying on the counterpane with his arms folded.

'You look like a corpse,' she said.

'I feel rather like one.'

'I thought you were a bit low at the Mappowders'.'

'I sometimes wish I'd never gone near that dyke.'

'What a funny thing to say.'

He didn't elaborate. She stood by the window, looking over the lawn where they had drunk the wedding toasts and Morgan had made his awful speech.

'I see Morgan from time to time,' she said. 'I've talked about him to Mamma. You should bring her to London one day, and I'll ask him round. He and Henry get on well together.'

'Is it true he's become a spiritualist?'

'That's what he says. He appears to make money at it, or to *have* money. But who knows, with Morgan? I suppose you've no idea why he went back to Rees Coal's and collected his lost property?'

'Hardly his property.'

'Figure of speech. He said he heard voices, telling him to do it.'

'Rees thinks it was me.'

'Why's that?'

'I was at The Mount one day. I had an idea she was being ill-treated. Rees knew that I knew. But I did nothing. The great do-nothinger, that's me.'

Margaret wondered what lay behind all that. 'Happens to the best of us,' she said, spreading a little balm.

She thought it more tactful not to say she meant to visit Miss Rees next morning.

It was their last day at Y Plas. She caught an early train, then used the tram to take her from the station to a terrace of tall, thin houses facing a park with a reservoir; her purse was never full these days.

The proprietress, a Mrs Thomas, a pensive lady in a silk dress, showed her up to Miss Rees's rooms on the second floor. A typewriter stopped clacking, and Miss Rees appeared, wearing a blouse and skirt, with her hair drawn back.

'You're Morgan's sister. I remember you at your wedding.'

'I should have written, but I thought I'd just come.'

'It's lovely to see someone. Let me take your things. Would you like to see the rooms? They're very comfortable. Morgan chose them.'

She spun around, kicking a spoon under a table and

opening a window with such a bang, Mrs Thomas appeared outside.

'Hello, Mrs Thomas, I'm showing my visitor the park. You can just see the band-stand, Mrs Penbury-Holt. They play there on fine evenings.'

'Margaret, will you call me Margaret? Then I can call you Aeronwy.'

'Isabel is in the park with Mrs Harry, they take crusts over to the ducks. Would you like to see her? Morgan is so good. He sends her dolls, he sent her a picture book of the Empire.'

'Has Morgan been down to see you since you've been here?'

'Not actually been, but coming shortly.'

Her history was in her face, thought Margaret. It was young, but at the same time not young at all, with a frown between the eyes that never went away.

The questions Margaret wanted to ask would have to wait, perhaps for ever. Instead, she asked about the typewriting.

'I do copy-typing for solicitors. I learned to type when I was young, when I was, before I was . . . They pay by the page, so although I don't have to do it, Morgan is so good, I feel, I feel I'm making my contribution.'

Wise girl, thought Margaret.

A young woman with bottle legs and a broad smile appeared, carrying Isabel. Margaret ate up the child with her gaze – a black severity of hair, and Morgan's deep eyes.

'And you are her auntie,' said Mrs Harry. 'Well, well. This is your Auntie Margaret, Sibli. That's what I call her. Tired, she is. One of them old swans went for her with his beak.'

Margaret gave her niece a shilling. She would have taken them all back to London with her if it was practicable. As it was, she said that one day they must come to stay, and

Aeronwy, the frown going up into her hair, said, 'Oh, Morgan is sure to arrange something very soon, so we may see your Aunt Margaret then, mayn't we, Isabel?'

On returning to Y Plas, Margaret found Henry in his topcoat and their cases packed. There had been a row. Dadda spoke to her briefly in the library. Her husband had tried to borrow a large sum of money. 'Why, Buckley,' he had told him, 'you are quite the tycoon these days.'

It made Margaret's toes curl. The fact that for the moment Dadda and his combine were hard-pressed by their expansion was apparent to her, so why wasn't it apparent to Henry? Perhaps, heretical thought, she was better at business than he was.

Refused, he had said, 'Well, Buckley, remember it's your daughter will suffer if my business goes down the drain.'

That was when they had the row.

'Henry's a good man, really,' said Margaret. 'You mustn't worry about me.'

'I'll try not to. If you need anything, you only have to ask.'

Mamma had either missed the row or was pretending ignorance. They had told her Henry was returning urgently for business reasons. She had a parcel of home-made cakes for Morgan.

Nothing had resolved itself. Margaret went to make sure the maid had packed everything. The bed looked too large for the room. Its pulsations of the first night hadn't been repeated. 'Traitor,' she said, under her breath, knowing it had failed her.

Late on a Saturday afternoon towards the end of winter, Will cycled out to see the piece of land that his father had given him, and realised it was where the famous picnic had taken place. The walls and broken chimney of the old powder works were unscreened by foliage at this time of year. He walked to the dunes and saw fishing boats with brown sails in Carmarthen Bay. The day of the picnic seemed part of his childhood now.

Riding back through town, he heard brass music and saw figures puffing and blowing in Market Street, carrying an acetylene lamp on a pole, collecting money for something called the 'New Dock Boys' Band'.

He thought he saw Flora with them. A man had his arm around her waist. Will wanted to rush up to them and ask her what she meant by it.

At the last minute he swerved down a side turning.

PART THREE
Ride a Tin Horse

10

Welsh Dragon and Union Jack flew side by side outside the marquee, and Buckley's surprise for the guests, a locomotive that was going to shunt wagons down the centre aisle, hissed in the sunlight.

It had taken more than a year to build and equip the Tir Gwyn works, link it with roads and railway lines, and paint the word *Buckley's* down the engine-house chimneys. The board had expected *Burry River*, but Buckley sent the painters up at a weekend, and when it was done it was done.

Tir Gwyn was a dream come true. Odd, thought Will, that he had grown out of dreams, while his father had grown into them. He squinted through an eye-hole in the canvas. All eyes were on the dais and the boisterous row of directors and their guests.

Lord Dillwyn of the Masters' Federation was speaking. He had just made a complicated joke about the Ark, comparing David Buckley to a Noah who steered his tinplate works to dry land. Men slapped the table-edges with their fingers, and ladies fanned themselves or wriggled inside their silk and whalebone.

Dillwyn made a passing reference to the venture recently embarked upon by Lewis of the Morfa, Egge the tin-stamper and some fellow with a coal-pit at Hendy. Masters were beginning to see the virtues of combination – 'Not,' he said, turning to Buckley, 'that the aforementioned gentlemen are in your class, Davy,' and loyal voices cried 'Hear! hear!'

Will saw his lordship raise his glass, ready to propose the toast of 'New Enterprise!'

'Right!' he called to the men, and as they drew aside flaps in the canvas, the engine began to edge the wagons backwards along the specially laid rails – a flat-car piled with bouquets first, followed by a dozen trucks carrying unboxed tinplate that glittered like treasure, all of them pushed by the engine.

A post by the track outside the tent marked the spot to an inch where the driver was to halt, when a rag lashed to the footplate came level.

It was all the old boy's dream, happening exactly as he had planned it, down to the choice wines they were drinking and the flowers for the ladies that would arrive practically under their noses at the top table.

Will saw him through the dusty half-light, standing like a block of concrete in a morning coat, smiling grimly as the guests first gasped, then applauded and finally cheered the slow clanking trucks.

Money was no object. Buckley had argued with the board, and no one, not even Mappowder, had been able to resist his vision of a grand send-off. What was three hundred and seventy pounds, twelve shillings and sixpence, the head cashier's figure? They were expensive dreams, thought Will; one way and another, we all have to contribute.

The old boy looked remote, brooding over his guests, arms folded, gazing, as far as Will could tell, not at the rumbling flower wagon but at some point in space where the balloon of canvas bulged towards the sky. There were times now when he was quite unlike the man that the word 'Dadda' still conjured up – as though his mind was running fast into the future, too concerned with 1911 to pay much attention to 1910.

A man shouted. The tank engine gave an unexpected

chuff, and from far away at the top table came a bang and a woman's scream. Then the brakes squealed and the wagons stopped.

The driver, an experienced man called Venn Jones, said afterwards that a wasp had gone inside his shirt, and he had touched the regulator by mistake. It was not impossible. The caterers' strawberries had attracted clouds of insects.

Miraculously, no one was hurt. The top table was jolted just enough to empty coffee and claret into laps. It made no difference. Buckley strode out of the tent and sacked Venn Jones on the spot.

Will tried to save him, but it was no good.

Nothing influenced Buckley any more. He had a plan to buy a cheap steamer as soon as one became available. The other directors weren't keen. But Will knew that when his father found a suitable vessel, he would go ahead and buy it.

The extra calls on capital to finance Tir Gwyn meant that Buckley's private means had almost vanished. He was prepared to stretch himself to the limit. The combine must do the same.

New Manchester engines from Daniel Adamson were installed in the hot mill at enormous cost. The first time they ran, Buckley allowed two hours for them to bed down, then balanced a penny edgeways on the engine housing. The vibration made it fall over at once. Adamson's had to send down a senior director with a new team of fitters to check the installation. Buckley wasn't interested in their excuses. He kept them at it for days until the penny stayed upright.

'This is my son. He's in charge of the works, day by day,' was how Buckley introduced him to visitors, but there was never any doubt where the real authority lay. When the old works was gutted for useful machinery and stores, the tinplate horse and rider came to light, and Buckley ordered them to be thrown away – 'yesterday's rubbish', he said. Will had to conspire with Trubshaw to salvage the figures and find them a safe corner.

When Guto wandered back to Tir Gwyn, Buckley made short work of him. He and Japhet lived in a cottage on the other side of town. The first time Guto was seen, Buckley had him frog-marched down the road. The second time, Phillips found him in a hut, striking matches, and came for instructions.

Will suggested they give him a job, collecting rubbish or scything grass. Dadda told him not to be frivolous and sent for the police; he was obviously an arsonist. Inspector Hussey came over from the station and agreed with him.

In court, Buckley said Guto bore him a grudge and knew exactly what he was doing. T. T. Rees, presiding magistrate, obliged with two months' hard labour in Carmarthen Gaol.

Hannah's birthday was in early September. She would be eighty, or eighty-one, or even eighty-three; no one had ever seen it written down.

Whatever it was, this year she demanded more than the usual tea. When she was a child, the family farmed near the coast at Pendine, a lonely village on a beach. That, she told her son, was where she wanted to go.

'Trust you to think of something awkward, Mother,' said Buckley.

But she knew he had to respect her wishes. He was her son; and he had expectations.

In Hannah's old age, forgotten images rose up – a donkey braying in a lane, her father driving a stake into red earth. Pendine was where she had found the piece of wood that became a toy house for children's games. Nowadays, if she was honest, it looked more like a skull.

With the new works only a month in production, Buckley

grudged eight hours for a picnic. Rain would have solved everything. But thunderstorms in August had given way to calm, hazy weather, with foghorns hooting in the Bristol Channel. He would have to grin and bear it.

Mappowder had insisted on lending his motor and its chauffeur; two or three of the men could travel in it. The rest of the party would go by train to the nearest station, where a wagon from the Beach Hotel at Pendine would meet them.

Everyone converged on Y Plas for an early start. Hannah made sure that Hywel took her there before she was expected.

'A very happy birthday, Nain,' said Margaret, who went out to greet her. 'We were just eating our breakfast.'

'I ate mine an hour ago. I'll wait here till you've all finished. I don't want to miss the train.'

'We aren't half ready yet. And there's your presents.'

Hannah let herself be taken in and made a fuss of. Sitting in the hall – she refused to go further – she received her gifts with nods and grunts. Her son's made her lean forward. 'It's another of those contraptions,' she said.

'It's a patent floor cleaner that the girl can use,' explained Pomona. 'They call it a Ukanusa Drudgee.'

'I don't care if they call it the Crown Jewels. I have told you and Davy till I'm blue in the face that those things are a waste of money. Now what's this?'

'Morgan has sent you some London boots,' said Margaret, and the old woman poked them suspiciously.

'He doesn't know my size.'

But he must have done, because they fitted her; she chuckled at the smart pattern down the side, and asked for a cardboard box to put the old ones in.

'He sent a letter as well,' said Margaret.

'Read it, girl, read it.'

Morgan wrote that it broke his heart not to be there, but

she would understand that, having chosen to be independent, and needing to make his way in a ruthless city, holidays were few and far between.

'Soft soap,' said Hannah, sticking out a leg to admire the boot.

On the train she behaved outrageously. Buckley, Abraham and Joe went ahead in the Colonel's motor, which had arrived at Y Plas with Aubrey at the wheel, wearing a chauffeur's peaked hat and saluting everyone in sight. The others shared two first-class rail carriages, Villette and Pomona placing themselves either side of old Mrs Buckley, while Margaret, sitting opposite, tried to forget her own problems and make her grandmother's day as pleasant as she could.

From the next compartment they could hear Theodore playing the flute.

'Mozart, I believe,' said Mrs Lloyd.

'When you reach my age, it's like needles in your head.'

Sun struck Hannah's face as the train pulled into the open; she looked like a wax doll. 'I'm beginning to wish I hadn't come,' she said. 'Davy was barely civil to me at the house. He's in one of his moods. Been crossing him, have you, Pomona?'

'Nain, you mustn't tease her,' smiled Margaret.

'Davy has a lot on his mind,' said Pomona nervously.

'That means money, I know. Well, he isn't getting any of mine. If he's bitten off more than he can chew, that's his own lookout. I don't know what's come over him these last years, what with combines and federations and getting thick as thieves with that old fox Mappowder. Mind you, I like a man with a temper. I hear Margaret's husband got the wrong side of him when he was here.'

'I must go and see Theodore is all right,' Mrs Lloyd said, and Pomona went with her, whispering that she had forgotten to wash her hands before they left.

'Now see what you've done, Nain.'

'Are we not allowed to mention Henry? I have nothing against him. As long as he treats my little sweetheart properly, I shall continue to give him the benefit of the doubt.'

She looked slyly at her granddaughter, but Margaret didn't rise.

'Davy, of course, thought you were marrying money – or as my sister Gwenno used to say, "Never marry money, but marry where money is." It must have come as a nasty shock to find that as far as Master Henry was concerned, it was supposed to be the other way round.'

Hannah's eyes slid shut, and Margaret drew the blinds against the glare of the countryside. Passing through the little stations, she was suspended between the two worlds of Wales and London. Did she belong in either? Henry's business affairs had worsened. Johansson's expedition, meant to 'astonish the trade', had barely covered its cost. The firm stumbled on. Yet that, she told herself, was where she belonged for ever and ever.

Will was by himself in the corridor, forehead resting on the window. She joined him and tried to make conversation by asking about the combine and the wonderful new works, but he wasn't responsive.

Always disinclined to do anything but accept her own life as it came, for better or worse, she was annoyed that Will didn't know when he was well off.

'What *do* you want?' she found herself saying. 'It strikes me you have a pretty comfortable time.'

'I'm sure. The young master must buck up and count his blessings.'

The edge on his voice made her solicitous. 'Do you want to talk about it?' she said, but he shook his head, and she gave up. If he was Morgan, it would be easier. Making demands was Morgan's stock in trade.

Best not to spoil the day by poking her nose into a life she no longer belonged to.

At St Clears, where the party alighted and the Beach Hotel wagonette stood in the sun, the stationmaster said that 'the gentlemen in the motor' had passed through twenty minutes earlier.

Soon they were on the road to Laugharne and the coast, a second vehicle with the servants following at a decent distance. Hannah was wedged between Villette and Pomona. Margaret, sitting next in line, told her mother the things she wanted to hear about married life in West Hampstead.

Pendine was a relief. The haze had thickened to a bank of blue, and the crunchy sand stretched to the horizon. The men were playing cricket with a driftwood bat and a soft ball. Aubrey Mappowder, defending a rock for a wicket, whacked it high in the air. Margaret stepped back and caught it.

'My pleasure, Mrs Penbury-Holt,' he said, holding out the bat. The gold wires of his moustache were more visible than they had been at dinner that night.

'Mr Lloyd will hit them better than I,' she said, making sure that shy Uncle Abraham wasn't left out.

The proprietor of the Beach Hotel brought deckchairs for the ladies. Margaret wandered off by herself, drawn towards a family that was camped a hundred yards away. A nursemaid had charge of small children, one of whom, a baby with a powerful turn of speed in its crablike motion, suddenly pistoned its way towards a stream.

The maid's back was turned. Margaret scooped up the child, which looked at her in surprise and then coo'd, fatally.

'The dear!' she said, and carried it back to the fold. The mother rose and apologised, the maid was in tears, Margaret jogged the baby aloft and remarked on his character. It was agreed that he had taken an amazing fancy to her.

To continue holding the child seemed a natural thing to do. The family were English, and staying at the hotel, where they came every year. The husband was a palaeontologist. He first went there in search of fossils. None of this mattered. Only the baby mattered, pulling at Margaret's blouse.

Theodore appeared, holding his flute like a gun, to say that Grandma Buckley and Aunt Pomona were going in search of the family farm, and would Cousin Margaret care to accompany them?

'No, thank you,' said Margaret, hardly thinking, and stayed talking to the family.

Lunch was laid outside the hotel, overlooking the beach. Hannah kept them waiting, and the champagne for drinking her health in had to be returned to the cellar. She arrived grumbling that the farm must have been pulled down. The one they found wasn't right at all. Behind her back, Pomona made signs of dissent.

'Come and sit next to me,' said Margaret. 'Look, the tide's coming in.'

Far off, the haze seemed to shift.

Her grandmother sat demurely. The new boots were white with dust. 'Like children, do you?' she said suddenly, when the toasts had finished. 'Couldn't tear yourself away and help me find the farm. Your mother's about as much use as a blind beggar. You could have found it for me.'

'It's changed, Nain, that's all.'

'You made an exhibition of yourself, you and that baby. It's time you had them of your own. Where are my great-grandchildren?' Her voice carried the length of the table. 'I've never seen the only one there is. The Lord punished Morgan. He punished me as well.'

'That's enough, Mother!' roared Buckley, and let the

company know, under his breath, that he had said all along it would be too much for her.

Margaret's food tasted like sawdust. Her anger with the old woman was trivial beside the rawness of the day. Then Will – a different Will, now – seized her hand and said he was taking her with them for a post-prandial spin along the sands.

'Why not?' she said.

Captain Aubrey, goggles pushed into his hair, offered her the front seat, and again, why not?

With Will and Joe at the back, the motor sped towards the line of sea, turned smartly and skimmed alongside it.

'Enjoying yourself?' shouted Goggles.

'Most exhilarating. How fast are we going?'

'Forty-five, I'd say.' The sand was like yellow paving. She felt better. Gulls rose shrieking from their path. Goggles braked gently and did things with the clutch.

'Why not take the wheel?' he said, patting it.

'Why not?'

Tuition in brake and throttle was necessary. The clutch was left to the owner, who had to do some leaning over and bending down. The back of his neck grew hairs as fine and blond as his moustache.

By the time Margaret took charge, they were already cracking along, still at the edge of the water. It was like a lake on the move, trickling faster in places, making bulges.

'Drive through it, do!' shouted Goggles, and the braking effect jerked the passengers forward from the waist. Behind the motor, spray fell like glass.

Margaret raced on, the two at the rear yelling encouragement, hard cushion catching her behind the thighs, air rushing through her skirt, aiming at some infinity beyond the end of the sands that seemed to go on for ever, set free by a machine, of all things, tied neither to Welsh family nor

English, a woman of tomorrow – she would tell Virginia, who would giggle.

The engine coughed, picked up, coughed again, and gave out. As Goggles jumped down, the tide touched the wheels. 'Drop of sea-water in the carburettor,' he announced with confidence. Whether or not that was true, in examining the insides he broke a petrol pipe. Rainbow-colours floated on the water. 'Damn!' he said, and took off his shoes and socks, mock-cheerful. 'We shall have to push the old girl.'

'Will, go for horses,' said Margaret. 'Quick, now.'

'That's one pair of hands less,' complained Goggles.

'She'll sink in the wet sand,' said Joe. 'Cousin Margaret's right.'

Already the wheels were settling. Five minutes of pushing and pulling had no effect. They retreated to dry land.

People were coming down the beach. As yet there was no sign of horses.

Dadda and Uncle Abraham arrived, and a waiter from the hotel, and the palaeontologist, and Mamma, using a stick because of bad legs, deep in conversation with Aunt Villette.

Far off, a small figure sat alone in the row of deckchairs. 'She's all right, just having a nap,' said Mamma, her eyes bright with champagne.

Margaret went back. The rescue party was coming down the path beside the hotel, heavy horses led by men carrying chains. Hannah was wide awake. 'Young Mappowder was showing off, was he?' she said.

'It's unfortunate. Joe reckons they won't shift it until the tide goes out again.'

'His engagement was broke off years ago, did you know that? He was going to marry one of the Sprewett girls.'

'The one who was in Haggar's film. I remember Mamma telling me.'

They gossiped about families they both knew. A puff of

cold air came along like a draught through a door. In the sea, men were shouting and splashing about. The horses stood patiently. Already water had reached the hubs.

'I'm sorry Morgan didn't come,' said Margaret.

'Morgan was always different. I respect character. I respect you as well. I shouldn't have spoken as I did. I was upset at not finding the old farm.'

'Would you like us to go and look now?'

Hannah shook her head. 'It isn't there to find.'

Instead, she took Margaret's arm, and they walked towards the sea. Men were straining at ropes. The horses shuddered on the water's edge.

'Wasting your time, you are!' cried Hannah, and the voice was shrill again.

'Heave!' and 'Gerrup!' rang over the sands. Inexorably, the horses moved forward. 'She's coming!' shouted Goggles.

The motor moved, but the angle was wrong. It shook, lurched, then toppled over and lay on its side, rainbowing the water.

A groan went up, followed by the shocking sound of laughter. It was Hannah. Her eyes watered, and she had to lean on her granddaughter.

'Behave yourself, Nain!' said Margaret, feeling the day turn sour, the glass thicken between her and them.

Dadda, in a fury, said they had better get his mother back to Rhydness before he did something he might regret.

In any case, the weather had turned dull. As the wag-onettes were got ready, Abraham thought he heard thunder.

Captain Aubrey was remaining at the hotel to supervise rescue operations next day. Looking bedraggled, he bowed to Margaret and said, 'I hope you don't think me too much of an ass. I enjoyed our drive.'

'And so did I.'

He stood waving. The vehicles rumbled off. Sand was

blowing across the road. To make more room, Will and Theodore were in the rear wagon with the servants, and the flute played 'Goodbye, Dolly' and 'A Bicycle Made for Two'. Margaret could hear her brother singing louder than the servants.

Lightning flickered over the sea, and the storm caught them before they reached St Clears. Coats were wrapped around Hannah to keep the rain off; she sat indifferent to what was going on, still chuckling to herself about the motor.

'We'll come again next year and bring umbrellas,' said Margaret, determined to be jolly.

The flute and Will's voice persisted in the rain. 'How romantic it all sounds!' Virginia would say, and smile at her sideways, and ask if Goggles had a manly figure.

On the train, Hannah seemed to suffer no ill-effects. But Dr Snell, called to Y Plas when they were home, wouldn't hear of her going on to Rhydness.

Overnight she weakened and grew feverish, and Margaret sent her husband a telegram.

Around midday Hannah called Snell a monkey and knocked her medicine on the floor. She prayed and demanded to have the Bible read to her. Then she fell asleep, and didn't wake.

Hannah's funeral at Bethania Chapel, at a crossroads a mile from the farm, was an event for the district. It wasn't one of the great occasions with a cortege half a mile long; neighbours, families with long memories and a handful of distant cousins made up the modest numbers. But it had an interesting core of the seriously bereaved. Buckley was much pointed-at by rural mourners, the big man with the works, 'Your broken-hearted son Davy' as it said on the white and purple wreath that covered the coffin.

Morgan was hoped for, but at first looked like letting

them down. Pomona limped into the chapel on her stick, accompanied by Margaret, the one who married the Englishman (*and where was he?*), followed by that Mrs Lloyd (not so many knew who she was), and the boy who was musical.

The male mourners and undertaker's men took a grip on the coffin at the gate. Onlookers shook their heads and said, No, that old Morgan wasn't going to show his face.

Then a closed carriage came down the road from the east at inappropriate speed, and out he got.

He had travelled from Swansea, leaving his arrival as late as possible to reduce the amount of time he had to spend with his family. The coffin was already halfway down the path.

Dadda, Will, Abraham and Joe made up the family bearers. In the middle were a couple of undertakers. Morgan tapped one of them on the arm, and waved him aside.

As the shoulders changed places, the coffin tilted. Buckley twisted his head and gave him a look of unfathomable rage.

'Hello, Dadda,' whispered Morgan. 'You have my deepest sympathy.'

Grief was a strange thing. In a way it hardened the heart. He might have been alone with the coffin, singing her favourite hymns in his low, out-of-key voice. The minister must have given an address, but he didn't hear it. Someone called Mamma was making a fool of herself. The eyes of someone called Margaret gleamed at him behind her veil.

At the graveside he whispered to the minister, 'I am Morgan, her grandson.'

'I know who you are, don't worry.'

'I wish to give a short address.'

'Out of the question,' said the old man, but Morgan was

already stepping on to the mound of clay, pocket Bible at the ready.

He opened it to a page marked by a London tram ticket, and read a passage about *Whatsoever things are true* and *If there be any virtue.* Cousins with rabbit-faces looked at him in wonder. He spoke of Hannah's piety and wit. 'I loved her. She knew the human heart,' he said, and stumbled off the clay.

The task had drained him. It was too much like the old days. This was God-country, not pagan, cheerful London, where the spirits were domestic creatures, there only by invitation.

A gawky figure with a squint, raising its hat in last respects, made him shudder. It was Gwilym, the lost soul at theological college; now, it turned out, managing his father's dairy farm not ten miles away.

So what was Gwilym doing here?

'Well, mun,' said the thick, vowelly voice, 'read it in the paper I did about the old lady, and I thought you might be here, like. Very good to me at Blaen Cwm you were, I don't care what they say about you. I remember you 'splaining "Son of Man" under a tree.'

He wasn't Gwilym, he was a supernatural force sent to torment Morgan. God was clever; God forgot nothing.

The farm without Hannah meant little to Morgan, and he wouldn't have gone back except that he had one more task to perform.

Cold food and hot tea were ready for the family mourners. Pritchard, the bailiff, hung about the yard, being obsequious to the Buckleys in general and Dadda in particular. Christmas Jenkins of Carmarthen, Hannah's solicitor, sat in a corner of the kitchen in his frock coat, guarding a deed box.

Morgan went straight to the ledge where the piece of oak should have been. It wasn't there. He looked in the hearth;

by Hannah's chair; on the dresser. The others were coming in. Rachel, the maid, red-eyed, was pouring tea.

'That piece of wood my grandmother kept here,' he said.

'It fell in the fire, sir. After she left here on her birthday.'

'What's that? I want nothing touched,' exclaimed Buckley.

'Too late,' said Morgan dryly. 'Unknown forces at work, no doubt.'

'I wonder you have the face to reappear like this. You have upset your mother – '

'No, no, I want to see him!' wailed Pomona.

Once more, a speedy departure seemed the answer. But as he went for his coat, Christmas Jenkins touched his arm and said, 'I think you should stay.'

He wondered what that meant. So, from his face, did Dadda. The funeral meal was gulped down in ten minutes. Pritchard could be seen in the yard, practising his smile for the new proprietor.

Rachel had opened the window of the parlour and waved a feather duster. Christmas Jenkins rattled the keys of the box as they filed in. He took out the papers, blew his nose, adjusted his spectacles, all in slow motion.

The will was dated three years earlier. It was quite short. Her dear grandchildren Margaret and Will received two hundred pounds each. Villette's two children, Joe and Theodore, also dear, each got one hundred. Her dear son received such pieces of furniture as he chose from Rhydness – from this point on, invisible emanations came from Buckley, as the blood rose up his neck and into his face.

Her dear daughter-in-law, Pomona, was to have 'all those valuable household contraptions that she and my son have given me over the years, which she will find in the loft as good as new'.

Pomona slumped in her chair. Margaret shouted for

cold water. The stricken woman began muttering about a Ukanusa Drudgee.

The solicitor paused for a full minute before Buckley said in a choking voice, 'Get on!'

Morgan's head had bowed lower and lower through the proceedings. He imagined he could hear the swish of the rocking chair and see the glint in the eye.

'I come to my grandson Morgan,' read Christmas Jenkins. This time there was no 'dear'. There was a reference to her lifelong affection for him, that was all. Oh, and he was to receive the farm, lock, stock and barrel, and the sum of six thousand pounds in cash. Any residues went to Bethania.

'Much good may it do you,' shouted Dadda.

'Thank you very much,' said Morgan.

In the confusion, and adding to it, the solicitor could be heard reading a codicil, sworn the previous spring, bequeathing one thousand pounds to Miss Aeronwy Rees, of Brynmill Terrace, Swansea, 'the mother of my only great-grandchild'.

Cold water was needed again.

Even in his black suit, Morgan looked flashy. He stood talking to the solicitor while the parlour emptied. Will thought: someone should tell him what we think of him.

He told Margaret to explain that he was remaining behind, and would make his own way home.

'Be careful,' she warned, but left him to it.

Buckley drove off with his party, black ribbons still dangling from the carriage. Christmas Jenkins followed in a trap. Pritchard was left in the yard, bowing and scraping to the new boss.

Will waited in the kitchen. His brother arrived whistling to himself and rubbing his hands. His surprise lasted only a second.

'I'm glad somebody stayed,' he said. 'I've been telling

Pritchard, I shall sell the farm as soon as I've got probate. That's ruined his day. He fancied having an absentee landlord while he cooked the books.'

'I want a word with you,' said Will roughly.

'We should never have lost touch, you and I. I've turned into a psychic. You've turned into an employer of men – don't deny it, I can see the Dadda look about you. What do we have to quarrel about these days? Our paths have diverged in a most satisfactory way. We can meet once a year and like each other.'

'That money,' said Will; the rest was hot air. 'I suppose it would never occur to you that Dadda is more entitled to it than you are?'

'Morally, you mean? You may be right. Hannah was a funny old thing. Am I benefiting because she liked me or because she wanted to spite Dadda? I don't know the answer to that. The trouble is, Will, morally, who's entitled to what? It gets very complicated. Is Dadda's combine morally entitled to the land at Tir Gwyn? You see, a little bird tells me things. But it was legal. Like Hannah's will is legal.'

'You could always talk. What I'm telling you is that you owe Dadda something. You've never even told him you're sorry for what happened. You ran away like a coward. You left him to comfort Mamma and pay your bills. There was Miss Rees. She had to be looked after.'

'Ah, I thought we'd get to her in the end,' said Morgan. He sat in Hannah's chair and rocked himself. 'Get it off your chest, then. Preach a sermon on sexual purity. I did the trick with her once. Just once. What about you and the ladies, Will?'

'You left her, that's all I'm saying.'

'She had a family. How was I to know her delightful uncle was a sadist? As far as I can see, she was a slave in that place for two years. She was in his bed as well, if I'm not mistaken. Dadda must have gone to The Mount. So must you. But nobody ever saw anything they didn't want to see. Rees Coal was a business partner. Well, I expect it was difficult. I understand. But why am I the one who gets moralised at?'

'You were the one who put her in the family way,' said Will. But he lacked conviction. He had no defence.

'Why not go and see her yourself? Brynmill Terrace, number seventy-two. You'd like her. She's a tough little thing, underneath – she had to be, to survive Rees Coal. Go and tell her about her thousand pounds. I have to get back on the express tonight. Anyway, seeing me only upsets her.'

'Seeing you upsets most people,' said Will, a parting shot that afterwards he regretted.

Morgan waved him off as Hywel drove the trap out of the yard, and 'No hard feelings' echoed after him.

By the time he reached Y Plas, Dadda was at the works, Margaret had left for London, and Mamma was in bed. A visitor was waiting for him in the morning room, an odd event – even odder when he went in, to find a stout rosy-faced man in a brown suit and farmers' leggings who said his name was Dr Pfizer and he came from Zurich.

He gave Will his card and said that he represented a group in Switzerland that was planning to manufacture cheese using revolutionary methods that required Welsh milk. 'I cannot go into them at present,' he explained. They were looking for land of a particular sort – something to do with minerals in the grass. He was on a trip to Wales. He had seen a possible site outside Port Howard, and only today had learned through solicitors that Mr Will Buckley was its owner.

'Five hundred pounds cash on the nail,' he said, and touched his pocket encouragingly.

Will wanted to know more; he might not understand

high finance, but there was something wrong with Dr Pfizer and his spotless leggings.

It was the offer or nothing.

'Nothing, then,' said Will.

'You won't hear from me again,' warned the Swiss, and presently his leggings were waddling off down the drive.

When Dadda heard of it later, he said it was Will's land and Will's decision, but if Pfizer came back, and Will had any sense . . .

But Pfizer didn't come back.

The first thing Morgan did in London was to rent a furnished house in South Kensington, so that he no longer had to rely on the Thorns for a roof over his head. Credit was no problem. Using papers supplied by Christmas Jenkins, he found that banks fell over themselves to accommodate a young man with a copper-bottomed legacy.

Armed with banknotes, he visited the house in Putney where he had served his apprenticeship. More than a year had passed since he was last there. His debt, Squale informed him triumphantly, had now risen, thanks to compound interest.

'I hear you left the Thorns in haste a week ago,' he sniffed. 'No doubt you have been seen through. That is why you have returned with your tail between your legs. I would hesitate to re-employ someone who repaid the kindness of his tutors by setting up in competition. But Mrs Squale has a soft heart. She may give you another chance.'

Her boudoir hadn't changed, except that it had more trinkets and boxes of crystallised fruit than ever. 'You have been a naughty boy,' she said, but she seemed to smell money about his person.

Raising her dress with one hand so he could fondle her, she patted his breast pocket with the other and looked at him knowingly. He stuffed a bundle of five-pound notes into her knickers, which made her sigh. 'You would do even better with me to help you,' she murmured. 'Science is turning against us. The great days of spiritualism are over.'

That was nonsense. He had too many ambitions to let them be compromised. She wanted to keep him with her, that was all. Morgan was flattered but unmoved.

A week later he was there again, this time to wheedle the recipe for Writhing Ectoplasm from her. As they lay naked on the couch, she told him that a spirit called Hannah had come through at a seance the previous night. 'She told me to stay close to you,' said Cordelia. 'An old person, not long out of the body. Do you know who she might be?'

'You fraud, you,' said Morgan. 'You sent a private detective down to Port Howard, didn't you?'

'What a cynical boy. Of course I didn't.'

'Of course you did.'

But in his trade, how could you be sure of anything?

11

Miss Rees's legacy gave Will the excuse to do what he should have done long before. In Swansea to bid for a consignment of tin, he took a tram to the suburb where she lived. It deposited him in the greasy November drizzle and went off leaving a trail of sparks.

She was about to go out. Isabel was being difficult over her dinner, and Mrs Harry was torn between making sure she ate up like a little lady and doing something with her mistress's boots.

Will stood inside the door. Everyone was talking at once, 'Obviously a bad time,' 'Not at all,' '*Up* with the spoon!' 'It's Uncle Morgan!' 'No it's not,' 'What pleasant rooms,' 'Try this button,' 'Do sit down,' 'So this is Isabel,' 'You aren't Uncle Morgan . . .'

'I don't have many visitors,' said Miss Rees, and the boot seemed to be straight at last.

'I have some good news for you.'

'Oh, I know about the legacy. I was amazed. I cried – Mrs Harry will tell you.'

Her eyes swam, an overpowering greeny-blue, with deep-curled lashes. Nothing remained of the scrawny child he had seen at The Mount.

She was about to deliver packets of typing to the firms of solicitors who sent her work. They were wrapped up in brown paper by the machine on the table.

He would carry them for her? That was kind. Here was the shopping bag she used. Be a good girl, Isabel. Your Uncle Morgan will be coming any day now.

In the tram, returning to the business quarter, she said

she might use her legacy to open a typewriting office and employ women. 'But then, would it be fair to Morgan? When his plans are complete, he'll send for us both to London. If I were to run an office, I should be tied down. There would be delays. That would hardly be fair to him, would it?'

She looked at him stealthily. 'You are the very first person I can talk to about Morgan. Margaret has been to see me. We got on like a house on fire. But brothers have a special bond between them. Are you and he very close? He never talks about his family. You *are* close, I can tell.'

'I'm the one who stayed at home.' Will wondered if it was possible to tell her anything approximating to the truth without hurting her. 'We make tinplate. Morgan and I have seen very little of each other for years.'

'But absence makes no difference,' she said. 'As I know from my own experience. Here we are, off we get.'

She let him help her down the steps, and hold the shopping bag open while she rummaged for the first parcel.

Her calls took half an hour, most of which Will spent standing in the drizzle outside solicitors' front doors. He was amused at the casual way she pushed his patience to the limits; it reminded him of Morgan. She would have taken him shopping if he had let her.

At the last minute, standing in High Street, he came to the point. 'There is something I have to say. I want to apologise here and now for having done nothing to help you in the past.'

'Silly boy,' she said, 'what could you have done? But you are very sweet. You must come again. We must be friends.'

When he returned to Tir Gwyn, his father asked what had taken him so long, and Will told him.

'Oh, very nice,' said Buckley. 'You are supposed to be in charge of the works. You are a director of the combine. But you disappear for hours in the middle of the day to visit a slut.'

'We can't pretend she doesn't exist. Mamma is always asking about the child. It's our flesh and blood.'

'I hope you asked her what she proposes to do with a thousand pounds of my money. She and your brother between them are living off the fat of the land at my expense. Do you realise what the demands on my pocket have been, as the major shareholder in the combine? Now to make things worse we have pit strikes. I've had telegrams from Rees.'

'I thought the strikes were in the Rhondda.'

'So they were till today. The board meets at five. And by the way, your precious Haycock is up to his tricks again. He wants a canteen for the men to eat their food in, with hot water and a stove. I've told him no. He's also fomenting trouble over that engine driver I had to dismiss. They have no vision, these men. They'd drag us down to their level, and we should never build a future.'

The board met and talked about money. Somehow there was less of it in the pipeline, or a fear that there was less. 'Business confidence,' that fickle barometer, was falling. Miners had been rioting at Tonypandy in the east. 'According to my newspaper,' said Sprewett, as if it was printed for his personal use, 'they had dynamite. They looted shops.' He dangled a cutting between thumb and finger. 'They stole white waistcoats and top hats. They paraded down the street in them, singing disrespectful songs.'

'Other end of the coalfield,' said Buckley.

'Some rascal 'ad a revolver at Glanamman yesterday,' said Rees. 'That's next door to me. They were cutting telephone wires and tramplin' over municipal flower-beds. That's bad for confidence, Davy, and it's contagious. I had ninety men wouldn't go underground this morning. I sacked 'em on the spot, but there's two seams idle as a result.'

Mappowder sat flipping through bank statements and invoices. Nearly two thousand pounds was still owing to Adamson's. Why was that, Davy?

'Withheld until we're sure the teething troubles are over.'

'Are they over, Will?' said the Colonel.

'They seem to be.' There was nothing else he could say.

'Come, come,' said Buckley, eyes glittering with anger, but honey oozing from his voice because Mappowder was the one director he daren't quarrel with, 'I think I can be relied upon to know about steam engines after all these years. Adamson's will be paid as soon as I'm happy.'

'Paid with what?' asked the Colonel.

'The bank will accommodate us. Once we begin to reap the benefits, we all know the profits there'll be.'

'I understand there are murmurings about a strike at Tir Gwyn. They are arguing that the engine driver Jones was unfairly dismissed.'

'Saul Haycock is a trouble-maker.'

'Of course he is. I agreed last week to let the copperworks have a canteen with hot water, so he'd have one less thing to make trouble about. I think the combine should do the same. Times are changing, Davy. Let the Venn Jones business go to arbitration.'

'We know a thing or two about Master Haycock,' said Luke Ricketts. He had big, shining teeth, like an advertisement for his brother's Dental Rooms. 'An embezzler when he was in Merthyr. He had to leave in a hurry. It was all the talk when I kept a shop there.'

'Was he convicted?' asked Will.

'He was certainly charged,' said his father. 'If he throws his weight around, I shall remind him of what happened.'

'These are dangerous waters,' said Mappowder. 'Please don't think I'm trying to tell you how to run the place. You have been the driving force behind the combine, and we are all aware that its potential for profits is very large. I would merely enjoin caution where Haycock and the union is concerned. If there is a particular wind blowing, we should be prepared to bend with it. The pits are in a turmoil right across the coalfield. Other workers may take advantage of that. Be careful, is all I'm saying. And let us keep an eye on our cash position. No buying cargo steamers for the moment, eh?', and Buckley raised an eyebrow at such an idea.

Dadda's dream had the substance of reality, but Will knew that a dream was all it was.

A summons to the North Dock at Swansea, when Buckley had been away from Tir Gwyn for half a day, made him gloomier than ever. He found his father showing Abraham Lloyd and cousin Joe around a rusty steamer called the *Hannibal* – plain as a shovel, built at a northern yard in the 1880s, an iron box for shifting things from A to B. Joe was fingering cloudy brasswork and dog-eared charts in the wheelhouse. When Abraham said he would be honoured to be her commander, Joe danced on to the wing of the bridge shouting 'Hurrah!', the sound echoing back from the warehouses and slums of the Strand.

'Don't resign from the pilotage yet,' Will warned his uncle, when he had him on his own.

'Your dad won't let me down. I know your dad.'

'Wait until you have it in writing. Just in case.'

When they were back at Tir Gwyn, Will tried to reason with his father. But Dadda looked through him and said that nothing was ever achieved by standing still.

Should Will tell the other directors? Before he could solve that problem, a worse one arose. Saul Haycock sought a meeting to discuss the Jones question and the canteen question. The night shift gathered outside the works gates, and somebody waved a red flag.

'I'll have him in here,' said Buckley, 'and I'll confront him with his past. I'll destroy him. I'll turn him into a Ben Ellis, and he'll say "Yes sir, no sir" when he speaks to you or me, like a man in his position should.'

Will made his decision. He went to see Saul Haycock after work.

He was in the kitchen, having his beard trimmed by Mrs Haycock.

Flora was there, and Will thought: what a fool I was.

'I'll be two minutes,' said Haycock. 'If you wait in the front room, Flora will light the lamp.'

Will went with her. She didn't look at him properly.

'You're still teaching?'

'What else?'

'And what happened to the band?'

'Mr Mokes died. I hope to restart it one day.'

'I shouldn't have deserted you.'

'Please don't blame yourself. The room was rented well beyond the time we continued to use it. I hope I was properly grateful at the time.'

'I mean you, not the band.'

He was aware of her warm skin and warm breath in the cold room. She seemed oddly uncomplicated, compared with everything else.

He said, 'Did you hear me?'

'You and I were poles apart.'

'You thought otherwise. If you kissed me now, I wouldn't need asking twice.'

Her father coughed in the passageway and came in fingering his beard. It looked slightly lopsided. She brushed past Will and closed the door behind her.

The men sat down at a table. An embroidered runner and a glass bowl lay on it.

Will asked if they were going to have a strike, and Haycock said he was the men's servant, not their leader. They were upset about Venn Jones.

'Not to mention their eating facilities. They seem to have a comprehensive slate of grumbles.'

'Something is stirring in people's hearts everywhere,' said Haycock. 'Laugh if you will. It won't change reality. They are at the point of deciding they want to be treated like men, not dirt. Are you here officially?'

Will shook his head. 'I'm here,' he said, 'because there's a rumour that you were involved in something shady in the Rhondda – embezzlement, no less. It might be used against you. I want no part of it. I came to warn you, that was all.'

'Why should you do that?' Haycock straightened the runner. 'It's an old story. I was supposed to have had my fingers in a strike fund. It suited an owner's nark to say so. The case was dismissed.'

'It could damage you here. The chapels are strong. The tinman isn't a miner.'

'I repeat the question. Why warn me? Do you mean threaten me?'

'No. I respect your case. I agree with it half the time.'

'I have a lot to learn, then.'

'The story will be used against you if the men come out at Tir Gwyn. I can't prevent it. Only you know if you can defend yourself.'

'Well, forewarned is forearmed. I shan't refer to your visit. I'm grateful.'

There was no sign of Flora as Will left. He wondered if she was his real reason for going there.

Sometimes Margaret thought herself back to the early days of the marriage, when Henry's key in the door made her stomach turn over. She would lie with her head on his waistcoat, feeling the muffled bumping of his heart, while he talked about – what, Gaddesden and the family? – and fingered her breasts. Six years wasn't long. What had they talked about, all those hours? They had been happy. When had they ceased to be happy?

She made lists of the things he enjoyed: such as the British Empire, weekends at Gaddesden, boiling baths and an after-dinner smoke alone in his study. Few of them required her.

At least he liked being looked after when he was unwell. Virginia said it was the one thing you could rely on a man for.

Henry suffered from colds in the head that gave him earache. Warm olive oil was the answer. She heated a silver teaspoon over a candle flame, half filled it, tested the temperature by letting a drop fall on the back of her hand, and tipped the rest into the ear.

Laid sideways on a table, and underpinned with a white towel, the head had a severed look. She closed the ear with a pinch of cotton wool, and Henry, snuffling and wheezing, turned his head so she could do the other side.

She had just finished a treatment when the evening letters were delivered. One was from Johansson; she recognised the writing.

He was supposed to be in Venezuela. The postmark was Hemel Hempstead. He said he hadn't gone after all. In fact, he was resigning from their partnership in order to join another firm, 'where I hope to have better opportunities, our business being in the doldrums'.

'That double-dealing Sander has poached him, depend on it,' said Henry, after reading it aloud.

He had to take out the cotton wool for her to repeat, 'I never knew whether to believe what he was saying.'

'I believed him. He was my partner.'

Olive oil trickled from his ear. He said, 'This is serious, Margaret. The rascal knows some of the finest sources in

South America. You recall the *Cattleya penburiana* that he almost succeeded in bringing back? I hate to think of it in the wrong hands.'

She wiped oil from his neck, wanting to say he was well rid of the dubious Swede. 'Never mind, Boy. He was a teeny bit of an adventurer, wasn't he?'

'He could be a swine, but he lived life up to the hilt. Women don't understand that sort of thing. We were a team, he and I. I shan't find another Johansson. I'm finished.'

Henry's cold got better, but not his misery. He pottered about the steamy hothouses, ignoring the occasional telegrams that still arrived with orders. Margaret did her best to despatch them herself. Searching for price-lists in his study, she found correspondence in a muddle, unpaid bills crammed at the back of a drawer, and, in a cigarette tin, yellowing photographs of can-can dancers.

Was it her own wickedness? Had she come to love Henry less because they had not been able to make a child together? Looking at the fat ochre thighs, love for Henry enveloped her. She tried being bold in their love-making. Finding him half-naked on his bed, sitting to remove socks and suspenders, she knelt in front of him, aroused him with her hand, and pressed down with her lips. She didn't care for it much. He made strange groaning noises. Next day he wouldn't speak to her.

Margaret persevered. If he didn't want that, she would concentrate on the hot baths and regular meals department. If he locked the study door against her, she could still find means of helping him put the business back on its feet.

She could have asked Morgan what had happened to the clients who used to order orchids, but shrank from anything that looked like begging, more especially since he had come into his legacy. They had not met in the months since Hannah's death. All Margaret knew was that he had rented a house in Kensington. He sent her a note on stately writing paper with an address in Peele Place.

Virginia, as usual, rescued her from the consequences of her fastidiousness. If Margaret didn't want to see the house, she jolly well did. They rolled up in a cab one morning, and Margaret felt a touch of pride at seeing a grander establishment than either of them had been expecting.

A mature parlour-maid answered the door, and left them in a reception room with an unusual number of upright chairs while she went for the master.

'This must be where they do it,' whispered Virginia. 'Do you think there's a presence about this house?'

'For goodness sake don't do anything to encourage him.'

The maid returned and took them to a study, where Morgan was studying piles of newspapers. 'That was Poppy,' he said, kissing both the women. 'You know about Poppy? She was the young woman who introduced me to spiritualism.'

He indicated a bonfire down the garden, being fed by a man in a cloak. 'The gardener's called Practical Hastings. He used to be a preacher.'

'The things you do say,' smiled Virginia.

'Every word is true. This is a house of spirits – there's nothing to be frightened of, it's bricks and mortar like anywhere else. The psychic phenomena are in the mind. But I must have employees I can trust.'

'In on the secret, you mean.'

'I forgive you, my dear Virginia,' he said, and Margaret couldn't tell if he was teasing. 'After that unfortunate experience with the wine glass and alphabet, what are you to think?'

'The less said about it the better,' said Margaret. 'We have come to see the house, not talk about your ridiculous spirits.'

'Sorry, Maggs,' and they began the tour of high-ceilinged

rooms with old-fashioned gaslight ('The spirits like it better than electric') and the characterless furniture that came with rented property.

So that they would be left alone, Virginia kept lagging behind or scuttling ahead – boldly opening cupboards, running taps, sitting on sofas, waving at her flushed reflection in mirrors. Then she drifted away altogether, on to another floor.

'You're angry because I've let you down,' said Morgan, stopping with his hand on his sister's shoulder.

'I'm enjoying looking at the house.'

'The orchid is going out of fashion. I don't seem able to provide the orders I'd like for Henry these days. Death of the King, I shouldn't wonder. These imperial English are obsessed with eras. They've had elegance and orchids. Now it's going to be socialism and suffragettes. Bad for Henry's business. Bad for mine, if I'm not careful.'

Like a conjuror, he produced a folded piece of paper and said, 'Here we are. Call it an advance order for hypothetical orchids.'

It was a cheque for a hundred pounds. When he refused to take it back, she dropped it on a table. It was kind of him, but out of the question.

'You're spending Hannah's two hundred on keeping him afloat, aren't you?'

'If I am, that's my business.'

'You're prickly, Maggs. Don't you love me, Maggs?' He balanced the cheque on a cushion and held it out to her. 'Still not up to scratch, am I? Not penitent enough. Too cocky by half. Why, the chap thinks he'll be the most talked-about medium in London before long. Really? Yes, he thinks he has powers. Powers from God? Now you're asking.'

'I hope you know what you're doing. They can prosecute mediums for fraud.'

Morgan sighed and put away the cheque. 'Come to one of my seances – just one, to see how much good they do people. Dear, sweet, incomparable Maggs!'

'Dear, sweet little spider with a web! Not even if you promised to materialise the late departed King Edward.'

'I haven't done a king yet,' said Morgan, and stroked her hand. 'Give me time.'

For a minute she lost herself in the endless maze of his attentions. He told her that her happiness was the most important thing in the world to him. He said he would seek a solution to Henry's problems that wouldn't embarrass them.

In typical Morgan fashion, he then upset everything, the minute Virginia rejoined them, telling her that a woman in a blue dress had been with her all the time she was walking about the house.

'How exciting!' she said.

'You make her unhappy because you laugh at the spirits. She says her name is Mrs Marmaduke, and she knew you when you were a child.'

'Stuff and nonsense,' said Margaret, seeing her sister-in-law go pale.

'There *was* a Mrs Marmaduke.' Virginia looked behind her. 'She was a cook,' and she burst into tears.

'Is that the best you can do, the cook's ghost? I've heard her talk about Mrs Marmaduke.'

'I'm sorry if I've upset you, Virginia,' said Morgan. 'It was a leg-pull, of course.'

But he said it in a way that suggested it wasn't.

A fault developed in one of the new Adamsons, a tension that broke the rope drive. The company refused to send its engineers until some of the outstanding bill was paid. Buckley despatched a shower of telegrams threatening legal action, and hoped the maintenance crews would find a solution.

That Saturday, cash was late arriving from the bank to pay wages. Anything to do with money made Will uneasy now. Every pound coming in had to be banked within hours of receipt, but bills to be paid were in a box in the cashier's office marked 'Hold'.

Paying for the *Hannibal*, a cash-on-the-nail job, had knocked a hole in the remaining funds. The board would find out soon, but by then, according to the old man, the steamer would be on the high seas with a cargo of tinplate, earning money. No cargo was forthcoming yet.

The South Wales Bank's motor car arrived with a sack of coin, and the men were paid for another week.

Will had arranged a walk with Flora. They might resume their friendship; or then again, they might not. They met near her school, where she had been visiting children ill with measles, which was sweeping the poorest streets with its usual thoroughness.

'Pa's still puzzled by you,' she said.

'He called off the strike, then. Or he persuaded the hotheads to keep quiet.'

'He did nothing dishonest in Merthyr. Only this is the wrong time to have to prove it.'

'Let's go on the beach,' said Will, and they took the old farm track at Tir Gwyn, alongside the works. The acid smell of the tinhouse made her nose twitch.

'Where do you sit all day?' she asked, and he pointed to an office window.

He held her hand. There was no one else on the beach. A blank sea lay under a blank sky.

'When we first met,' she said, 'I used to think I might convert you. I was very practical about it. I thought, I hardly know this man, and already he's giving me money for brass-band lessons. I had you down for all sorts of good causes.'

'Tell you what,' said Will, 'I could put you on to an old tinplate works that nobody wants.' Along the beach, their tracks disappeared into greyness. Above them loomed the dyke, shored up with steel piles. 'Room for brass bands, working-men's libraries and a nice doss-house for tramps. Bracing situation. Doesn't get flooded all that often.'

He helped her up the stone face of the dyke, using gaps where stone had fallen away.

The works looked smaller now, gutted and derelict. Brick-dust from the main chimneys, brought down months earlier by fires lit at the base, looked like a pool with ragged edges. Sheep grazed outside the shed where the hot-mills had stood.

Will found himself talking about the dragon whose roaring he heard in his sleep when he was a child.

'The dragon that eats up men,' she said.

They tramped around the ruins, and picked their way up dirty stone steps to what had been the office, now windowless and smelling of cats.

'Look on my tinplate works, ye mighty, and despair!' she declaimed, and Will said, 'My sister used to quote poetry. I want to kiss you.'

'Remember, you and I aren't on the same side. You think this is lovely – this monument to the great god money.'

'Stop talking socialism.'

'Poor tinplate men. Poor miners digging coal, and for what? For the British Admiralty to use in Dreadnoughts, ready to fight wars with. Would you fight in a war?'

'There won't be one.'

'The armament firms are counting on it. Did you know, somebody wants to build an explosives works in South Wales? *Now what are you doing?*'

'Making sure you're comfortable.' He sat her on a packing case and squeezed precariously beside her.

'Pa has a friend in the Anti War League. *You mustn't do that*. They are looking for somewhere round here in secret, not telling anyone.'

He held her tightly. She stopped talking at last.

Walking back, as the day thickened into darkness, they went across the marsh road and so past the gates of Y Plas. Lights shone between the trees.

'I saw a man with you once in town, collecting for the band,' said Will.

'And don't you have sweethearts?'

'I'd rather have you than anyone.'

The town was full of shoppers, cardboard men and women against the flaring windows. He didn't want her to go, but she had to take her sisters somewhere.

As he was leaving her, he remembered what she had said about the arms factory. He asked her to find out if her father or his pacifist friend had ever heard of a fellow called Pfizer. It was just a thought.

The disaster came quickly. The Old Castle works was having an Adamson engine fitted; they had people there from Manchester, and soon the rumour that Buckley couldn't meet his debts was circulating the town like steam in a boiler.

Mappowder heard about the *Hannibal* at almost the same time. Within hours there was talk of a row within the combine. Creditors became aware of other creditors. The South Wales Bank sought clarification, the first step before seeking its money.

Events gathered speed. The first thing the board did was to strip Buckley of all fiscal powers. The second was to put the *Hannibal* up for sale. Sprewett knew of a buyer. The Lewis–Egge combine, smelling opportunity, was offering a few thousand. The steamer was sold in a flash, as if Buckley and his vision had never been, and Abraham Lloyd, commander, lost his job before he started it.

But that was merely a gesture. Fresh capital to the amount of twelve or fourteen thousand pounds was required.

Did Davy happen to have that amount tucked away in an old sock? No? Then they would have to accept the kind offer of Colonel Mappowder and Rees Coal to make loans to the combine, in a form that diluted Davy's shareholding and meant that he lost his controlling interest. Otherwise the hands couldn't be paid next Saturday.

When the documents were signed and the other directors had gone, Will waited for some explanation, some expression of regret, some evidence that his father had come to terms with the disaster that had overtaken him. Instead, all the old boy could say was that he had been cheated by envious men.

'I shall rise again,' he said. 'I shall make this combine a byword.'

That afternoon he walked to the Conservative Club, to show them he wasn't broken. At the market, winter vegetables were laid out on benches; the red necks of turkeys hung over the sides of baskets. He had a far-off memory of visiting the market as a child, with his mother. Ice hung from a tap, and a woman gave him a cockle on a pin.

The old works was barely a memory – chimneys and a huddle of sheds on a saltmarsh. He imagined his empire as it would be, spanning Glamorganshire. He would find a way.

He marched into the Conservative Club as if he owned the place.

Henry didn't mend the glass when boys threw stones at the hothouses. Margaret knew then that it was time for drastic action.

They were invited soon after to Gaddesden, to celebrate the fortieth wedding anniversary of Arthur and Elizabeth Penbury-Holt. She hoped to find someone to talk to in confidence – Charlotte, perhaps, the senior daughter-in-law, who could gauge the chances of Henry being taken back into the firm. A hint should be enough.

The old, unreconstructed Margaret would have gone straight to the point, doing more harm than good. She was subtler now; she stalked her prey.

The rambling house was packed. Grandchildren were everywhere; Henry's generation was still breeding, though Charlotte's fourth (a little howling-machine, like the rest) was expected to be her last. Virginia was pregnant with number three, and Daisy, the doctor's wife, had three already.

Margaret would have liked to hug the smaller ones, but they were not a hugging family. The larger ones had been ordered (she suspected) to have polite conversations with their Aunt Margaret, and, having done their duty, kept their distance.

One of Charlotte's brood, the boy Stuart called 'Old Hat', addressed her as 'Aunt Esther'. Esther herself wasn't there – away on some Suffragette mission that no one referred to. Mixing up the names was a harmless enough mistake. How foolish of her to be made unhappy by it.

Her chance with Charlotte came early in the evening on Saturday. Sons and daughters had been looking at the presents, laid out in a small drawing room where the parents would be brought – unawares, everyone pretended – before the celebration dinner. Charlotte stayed behind, adjusting a candlestick, wiping a fingerprint. Margaret stayed with her.

The room had a reddish tinge, red glass and red silk among the silver plate and silver cutlery, red roses magnificently splodged in bowls, even an actual ruby here and there, staring from a necklace, a brooch, a tiepin. The place was like a shop-window, and Charlotte, big-hipped, was the manageress.

'There,' she said, 'that should do. Handsome, isn't it?'

'Exquisite,' said Margaret. 'Is it tonight that the Father will announce his retirement?'

'We must wait and see. But Tristram has been doing much of the work of senior partner for the past year.'

'Henry misses the office, you know. Very much.'

That was it; the deed was done. Charlotte said, 'Mm,' and shut up the shop.

All Margaret could do was wait, letting the weekend rush past her. She had an odd encounter with Daisy, the youngest daughter, married to the medical man from the North, Munro Parton. Margaret hardly knew her. Her latest child was a baby with a domed head like a monk. For a while on Sunday his mother had him away from the nursemaid, and dumped him in Margaret's arms. His ungainly features touched her even more than the usual pretty baby-face; she couldn't leave him alone.

The two women were by themselves in a conservatory. Daisy had blonde curls and blown-out Penbury-Holt features, but underneath was warmth and sisterliness. She kept a shrewd eye on Margaret and the baby; spoke of a miscarriage she once had; remarked that her husband took a special interest in problems of gynaecology; mentioned that he was thinking of hiring rooms in Harley Street.

'He's an excellent doctor, should you ever wish to consult someone,' she said, and Margaret, who had not previously thought of Munro Parton as anything more than a pair of skinny bow-legs and a nose like Mr Punch, found herself saying, 'Thank you, Daisy. You're very thoughtful.'

The weekend made her feel better. Old Saracens itself was a lovely house – not that one needed lovely houses to be happy in. She and Henry could be happy anywhere.

That is, if they would ever be happy again.

On the journey back to London, Henry was morose, staring at fields and brickworks from the train, eyes closed in the cab. It was no more than she expected. Home at last, she waited for the storm. They ate a light supper in silence. Lake cleared the remains and retired.

On the sideboard, an orchid wilted. Henry cleared his throat. 'I have been humiliated,' he said.

'I made one remark only.' She meant to have it out. There was nothing to be ashamed of in helping one's husband. 'I made an oblique reference to you and the firm. I did it on purpose, to alert Charlotte and thus Tristram. With your father retired, they might welcome your return. The fact is that the orchids are going to make paupers of us. So be it, if necessary. I love you and I shall stand by you, whatever happens. But I decline to sit like a dumb animal and say nothing. What I did, I did as tactfully as I could. I am sorry you feel humiliated.'

'Charlotte?' he said. 'Who said anything about Charlotte? I was talking about Munro Parton.' He rubbed two fingers up and down his forehead. 'You have had a field day with my family.'

Margaret winced at her mistake. The doctor, said Henry, that damned doctor had approached him. 'As a matter of etiquette,' thundered Henry. Munro Parton had said, 'I hear your good wife is having trouble conceiving. I would be delighted to see her.'

Henry's face was bruised with anger. 'The most intimate, the most delicate secrets between a husband and wife – bandied about at my parents' house,' he said.

'It's hardly a secret that we have no children.' She was both angry, and anxious to comfort him. 'Please listen, Boy – '

' – and stop calling me Boy!'

'I made no overtures. Daisy spoke to me, and must have spoken to her husband. It was not on my authority.'

'Blaming my sister hardly helps your case.'

'You make it sound as though I'm accused of an offence.'

'Two offences, it turns out.'

The quarrel ended in silence and hostility. For days Margaret saw little of her husband. He left in the morning, as he had done when he worked in the City, and came back at night. Perhaps, after all, he was talking to his brothers. Virginia knew nothing.

At the end of the week he returned home with Morgan. He was all smiles. So was Morgan. She was taken aback; sent Lake out for a joint and a bottle of claret; held her breath; watched their faces.

'Henry is going to be my business manager,' said Morgan.

'So buck up, old girl. We are going to live in Peele Place.'

'The rooms you liked on the second floor, Maggs.'

She wanted to faint or scream, but nothing was appropriate, except despair. Where would the nursery be in Peele Place? She said, 'This is my home.'

'We can't afford it, old girl.'

For the first time in her life, Margaret knew what it was like to be poor. The lease had been paid until the renewal date, in spring; she begged Henry to let them remain until then, and Morgan, seeing her distress, said he saw no objection.

Overnight, she was a poor relation. Morgan gave no hint that he saw things in this light. He had the same mischievous respect for her; continually sought her approval; said as little as possible about spiritualism. It was no use, his cry of 'Maggs!' grated on her now.

Henry was at Peele Place every day. She had no idea what his duties were; had no wish to know. Often he was late returning. One night a telegram came instead, to say he was detained and would sleep in Kensington. 'Your loving Morgan,' it signed itself, as though Henry had resigned control over his own life.

It was after eleven o'clock, a cool night, wind sighing over the London hills. She went out to the first hothouse – unlit and unheated now. It smelt of decay. A few blooms were still alive. She picked a velvety purple one and held it tightly.

The cold smell of London soot and London stone poured in through broken glass. It was terrible to feel so alone. She thought she was probably going mad. She pressed the bloom against her, saying 'Poor cattle's-ear, poor cattle's-ear,' over and over again, until the words lost their meaning.

12

The Lloyds were penniless, Joe and his father reduced to cockling and shrimping. Buckley bought them a decrepit fishing smack, an expense he said he couldn't afford, and left them to get on with making a living from Carmarthen Bay. Joe said he would happily be a fisherman, and pretended to put away his text-books about marine law and navigation.

They sold skate and codling to local traders. Villette said she would never hold up her head again.

Then Egge the tin-stamper sent a curious message. He would be pleased to see Captain Lloyd at seven o'clock in the evening.

Abraham waited in the drawing room where marble heads stared at him, and a pier-glass reflected a weather-beaten skull and a pilot jacket that had seen better days. When Egge appeared, so did his partner Lewis.

Abraham was uneasy, remembering that the same Rhodri Lewis had stirred up trouble on the Harbour Trust. But Lewis said severely that bygones were bygones.

Sherry was poured into a tiny glass that grew hot in Abraham's hand. They knew something about his history. They were in a position to offer him command of the *Hannibal*.

The *Hannibal*?

'Flagship of our fleet!' cried Egge.

Abraham said honourably that he would need to consult one or two people. But they told him he had to decide on the spot. A cargo for the Continent would be made up by the end of the week. That was the way with busy men.

'Someone of your experience is a cut above fishing boats,' declared Egge.

He had a smart son, Lewis believed, studying for the merchant marine. Catching fish wouldn't be much help in that direction.

To be known about was a compliment. Abraham's head was in a muddle. They showed him a piece of paper on which was already inscribed, 'Abraham Lloyd, Commander'.

'Mrs Lloyd will be pleased,' said Egge encouragingly.

'She will, she will,' agreed the captain, savouring his desirability.

'Do we shake hands on it like gentlemen?' suggested Egge.

'And sign just here,' said Lewis, pen and ink ready.

Buckley was incensed. The fact that Abraham went to tell him, and handed back the fishing boat, made no difference. Hadn't he been aggravated enough, without a member of his own family going behind his back to negotiate with his enemies? They had done it on purpose to slight him.

Will's attempts to defend his uncle only made matters worse.

'I'm entitled to ask for loyalty,' said Dadda. 'Ingratitude is a terrible thing.'

Were the words aimed nearer home? Will stuck to his duties. The combine made its tinplate and mined its coal. Rees's pits were back at work. The Adamson engines thundered as per specification, their monstrous flywheels spinning till they might have been standing still. But Will could no longer pretend that the aims and objects of the undertaking were of any consequence to him. Each day was drudgery; the shapes of workmen who came and went along the road in two-legged herds gave him more to think about than the boxes of tinplate that were the point of their existence. His father, rambling on about his 'empire', the mills and steelworks that he meant to bring together one day on vast campuses to rival the Americans', might have been describing the lost city of Atlantis or the creatures that lived on Mars.

With the spring came Dr Pfizer, driving up to Tir Gwyn one morning in a horse and trap, still in his leggings, still talking about cheese.

Months earlier, Flora had given Will a reply to his question about Pfizer. Haycock had mentioned it to his pacifist friend, the one who said the warmongers wanted to build a munitions works in South Wales, where steelworks were handy to make the shells. But the friend knew only that an agent of Nobel & Co was rumoured to have been in the area. His name wasn't available.

Now the offer was repeated. The site outside Port Howard, Pfizer said in his stiff voice, appealed to his principals. He spoke knowingly about grass. His wallet, secured with straps and buckles, lay temptingly on the table. He was authorised to pay nine hundred pounds.

It was a lot of money for cheese.

'Nobel Explosives can afford to pay more than that,' said Will. What did he have to lose?

'If you make fun of my offer, I go this minute.'

'Goodbye. Trubshaw, will you show this gentleman out?'

But the gentleman stayed. He said these were delicate matters. He would prefer not to hear the name 'Nobel' spoken aloud at this stage. It was time, perhaps, for lawyers to talk.

Dadda was off on one of his expeditions, probably trying to purchase a small passenger liner on credit, or something equally silly. Will told him nothing, and was careful not to instruct Oscar Harris, who gossiped. Instead he went to see Christmas Jenkins, Hannah's solicitor.

In his dark old-fashioned clothes, he looked about a hundred.

'They'll want to drive a hard bargain,' warned Will.

Christmas grinned and said he had been driving hard bargains since before Mr Nobel discovered dynamite. Who did Will think stood out for thousands more, and got it, when the Great Western wanted to build its viaduct over Tomos Buckley's fields at Rhydness?

If Nobel had come back for Will's piece of land, it was because the site suited their purpose better than anywhere else. 'Near to railway lines, don't y'see?' he chuckled. 'Towns with experienced labour they can draw on. Sea water for cooling. Isolation, very important. That's why they built the old powder works there.'

He thought he'd ask for twenty thousand and be prepared to come down a bit.

Negotiations lasted almost to the summer. 'Strong nerves,' urged Christmas. Once, a man in a black hat and a coat with an astrakhan collar came to see Will and implored him to intervene, because his solicitor's demands were outrageous and the deal was about to fall through.

Will hung on. He bicycled there with Flora on a hot Sunday afternoon (He said, 'That used to be a gunpowder works.' She said, 'You capitalists see the landscape in terms of works'), and they curled up talking and kissing in a hollow of the dunes. He loved her; he told her so; he had told her before, but in the warmth and quiet, with the sea scratching the sand beyond the lip of grass, it had different consequences.

Half naked, they lay in the sun afterwards, drifting under strips of cloud. Suddenly a man appeared above them carrying a striped rod. He said 'Pardon me' and thrust it in the top of the dune.

Will threw a coat over Flora and pulled his trousers up. There were two men, surveyors, with chains and tripods.

Will told them they were trespassing, and the man who had surprised them laughed and said, 'Well, at least that's all we're doing.'

'I own the land. Now remove yourself from it, or there'll be trouble.'

His manner made them pack up and go.

'Why did you tell him that?'

'Because it's true. We capitalists are devious creatures. But don't worry. I'm selling it.'

She did up her cuffs, looking solemn. 'I was right,' she said. 'We *are* poles apart. What does loving me mean?'

He said things would be different soon, but she must be patient. He wouldn't elaborate; he wanted to be sure. He guessed, though, that Christmas Jenkins had done it again.

Margaret went to live at Peele Place because she had no alternative. Ragged bits of philosophy ran through her head – 'If you can't get what you like, you had better like what you get' went round and round like a popular song till she was weary of it.

The lease expired; the furniture men came; Lake left with a good reference and five pounds. Margaret stood in the nursery for the last time, watching the spring sunshine slant in through the window on to the bare boards.

Asking Dadda for help was out of the question. She wouldn't have done it, for shame, but in any case she knew something of the combine and its troubles from Mamma's letters, fiercely defensive of her Davy. So there was nothing for it but Peele Place and a new life that one ought to be thankful for, brothers as thoughtful and well-off as Morgan not being found on trees.

The rooms were agreeable, if only they'd been hers; she missed the shabby villa in West Hampstead. She kept to what Henry called 'our private apartments'. Coal, clean linen and food cooked by Poppy were sent up from the nether regions. There was no shortage of amenities. They came and went as they liked.

Henry's office was on the ground floor. He kissed her goodbye in the morning and she rarely saw him again until the evening. He never spoke about orchids now. That was a closed book, a life that had gone. She thought of him as a kind of conjuror's assistant.

It was Morgan's first season as a practising psychic with a manager, a carriage and a fashionable address. His regular sittings, never fewer than three evenings a week, were well subscribed. No money was sought or accepted on the premises, but cheques sent later through the post were treated as gifts and paid in smartly to Parr's Bank.

Other evenings were kept for visiting. The Thorns were practically old friends, their faith in their young provincial justified. Lord Leuchars invited him to Charles Street more than once, and so did a friend of Leuchars, an Irish peer called Rathlackan, who was unfortunate enough to have a seizure and die during a manifestation of spirit lights. This ensured reports in the morning papers, one or two of which referred to 'Mr Morgan Buckley, the Welsh spiritual medium'. God might not be on his side but was at least prepared to be decently neutral. Rathlackan had no sooner crossed over than his ghost was visiting Charles Street, more eloquent in death than he had ever been in life.

'You mustn't think me a snob, Maggs,' he told his sister. 'My reasons are tactical. Names breed names. What with the Coronation coming, they say it's the most brilliant social season there ever was. I am feeding on the edges of high society – don't look so shocked, the voices tell me to. They have no class distinction on the other side. Then again, we have thousands of colonials coming here to gawp at the king-making. Think of all the reunions with family spirits who didn't emigrate to Australia.'

For Margaret, the hardest moments came after dinner

when the lights flared up more brightly, a signal that in the drawing room below, the gas had been turned down and her brother was starting to talk in strange voices. She would have nothing to do with the seances.

Henry was always urging her to attend one.

'So I can rattle a tambourine or tug a thread?'

'You have an entirely false idea of what goes on. Pull yourself together. Try to realise it's your duty.'

'I won't take part in something I despise. I wish you would resign your post. I would rather you were a clerk and we lived in lodgings.'

She was cleverer than Henry; usually she concealed the fact, but during arguments it was liable to slip out and enrage him. In a temper, his eyes were smaller in relation to his cheeks. She tried not to dwell on this and other physical unpleasantnesses – rims around the bath, that sort of thing. Love offered emergency solutions, if only they worked. She had spells both of approaching his bed every night, and of not approaching it at all, depending on what she thought he wanted. Either mode seemed to get on his nerves. If he had caught cold she could have cossetted him with warm oil in the ears, but during the fine weather he was strong and healthy.

Word came that Dr Munro Parton had put up his plate in Harley Street, and Margaret went to consult him, taking Virginia with her, sworn to secrecy. He examined her in a room with grubby net curtains, chatting to her about Old Saracens and the ruby wedding. His nurse was on the other side of the screen, washing bottles in a sink. After half an hour he said there was no apparent reason for her failure to conceive. The fault might conceivably lie with Mr Penbury-Holt.

The droll face with its red hooked nose loomed over her. 'What is the frequency of intercourse?' he asked, and the bottles rattled in the sink.

'Two or three times a month,' Margaret answered.

'These days we know more about the male aspect of things than we did. Would he be willing to consult a medical man?'

'He would not.'

Virginia insisted on hearing every detail, hooting with laughter. 'He *didn't* say that? You are a goose, going to see him instead of Sir Somebody Snooks.'

'I expect he was as much or as little use as anyone else. It's my fault, I know it is.' They were in a private corner of the ladies' luncheon club that Virginia belonged to. 'What shall I do, Virginia?'

'Keep trying. There are more ways than one of loving a man. They have an Indian book at Old Saracens, locked up in the library. Stuart showed it me once. You would never *believe* such inventiveness.'

'I mean, about everything.'

'What are you grumbling at? We all know Henry is a baby at business, so be thankful you have a brother who isn't.'

'I want Henry to be *himself*, not dependent on Morgan. It makes me angry. I can't help it. Spiritualism is such nonsense. It's one thing for Morgan. He has a religious twist. Henry is down to earth. I think that's what attracted me. He was the opposite to someone like Morgan. He was solid and English and not particularly clever. What he believed was what he could see.'

It dismayed Margaret to find tears in her eyes. That wasn't very Penbury-Holtish. Virginia chose to pretend not to notice. Her advice was to support Henry: what else was there?

But the harder Margaret tried to forgive him for making such a mess of things, the angrier she grew with Morgan. His visitors were impossible to avoid all the time. Seances she could refuse, but sometimes there would be an At

Home or a supper party, and she would do her duty and accompany her husband.

More than once she met Mrs Squale, to whom she took an instant dislike. Mr Squale was present on the first occasion, but not thereafter. The Squale woman confided in her that Morgan was 'my young protégé who has outgrown the nest, bless him'. Her coils of hair reminded Margaret of snakes.

Before breakfast one morning, after there had been an evening seance, Margaret saw her walking in the garden, and realised that Cordelia Squale was in the habit of staying the night. She felt it was the last straw.

Morgan knew at once that she knew. 'It's time we had a day out, Maggs,' he said. 'Just you and me.' He wouldn't let her say no. Henry thought it a splendid idea, or thought he should think so. It was her duty to go.

Part of her wanted to, in any case. London was still London; she had read few of its stony pages.

The Fulham Road was brisk with carriages and motor buses. An aeroplane crawled across the sky. People stood, pointing.

'I've neglected you, I know,' said Morgan.

'You've corrupted Henry, that's what I can't forgive.'

'Now, Maggs! You were always inclined to exaggerate. He runs the office, that's all.'

'He's in your web. So am I, for the moment, but I can look after myself. I don't know that Henry can.'

He pretended to be downcast. Sighing, he took her to Shepherd's Bush and the White City. Street hawkers and traders were all along the Uxbridge Road, catching the crowds as they followed the signs to the turnstiles, 'Coronation Exhibition' and 'Wonders of Empire'.

Hands in pockets, he went where she went, standing meekly outside pavilions like a henpecked husband while she made up her mind which way to go. It was only Morgan playing tricks. He stood mute in front of the Taj Mahal and gold-dredging in New Zealand, smiled at her smiling at the bears and tigers, waved at her through the rainbowed arc of Niagara Falls, frowned at the Welsh coal mine when she frowned.

'Am I forgiven?' he said at last.

'When I was married, you could hardly bear to speak Henry's name. Now it suits you to make use of him.'

'There you go, Maggs, putting the worst interpretation on everything I do. I was a callow youth in those days. I have come to like him. Is that a crime, liking my sister's husband?'

'You think you can talk your way out of anything. So you could, with me, once. You've talked your way out of Miss Rees. We never hear anything about her now.'

'She would hardly fit in at Peele Place. Be reasonable, Maggs.'

'You mean because of Mrs Squale.'

'Don't be naughty.'

'You could invite them here for the Coronation. Wouldn't you like your daughter to see it?'

'No, no, quite impractical,' he said, pausing to watch Indian women making lace and buy her an extravagant length. But his refusal gave her an idea.

Colonel Mappowder looked in at Tir Gwyn on a Saturday morning to see if the men's canteen was open yet, cold water tap with sink to be installed, coal stove provided with a ton of nuts and sweepings free every year.

Buckley said he had been too busy to do anything yet.

'It requires an instruction from you,' said Mappowder. 'Do you want the board to go over your head?'

'All in good time, Lionel.'

'The board decided on it five months ago. You make it very difficult. Is Will here? Let me talk to him.'

'He's away on his bicycle somewhere. Now if there's nothing else, I have letters to write.'

'You're a servant of the board. You are no longer the controlling shareholder. Come back to earth, man!' and Mappowder went away shaking his head.

Buckley did what he always did when provoked, and took a stroll around the works. But these days nothing could be relied on.

He came across a rail wagon bearing messages of support for striking seamen. 'Get this filth cleaned off!' he said. He wasn't having anarchist slogans, chalked at Liverpool and Cardiff, in his sidings.

Sailors, dockers, railwaymen, miners, they were all being bloody-minded this summer. It was worse than last year, a strike here, a strike there, men testing their strength. Why now, why 1911? No one knew.

Will arrived, out of breath, and Buckley ticked him off for walking through the works wearing bicycle clips. And where had he gone to?

Will put a slip of paper in front of his father. It was a banker's draft made out to Buckley in the sum of sixteen and a half thousand pounds.

'What's this?'

'Money. It was mine for thirty minutes. Now it's yours.'

Buckley's brain garbled the details as he heard them. He looked at the draft, and Will, and the clock, and the draft again. The words 'Nobel & Co' burned themselves into his brain.

'It means,' he said, racing ahead down the long vistas of his dream, 'it means . . .'

'That's it.'

'We can buy back control.'

'You can. You know better than I what to do with it.'

'You, me, what difference does it make?' One minute he

was embracing his son. The next, he was toying with figures on a pad.

It was as if he had known all along it would happen like this.

Only Will was a discouragement. During a lull in the telephone calls and dictating of letters, his son came in and said quietly, 'I must talk to you. I mean to leave the firm within a year.'

'You do, do you?' said Buckley. He knew at once that it must be strain. The secret negotiations had pushed him to the limit. 'What you need is a long holiday. Go where you like. Take a month. Go to your sister's. Go to the Continent. You'll feel different after that.'

He was called to the telephone. For him, it was the end of the matter.

For Will, it was the start. He was free now; he owed his father nothing.

The news about Nobel & Co would be all over the town by Monday. He had to see Flora first, to tell her himself. That evening the old man was at Cilfrew Castle, to meet Mappowder and Sprewett. Will declined to join them ('Mind you plan that holiday,' said Dadda). Conscientiously, he saw the weekend work get under way at Tir Gwyn, and set off on foot to visit Saul Haycock.

New Dock glittered in a mist, declining sun versus dust. A solitary locomotive shunted past, air vibrating over its funnel; on the boiler was chalked, PUNISH SCABS.

In the town were tram cars, horse traffic, a motor, smell of beer, Salvationists in bonnets, striped shop-blinds, soldier's statue, crowded park, clouds of insects; two colliers with black faces, laughing by a tulip-bed; a feeling of unease.

Flora was in the kitchen. The doors were open and he walked through. She was cutting sandwiches, wearing an apron over her dress.

'No time for anything,' she said. 'Put some more butter on the plate, if you want to help. You can't stay, either.'

Her father was coming back with two friends. The rest of the family had gone to a singing festival. She was woman-in-charge.

'You may have a piece of bread and butter, a quick kiss and then off you go.'

'You're beautiful,' he said, sitting at the table. 'Feed me till I want no more. Do you believe that I love you?'

'I believe you have certain notions about the romantic side of life. I believe that if I belonged to your class or you belonged to mine, you'd see me differently.'

'I'm tired of my class, as you call it. I've a mind to resign.' He tried to stroke the front of her apron, and she threatened him with a pickle jar. 'Shall I place an advertisement in the *News*? "To whom it may concern. I, William Buckley, hereby declare that I have left the capitalists and joined the other lot." Will that do?'

'You make it sound like a game.'

'That's all it is. I gave away sixteen and a half thousand pounds today. I'm serious.'

'Barmy, more like.'

He explained about the powder-works land and Nobel, but she wasn't impressed, even when she realised he was telling the truth. It was what capitalists did all the time, shifting their wealth around from one immoral purpose to another.

He was still trying to make her understand when figures appeared in the passageway.

'Quick,' said Flora, 'run down the garden, or you may have to shake hands with socialists.'

Will stood up to greet them.

'My word,' said Saul Haycock.

He had two companions. The man with pitted cheeks was Benny Nolan, the brother-in-law from Liverpool. The man in the clerk's blue suit with half a tattoo showing under a cuff was Tommy Spit.

'Long time since we met, Mr Buckley.'

'You found work.'

'You'd be surprised. I write a nice copperplate with my left hand. Funny thing, I still miss the old mill. Buckley's has come on since then.'

'You had a raw deal from us.'

'No worse than average. I don't bear no grudge.'

'They did you a good turn!' cried Saul, and winked at his daughter. 'Is the beer nice and cold?'

'In the scullery, in the sink.'

'We'll go in the parlour. Care to join us for ten minutes, Mr Buckley?'

They crowded into the room. An exercise book with homework had been left on the table. Benny Nolan crumbled tobacco into a paper and rolled a cigarette.

'The newspapers say Liverpool is having the worst of the strikes,' said Will, and realised his mistake at once.

Nolan picked tobacco off his lip. '*Worst* of the strikes? They are running food convoys from the docks. Soldiers at front and rear. Every man-jack with twenty cartridges. They are shoeing cavalry horses to use in the streets. *Best* of the strikes, I'd say.'

'It depends on your perspective,' said Haycock, and drew the curtain to hide the street. His daughter brought in the food and lighted an oil lamp. Haycock said, 'There are plenty of radicals who abhor violence.'

'I abhor it myself,' said Nolan, 'but the authorities keep on provoking it.'

'What does Mr Buckley say?' asked Haycock.

'If everything else failed, perhaps. But with democracy, the right thing gets done in the end.'

A moth fluttered at the lamp, and Tommy Spit killed it between the black glove and his good hand. 'A boss's son can't help,' he said. 'Born into a class, he is. The track is laid down. He has to follow.'

'Dogma,' said Will.

'Why's he here?' asked Nolan belligerently, chewing bread.

'He's a guest in my house, that's why.' Haycock stuck a leg over a stool. 'He came to the Chartists' Cave and cheered with the rest of us. Of course, he might have come as a spy ('We chucks that sort in the canal at Bootle,' said Nolan). But he and Flora are great pals. I sincerely think that he knows the old order trembleth, that this society can't last, that oppression can't last. He knows there are plans afoot.'

'To do what?' said Will. Far off, a locomotive squealed, a door banged, a woman laughed; the town seemed at an immeasurable distance.

'Use the weapon we've had all along,' said Tommy Spit. 'The general strike. Act together, we have to. Every industry, every trade. It would be over in a week. Asquith would sue for peace.'

'Keep your trap shut!' growled Benny. 'You Welsh never know when to stop yapping.'

'What's the secret?' cried Saul. 'Winston Churchill knows all about it. He kept troops at the ready for months in case they were needed at Tonypandy. At this moment Liverpool is encircled by the military. You know as well as I do, Benny, keeping order is only part of it. Some of them are ready to work the gasworks. The power station. The lockgates.'

'Try to work them,' said Tommy Spit.

Footsteps sounded in the street. A rustling crept along the walls of the house.

'Something up,' whispered Haycock, and Nolan got to his feet.

Suddenly the house shook. The parlour door burst open.

Uniforms rushed in. Benny had a poker in his hand, roaring abuse. A truncheon caught him under the elbow. He gasped and fell on his knees.

Inspector Hussey was holding a photograph under the oil lamp and comparing it with Benny's face, twisted now with pain. 'Benjamin Nolan,' he said, 'I have a warrant for your arrest issued by the Liverpool magistrates.'

'This is my brother-in-law on a family visit. There is a woman in the house.'

Will could see Flora in the passageway. He tried to go to her, but an arm barred his way.

'You are charged with a serious assault on a police officer,' Hussey was saying. 'You will be held here overnight and taken to Liverpool in the morning.'

He was hustled out. A crowd was gathering in the street. The inspector peered at the exercise-book; he looked disappointed to see arithmetic.

Names were taken. Saul Haycock, trade union official. Thomas Jenkins, railway clerk. Will Buckley – 'Iesu mawr, Mr Buckley, what are you doing here?'

'I looked in to discuss union matters at the works. Ventilation during the heat wave.'

'We'd better get you out the back, sir. We don't want tongues wagging.'

'Why should I want to leave? I'm here on lawful business.'

'As you wish.'

The heavy figures walked out one by one. Flora was still shaking. 'Go in five minutes,' she whispered. 'I love you, do you know?'

He poured beers for the four of them. His hand was trembling, too. Tommy Spit looked at him ironically and said, 'Iechyd da, Mr B,' the glass almost hidden inside the black glove, steady as a rock.

* * *

Morgan had just heard from a millionaire that a welcome awaited him when he visited New York. He waved to the departing taxi and stood on his broad stone steps, shirt-sleeved, like a servant. The sun was behind the chimney pots, but warmth still rose from the pavements.

He had kept in touch with Walter Marshall, and the American, in London to see the English crown their king in two days' time, had come to Peele Place.

Marshall sat with him in a darkened room, and nothing happened. This time there were no messages about East Coast rivals. Morgan waited to see if any wraith or extra-sensory antenna would oblige with a successor to that trump card of the last occasion, the Little Imp. When none did, he opened the curtains and smiled regretfully.

Pretence could only do harm. Marshall had been told one thing that was incontrovertible, and he would wait years to be told another. Under those conditions, failure was itself a kind of evidence. He remembered the words as Morgan spoke them, no more and no less.

He even remembered the message that came after, about the sick child.

'That was a funny business, too,' said Morgan. 'It was my daughter, who was born outside wedlock. She had pneumonia. I suppose I was meant to save her. I had never seen her. Something made the spirits work overtime that afternoon. I wish I could repeat the performance to order.'

It was then that Marshall said he could come to the United States as his guest whenever he chose, and Morgan said, 'In a year or two, perhaps. I shall know when the time has come.'

As the taxi vanished around the corner, another one appeared. He watched to see if it would go to the house opposite, where a Spanish-looking woman in tight clothes came and went from time to time. He liked full-bodied women with a hint of thigh below the skirt, and looked forward to excursions with some of them, when he wasn't so busy.

The taxi stopped by the steps. A small arm waved and a small voice shouted, 'Uncle Morgan! Uncle Morgan!'

Isabel, Isabel's mother, Mrs Harry and Margaret emerged from the taxi. Morgan retreated backwards up a step before taking hold of himself. Aeronwy, carrying the child under one arm like a parcel, thrust herself at him. 'How good and wonderful of you to invite us!' she gasped, and Isabel grabbed him by the waistcoat pocket.

His sister, looking pleased with herself, told the driver to take the suitcases into the hall.

'Just arrived at Paddington, have you?' said Morgan, with an attempt at cheerfulness, patting Isabel on the head and disengaging her. 'You'll be able to stay overnight, I suppose?'

'He's forgotten you've come for the Coronation, the goose,' said Margaret.

Mrs Harry greeted him respectfully and made Isabel clean her shoes on the foot-scraper, just in case. The taxi driver saluted, waiting to be paid, and Morgan handed over coins.

His visitors were all in the house by now. Had some spirit been working overtime to make a fool of him? But it was only Maggs, tormenting him because she loved him, because they loved one another. He often wondered if she knew how much he relished her presence under the same roof. From the garden on summer nights he would watch the lights in their bedrooms, and look for shadows on the blinds.

Margaret was surprised at how well Morgan took the visit. He beckoned her into his private sitting room, where a coal fire burned and Hannah's rocking chair stood in a corner, and said he knew what she was up to: she was cruel, she enjoyed tormenting her poor brother.

'Wrong as usual,' she said. 'They deserved a treat. Why shouldn't you give them one?'

'So you tell her I've invited her here and give her ideas. Come on, Maggs, that's not the way to make her happy.'

'You make her sound like a schoolgirl. She has no illusions. I expect she knows quite well that it was I, not you. But she likes to pretend – why not? Since your entire life is based on a fiction, I don't see you have any cause to complain about hers.'

'What a tongue you've got these days,' he said, admiringly.

Henry, she knew, would not be as tolerant. But Aeronwy was to sleep in their apartment (the only decent course), leaving the child and her nurse to occupy a room elsewhere in the house. Henry would have little chance to make his views felt.

He was awkwardly polite to Miss Rees, and left the two women still talking when he retired. They sat up late. The visitor was too excited to be tired. She talked about a trip that she and her mother, now dead, once made to London. She spoke continually of Morgan, and how she had always known he was fond of her.

Despite her confident words to her brother, Margaret began to wonder. She had interfered in an equation she knew little about. 'Well, there it is,' she said lightly, hoping to be taken seriously, 'men have peculiar ways of being fond. I'm glad you have your typewriting career.'

'I'm not as dull as I look,' said Aeronwy, her greeny eyes very round and dry. 'Sometimes I loathe Morgan and sometimes I adore him. But I never underestimate his power to do as he pleases.'

Lying in bed afterwards, Margaret thought she couldn't have put it better herself.

Next day she took the visitors and showed them London. There was time for a park (brass bands and summer dresses), a waxworks (Isabel was terrified, imagining they were dead people), a department store (Aeronwy bought some silk for herself and a box of dark cigarettes for Morgan), a man in chains on the pavement (he undid himself inside a sack, collected pennies in a hat and called Isabel 'my young beauty'). Margaret had forgotten how easy it was to be happy. Watching Aeronwy, she caught an echo of her own excitement when she first came to London.

Coronation Day was fine and clear. The streets were busy before dawn. Newsboys with early editions could be heard shouting in the Brompton Road. Henry, inexplicably, was unwell with one of his ear-aches. He delayed their departure, and in the end, Morgan took the visitors, leaving Henry and Margaret to follow.

The house was empty. Henry, his ears oiled, rubbed his neck with a towel, frowning. Through open windows came a sound like trees rustling in wind.

'Listen, that's the crowd,' said Margaret.

Henry banged the window shut. 'Now that we are alone,' he said, 'I have things to say to you. Your behaviour has been a disgrace. How dare you bring that woman and her child to your brother's house. It was unforgivable.'

She laughed at him. Henry defending Morgan was absurd. Henry was nothing to do with Morgan. Morgan was her brother. He was as remote from Henry's understanding as a sentence in Welsh would have been.

The more Henry shouted, the less inclined she was to take him seriously. His brick-red face was like a mask, hiding the flesh and blood of jolly old Henry.

When she tried to walk from the room, he thrust out his arm.

When she went to push past him, he flung her backwards. She crashed into a table, broke a framed photograph of Mamma and Dadda, and hurt her hip. Through the pain, all she could see was the mask, floating in mid-air.

'You can spend the day here thinking over what I've said,' he panted.

Next minute she heard the door being locked from the other side, and the sound of jolly old Henry receding.

The windows overlooked the garden. It was empty, as were all the gardens. Bursts of cheering floated over London.

Hastings appeared below, in his shirt-sleeves, drinking from a medicine bottle.

She called to say she had been locked in by mistake. He hid the bottle and came into the house and upstairs at once.

'Thank goodness you were here,' said Margaret.

'Poppy wanted me to go with her, Madam. But I can no longer keep up with the Poppies.'

Henry appeared behind him. 'Back inside, Margaret, if you please.'

'I wish you to call the police, Hastings.'

The butler seemed unperturbed. 'They'll be busy today, Madam. I am on duty here – I, Practical Hastings.'

'Clear out,' snapped Henry. 'You're drunk.'

'Is the Atomic Elixir strong drink? Nay, verily I say unto you, inasmuch as the transcendental chemist has stirred the universe with his finger, so shall his tincture be blessed. Now permit Madam to pass, sir, or I might have to give you one.'

He was a big man. Henry made a lunge, thought better of it, and went downstairs. 'Bless you,' said Margaret, and packed a hand-case while he stood guard. He escorted her to the hall, where Henry, emerging from the office, demanded to speak to her alone.

'Goodbye, Henry,' she said.

Hastings found her a cab, with difficulty, and it took her by a roundabout way to Esther's flat in Victoria. The cheering was louder here; bunting swayed above the empty street; church bells were ringing.

Esther was preparing lunch for a party of Suffragettes who were coming back from the morning's festivities – for the moment, there was a truce with the Government. In the rimless clip-on spectacles that militant sisters were advised to wear, she looked thinner and harder these days.

'I have done something of which you will not approve,' said Margaret. 'I have left Henry. It would be a great relief to be allowed to stay here for a few days. Failing that I must go back to Wales.'

The pure sound of trumpets from inside the Abbey made her spine turn to ice. She wished she had seen King George V. But there were more important things.

'Help me mix this salad,' said Esther.

At the start of August, works shut down for the annual holiday. Chimneys stopped smoking and the air cleared. Cottages and even cattle could be seen on the green flanks of Gower across the estuary. There was time to do things. Eisteddfods, chapel outings, cricket matches and fairs obliged. The railways ran excursions. Shops near the sands laid in extra ginger beer. People said what a nice change it all was. But with the enjoyment came a sense of disruption. The place lost its rhythm. Without hooters sounding, gangs of men going past in clogs and the clamour of mills in the background, the town seemed to hesitate; what was the point of anything, without the central purpose of the works?

Will and Flora cycled out to Pembrey to see how Nobel & Co was getting on. Rail sidings were being laid on the scrubland, and twin tracks already swept away to connect with the main line. Men with a bucket crane were levelling a dune.

They had not been back since the day they made love there. A rough fence with a single strand of wire ran along the shore, and signs said 'PRIVATE. KEEP OUT'.

'What will you do, if you leave the works?' said Flora.

'I could be a teacher.'

'You'd need a diploma. You wouldn't have the patience. Where would you teach? *What* would you teach?'

'I'm on holiday. I don't have to know the answer this week.'

They sat on their bicycles, arms entwined. The Buckleys had gone to Llangammarch Wells. Will was supposed to go with them, having stubbornly refused to take himself off on any other kind of holiday. But he remained in Port Howard.

'I think I liked you better when you were a capitalist,' she said. 'At least I knew where I was. Now you say you're something else, but nothing's changed, really. You live in a big house and you sit behind a desk in a big works. You have some romantic idea about teaching. It's hard work, I can tell you. You try teaching sums to kids with nothing in their stomachs.'

Will rang his bicycle bell to shut her up. 'When we go out on the pleasure steamer tomorrow, if you carry on like this I shall pick you up and drop you over the side, and you can swim back to Swansea Docks.'

'We may not go, come to that,' she said. 'The railwaymen are coming out, you know that?'

'Not tomorrow they aren't.'

'Nobody knows what they'll do. My Pa doesn't know.'

'Says he doesn't know. He's deep, is your Pa.' He touched her breasts but she pushed him away. 'It's stop week. People are enjoying themselves. The railwaymen can't come out tomorrow. We're taking Aeronwy and Isabel. Tell your Pa to inform the Workers of the World accordingly.'

But something of her bleak uncertainty rubbed off on him. Flora touched on other worlds. She still had the same look in her eye that he remembered from New Dock School, the day he spilt the porridge.

Early next morning, as he set off from Y Plas for the

railway station, he found the silence disturbing. The town had no focus. Its corridors of stone and brick, lit by the sun, were the cave dwellings of another race.

'Cheer up,' she said, when they met on the platform. 'I was wrong after all. The trains are running. And what d'you think? Uncle Benny's out of Walton Gaol – Pa had a telegram last night.'

'They can start the revolution now, can they?'

'Poor Uncle Benny. Such a temper. We're all ashamed of him really.'

The others were waiting for them as arranged, on a convenient street corner near the river at Swansea, where the paddle steamer left from a jetty. Flora had met them once already, when Will took her to Brynmill Terrace. Now, together on an outing, they were like a family, of sorts, with Mrs Harry bringing up the rear, telling everyone she had taken arrowroot for breakfast so as not to be sick.

The ship crossed the Bristol Channel in dense fog, its own and other sirens mooing like stricken cows. But there were few ships; many seamen were on strike. In the English town on the other side, they walked up steep streets into sunlight, and fed a goat in a garden with handfuls of grass, before eating in a wooden chalet.

It seemed to Will as if his new life, whatever that would be, had begun already. He half listened to Aeronwy telling Flora about the Coronation. Mrs Harry dozed, and he took Isabel to see a Waterfall and Grotto. Wooden figures of goblins and dwarves stood everywhere. The two agreed they didn't think much of it.

'Why are you my Uncle Will?' asked the child as they walked back. Already her fine black hair made people look twice.

'Because I'm your Uncle Morgan's brother.'

'He's my father,' said Isabel.

'You must talk to your mother.'

The girl shook her head. 'I know he is.'

'You know a lot for six.'

'Uncle Morgan showed me paint that shines in the dark. He makes ghosts with it. I'll make ghosts when I'm grown up.'

Their futures were beckoning them.

The fog had lifted and a breeze made blue-black waves. Mrs Harry was sick. Will and Flora kept warm by the funnel, holding each other tight.

'What a lovely, lovely day,' Flora said, when they had seen the others on a tram, and were walking to High Street station.

The yard was crowded. Trains were running late. An official distributed handbills from the railway company, explaining that porters and shunters had withdrawn their labour. Inconvenience to the public would be kept to a minimum, it announced at the bottom, between two hands with pointing fingers.

A constable stood by as the London mails were taken on to the platform. A motor van dropped off a late edition of the *Post* for the High Street newsboys. 'Riot Act at Liverpool,' Flora read out, and Will said, 'Now then, Uncle Benny.'

13

Men were up at dawn, watering the shrubs and flower-beds by the lake at Llangammarch, so that guests at the hotel would get the nice wet smell as they walked out before breakfast. Every morning Buckley strolled and sniffed, and went inside for bacon and eggs and *The Times*, crisp off the train except for one morning when it failed to arrive; railway trouble, said the manager.

The holiday was excellent. But then, a boarding house by a gasworks would have done. Buckley was in charge again. The board had had no option. A man didn't pump a small fortune into a company without setting out his terms. Rees Coal's loan was repaid. The banks bowed and scraped. Buckley had his controlling interest back. Mind, he had signed a piece of paper promising to submit anything costing more than five hundred pounds to the board. But he would find ways round that.

Pomona's neck and wrists got quite sunburnt. Her legs were better. She accompanied her husband to a horse show and an excursion on the moors. To please him she even drank a few glasses of the sulphurous local water, as recommended by Snell before they left. Build her up, that was the thing. Buckley didn't tell her – he wouldn't, if he could help it – that Margaret and Henry were having troubles, *going through a bad patch*, as people put it.

In the afternoons she lay on a chaise-longue and watched him play croquet. Looking back at her along an avenue of trees, he would see her wave a handkerchief. Far off in the converging green, it was like a signal for help.

They returned on a Sunday. The train meandered

through rural Wales, then halted in open country a dozen miles short of Port Howard. After a while the carriage was unpleasantly warm.

Next to the railway was a field of corn, harvested up to an invisible boundary, as if a plague had struck; Carmarthenshire farms still took Sunday seriously. Beyond the fields a pit-wheel and slag-heap could be seen.

Buckley saw the guard walking along the ballast, and got down to join him. 'Don't go far,' begged Pomona.

The guard confided that an iron bar had been found on the line, and the track was being searched. There were ruffians in the union, talking of a national strike. It was the second iron bar in a week.

'If they derailed a train and killed someone, that would be murder.'

'True words, sir.'

Buckley told Pomona it was cows. But she said men had been gossiping in the corridor. Only the day before, miners from the nearby village had thrown a gate on the line.

'Stupid rumours,' he said.

He couldn't bear to see her so upset. She looked her age these days. The world frightened her. He made her get down for some air, which wasn't easy. He held up his arms and she fell into them with a squeal.

Other passengers had alighted and stood chatting, but he led her through a gate and along a hedge, as if they were lovers, out for a Sunday stroll. 'Do you remember before we were married, walking on the hill at Rhydness?' he said. 'The day I kissed you, and you said I was a devil?'

'So you were,' she said, for a moment the old Pomona. He kissed her cheek; it felt hollow. In the field, in the silence, he had the old feeling of permanence between them, as though, sustained by one another, they and their marriage would last for ever, through death and beyond.

The guard blew his whistle. The holiday was over.

* * *

High tide on Wednesday, soon after dawn, saw the *Hannibal*, commander Abraham Lloyd, going down the dog-leg channel in a summer sea-fog that Joe said you could cut with a knife and put on your bread like dripping.

Abraham was short-handed. The crew was missing three deckies and a greaser, pulled off the ship by delegates sent by the Swansea strike committee. By rights it shouldn't have sailed at all. Shouts of 'Blackleg!' and a shower of stones came out of the fog as the vessel cleared the lock gate. But Egge had been round the night before to say that company orders were to get away at all costs. Five hundred tons of tinplate were loaded already, and another nine hundred were at Briton Ferry, if he got up to the quay when no one was looking. En route he could pick up a couple of non-union men at the Mumbles Pier.

'You are the captain, of course,' said Egge. 'If you were to advise us that you couldn't sail for safety reasons, we should have to respect your judgement. But Mr Lewis and I would like you to take a positive view. Get this cargo to Gothenburg by next week, and there's a fifty-pound bonus in it for you.'

That meant enough in the bank for Villette to have her house with an inside lavvy. But it was Joe who swayed him. Joe was bo'sun of the *Hannibal* now. He wanted the glory of this being the only vessel taking cargo out of the Bristol Channel. She was an old tub overdue for the breakers, but Abraham knew that his son lived for nothing else.

In his cabin, the neatly folded jerseys and oilskin trousers would have astonished Villette. The almanacks and navigation tables that he was studying for his mate's ticket were laid out ready for idle moments, together with ink and paper. His tally of ship's tasks hung from a bulkhead; the stores ran through scrubbing brushes and lead paint at a fearful rate.

If anything he was over-keen. Abraham knew what it was

like to make a life out of a ship. Yet Joe took him back to an earlier self, when nothing mattered but the adventure of the sea.

As they pushed through the fog, dead-slow, siren blasting across the bay, Joe was the bow lookout, standing at the rail with his head on one side, hearing as well as seeing. Abraham had thought twice about sailing with a depleted crew, a couple of them blacklegs who didn't inspire confidence. Joe swung the balance. Youth could change anything.

Joe swivelled and cupped his hands. Abraham stuck his head through the wheelhouse window, and the shout came back, hollowed by the fog. 'Number Four buoy off the port bow.' Half a minute passed before Abraham saw it.

Rees Coal, in Port Howard to preach at a seaside mission, was at Y Plas for supper on Thursday evening when the coachman, who had been told to listen out for a special edition of the newspapers, sent in a *Star* on a silver tray.

'The worst has happened,' said Buckley. 'The railway unions have despatched the telegrams from London. They are forcing a national stoppage.'

'World has gone mad, Davy,' said Rees.

'Let's be philosophic about it. There are goods piling up at the docks as it is. We've got tons of plate that need shipping. Railways take second place for the moment.'

'Let's hope the military is ready. I trust I'm as good a Christian as the next man, but ye can't do better than a line o' men with cartridges in the breech, advancin' on a riff-raff.'

'Have those trade unionists no feelings?' asked Pomona.

'They want a living wage, Mamma,' said Will.

'What, are they dead, then?' cried Buckley. 'Frequently idle, I agree. But they appear to draw breath. They have two legs that could take them elsewhere if they don't like it.'

'I'm not well, Davy,' came from the end of the table, Mamma's way of stopping a quarrel. Soon she was lying on a couch, Dr Snell in attendance. He gave her one of his powders and remained for a whisky and a chat. He said he had heard shouting and police whistles when he was on his way to Y Plas.

Curious to see what happened in a railway strike, Will wandered into the town. Men were running down Station Road. A crowd had gathered on the main-line level-crossing outside the station. Jeering and whistling under the lights, they were like a shadow without an edge. A locomotive loomed above them, buffers up to the gates.

'We appeal to the driver and fireman to join us!' a voice was shouting from the gates. The fist in the air was a black glove. 'Come on, boys!'

Will couldn't catch what was said from the cab, but Tommy Spit's voice rang out again, 'Boat train, mail train, makes no difference. Nothing goes through. That's final.'

A group of uniforms advanced warily on the crowd. The sergeant in charge held a truncheon over his head. 'You are breaking the law!' he shouted. 'They will be sending soldiers, mind.' The truncheon bent in his hand. It was a rolled-up mackintosh. The crowd cheered him and sang 'Sospan Fach'.

The train steamed slowly backwards. Will realised he was cheering, too.

The town was busy with rumour. 'They are looking for a magistrate to read the Riot Act,' he heard a man say in Market Street. Sprewett and Inspector Hussey stood talking on the Town Hall steps. Electric lights designed to look like torches of learning shone down on them. Sprewett seemed to be drawing a plan in the air with his walking stick.

Will slipped down an alleyway and emerged by Saul Haycock's office. The windows were dark. What had he expected to find, a red flag and a committee in session?

Flora would be home, at any rate. The front door stood open, light coming from the kitchen. She sat cleaning knives with bath-brick on a board. Her eyes were deep-sunk; a curl was coming loose.

'Why are you doing that?' he asked, standing behind her, playing with her ears.

She reached up and ran a finger along the back of his hand. 'Somebody has to.'

'It's after ten. I looked in at your Pa's office but he wasn't there.'

'Why ever did you do that?'

'They've cut the railway at the level-crossing. There are hundreds down there.'

She worked furiously on the knives. The kitchen was unnaturally clean; the floor had been powdered with red chalk, and the children's dolls and crayons all put away.

He said, 'The Irish boat train is stopped. Others as well. I want to know what's going on.'

'A railway strike is going on. They've been talking about it for long enough. Thank goodness they've had the nerve to do it at last. What else is there to know?'

'Seamen are out, dockers are out. Who's deciding what happens next?'

'Nobody, as far as I'm aware. You're making such a fuss. Sit down and do some forks.'

He couldn't fathom her. 'This isn't Liverpool,' he said. 'Men don't go on the streets down here. Somebody planned it. The union only sent the telegrams this evening. There were people ready – Tommy Spit for one. He's down there now. Is that where Saul is?'

'I'll let you into a secret,' she said, and wiped her hands on the apron. 'He's upstairs, asleep.'

'As if nothing had happened. And you're cleaning the cutlery – that's as if nothing had happened, too.'

'What is he going on about now?' she said. 'Ma isn't here, that's all.'

'Ma being where?'

'Taken the children to Merthyr to stay with the old people.'

'Where they'll be out of the way,' Will said triumphantly. 'If the railways don't run and the docks are closed, who knows what'll happen? It could be the start of the general strike. They say one of the trains is the London milk. See how they like it up there.'

'Open the eyes of the capitalists, will it?'

'Why do you try to be so superior?' he burst out. 'You aren't really indifferent. Come to the station with me. I want to see things happen.'

'Leave it alone. It's not your concern.'

'I suppose your Pa's been talking to you. *Don't trust that Will Buckley. He spies for the combine.*'

'Go back to Y Plas,' she said. 'Nothing will turn out as you expect. Come here on Sunday. We'll go up Swiss Valley. You can kiss my lips if you're good.'

He stormed out into the street. Far off he could hear men singing.

There was a movement at the upstairs window. Haycock was standing in his nightshirt.

'Saul!' cried Will, but the man only smiled and shook his head, and pulled down the blind.

By breakfast-time on Friday a company of the Lancashire Regiment had arrived. To the delight of Rees Coal, they were too few to hold all the level-crossings against the crowd. They retreated peacefully to the station, where they cleaned their equipment and mounted guard on empty platforms. But English officers didn't like retreating. The strikers were playing with fire. It was a happy thought.

Mappowder called an informal meeting of masters in the back room of the Conservative Club at noon. Rees was still at Y Plas, and meant to attend. 'Will is coming with us, aren't you Will?' said his father. 'We stand together on the deeper issues, he and I.'

'What if 'e says 'e's on their side?'

'He isn't. When it comes to fundamentals, he's a Buckley.'

But Rees Coal shook his head, deeply mistrustful of anyone who could give sixteen and a half thousand pounds away, whatever his motive.

The Colonel wore uniform; the situation must be grave. 'Gentlemen,' he said, standing on the hearth, 'the town is in the middle of unprecedented events. I have information that a further three hundred soldiers and their officers are expected in the late afternoon. These are modern fighting men, armed to the teeth.'

'I hope their brains are in working order, as well as their guns,' said a voice. It was Rhodri Lewis, the old enemy.

Jeering broke out. Mappowder said he hoped there would be no seditious talk, and called on Mr T. T. Rees, magistrate, who was there to tell them something that should put an end to carping criticism.

T. T. had cut himself shaving, and looked as if he hadn't slept. 'I was at my grocery business at half past eight this morning,' he said in a low voice, 'when the Town Clerk came personally with a copy of the Riot Act and said my services were required.'

The great Sprewett intervened to say that that was entirely accurate. He added, in the utmost confidence, that the police were down to a skeleton force, numerous constables and three sergeants having been sent to Cardiff earlier in the week, since who would have thought that Port Howard was in danger?

'Pray continue,' he said.

'I went to the level-crossing with Mr Sprewett, a Captain of the Lancashires, and a party of fifty men. I then attempted to read the Riot Act, but I was shouted down. Some of the remarks were insulting. The Captain said he would order the soldiers to fix bayonets, but rather than risk bloodshed, I begged him to withdraw them to the station.'

'I hope that that example of restraint will satisfy the critics,' said Mappowder. 'Unless absolutely necessary, the authorities will not meet force with force.'

Tom Egge declared that there was more than one way of outwitting the mob. He could tell them now that the *Hannibal* was at sea, or soon would be, jam-packed with tinplate which the strikers had been unable to stop, thanks to the determined seamanship of local men.

'Stick to the point!' came a rebellious quaver from Rees Coal. There would have to be a battle, sooner or later, he said. The sojers would teach the mob a lesson. But the rest of 'em had to be prepared as well. If they 'ad any sense, they'd use tinplate men as vigilantes.

'Lead us in prayer, Rees!' called a voice.

'You watch yer godless tongues,' barked Rees. 'Coal's been my life, an' I learned long since you can't trust the miner, ever. He's a devil, is the coal-miner. But the tinplate man's a peaceable sort. Do what you like with him. He don't want trouble. He'll guard yer works when the mob comes a-shoutin' and a-screamin'.'

Some of the masters laughed. Others thought he had a point. Hughes of the Old Castle said self-protection should be on everyone's agenda. Mappowder agreed, as long as the role was purely defensive. Fighting was for trained men.

Will raised his arm for the Colonel's attention, and there

was some pointing and shushing. Buckley was expressionless.

'The meeting ought to be aware,' said Will, 'that not a few of the mob, so-called, is made up of tinplate workers. ['*Shame!*'] I counted more than twenty faces known to me at the station crossing at eight o'clock this morning. ['*Let's have their names!*'] Never mind their names. They are trade unionists making a common cause with the railwaymen. Examine that crowd, and you'll find men from all quarters – from iron works, from tin works, the pottery, the docks, and, yes, the coal mines as well. The meeting should realise it. We are not dealing with a few strikers. We are dealing with a united body of workers.'

'Of hooligans,' shouted a master, and the cry was taken up, 'Hooligans! Hooligans!'

'And what does Mr Will Buckley suggest?' asked Colonel Mappowder above the din.

'All friends here, I'm sure,' chuckled Egge.

'Moderation and good sense. Pray that the railway companies will come to their senses before it's too late.'

Order collapsed. Everyone was shouting at once. But Buckley took no notice. Will was young. 'What are you grinning at, you silly fool?' he shouted at Rhodri Lewis.

The announcement of the *Hannibal's* coup was premature. The promised blacklegs failed to materialise at the Mumbles Pier. Abraham lost twelve hours at anchor there, before he decided, with misgivings, to make the river passage up to Briton Ferry. It was too late. The quay, when they arrived, was blocked by a pair of mud-hoppers, in charge of some unsavoury customers from the Cardiff docks who threatened to come on board with hand-spikes.

Abraham turned the *Hannibal* round and went back to Swansea Bay to think. 'Sorry, Joe,' he said. 'We've got half a cargo and half a crew.' The Mate, an elderly man who had been in dredgers, rubbed his stiff fingers and said they would be home in time to catch the Saturday-morning tide.

Late on Friday, they began the short haul back to Port Howard.

It was the Captain's watch, Joe alongside him as helmsman. Their shortest passage would have been the inshore channel, following the Gower coast. The night was clear, with a slice of moon in the water. But Abraham's caution asserted itself. It was a falling tide, and what inshore chart ever marked every reef and bank? They were in no hurry.

'Steer two-one-five,' he said.

'Two-one-five, Cap'n.'

'Going outside the Helwicks, Joe. Just to be on the safe side.'

Joe didn't answer, fixed to the wheel like an extension of it, his face lit in scratches by the glow of the binnacle. Left to himself, Abraham knew, Joe would have sailed for Sweden. But he got on with the job and didn't complain.

Soon, now, he would have his first ticket, and be away to Liverpool or Rotherhithe to find a ship. They had that understanding between them. These days there were too many fleets of cargo liners steaming up and down the oceans for a smart young officer to stay at the short-sea end of things. Joe had a future with gold braid and a big company. Abraham would send him off with his blessing. Old tubs were for old men.

The *Hannibal* rolled in a trough, creaking at the joints. Even the flattest sea had mysterious lumps and dents in it. Abraham stood on the wing of the bridge, listening to the thud of ancient engines.

The watch changed, and their pounding followed him into his sleep. Three and a half knots would bring them off the Burry Estuary by breakfast. He didn't need calling. The first change of engine-noise brought him awake and on his feet. They must be off the land. Milky light came through the porthole.

Joe, quicker off the mark, went pounding up the companionway to the bridge. Abraham was close behind, grunting at what he saw, white cliffs of fog.

'We're a cable inside it,' said the Mate. 'I got a bearing on Llanmadoc Beacon and the Worm.'

'Stop her man, stop her!' cried Abraham.

He brooded over the chart where the pencil lines crossed. Swinging at anchor, they could hear sheep on Llanmadoc or another of the Gower hills. If they were to catch the tide up to Port Howard, invisible on the far side of the estuary, they had ninety or a hundred minutes' grace before entering the fairway.

Abraham waited a full hour. The fog showed no sign of thinning. Joe was restless, working with chart and slide-rule. In the bows, the Mate tested a lead-line. A seaman stood ready at the anchor-winch.

'Pretend you're the Master,' said Abraham. 'How do you proceed?'

'I'm familiar with local conditions. Our position is known, pretty near. Visibility . . . two and a half cables. That's enough if we look where we're going. Tide sets from the west-sou'-west at one and a quarter knots. I've done a course around the Hooper to bring us up to Number Seven buoy. After that it's straightforward.'

'Show me.'

The calculations were in order. Joe sharpened a pencil, whistling as if he didn't care. Abraham's pride welled up. He said, 'Very well, Bo'sun, them's your orders. Take the wheel and take her in.'

He shouted through the window to get the anchor up, and Joe asked if he could ring for dead slow. Abraham told him, 'You're the pilot.' There were no more questions.

It should have worked. The tide was still rising. The worst they could expect was a bump on a sand-bar.

Whistle blowing every half-minute, the *Hannibal* edged through the fog, decks shining with moisture. Who wouldn't be proud of a son like Joe?

The Mate, swinging his lead over the bows, yelled that it was shallowing. Joe rang for slow astern, and Abraham shouted for a second leadsman at the other end of the ship. He had to leave the bridge to instruct him, sign of a second-rate crew.

He missed the fatal calculation. Afterwards they went over it a thousand times.

Joe saw Llanmadoc Beacon through the fog, just the tip, a green crest that vanished a moment later. The bearing should have been near 30 degrees. It was 160. They were far up the estuary. The shallowing water meant the tip of the Hooper bank.

Where the barque *Jerusalem* ended up, where the nightmares came from. In the white coils of fog he lost his nerve or his judgement. He rang for quarter speed and dragged the wheel to starboard, looking for the safety of the channel.

It was minutes before Abraham returned. 'Steady at two and a half!' the Mate was calling. 'At two and a half! At two!'

'I saw Llanmadoc Hill,' said Joe. 'Bearing one-six-o.'

Abraham looked at the chart. 'You saw Rhossili,' he said.

He rang to stop engines, and at that moment the Mate screamed, 'Rock bottom!'

Joe had been right to begin with. That was what they dwelt on, time and again.

Before Abraham's order had time to take effect, the *Hannibal* crunched on to a reef off Bluepool Bay. A sounder ship might have survived. But her plates buckled and she took water at once. There was no stopping it. The tide floated her off minutes later, filling at the bows and already difficult to handle.

Abraham beached her on the steep sands at Broughton. A sheepdog ran out of the fog, barking at them. 'Now remember,' he said to Joe, 'you were the helmsman, under orders. Your career's in front of you.'

Coal dust was floating on the water. A man in leggings came after the dog. Abraham put the crew to work moving boxes of tinplate out of the hold before the water got at them.

'A few precautions are in order,' said Buckley. 'A couple of men will keep an eye on the sidings. We rig some lamps up, ready for tonight. Phillips suggested we have a fire-hose screwed into the main.'

'He would,' said Will.

'I think I deserve to know where you stand. Tir Gwyn is as much your works as mine.'

'I'd defend it, if that's what you mean. But it won't arise. Listening to them at the club yesterday, you'd think the mob was out for blood. They're working men with grievances, that's all. If they came here, they'd listen to reason. They don't have any quarrel with us.'

'Workmen who talk about a general strike have a quarrel with everyone.'

'They show discipline, Dadda.'

'You see them through rose-coloured spectacles. I went to the level-crossing at six this morning. There were bright sparks coming off the night shift. They rolled up their aprons, splashed a bit of water on their skinner cuts, and started taunting the soldiers. They weren't disciplined. They were vicious.'

'We shan't agree,' said Will.

He had been there, too, and seen his father across the street, leaning both hands on his ebony stick. There were bystanders, even at that hour, in the sea-fog that curled along the streets from New Dock. Deacons and shopkeepers walked up and down the fringes of the boiling crowd. Mob and bourgeoisie ignored one another. An invisible barrier lay between.

In mid-morning the fog stopped drifting in, and the sky cleared. Phillips said the sun was definitely flashing on bayonets near the copperworks. He also claimed to have seen a goods train approach Port Howard from the west and leave it to the east, moving away towards Loughor Bridge.

Did that mean it was all over? If so, Will knew the railwaymen must have lost. He didn't want that. He wanted victory so that he could say to Flora: That was what I wanted. He wanted them to roam the town together, to see the crowds through her eyes, to feel them press up against him in the shape of her figure.

Rumours festered. They were tearing up the rails. They were negotiating. Other towns with level-crossings were joining in. Soldiers had broken up the rioters (the word began to be used), or the town's dairies had run out of fresh milk, or the magistrates had ordered the public houses to stay closed.

Chimneys continued to smoke, locomotives to shunt in private sidings, steel bars to metamorphose into silver sheets of tinplate. Normality couldn't be switched off. Children with towels ran on to the sands. The shops in Stepney Street were full.

Will washed his hands and put on a straw hat. It was two o'clock. The week ended.

'Mind your step, now,' Dadda said gruffly.

'I shall come back later.'

From a distance, the crowd outside the station had a holiday air. There was even a roar of laughter. Someone standing on the gate – could it be Tommy Spit? – was pointing down the road. A fresh column of soldiers came marching four abreast from the direction of the goods yard, where the troop trains were shunted.

Sun flickered on their rifles. As they approached, they changed to single file, and doubled round the back of the station, reappearing on the end of the platform, which was already crammed with troops.

They leaned on the rifles, looking hot. The crowd cheered.

Officers appeared. One of them was Mappowder. He shouted that an important train was coming down from Cardiff. Those who had any sense wouldn't try to delay it.

This brought groans and whistles. Will edged nearer. 'There are magistrates present,' could be heard, 'Riot Act in their pockets . . . good run for your money . . . be sensible, like this morning.'

'That was a cattle train,' shouted Tommy Spit, his face bobbing into view. 'Took pity on the cows, we did.'

A railwayman with whiskers called for restraint. They could win this fight without resort to rough measures. The railways would be nationalised before long.

'Go home, Whiskers!' shouted a young man.

A lump of coal came from nowhere and hit a wall.

Did someone decide, now is the time to throw lumps of coal?

He could get to the Haycocks' and back before the Cardiff train arrived. But when he reached the house, it was locked up. He banged the knocker, and a woman with a baby in a shawl appeared from next door and said there was no one at home. Flora had been gone an hour, to help with a Sunday-school outing.

Shoppers drifted along Stepney Street. Pavements rippled in the heat. T. T. Rees had put a lifesize plaster pig in his window, festooned with Palethorpe's sausages.

This time Will approached the station from the east. The

copperworks crossing had a guard of soldiers. A passenger train was moving away, towards the platforms in the distance.

Sam Lewis in a smart grey suit stepped between the lines. They couldn't avoid one another.

'That's the special from Cardiff,' said Will.

'Is it, now?'

They inspected one another. Sam's face was heavier, his lips thicker. He said, 'I hear you were nearly lynched at the Conservative Club.'

'Old men with wrong ideas. What's your view of the dispute?'

'Haven't got one, my dear Will.' He lunged with his straw hat and killed a wasp. 'I was supposed to be meeting a little girl, but it seems she's on strike, too.'

They walked down the track together. Approaching the station, there was no sign of the train. Soldiers could be seen. Beyond the platforms, the level-crossing gates were open.

'All over,' said Sam. 'So much for your brave boys.'

'Wait a bit.' In the glare, a column of troops was doubling along the ballast, westward from the station. 'Old Castle crossing! That's the strategy.'

It was a quarter of a mile down the line. The brown and cream coaches were in a cutting. Backyards and bits of grass behind poor houses overlooked the railway. Crowds of men and boys were up on the skyline, throwing stones. Soldiers were all along the track. They ducked and waved their rifles.

'Ambushed,' said Will. It was like the Boer War. He remembered the illustrated magazines. Someone, not the magistrates and not the Army, had learnt the lesson.

A thin voice that could have been T. T. Rees's rose above the shouting. 'Lawful order . . .' could be heard, and 'hereby give warning . . .'

An officer had climbed to the top of the embankment to talk to men in the back gardens. Figures leaned towards him, gesticulating. He scrambled down again, and a stone whizzed over him and hit a soldier on the head. The soldier's cap fell off. He disappeared from sight.

'Hooligans,' said Sam. 'If this was America, they'd have clubbed some sense in them by now.'

What could men do but use the means at their disposal?

'Because a few of them are throwing stones – '

'Christ, look!' said Sam.

Rifles were pointing upwards. The threat was greeted with jeers.

'They only give 'em blanks, boys bach!' someone shouted.

The rifles popped. A man fell backwards off a wall. There was screaming, a sense of darkness, of people fading from the scene.

14

By the afternoon, Abraham could do no more for the *Hannibal*. Coastguard and police had found their way to the remote beach at the end of the Gower peninsula. Messages had been sent to the owners and the insurers, reporting the loss – 'Aground at Broughton, Glam. Badly holed. All hands safe.'

Captain and crew were taken to Swansea in a farm cart, where Abraham inquired about trains, and was asked where had he been living? He even had difficulty hiring a brake. The carrier said two anarchists had been shot dead in Port Howard and others wounded. He demanded an extra five shillings for the danger. Joe called it a typical Swansea trick.

Joe's finger-ends bled where he had bitten them. He was to go straight to Bank Cottages, to tell Villette they were safe. Abraham had the owners to deal with.

At Egge's house, windows were shuttered, the servants nervous. The master was across at Mr Lewis's, where the women of both families had gathered. He was sent for, and the owners arrived together; Egge's teeth seemed to rattle in his mouth, he was so angry.

Captain Lloyd was sorry? He would be sorrier. There was such a thing as a Board of Trade inquiry, and Egge would see to it that criminal negligence wasn't overlooked.

A commotion was heard outside. The door burst open. Joe was there, with a manservant behind, trying to grab him.

Joe said, 'They aren't at home, Pa. They should've been

back from Theo's lesson at seven. There's soldiers with bayonets in the town.'

Lewis said it was all right to go. The world was upside down.

Abraham insisted they went home first. The others might be there by now. But it was as Joe had seen it. The kitchen table was laid for supper. Flies were trying to get at a piece of cheese in a glass dish.

The piano was open, the sheets of music ready to play.

They tried to go down Market Street, but a constable advised them to keep clear. Figures could be seen in the dusk, running to and fro in front of the shops. Glass broke with a chilling noise.

A dozen colliers barged round a corner – white teeth, black faces. They had bottles of beer. They were singing. One of them had a woman's corset on a stick, waving it like a flag.

A dozen soldiers marched past, in the charge of a corporal. The colliers booed. The soldiers went on marching as if they hadn't seen them.

Police whistles blew. The soldiers began to run.

When the Lloyds reached the Stoker residence, no one would answer the door. Abraham had to go round the back and shout.

A curtain moved. Mr Stoker, his cravat come loose, said through the glass that Mrs Lloyd and her son had been gone two hours at least. Old Mrs Stoker's hand appeared and closed the curtain.

They were not at Y Plas, either. Gardener and coachman were on watch in the grounds. Mr Buckley was at the works.

Redness filled a corner of the blue-black sky. The coachman said a goods train had been set on fire.

Abraham went to the police station, but they knew

nothing. A bell rang continually; a captain of the Worcester Regiment was talking to Inspector Hussey.

Suddenly a smart fellow in a bowler brought Villette in from the street. She ran to Abraham and began sobbing about Theodore.

The fellow in the bowler had to explain. He was Jonathan Boulton, the town librarian (Abraham couldn't help thinking it was typical of Villette to take refuge with a librarian). Terrified by a patrol of soldiers, the lady knocked on his door, which she happened to be passing. Lady and little boy were made welcome. Piano was played. Young daughters entranced. Talk turned to books. Boy went to use water-closet. Boy vanished.

The desk sergeant made notes; librarians had to be taken seriously. 'We'll do what we can, Mr Boulton, sir,' he promised. 'But I only have a handful of men, and as for the military,' and he dropped his voice, 'they don't know if they're on their arse or their elbow.'

The light from the lamps strung between poles outside was so brilliant, Buckley could pick out stalks of corn that had sprouted along the private sidings.

The fire-hose was ready. The fitters and engineers, middle-aged men with no interest in strikes, had staves ready in case anyone thought of wrecking the machinery. There was no telling.

Shops and railway wagons had been looted, Buckley knew; stolen liquor was in circulation. Drunk or sober, he would see off any louts who came near. Phillips, in town earlier, had encountered a line of youths dancing along Copperworks Row, chanting 'We are the hool-i-gans!' to the tune of 'Ta-ra-ra-boom-de-ay!' He said you could have lit their breath with a match.

Buckley was relieved when Will appeared out of the dark. How could their differences be permanent? His heart quickened. Will must have seen how ruthless the mob could be.

His son had drunk water from the tap and let it run over his shirt. 'You know there were two men shot dead?' he said.

'One of them from this works. We know. John Johns. Was he a ringleader?'

'Never liked him, sir,' said Phillips, from the window. 'And the other chap was a Londoner. Come down here to make trouble, I wouldn't be surprised.'

'They'll do anything now,' said Will. 'The military expect worse things before the night is out.'

'You're safe here,' said Buckley, and Phillips called, 'Men heading this way. There, in the grass, other side of the lights.'

The point of coming was to warn his father, not to join forces with him. Will could just make out the ugly red in the sky, beyond the lamps. The town might be full of terrors, but it was the town that drew him.

Long after he and Sam Lewis parted company, Will had been following the mob. It had swept him into the People's Park to hear Tommy Spit call his listeners 'Today's Chartists'; down back-alleys where boys were drinking rum out of tin cups; to T. T. Rees's shopfront where the pig was in pieces, to see looters emerge calmly with bottled pears and bags of flour; past soldiers with faces as shiny-white as their bayonets; among colliers and tin-workers swearing vengeance; by men masked in scarves who were tearing up the main line with crowbars.

The figures came crawling through the grass. Phillips picked up an ebony ruler and said, 'Right, sir, action stations, is it?'

It was too late to run. Will picked his way past the sleeping furnaces. A fitter was sharpening a wooden stake on the shears. The mill had the vast hollowness of a cathedral. The god had fled, leaving shadows and a smell of iron. For the last time, he stood beside his father.

'Hosepipe ready!' cried Phillips from outside.

'I can see six – seven,' said Dadda. 'Eight, there by the wagon.'

Fitters heaved at the doors that stretched to the roof, rolling them together on their oily wheels. They left a slit for father and son to stand in.

'I warn you!' shouted Buckley. 'We shall meet force with force. Clear off. John Johns getting killed isn't my business. You know me for a fair man. I won't call on the military unless I have to.'

There was a derisive cackle of laughter. The figures were standing, forming a column two abreast. They had a military look. They wore soldiers' caps. Will saw a criss-cross of webbing on a fat man's chest.

He saw something else, and stepped forward.

'Will!' shouted Dadda, but he didn't stop.

The column marched into the light, swinging their arms – eight of them, two by two, with the fat one at the front. They were half soldiers, half scarecrows. Puttees here, a tunic there, some greatcoats, an ammunition belt, black boots, a rifle, a mess tin.

They were all women. The one at the front was Fat Sara.

'Look who it is!' she said. 'Squad, halt!'

'Mind out the way, Mr Will,' shouted Phillips, but Will planted himself between the hosepipe and the visitors.

'Well, Sara Jenkins,' he said quietly. 'Been stealing from the troop train, have you?'

'That's right. Smart lot, we are.'

'What is it you want?'

'The tin statue. General Roberts on his hoss.'

'For what reason?'

'Wouldn't remember, would you?'

'Mr Johns it was who made it,' said a soldier with a hook

nose and a tunic over her dress. Will recognised Kitty, the girl on the sands, that day, years ago.

'His fam'ly ought to have it.'

'So they ought,' said Will. It shamed him to have forgotten the connection. Men were just names.

Waving to Dadda that everything was in order, he led the scarecrows away, past the mill shed, to the despatch yard and store rooms.

He had his keys with him. The room where the General had been hidden smelt of rats. When they pulled the sacking away, the metal was dulled and lead-like. The horse's rump was dented. General Roberts had lost his nose, too.

'You mean we can just take it?' said Fat Sara. 'Isn't he nice, girls? Which of us would you like to kiss?'

He thought how dangerous they might be, these people who were beginning to rouse themselves. For a second he was alarmed, as they crowded around him and the statue.

'Take it now, before Mr Phillips comes with his big stick,' he said.

Laughing and chattering, they dragged their prize outside.

'Tell me one thing, Sara Jenkins,' he said, 'was it your brother who played that trick?'

'You mean the bucket of hoss manure? No, that was me, lovey,' and she rubbed her leg up against him as she passed.

He watched them disappear down the road towards the town. The air smelt of fire.

'Earl Roberts belonged to the combine. You had no right to give him away,' said Dadda.

'We didn't want him. They did.'

In the room next door, Phillips was trying to telephone the police, to say a statue had been stolen.

'Those women will be laughing their heads off.'

'I doubt it. They were more serious than you think.'

'That only makes it worse. You gave in to them. It grieves me to listen to you, Will. How can you be blind to the dangers of mob rule?'

'The mob is more than drunkards and hooligans.' But he knew it was too late to argue with Dadda; it had always been too late.

'You're entitled to opinions. I never said you weren't.'

Dadda relaxed. Dadda was smiling, face still iron, more threatening than ever. 'You were proud of that statue. I'd forgotten. One forgets so much. What were you, then? Sixteen? Seventeen? Starting to find your feet. Finding the world a more wicked place than you'd realised. Becoming a Buckley.'

The dragon was still there. The past was never erased. Will knew he could still be tempted back to what Dadda called his 'destiny'. ('You guarded that statue with your life,' the voice was saying. 'The old chap's still alive, you know. He must be nearly eighty.') The town was where he should be. The streets were a protection. He had work to do there, visions of his own to cultivate, theories to prove. In the restless shifting of people who had tasted power, and had seen the response they drew by way of bullets, was the hand of desperate men who knew there was no other way.

The riots had been planned, he was sure of it. ('When we get Earl Roberts back,' Dadda was saying, 'he can have a place of honour. Why, we can bed him down in concrete and have railings and a flower-bed. I can make concessions, you see.')

'I'm truly sorry for the way things have turned out,' said Will.

'You mean the shooting? We all regret that.'

'I mean Buckley's and me. I've finished with it – with the works, with the combine, with everything.'

'Never!' said Buckley. 'Here you belong and here you'll stay. You have no option. You are part of my plans. You – '

They didn't finish the conversation. Phillips was at the door to say Buckley's nephew Theodore was missing. Moments later, Will slipped away under cover of this new crisis.

Outside the police station a search party of Territorials had gathered. Aubrey Mappowder was in charge, looking fierce and saying the socialists had better watch out. He said Abraham Lloyd had gone with a party of men to the railway station, in case his son had wandered there. Others, Joe among them, were at New Dock.

Will went up Market Street, where a bayonet charge had just ended. A minute later, looting resumed. It was like a game where everyone took turns.

A young man had a leg wound. Haggar the film-man would have shouted, 'Distort your face with pain!' The features were grey and expressionless. Drops of blood left stars on the pavement.

Captain Aubrey's Territorials were wandering up back-alleys, shouting the boy's name.

At the railway station, hundreds of soldiers lined the platforms and stood on the footbridge. A picket with fixed bayonets guarded the crossing gates. A crowd, girls among them, watched in silence. Will saw no sign of Abraham.

The smell of burnt wood was strong. Smoke drifted from the goods yard, half a mile away. When he reached it, figures were scurrying about the sidings, and Will thought it must be the military, moving supplies, until he realised most of them were women.

As he watched, a man used a sledgehammer to smash the locking bar of a wagon and open the side. Immediately women converged and helped themselves to smoked meat and cheeses. A group came up with a porter's trolley, already piled with booty. A clothes mangle could be seen, next to a chest of tea. The new provisions were thrown aboard. Some of the cheeses rolled away. Nobody bothered to go after them.

'Opening a shop, are you?' called a man who had climbed into another wagon. He began to throw down boots. Some of the younger women lost interest in the food. Soon they were dressing up in hats and stockings.

Joe was there. They saw each other at the same moment, and moved away behind a burnt-out wagon to talk.

'It beats everything,' said Joe.

'Is he down here, do you think?'

'I wouldn't put it past him.'

They began to explore the yard.

'I thought the *Hannibal* had got away,' said Will.

'That's another story. Tell you later.'

At the far end of a line of trucks, fresh flames had broken out. The glare was like daylight. Figures danced around it.

'Why aren't there police?' asked Joe. 'Or soldiers, or somebody?'

'They've lost their nerve.'

The light seemed to break into pieces, which flew silently over their heads. Will found himself lying on the ground. A noise like thunder was receding. He felt sick. A woman was screaming.

'They're using artillery,' he gasped. 'Joe? Are you all right?'

'I've shit my pants. Thought I was dead.'

'The shell has put the fire out.'

Amid crying and screaming, most of the ants were running, escaping. Abandoned food and clothing were everywhere. Joe uncorked a bottle of whisky and used it to clean himself with.

Hot ash still glowed in a circle, and within it, people held out burning sticks to give more light, and tended the injured.

'Two dead,' someone said. 'More like five,' said another.

Worst of all was a woman who lay on a mound of hats and dresses. Her face had been stripped from the bone. A woman knelt beside her, holding her hands.

A boy crouched by a wagon, observing intently.

'Theo!' shouted his brother.

'Sh-h-h,' he said. 'She's on her last legs, can't you see?'

Had the deaths been allowed for, too?

The scent of fire and explosion was on Will's skin, like written evidence; he had been under attack. Some of Joe's washing-whisky had splashed him, so he smelt of that as well. He felt as light-headed as if he had been drinking it.

Near the town centre, everything was quiet; undoubtedly the calm before the storm. Hundreds, perhaps thousands, of colliers had come into the town. They were linking arms somewhere with the tinplate workers and railwaymen.

Market, town hall and post office were silent and undamaged under a smoky moon. Military guards had been posted outside the broken shop fronts. A boy jeered at them from a doorway, then ran for his life, unpursued. A shopkeeper swept up glass.

A woman came down Stepney Street, pushing a pram, and turned into Skinner Lane. A tramcar passed, almost empty. As the noise faded, Will heard a cry, and ran back.

The lane was lit by a single gas lamp. He saw the woman crouched over the pram, and a policeman trying to hoist her up by the waist. 'Thieving little cow!' he was saying.

She must have kicked his shin. He let go and jumped backwards, swearing and rubbing his leg.

Her shawl caught in the pram, or she might have got away. But as she freed herself, he hit her shoulder with his truncheon and she fell in a heap.

Will had no alternative. The moment had come. Skinner Lane was the appointed place.

He was on the constable before there was time for more truncheon-work. A blow in the face sent him staggering. Another in the belly brought him down.

'Quick, Missis!' said Will, and helped the woman to her feet. She looked young-married – coarse hair, full hips. She nodded her thanks, then ran towards Stepney Street, hoicking up her skirt.

The policeman was groaning, fumbling in his top pocket. Will tore the blanket off the pram. He felt gingerly under the hood and found himself holding a York ham with a T. T. Rees price ticket still pinned to it.

Whistle-blasts followed him down the alley. Another whistle answered them, ahead of him.

'Over by 'ere,' said a voice softly.

It came from a crack between buildings. He saw the white of teeth and the shine of a bald head.

'Quick, now. Follow me.'

There was barely room to run. They came into a back-yard, and a dustbin toppled over with a crash. Will twisted his ankle.

'Tell yourself it doesn't hurt,' said the man. 'Across this wall now. They'll skin you if they catch you. Policemen are sacred, didn't you know?'

The man caught him as he came over the wall. He supported him as they ran three-legged down Nevill Street to a flap in a stable door. He whistled, and a whippet ran up. 'In we go,' he said, and they were all inside a stable-yard behind Nevill's Hotel.

'Be safe here for a bit,' said the man. 'There's horses at the end. This one's empty.'

Will sat on the floor and pulled off his shoe.

'Didn't I see you once before?' he said.

'Why, who are you, then?'

'Will Buckley.'

'Means nothing to me.'

'Three years ago. The Chartists' Cave.'

The man tied a rope to the whippet's collar. 'You stay put,' he said. 'I'm all right, see. A dog on a lead's as good as an alibi.'

'Will you tell Saul Haycock where I am?'

'There's a tap by 'ere. Try cold water on it.'

Man and dog disappeared through the flap. Will soaked his handkerchief and wrapped it inside his sock, then crept into a stall and lay on the straw.

The police whistles had ceased. He heard the wheels of a cart. A man started the chorus of 'Sospan Fach', but it was cut off abruptly. A tram-car crackled on the rails, far off. The calm went on and on, a smooth skin of night, undisturbed by the tumult of voices that Will hoped for.

He heard a click and a scratch and the rustle of clothes. A woman's voice whispered, 'Will?'

'Here,' he said.

It was Flora. She knelt beside him.

'This is a fine thing,' she said, and sniffed suspiciously. 'Have you been drinking whisky?'

'It's on me, not in me.'

'You must stay here for a while. You'll have to be carried. Too many police about just now.'

He wanted to know what was happening. Had the artillery fired more shells?

'Shells?'

'They fired on the goods yard. I was there. Hit a railway truck and killed people.'

'No, no,' she said, stroking his head, 'the looters burnt a truck that had chemicals in. Blew themselves up, they did. Four dead, maybe five.' She took his hand and held it against her face. 'It's like a nightmare. It shouldn't have been like this.'

'Surely it's inevitable?' said Will.

'What do you know about inevitable? You haven't begun to learn. Do you think my Pa wanted riots and bloodshed?'

'Not wanted, perhaps. Was prepared to consider.'

'Stay there and shut up,' she said roughly, and a moment later he heard the flap-door click behind her.

A moment after that, a police whistle sounded, very close.

Then running footsteps, a man shouting, laughter – incongruous – and what might have been Flora's voice. Then an eerie silence. He crawled to the back of the stall and pulled some of the reeking straw over his legs.

He knew someone had seen her leave.

He heard the flap open. The rays of one lantern and then another made the horses stir. He tried to stand up, and the lights shone in his face.

'Over here. Is this him? Stinks of whisky.'

'No question,' said a voice with a slight sibilance, as through broken teeth. 'I'm the one you struck, sonny Jim.'

Will thought there were three of them.

'Charge him, will we?'

'Cells are full up.'

'I want this heard in court,' said Will, mortified that his voice was so unsteady. 'You assaulted a woman.'

'That wasn't a woman, that was Annie Pisspot, supplies the Copperworks with flew-id. Get his trousers off, boys.'

Will tried to shout for help. They flung him face downwards on a bale of straw, and put a coat over his head. Hands pressed him into the straw; it scratched his bare legs.

Something harsh and leathery cracked across his skin. The pain took his breath away. It cracked again, and he began to scream.

'That's it, you yell for Mammy,' and the whip curled around him like liquid fire.

When it was over, they dragged his clothes back on, and

he nearly fainted as the cloth touched him. They dumped him in the back street, on his hands and knees. He tried to stand. Some boys saw him swaying on one leg and hopped after him, cat-calling.

Two men came round a corner and ran towards him. 'Are you Buckley?' said one of them. He tried to speak. He could feel the blood dripping into his shoe. They caught him as he fell.

They sent Joe over to Tir Gwyn to tell his uncle that Will and he had found Theodore, who was safe.

'I'm glad to hear it,' said Buckley. 'But your father's in trouble. Wrecked his ship. Lost his certificate, I dare say.'

'Yes, Uncle Davy.'

'Tell your mother not to worry about the musical genius. He'll go to college as I promised. But I shall do nothing for your father.'

'He expects nothing, Uncle Davy.'

The lad was well-spoken. Given a chance . . . but one could say that of thousands. He was just Joe Lloyd, whose destiny was to be a fisherman and live in a house like a matchbox.

'The town seems quieter now.'

'It was the wagon blowing up that did it.'

'Where was your cousin Will when you saw him last?'

'He went back into the town.'

'Well, thank you for coming over,' said Buckley. 'I daresay we shall all be glad to see tomorrow.'

A minute later he was watching Joe through the window as he ran under the lamps and out of sight.

The sound of metal-cutting came from the mill, where the fitters were at work. Buckley was reluctant to leave. He sat with his eyes closed, trying to fathom what had got into Will.

Phillips cleared his throat next door and spat through the window, and Buckley went to tell him he could go.

'Beg pardon, I'd like to stay, seeing you're here, sir.'

'You're a tidy man, Phillips. But I like to be on my own. We'll have no more trouble tonight. There are men here if there is. I'll see you Monday morning.'

He thought to telephone Y Plas to make sure Will was home. But it was late, and he didn't want to disturb Pomona.

He went outside, still thinking about Will. The moon gave enough light to see the path behind the mills, away from the lamps. He tried to remember exactly what it was that Will had said.

His foot caught in something, and when he stooped it was a noose of wire, like a rabbit snare.

The men carried Will back to Haycock's house. He was aware of pain, but unable to tell if it had lasted five minutes or an hour. A woman tended him – they told him afterwards it was a neighbour who was a nurse at the infirmary. The world smelt of iodine. He seemed to lie in a bath of it, taking his skin off in strips. But after it came cool bandages, and the worst was over.

Lying on his side on a bed, he was aware of Flora. The only light came through the window. Voices murmured downstairs. He heard 'Lloyd George' and 'ultimatum'.

'Did they hurt you?' he said.

'No, my sweetheart,' she whispered, and he could see the tears glistening on her face.

'They followed you.'

'I suppose so. Do you still love me, after all this?'

'I shall never stop loving you. Is it all right if I stay here tonight?'

'Won't they have search parties out?'

'I shan't be missed till morning.'

The front door banged, the stairs creaked.

'How's the casualty?' said Haycock.

'I want him to sleep. I'll stay here with him.'

'Enigma, aren't you, Will Buckley?'

'I changed sides, that's all.'

'Didn't need to get yourself half killed in the process.'

'What's the news?' said Flora.

'Depressing,' and paper rustled in his hand. 'There's a Board of Trade telegram gone to every town in the kingdom. Terms of settlement of the railway dispute, as agreed with the union leaders. Six conditions, but what they boil down to is another damned commission of inquiry.' He scrunched the paper into a ball and flipped it on the bed. 'All over and done with.'

'There'll be other times,' said Will. Yes, they said, there would be other times.

Buckley thought the breathing he could hear to one side of the path was an animal, and stopped to listen. But it was Guto. He smelt the dirty clothes and the sweat, and saw the narrow eyes shining.

'What are you doing here?' he said sharply. 'This is a tinworks now. There's nothing here for you. You won't catch any rabbits. Go home to Japhet like a good boy.'

'D-dead,' said Guto.

It was the only word Buckley had ever heard him speak.

'If that's so, I'm sorry.' He rather wished he hadn't walked so far. 'I am going back, and I want you to walk in front of me. Come along. I shan't hurt you.'

He stood aside for the shadow. As it passed him, something flashed under his eyes, and he felt the knife go into his throat.

15

Morgan sat in a private room with a skylight and a greasy carpet at the Lamb Hotel, in the Rhondda Valley, and thought how agreeable life was. He had been telling a succession of women about their dead husbands. The room, at twilight, was full of shadows. He poured a glass of dusty water from the carafe and closed his eyes.

Spirits didn't worry him. The world was a mystery, behind closed doors. He no longer looked for explanations. Once in a blue moon he heard a voice or had a dream that hinted at the supernatural. Very useful it was, too. But the spirits were voices calling from far away.

He thought about his father, something he did more often than when he was alive. At the time, the savage manner of his death had tempted Morgan to see if the tormented spirit had any message to send from the hereafter. He told Margaret how he waited patiently, alone in a locked room, on the night they hanged Guto in Swansea Gaol. But no one spoke.

'Poor Dadda,' Margaret had said, 'if he wanted to tell us anything, you're the last person he'd go to.'

'Then sit with me. See if he'll tell you. Just suppose the old chap is up there somewhere, aware of what's going on. What does he see? Chaos and confusion. His son and heir doesn't want his inheritance. Nor do I – not that anyone's offering it to me. So what about you? Wasn't there a Miss Dillwyn who ran a works in Swansea for years? Perhaps Dadda's spirit has a memorandum he wants to send you.'

'I'm sick of your warped sense of humour,' she had told him. 'Let him rest in peace.'

'Whatever you like, Maggs. But remember what I've said.'

That was more than two years ago. It was 1913 now; late in the autumn.

Something moved and he opened an eye. No doubt mice lived behind the mouldy furniture.

He was in Wales to hold a series of private sittings – one of Henry's bright ideas. Good old Henry; with his waxed moustache and cravat, anyone could see that Henry had found his vocation as a showman, and if he had ever pined for orchids or Margaret, he had got over them now. He was even accumulating capital.

A pit blew up in the Rhondda. Hundreds of men died. 'You would be doing a service,' said Henry. He hired a room at the Lamb, and paid boys a shilling to stick up posters. 'Mr Morgan Buckley, the Famous London Medium, offers his sympathetic services FREE to widows and others Bereaved in the Terrible Lancaster Pit Disaster, who may wish for contact with the Beyond.'

A succession of women came, and Morgan had messages for them all. No one was charged a fee, a point Morgan emphasised to a special correspondent of the *Daily Mail*, where the article, together with a photograph of the medium, appeared as 'THE GHOSTLY MINERS OF THE RHONDDA'; it was said that Northcliffe wrote the headline.

Now, his last day at the Lamb, women were still waiting to see him. Because he was tired, he had told Henry he must have ten minutes on his own before continuing.

He took another sip of water and dozed again. Almost at once, he saw a procession of miners, limping and bandaged. They walked slowly, helping one another, across a landscape blurred with mist or perhaps smoke. It was odd. He knew they were miners, yet they wore the tattered remains of khaki uniforms. Some of them carried rifles. They were soldiers.

Shuffling past, they unnerved him, though he couldn't say why, exactly. Where had they been? Who had they been fighting?

His mind froze at what he was seeing, yet he knew all the time that he was in a room at the Lamb, dozing at a table covered in a green velvet cloth.

His father's voice cut through the dream. 'This is a scandal!' it said, and he woke with his flesh crawling.

There was a scuffle in the passageway. It wasn't his father. It was a flat-nosed collier who was arguing with Henry, telling him to get himself and that bugger Buckley off the premises in ten minutes.

Morgan forgot the men in khaki. He introduced himself to the collier and explained that his mission was humanitarian.

'Ten minutes,' the man kept repeating.

Something called the United Lodges had met and condemned his intrusion into the private grief of the valley. He represented the committee.

'I shall remain tonight as long as I'm needed,' said Morgan. 'Tell your committee that.'

'We'll be here in ten minutes. So watch out,' and the collier disappeared down the murky street where rain was beginning to fall.

Henry was for them leaving. So was the landlord, who tried to order Morgan off the premises.

'See this?' said Morgan. 'It's your receipt for my money. I have no intention of running away from ignorant men. Send your pot-boy for the police if you're worried.'

'I'll go,' said Henry, and set off with his collar turned up.

A young widow, numb-looking, sat shivering across the table. Morgan held her hand like a doctor and insisted she drink a brandy. Beyond any shadow of doubt, he said, her husband had not suffered. Death had been instantaneous.

Outside the window, voices were muttering.

'I see him now,' said Morgan. 'A slight figure – was he slight?'

'Tall for these parts, sir. Tall but thin.'

'Thin, that's right. The thinness is what I'm getting. And a most beautiful smile.'

'That's him!' she cried. 'My poor Tom!'

'Tom is smiling at you.'

A stone came through the window and fell, with the glass, on the other side of the curtain.

The landlord rushed in, followed by men in grimy clothes with white scarves.

'He knew his name, even,' the woman was sobbing. 'He knew Tom's name.'

'You've had your warning,' said the flat-nosed collier. 'You're going in the river.'

The landlord gabbled that he was returning half a crown for unexpired use of room. The coin rolled on the floor.

'I think you should know I can't swim,' Morgan said.

'Then you'll have to sink, won't you?'

They dragged him out. He assumed that the *Daily Mail* would portray him as a martyr if they killed him or a charlatan if they didn't; newspapers were like that.

The crowd of men outside was bigger than he expected. They jeered when they saw him.

Why had he come back to this barbarous country? And where were Henry and the local constabulary?

A clod of earth hit him on the shoulder. He was frightened. He was being dragged down the street.

'Hang on, boys,' said a voice, and Will was standing in their path, arms folded.

'How do, Will,' they shouted, and 'Got your namesake here, we have.'

'You've got my brother,' said Will, and eyes looked between the two. 'I don't hold any brief for what he's done.

I don't like spiritualist tricks any more than you do. But if I guarantee there's no more of it, and he's back in Cardiff tonight, will you let him go?'

'In the river, he deserves,' said Flat-nose, disappointed, but Will seemed to have their confidence.

'Ay, all right,' they said.

Back inside the Lamb, Morgan could still feel the grip of their fingers. He couldn't bring himself to thank his brother. He cursed the police for not coming. For all they knew, Henry was dead in a ditch.

'Hiding at the railway station, more like. As for the police, they've got better things to do.'

'What a God-forsaken place you've chosen to live in,' said Morgan, waiting at the foot of the stairs for his bags to be brought down.

'It suits me. It suits my wife.' His brother's contempt was a measure of the distance between their worlds. 'Did Maggs tell you I was a conciliation agent for the miners? I tell the bosses not to try things on, I used to be one myself.'

'I may bring charges yet,' said Morgan. 'Assault on the person. Breach of the peace. Attempted murder. Abduction.'

'They live with death round here. You insult them with your mumbo-jumbo.'

'The women were glad enough to come. I gave them comfort.'

'Told them lies, you mean.'

'I could tell you things that would make your hair stand on end,' said Morgan, and followed the luggage out to the landlord's pony and trap.

Will watched him go down the street until a corner cut him off. Rain and coal-dust and cobbles shone in the pitiful gas flames that hesitated behind the glass as though the wind would blow them out at any minute.

The rain was falling all along the great vee of the valley,

washing over the blue slate roofs, down the gutters of endless terraces. Tens of thousands of lives were clustered in the dark, their habitations like cells hacked in the valley walls. Flora was in one of them, not far off, the baby fed and asleep, her blouse smelling of her milk; sometimes it oozed from a nipple and stained the fabric.

He longed for her company. If he ran, it would only take ten minutes.

Groups of people, mostly young, went on reliving the riots at Port Howard, but the respectable thing to do was forget them. When the statue business was brought to Henry Sprewett's notice (he wasn't the sort of man to notice things unaided) he went in person to remonstrate with the Woman, as he called her. She was polite but unhelpful.

The day the statue was unveiled, he urged Will Probert of the *Star* not to dignify it with a report. But Probert couldn't oblige, either. A woman tinplate owner was too valuable a property to ignore. As he said to his pals at the Conservative Club, if someone brought irrefutable evidence of the colour of Margaret Penbury-Holt's drawers into the office, he'd be tempted to publish it.

'Of course,' he wrote, 'the fewer reminders we have of the dreadful events of that weekend, two years ago, the sooner they will be forgotten. But one must concede that the proprietor of Buckley's is moved by genuine principles. She is a remarkable woman. We are still in the process of growing accustomed to such a phenomenon in this masculine old town of ours.'

It was only Earl Roberts on his horse. The warrior had reached his last resting-place, a concrete plinth outside the general offices at Tir Gwyn. Railings and a flower-bed surrounded him, as David Buckley once suggested. Coated in stone-coloured paint as a preservative, he had the battered look of a knight's effigy in a village church.

What Sprewett objected to was the plaque underneath – 'This tinplate figure of General Roberts was made by John Johns, who died with five others during the riots of 19 August, 1911.'

Were rioters and hooligans to be commemorated as if they were heroes?

'They were townspeople, surely that's enough, Mr Sprewett?' said Margaret.

She had a habit of directness that made friends and enemies in roughly equal numbers, and had done so from the moment of her return to Port Howard.

That period, following Dadda's death, had taxed her more than anything in her life before. His loss, coming after Henry's (she never went back to Henry – couldn't and wouldn't), seemed to echo through the house when she was there consoling Mamma. Will had already planned his getaway. Y Plas was a house without men.

Will refused to inherit the business. He said things about class and equality that didn't matter to her, and things about Flora Haycock that did. He was harder and more passionate than she remembered. He had it worked out – sell his shares, give Mamma the proceeds.

No one had any better suggestions, except for Morgan, with his evil sense of humour, saying she ought to try running the works herself. You could never shake Morgan off. Wasn't he at the root of all that had happened? He was the first defector. 'He broke Davy's heart' became one of Mamma's choruses, as though blank-faced Guto with his knife had been at most an accessory.

Next day she began to think Morgan was right.

Will said, Certainly, if that was what she wanted. He signed away his shares and spent weeks telling her what he knew about running a works.

The combine's board was shocked. Realising that this woman (soon to be a divorced woman, if the rumours were true) meant to exercise her power, they begged her to consider letting them buy out her interest, detaching Tir Gwyn for her to do what she liked with.

It was expected she would ruin it in a year. What no one allowed for was that as a woman and a newcomer she could go where she liked for advice, and between flattery and surprise, would get it.

When the works had problems with impurities in a batch of steel bars, she arrived at Morfa unannounced; Rhodri Lewis almost had a fit, but an hour later he was at Tir Gwyn with his works chemist.

When Phillips posed a threat to her authority because it suited him to be secretive and not keep her in the picture, she made an excuse to meet the Mappowder son (still not married, she was surprised to find), and benefited greatly from his advice: sack Phillips, promote Trubshaw.

She still thought of him as Goggles. He drove a motor of his own now, a green and black monster. The day the statue was unveiled, he came purring up and honked his horn outside the general offices.

Margaret was in the Despatch department with the manager, Abraham Lloyd Esq, discussing freight charges. Uncle Abraham had turned his back on the sea with few regrets. When the message came that Captain Mappowder wished to see her, she made him wait a bit. 'How is Joe getting on?' she wanted to know, and Abraham showed her a postcard from Yokohama, where Third Officer Lloyd had been lately in a Blue Funnel ship.

Goggles was waiting in her room. He looked thinner and sprucer than ever. He had come, he said, to take a look at the famous statue. But since he was here, there was something he would like to discuss.

'Me, too,' she said, noticing that the gold-wire hairs on his wrist were darker now than that day at Pendine.

'You first, Margaret. I insist.'

Hers was simple. She was dropping Rees Coal as her main supplier, the quality having deteriorated, so could he recommend a reliable colliery? Goggles gave a good imitation of Rees Coal asking the Lord to punish difficult customers, and wrote her an introduction to a pit that sometimes supplied the copperworks.

'Your turn.'

'You ought to have a motor,' he said, and flushed slightly. 'I mean, someone in your position these days would find it useful. It so happens that one of the motors at Cilfrew is being replaced – excellent condition – very cheap – I mean, you can have it for nothing.'

She thought how quaint men were, or, as Virginia put it, '*suspiciously* quaint'. She said, 'I suppose if I needed a motor I should go to John Brown's in Swansea.'

Goggles stood up.

'I'm sorry if I've offended you.'

'Don't be ridiculous. Sit down.'

'All I meant was that we had a car knocking about, but, and this is the point' – his face tightened around the eyes – 'I could teach you to drive, if that was what you wanted to do. Of course, you can have a driver, but it's tremendous fun to do it yourself.'

'The only time I drove a motor car, we know what happened.'

'I was egging you on. I was showing off.'

'Shall I say that if I do learn to drive, I'd like you to be the instructor.'

'Excellent,' said Aubrey. 'When you're ready to leave, I could run you up to see her in the garage – a Darracq, nineteen eight, silver-grey.'

She shook her head. 'I have some ladies coming to supper. At the weekend, perhaps.'

'At the weekend, then.'

She rather wanted to see him drive off, but kept away

from the window. She was a divorced woman who had reached her mid-thirties. That side of her life was over.

Probably over.

The supper party was in honour of Esther, who was staying for a few days. Enid, the Captain's daughter, had faded out of her life, moving to share a cottage in Sussex with a bank manager's widow, and Esther, despite the Suffragettes, had a lonely look about her these days.

'We can all wear our silks and satins,' said Margaret. 'My cousin is home from music college, and if he isn't having one of his peculiar days, he'll come and play for us. He likes being made a fuss of by women.'

It was a cold, wet time of year; she liked to give little parties that cheered people up, herself included. Mamma began by wanting to be excused, but Margaret got round that by making sure Ada Lewis was there. Ada and Mamma sat side by side on a sofa before going in to eat, disagreeing contentedly in whispers about things that had happened decades ago.

A storm was blowing. Aunt Villette arrived complaining that rain had got into the carriage that was sent for them. Theodore's sleeve was wet.

'A chill in a pianist's arm could have unforeseen consequences, Margaret,' she said, and he ate supper in his white waistcoat while the garment was dried and aired.

Aeronwy was there, too, quick to insert Morgan's name into a conversation when she saw a chance. A jewel flashed on her neck, and she hinted to Margaret that it was his. She asked if Esther had read 'The Ghostly Miners' in the *Daily Mail*.

Villette found her behaviour improper, but since Margaret and her mother permitted it, she had to keep quiet. Pomona had long since lost any resentment she might have felt towards the girl. Besides, she had her grand-daughter – asleep upstairs, at the moment, since mother and child were staying the night. Pomona didn't like admitting it to herself, but some things were easier without Davy. She dreamt of him most nights, and in the dreams he always forgave her.

The shutters rattled in the wind, and when he came to play for them, Theodore asked that they be secured properly before he begin. He paced up and down frowning while servants got soaked outside, and failed to stop the noise.

A crisis threatened. Margaret's patience with the ugly bad-mannered youth was limited. Aunt Villette was talking unhelpfully about the problems of the Artist.

Then Aeronwy went up to him and said, 'Please. What offends you doesn't offend us. We so want you to play. *I* so want you to.'

The famous eyelashes moved, and in a moment Theodore had whisked up his tails and was seated at the piano.

He began peacefully (he said it was Weber), became frenzied (Ravel, a name Margaret had never heard), and drifted into sadness and melody (they all knew it was Chopin). Whatever Theodore had been, he was transformed. The storm, driving in across the marshes, only drew attention to the purity and violence of the notes.

He played on and on, and much later, when the evening was over, the guests gone or in bed, and she was alone in the library, Margaret could hear the music in her head, like a vindication.

She thought of her childhood at Y Plas, and the last night she spent there as Miss Buckley. Morgan would have looked for something in the shadows. But the room was empty. The dead were dead – persons or marriages. She glanced at her father's writing in the front of a book – 'David Inkerman Buckley', with a date before she was born – and turned out the light and went to bed.

Next morning Isabel came into her room soon after dawn.

'I didn't hear you knock,' said Margaret.

'Look through the window, Aunt,' whispered the girl. Already she had something of her father's self-possession.

Margaret drew back the curtains and caught her breath. Sea had flooded the marshes. The remaining sheds and walls of the old Buckley's were lapped by water. Gulls floated on the surface. Rays of sun came through broken cloud.

'Isn't it beautiful, Aunt Margaret?'

'Isn't it,' she answered, and put her arms around the child, weeping for the past and the future.

Wales and London
1986–1987

The Divining Heart

Paul Ferris

The Divining Heart reveals the changes that befall the Buckleys from the 1920s to the 1940s, as ambition, love, pride and dissipation whirl them between high and low society, from a close-knit Welsh community to a Europe threatened by chaos.

Morgan Buckley is an opportunist, a chancer, dabbling in book publishing: his forte may be literature, or it may be pornography – the line is thin and Morgan is the man to walk it. Maddening, charming Morgan is not one for the caution urged upon him by his sensible sister Margaret; nor does he play the role of heavy conventional father to his wild daughter Sibli.

Sibli is a child of her time, a good-time girl with a brain, a girl who takes her chances and her men among the bright young things who flourish in the new London, who espouses causes as passionately as her father, who loves and leaves with seeming insouciance – but whose heart is more fragile than she cares to admit. Her story, dramatic and heady, is at the centre of a novel which unforgettably matches tragedy with comedy.

ISBN 0 246 12977 8